KING
OF THE
STORM

B. A. BROCK

DSP PUBLICATIONS

Published by
DSP PUBLICATIONS

5032 Capital Circle SW, Suite 2, PMB# 279, Tallahassee, FL 32305-7886 USA
www.dsppublications.com/

King of the Storm
© 2015 B.A. Brock.

Cover Art
© 2015 Anne Cain.
annecain.art@gmail.com
Cover content is for illustrative purposes only and any person depicted on the cover is a model.
Map Art by B.A. Brock

ISBN: 978-1-63476-157-4
Digital ISBN: 978-1-63476-158-1
Library of Congress Control Number: 2015906692
First Edition November 2015

Printed in the United States of America
∞
This paper meets the requirements of
ANSI/NISO Z39.48-1992 (Permanence of Paper).

This novel is dedicated to David and Rand.
Without you, this gay fantasy would never have been possible.

Acknowledgments

I'D LIKE to thank David for giving me permission to write a dirty story. None of this would have been possible without you. I'd also like to thank Keira Andrews for writing the first M/M romance book I'd ever read and giving me hope, and Leta Blake for all her support.

Thank you, Scott Coatsworth, and Max, Jim, John, Dawn, Zach, Shannon, and the rest of the members of Queer SciFi for looking at my first drafts. You are all talented and amazing, and I am honored to be a part of your purpose. Thank you, Josh and my gaming group, for your help creating the fantasy world of Gaia, and thank you, Jamie and Erich, for your wonderful insight into Ancient Greece.

And finally I'd like to thank my family, with a special thank-you to Boo Bear and Bunny Rabbit, for all your love and understanding. My sky would be dark without your light.

Author's Note

THIS STORY is a work of fiction, and though it resembles the great hero's tale, it is not Perseus's tale from legend. The fictional world of Gaia is not our Earth, and the time frame isn't that of Ancient Greece, rather roughly equivalent to our medieval period.

In the Ancient Greek legend, Perseus was probably one of the happiest of all the great Greek heroes, and I imagined a world where he wasn't. I'm sorry, Perseus (the legend).

Continent of Greece

Part One
Seriphos

Chapter One

I SHOOK out my hands and stepped from foot to foot, the sand and grass squishing under my sandaled feet. My skin was slick with an overly sweet sweat, and my stomach churned. I adjusted the metal helmet on my head, the heavy horsehair making it feel unbalanced, and patted the clasps of my cuirass and fingered the leather flaps. Earlier, my slaves had shaved my body and rubbed me down with pomegranate oil, polishing my skin into living bronze.

I stood in the middle of a chaotic mass of students, all outfitted for battle. The match took place on a bluff overlooking the Vathia Ocean. A dangerous and welcoming storm churned above, and the wind whipped the sparse grass on the wide plain. Through the roiling black clouds, his presence lit my soul, and I closed my eyes and drank in the radiance of being this close to my father. Zeus's realm was in the heavens, and today we would share its power.

My father rarely monitored these matches, since they were only small contests for the academy, but he had agreed to preside over this one, because I had turned eighteen a week before and was finally able to compete. As coming-of-age gifts, my mother had given me the golden wool cloak I wore, and my father had given me my sword, made by Hephaestus.

A god-blade fit for Perseus, a son of Zeus. I was a man.

Lightning cut through the clouds, and thunder cracked. That was the signal.

The ranks shuddered, and as a mass everyone sprinted toward the middle of the clearing. The skirt of my tunic slid across my legs as I flowed with the tide, my sword and shield at the ready. I took up the battle cry, our shouts covering the noise of our rattling armor. I knew I was yelling at the top of my lungs—I could feel my breath in my chest, throat, mouth, and as it passed my lips—but I couldn't hear myself through the cacophony of voices.

I sent my consciousness into the sky, and the air pulsed and churned around me. Zeus's voice was the thunder, and his presence saturated the clouds. With each boom my insides trembled with the fear of being among the gods ingrained in all mortals, but I also felt a pleasant sense of nostalgia, memories of playing with my father in the storms as a boy. We hadn't played together for a long time. I ground my teeth and grinned.

The teams collided at inhuman speeds. With little thought, I created a gradient in the air currents and used the resulting tunnel of wind to sweep away all those with red tabards in my path, plus one unfortunate teammate in blue. They tumbled from me, pinwheeling wildly from my course, and I laughed.

As I opened myself to the air, my ears popped and the hair on my arms tingled and stood up. Bortos, a boy in red, charged toward me and then disappeared into a cloud of darkness. Quickly, I drew a line from the sky to where I guessed he would be and split a path for the energy to follow.

Lightning seared into the inky cloud.

The air crashed back to equilibrium, and I felt rather than heard the concussive force of thunder that resulted. The black cloud dissipated, and Bortos slumped to the earth, smoking, and was still. As I stepped past him, the smell of burned flesh tinged the air.

My father would make sure none of us died from our injuries.

Tremors in the ground were my only warning before a towering figure, who could only be half giant, stomped into view, and I barely leaped to the side before I was almost kicked like a ball. I rolled to my feet and readied my sword and shield.

Wearing blue, Zoticus, the dark and gargantuan son of Ares, stalked up and took on the challenge instead. With a manic gleam in his black eyes, he charged, slamming into the giant. I raised a brow and turned to find another fight. Those two could handle it without me.

A shift in the air sent me into a reflexive crouch, and I flung my shield up. Metal clanked against metal—a blur flew past overhead. Seizing the storm, I anchored lightning through my flying opponent.

With a *flash* and a *crack*, the flyer plummeted out of sight. The air bloomed with the sharp smell of heaven's smoke.

I had only a moment to recover when Selene, a daughter of Poseidon, marched in my direction, her pale blonde hair tied up in a Thessalian knot and her silvery arms covered in rust-colored smudges. Moving as quicksilver, she pulled back her arm, shaped it into a sword, and thrust it toward my head.

I flinched and squeezed my eyes shut as her sword arm breezed by my face.

Opening my eyes, I glanced to my side and followed the length of her weapon. Her arm seemingly disappeared into translucent space near the ground. She leaned forward as if she was pushing something down. I stared, fascinated. Invisibility was rare—it seemed as though I was looking from the other side of a glass, the grass indenting and light bending.

Selene jerked her arm back, her silvery fingers now dripping with blood. She wiped them on her blue tabard, leaving dark red smears.

"Thanks," I said.

She considered me for a moment with mercurial eyes and then nodded. "You're welcome, Perseus." She moved back into the masses with her liquid grace.

The world rocked and pulsed, and color flashed everywhere. Explosions of fire dotted the hillside, and the giant hurled someone over the side of the cliff and into the sea. A flash of blond hair and a blue tabard disappeared over the edge. Palamedes, maybe? I wasn't sure what had happened to Zoticus.

Thinking no one would challenge me on whether or not it was cheating, I shot my awareness into the storm, asking for a cyclone from my father—one of the benefits of sharing a similar power with my divine parent.

Immediately, gale-force winds dropped on my head, squeezing me. I used the currents to swirl myself up into the air, spinning as I reached the top. Getting high enough so I could observe the entire field, I stabilized the flow of air to keep myself stationary. Sheet lightning periodically blinded me, and thunder threatened to tear me apart. The storm stretched all the way to the coastal mountains and far out to sea, the water gray and roiling. My hair whipped my neck, and I laughed as I scorched the landscape with lightning, attempting to only hit the red team.

The winds wavered, and I panicked and juggled the currents but was no longer able to support myself.

I dropped out of the air. The wind rushed by my face as I fell, and I couldn't get my legs under me. I hit the earth with a thump.

I barely managed to hang on to my weapons as my vision blurred. I gasped in a few breaths and leaped up into a defensive stance, trying to recover my wits and warily looking around me. My face flushed. I hoped no one had seen that.

The way clear, I kept an eye to the skies and shot down another flying opponent. Absorbed in throwing bolt after electric bolt, I didn't notice the hissing approaching me until it was almost too late. I turned to face the rearing mass of green and black and narrowly dodged a viper strike. In one smooth motion, I dragged my blade across two of the snakes' necks, but the instant my sword penetrated their scales, they vanished. Too late, I realized the snakes were illusions.

I sensed movement behind me, but before I could turn, I was hit. A clanging rang through my head, and my vision exploded with colors. The ringing overwhelmed my ears as my world faded to black. The last thing I remembered was how sharp the grass was on my face, as if they were tiny swords.

A ROCKING motion jarred me. The movement was followed by a clanking of metal and then another bump, and distant talking. I awoke on the floor of a wagon. The sun was out, and birds were singing. The storm was gone, and so was my father.

I opened my eyes slowly, my vision blurring. The wagon jolted me again, and I puffed out a groan, trying to move my arms. I became aware that I was lying on them, now awkwardly askew and numb. I shifted and released my limbs, grunting as pins and needles spread and faded. I had been dumped on my weapons, and my helmet had been removed.

I hauled myself to a sitting position against the side of the wagon, and my head spun sickeningly. My stomach lurched, and I threw my head over the side, gut spasmodically heaving hot, sour liquid into the swirling dirt below. I scrambled to get my knees under me, clenched my eyes shut, and tried to wait it out, my breath hitching.

Light laughter, maybe my name, and some words I couldn't process drifted to my ears as my head seemed to swell with hot air. My stomach lurched again, and I dry heaved before my head stopped spinning. The bumping of the wagon wasn't helping. I panted, spitting in the dust.

At last the dizziness passed, and I slumped to the floor with a groan. I wiped my mouth on my leather arm guard, and then slowly moved my head around, and when that went all right, I felt gingerly at the sore spot on the back of my head. It was tender, and pressing on it sent a sparkle of lights across my vision, but otherwise I appeared to be all right. I ran my hands through my long wavy hair, but there wasn't any blood, and I didn't think I had any broken bones.

Lying next to me was my helmet, and I picked it up, marveling. It had a huge dent in the back, and with its concave shape, I couldn't figure out how they had taken it off my head. I dropped it in disgust.

Realizing I wasn't alone, I lowered my gaze. In the wagon were several people curled up here and there and piles of armor. A hairy dwarf was balled up an arm's length away from me, his weapons dumped over him. Across from me sat a woman with flaming red hair and a man wearing full plate. I didn't know either of them. My mother had told me that in order to get enough participants to create two teams, she'd had to send out invitations to all of the kingdoms.

My heart sank. I was the only student from the academy in the sick wagon. I rested my forehead on my knees, feeling my cheeks burn. At my age and with my abilities, I should be in Advanced Gymnasium, but I knew I was short for a demigod… and weak. My slaves had shaved my face this morning, but they hadn't needed to. I was sure there was something wrong with me, and my mother strongly hinted for me to go see a cleric, but I had refused.

The woman's arm was a bleeding mess, with rags wrapped around it and her blue dress stained brown, and the man had a makeshift splint on his leg over his armor. They were both covered in bloody scratches and had crumpled red tabards next to them. They caught me eyeing them.

"Hail, Son of Zeus!"

I lifted my hand in greeting. "Hail. Are we heading back? Is the match over? Who won?"

The blue team had won, so my shoulders eased a bit. The human man and the woman, a daughter of Eos, were from northern Epiro. They seemed to be enjoying themselves, even though they admitted that they had gotten completely cut up by a fair-haired boy in blue who wielded swords like spinning shark's teeth.

I laughed. "That was Palamedes. He knows how to use anything as a weapon." I made a face. "Sometimes he shows off and attacks us with grapes and candlesticks."

Palamedes and Zoticus were both in Advanced Gymnasium, but I was in Intermediate, so I rarely got to see them fight. On top of that, they trained separately and weren't allowed to fight against one another, since their island realms had been at war for centuries. It had been a treat to see them in action. I was sorry I had missed them attacking the giant.

By the time we arrived at the academy, I had pretty much recovered. We rolled up to the white-pillared buildings, and I hopped out of the wagon. I only had a slight headache, so when the clerics approached me in their long robes, arms outstretched in an offer of healing, I waved them away and went inside. I marched upstairs to wash up, and then met everyone in the mess hall to celebrate.

Picking a table near a corner, I slid onto a bench with my tray. My food was lit by the white light coming from Antolios's eyes, exposing all of the shadows of my stewed greens and fish.

"Hey." I glanced at him as I shoveled in a bite.

"Hey," Antolios said.

A roar went up, and we both turned our heads toward the middle of the room. Visitors and students held up cups of wine and challenged each other to drink. Leonidas stood on a table and spread his wings, spinning around and slapping people with white feathers. Antolios picked up his cup with long pale fingers and drank deeply of his wine.

"Weren't you on the blue team?" I said.

"Aye." He took a bite of fish.

"I didn't see you."

"I was there," he said around a mouthful. He brushed a loose strand of curly golden hair from his face and put it behind his ear.

I grunted. I wasn't sure why I bothered with the son of Apollo. My head throbbed at my temples and I lost my appetite, so I slid off the bench and ambled toward the kegs of wine.

Palamedes stepped in front of me. His golden hair was wet against his head, but his clothes were dry, and the only thing marring his handsome face was the sneer tugging at the corner of his pink lips. "Hey, Sparky, I heard you got dumped in the sick wagon." The students collecting around us laughed. "And you threw up." His smirk grew.

"Get out of my way, Palamedes." A flush crept up my neck as I tried to push past him.

Palamedes thrust a hand out, and I crashed into it. He glared down at me with the most beautiful green eyes I had ever seen. "You shouldn't have been allowed to play. You could get hurt." He formed a fist, and when I balled mine, he threw his head back and laughed. "What are you going to do to me, Sparky?"

A deep voice rumbled behind me. "Leave him alone."

I gazed up into Zoticus's black face and forked black beard. Even though he was younger than me, he was humongous. Turning to Palamedes, I smiled and placed my fists on my hips.

"You had a nice bath in the ocean, Son of Aphrodite," Zoticus said. "Was that not enough to cool you off?" His voice was mild, but it vibrated through my chest.

Palamedes scowled and stomped past us, leaving the mess. Now that the altercation was over, the group around them broke up with a disappointed sigh and wandered back to the party.

I turned to Zoticus. "Thanks."

"Any time." Zoticus slapped a huge palm on my shoulder. His skin was so dark it reminded me of obsidian, and his big black eyes were soft as he bent his boxy head to mine. "How long were you out?"

I shrugged and dropped my gaze to my feet. "Since after I was in that cyclone?"

"Did you get healed?"

His thick brows were lowered in concern when I glanced back up. "My father would have healed me if I was in trouble."

"Hm." Zoticus straightened and guided me to the door. "Let's go to the infirmary anyway."

"I'm sure I'm fine."

We strolled out of the mess toward the medical wing. "Probably," Zoticus said.

After getting healed, my headache disappeared, but in more ways I felt worse. Even though my team had won, as I walked out of the infirmary, I couldn't help but feel as if my first match had been a failure. I had known most of the students since we were small children, but I was still getting picked on by some and coddled by others. I trudged upstairs to my private rooms and spent the rest of the night alone.

CHAPTER TWO

I WAS sweating under the midmorning sun and already sporting a few bruises as I circled Antolios in the fighting pens. Antolios was silent as usual, a tower above me that neither blinked nor smiled. His flaxen hair was tied up in the complicated knot of the pale people of the north, where there were tall trees and ice. I was stuck fighting him for another half hour.

The first class of every school day was Gymnasium, where we worked out and then sparred until the midday meal. I ducked another well-placed swing by Antolios's sword, grinding my teeth. This was why I hated fighting him. It was rumored that he could read minds, and even though the son of Apollo never discussed his powers, he'd had a few slipups when he was younger.

Though I had lived here my entire life because my mother ran the school, most demigods attended the academy after eight or ten years old, when our powers manifested, and most of our powers were fairly obvious.

Besides Antolios's creepy eyes, no one knew for sure what he did, but he had frequently responded to people when they hadn't said anything, and one time in Reading he had lost it and told everyone to shut up—in a completely silent room. We all pretty much assumed he had some kind of mind powers and naturally had mental issues, but next year he would turn twenty-two and graduate, so I wouldn't have to fight him anymore.

I tried to focus, but when focusing got me as many bruises as not focusing, my mind began to wander. I caught a glimpse of Antolios's hard thigh under his tunic.

I frowned and danced away from one of his attacks, halfheartedly trying to bash him in the back, but he stepped aside. His tunic hiked up his leg, the color reminding me of white alabaster.

A thud against my shoulder sent me sprawling—I barely caught myself before I face-planted in the dust. I jumped to my feet, now covered in brown. Antolios leaped close, and his sword whooshed by my midsection. I sucked in my gut, dodged the blow, and inhaled, my nose flaring.

Antolios's scent was heady and earthy. Warmth flooded through me, and my penis throbbed. I flushed. We weren't wearing armor, and tunics were notoriously poor at disguising erections. I could have sworn I had seen Antolios like this a thousand times before today, so I was a bit surprised by how I was suddenly noticing the color of his skin and the way he smelled. I shifted into a defensive stance and successfully blocked two swings.

My blush crept all the way to the roots of my hair, but I told myself I didn't have anything to worry about. Since the academy was full of lustful demigods in various stages of development, an understanding had quickly formed among us. However, despite my assurances to myself, I shivered as the ocean breeze brushed over the sweat on my nape, and warily danced around Antolios, feinting back and forth.

As I fought, I remembered last month, when I had been walking toward the yurt where Professor Oston taught music class on the outskirts of the forest. I mistakenly took the wrong path, nearly running into Leonidas rutting against a tree. His wings were folded across his back, hiding what he was doing from sight, but I knew he wasn't alone. I could smell Nicanor beneath him and hear them both groaning.

Getting clobbered on the hip startled me out of my ruminations, and my face grew warm again. Antolios could read minds or something, right? Either he hadn't noticed, or he was ignoring my mental musings, because he continued to fight, occasionally whacking me with his padded sword and neatly dodging every one of my attacks. Why wasn't he in the advanced class?

I tried to concentrate on my technique, but my groin glowed in this oddly exciting but uncomfortable and distracting way, and I couldn't think of anything else, which seemed to make it worse. I caught another whiff of Antolios, and my lips dropped open. I had a strange desire to roll in the dirty scent, to roll *against him.*

After almost bashing me in the head for the third time, Antolios lowered his practice sword, his face blank. He returned it to the weapons rack.

"Where are you going?" I stuck my sword into the ground and leaned on it.

His back was still to me when he spoke, low and flatly. "Son of Zeus, please follow me."

I rolled my eyes at the overly formal address, and Antolios turned and looked pointedly at my crotch, his white light illuminating the bulging area of my tunic.

I froze. Oh shit.

Antolios started off toward the latrines, and I stood rooted in place. I hadn't really had this problem before, and I wasn't sure what to do about it, but a growing part of me was extremely interested in seeing what Antolios had to say. It couldn't be bad, right? I hadn't done anything wrong, exactly....

My heart beat furiously as I put my sword away and trailed after him, trying to look inconspicuous as I headed toward the latrines and then past the storage buildings. My mouth went dry, but I kept my head up. I was a son of Zeus.

When I came around to the back of the storage building, Antolios was pulling his tunic over his head, revealing hard, flat muscles. My breath caught and I stopped. Before I could recover, he reached for me with long arms, grabbing me by the collar. He slammed me up against the stucco wall and wrenched off my tunic.

I quickly crossed my arms in front of my chest to push him away, but he thrust his hand between my legs and wrapped it around me.

My breath huffed out, and my hips lifted without my control. I lost all desire to get away and dropped my hands to the side, thrusting against his fist. He joined our cocks together and stroked them, and I groaned.

Don't be alarmed, a voice spoke in my head.

I jolted, and then another wave of pleasure hit me, and my eyelids lowered. It was Antolios's voice. "Wha—"

Shhh, don't talk. Just think, and I'll hear you.

I closed my eyes and hoped I was thinking clearly enough. In the back of my mind, I wasn't sure why I was going along with this... but it felt good. *What's going on?*

We're communicating telepathically, he told me.

I meant to laugh, but the noise I made was an embarrassingly high and breathy whine.

And I want to try something.

Another wave of arousal crashed into me, and another. Oh gods.... *Whatever you like,* I said in my head, hoping he would "hear" it. Not sure what to do, I balled my hands into fists and dug my feet into the earth. He clutched us so our foreskins slid roughly together. I bit back another moan.

Suddenly I had a vague sensation of my mind being scrambled, and then my brain flooded with the storm. Instead of me reaching out to the storm, it was *in* my head, pulsing and swirling, and it got louder, and louder, and *louder*....

"Fuck!" I cried out, and Antolios's chest smashed my head back into the wall. I screamed, but my mouth was full of his salty skin, so I let out my scream through my nose and convulsed as my vision went white. Hot spurts shot out of my cock, over Antolios's hand, and in between our stomachs.

He groaned softly and stiffened, the wet spot growing between us. We both shook, and then he stepped back, releasing me. I almost fell forward, and I shivered as the cool ocean air hit my damp belly. Antolios's cock slowly lowered until it was hanging long and thick and dripping. I swallowed, my throat raw.

Antolios gave me a smile and then frowned slightly. *Let's get cleaned up.* His voice was in my brain but seemed to come from all directions at once. He turned and walked toward the latrines.

I inhaled deeply, recognizing the wonderful scent. It was us. The others would be able to smell it too, so Antolios was right. We had to clean up. I picked up my dirt-stained tunic and went to join Antolios at the wash bucket.

We rinsed our chests. Antolios's dark nipples stood out on his pale, almost hairless chest. I wondered if he even needed to shave. He snagged his tunic from the grass and threw it over his head. *I'll go first.*

I nodded and watched him leave. Numbly, I took the soap ball off the hook and ran it across my body. The scent of us was in my nose, in my brain, and I was sure it couldn't be washed out. I didn't want it to be.

What had just happened? Whatever it was, I was still reeling from it. My body buzzed faintly, still connected to the air around me even though I hadn't reached out to make that connection. The wind had kicked up again, and the sky was darkening. I shook the dirt from my tunic, dried off, and then pulled it on, adjusting the waist.

I met Antolios back in the pen. No one even glanced at us. We took our weapons back up but only finished a bit more sparring before Ramios called for us to switch partners. He shouted out the next group of sparring assignments. Same rules: no armor, no overt powers, and no bursting. I was paired up with Selene.

Selene's sparring partner, Page, left her to join up with someone else, so I headed into Selene's pen, giving Antolios one last look. He stepped over the fence, completely oblivious to me. That was the way it went, right? Quick pleasure, and then it was done. You wouldn't want to show weakness to the pack.

I was staring in the direction of the ocean, trying to decide how I felt about all of this, when Selene gasped. I peeked at her silver face, her white-blonde hair tied in the Thessalian knot. Her eyes were wide, with swirling, silver irises. She pointed. "What's wrong with your eyes?"

I raised a brow at her. She morphed her hand into a flat mirror, lifting it up so I could see. I took a look at myself, and then another. "What the fuck…," I said. My eyes were a churning gray tempest, and it consumed the whites and pupils. I poked a finger at my eyes, but they still felt firm and wet.

Jerking my head over to where Antolios fought Leonidas, I frowned at him. He was leaping into the air and then ducking low, dodging Leonidas's powerful wings. I didn't want to cause a scene, so I faced Selene again and shrugged. "It's nothing," I said, but my voice was high and tight, and the air shuddered around me.

Both of us looked up when the sky grumbled and darkened, and she gave me another wary look. "No powers, Perseus."

I closed my eyes, trying to separate myself from the storm, but my heart pounded, and the air pulsed with the beat of my blood. I practiced my meditation, breathing in the sky and blowing it out. Another gust of wind tossed my hair, and I clenched my fists.

"Professor!" Selene strode out of the pen. "Perseus is cheating!"

Shit. I sighed and gave up, opening my eyes. I had no idea why I couldn't detach myself from the storm or why I couldn't calm it down. I observed Antolios as he sparred. Leonidas extended his wings and tried to herd Antolios into a corner, and Antolios basically ran away.

Ramios marched up to my pen and beckoned to me. The professor's salted-black hair was cut close to his head, his beard was short, and he wore a bronze cuirass over a green tunic. Selene stood next to him on our side of the pen, her silvery arms crossed, looking bored and annoyed that I was being difficult. She was wearing the standard white tunic today, but her feet were bare.

I plodded over to the professor, feeling heat in my face, and the beginnings of thunder cracked above us.

"What's going on, Perseus?" Ramios eyed me and the darkening sky.

"Nothing, Professor. I'm not cheating." I rubbed my arms, trying to push the hairs down.

"Look at his eyes, Professor, and—is that rain?" Selene scowled at the droplets falling to the dirt.

Ramios regarded me and frowned. He held up his arms and gestured for me to come closer, and I sighed and moved forward. Taking my head in his hands, he peered into my eyeballs, tilting my face this way and that. After a minute he let go. "Huh. Well, go to the clerics, then."

I shook my head as thunder boomed. "I'm fine. Really."

Ramios glanced up and then at Selene.

She shook her head. "No. I'm not getting struck with lightning."

Ramios sighed and nodded. "Okay. Perseus, go throw some boulders or something. I'll fight Selene."

"Yes, Professor." I trudged over to put away my sword, shooting Antolios dirty looks that he probably missed.

I hung up my sword and headed toward the end of the field where we had the gym equipment. I tried to work on my bursting power as I tossed boulders, giving them that extra bit of speed before I released, but I couldn't concentrate. Each time I blurred my arms into motion, I threw the rock either too high up or it hit the ground at my feet. It wasn't until the end of class that the storm dissipated.

After class I waved to get Antolios's attention, but he and Leonidas had been sparring closer to the entrance to the main building and were the first to get inside for the midday meal. I jogged after him and entered the house, everyone's footfalls echoing off the walls. People laughed and talked, and Zoticus and the kids from the advanced class joined us in the hall, everyone filing into the mess and grabbing a tray.

I barely remembered getting my food. Antolios was sitting in his corner, so I stalked up and slammed my tray in front of him. "What the fuck did you do to me?"

He looked up at me, his bright eyes searing a hole in my brain. *Nothing. Sit and keep it down.*

I sat, glowering into his white glare. *Bullshit. You did something psychic.*

He dropped his gaze and resumed eating. *Your eyes are back to blue, so no harm done. A part of you was… hanging in your mind, and I simply jostled it lose.*

You what!

A part of you. It was probably going to happen anyway.

I stared at him in stunned silence. No one had ever dared hurt me before, yet I was fairly calm about it.

I'm sorry, he said. *I didn't mean to alarm you, and I don't think it's dangerous. It felt like a part of your mind, and that it was... out of place or wrong for it to be hidden, so I let it out. It doesn't feel bad, does it?*

I shook my head slowly. No... it didn't feel bad. It was the storm, the same storm I had always known. Instead of reaching for the connection, I could feel it all the time. If Selene hadn't said something, I probably wouldn't have noticed it for a while.

I should ask my father about this, but I wasn't sure when I'd see him again. The last time we'd had a conversation was... five years ago? Since then I'd been lucky if I spied him in a summer storm or caught him at the end of a conversation he was having with my mother on her balcony. I'd probably be fine.

I grabbed the flatbread from the table and dropped shrimp and sauce onto it from my plate. I took a bite and snuck a glance at Antolios, who looked completely unperturbed. Maybe he did this to people all the time.

I wasn't sure what to say, so we finished our meal in awkward silence. After, I followed everyone upstairs but stopped at the top of the landing. I wanted to follow them into the public baths, but someone nudged me from behind, so I walked to my suite.

Sarah and Marta were finishing drawing my bath, and they offered to wash me, but I waved them away.

I stared at the ceiling, getting used to the new connection I felt. My thoughts swirled until my bath grew cold and I was almost late for class. Running out of the tub, I threw on my clothes, snatched up my bag, and raced out the door.

AFTER SCIENCE, I had Art with Antolios and made sure to sit at his table. We were doing sculpture, and I stared at Antolios's long pale hands and how they shaped his dark clay. My throat went dry. I shifted in my seat and tried to concentrate on my work, putting my fingertips onto the cool clay. Frowning, I dug my thumbs into my sculpture, my heart pounded, and I began to sweat.

I looked up at Antolios. *Do you want to... come to my room after supper?* I held my breath.

Antolios tilted his chin. *Okay.*

I smiled. *Okay.* I looked at my work, a misshapen blob, and tensed up again. Now what was I supposed to do?

I spent the rest of the class trying to engage Antolios in conversation, but that was just as difficult as before I had taken my pleasure with him. Scratching my head, I was feeling out of sorts when class ended and I had to go meet my private tutor for History.

I SAT on my bed and stared at the door of my suite. It was after supper, and I had told my slaves to not come in unless I rang the bell for them. I had gone to the mess to eat but quickly left, the smells making me nauseated. I shouldn't feel this nervous. I was a prince, a son of the king of the gods. People did this all the time. Antolios probably did this all the time.

There were rumors that my mother put herbs in our watered wine so we couldn't conceive. The corner of my mouth twitched with the thought of my mother trying to explain to someone's family why their daughter was pregnant. Knowing the kinds of parties thrown by the students, finding the father would be… difficult.

This behavior was completely normal, and I probably should have been doing this years ago, so why did I feel lost?

A knock sounded on the door, and I jumped off the bed and went to open it. Antolios stood there, his light searing into me. My heart skipped a beat. How could I feel ill and excited at the same time?

"Come in." I stepped aside so he could duck through the door. I shut it behind him and latched it. "This is my room. Uh, the bathroom is over there, and my dressing area is just past it." Antolios briefly turned to where I pointed and nodded politely. I fumbled for my words. "I have some games. Do you want to play something?"

Antolios didn't answer, but stared straight at me. He stepped up and seized my shoulders, bending to kiss me. Our lips touched, firm and warm. My muscles were jelly as he moved into me and mashed our mouths, crushing me.

Acting on their own volition, my hands roamed up Antolios's back and then down, down, down. My heart beat faster and faster, and my cock twitched and filled. He pushed me toward the bed, backing me up until I hit the edge. Pulling away from my lips, he let me balance there until he shoved me with his palm and I fell to the bed. I bounced on the dense goose down as he removed his tunic and tossed it to the ground. I yanked my own tunic off and discarded it. His eyes never left mine. Their light lit my body as the moon on the sand.

I trailed my gaze up to his penis, the tip rosy against his light foreskin. It lifted toward his navel, nested in a patch of dark blond curls.

He knelt on the bed, and I closed my eyes. A finger dragged down my chin and all the way to my throbbing cock. "Do you have oil?" he whispered.

Before I could speak, he was up and striding into the bathroom. He came out with the jug, and I propped myself on my elbows, watching him work his penis over with oil. The skin glistened as a freshly shucked oyster, and I swallowed, licking my lips.

He smiled and kneeled back on the bed. "Go ahead," he said softly.

I crawled toward his penis, bringing it to my mouth to taste the warm olive oil and the salt from his sweat. I lapped at the exposed tip and danced around the slit, my body thrumming. Gods, I had never touched anyone this way.

Antolios sighed. Neck flushed all the way to his chin, his eyes were closed, and his thin lips were parted slightly. The thick golden curls and surprisingly fine eyebrows softened his angular features, but even with the glow muted by his eyelids, every once in a while I caught a flash of gold from his eyelashes where they glinted in the light. The capillaries on his lids popped out like small red lightning bolts.

I pulled down the sheath of his penis, taking the entire head into my mouth and sucking it hard. Antolios gasped as his hips thrust forward, his cock hitting the back of my throat. I pulled away so that I wouldn't choke, and moved my hands clumsily up and down his shaft.

Antolios clenched the blankets and groaned loudly, thrusting harder. *I'm close*, he sent.

Licking and sucking with renewed vigor, I wrapped my hands firmly around his shaft as my eyes watered with effort. I swallowed repeatedly, and Antolios's hips stuttered. He held his breath. The head of his penis swelled in my mouth as his salty seed rolled onto my tongue.

I gulped it down, and Antolios moaned and jerked. When he put his hand against my head, I released him with a plop. He fell back on the bed, ripping his legs from under him and spreading them off to the side. I swiped a hand across my face, but I couldn't wipe off my big grin.

He was mouthing words, but nothing came out. *Thanks.* He blinked, making the room flash. He regarded me and held his arms open. My stomach did a somersault, and I eagerly rolled into them. Our mouths touched, hot tongues darting around each other.

I didn't know how long we had been kissing, my body lost in the sensations, but when he laid me on my back, the heavy presence of the storm was in my mind. Antolios pulled away as I trembled with a desire I didn't know quite what to do with. I breathed and tried to catch up with what was happening. He slapped on more olive oil and then came back to me, his lips ghosting over mine.

I want to try something, he said.

I smiled. "Whatever you like."

He slid down my body, kissing his way past my painfully hard cock. Then he kept moving on, kissing my tight balls and going down, down, down.

A hot, wet tongue licked my crack, and my back arched reflexively. "Oh fuck!"

Antolios smiled at me from between my legs. He pushed my knees to my chest, urging me to take them, and wedged a pillow under my hips. Then he went back down, licking up and down my ass and swirling and poking his tongue. I jerked and groaned, eyes rolling into the back of my head.

"Oh my gods!" I bashed my head against the bed and tossed it side to side. I had no idea why it felt good, but I didn't want him to stop. My stomach muscles shuddered, and my cock was so hard I was going to rip apart.

Antolios pulled his face away, and my ass tried to follow him. I looked down, confused and panting.

His voice was uneven, cheeks flushed, and his pulse jumped in this throat. "May I fuck you?"

My cock throbbed, and I couldn't think through my fog of lust, but I didn't want to stop being touched. I barely managed to clarify my thoughts. *Whatever you like.*

He sat back on his feet, pulling me into his lap. My ass on his thighs, he reached down and rubbed the wet head of his penis against my anus. That frantic, urgent feeling of earlier left, and I got quiet. Antolios's brow furrowed as he tried to push into me, but I tensed. He didn't manage it. He pushed harder as I squeezed the tip of his penis. I stared at the ceiling and bit my lip.

"It's okay," he said. "Relax."

Trying to loosen my muscles, I took a few breaths and laid my head back. The stretch of my ass was weird to the point of discomfort, and I began to subconsciously scoot away from him, but he held me firmly in place. I felt the embarrassing urge to expel him from my body, and I tightened harder. Shivering, I broke into a cold sweat.

It's okay, Antolios said again. *Go ahead and push.*

I shook my head. I couldn't do this.

Antolios bent at the waist until his face was hovering above mine, the white light of his eyes glaring into me. I looked through the whiteness, on and on. In the depths I saw a kaleidoscope of rainbow colors, and my thoughts became louder and louder in my own mind until I was listening to myself talk. An eerie feeling grew in the pit of my stomach, but then the echoing consumed everything, and I listened raptly to it.

I was heir apparent to a land I had spent only one day in. Argos, a land I wasn't wanted in. And I was a bastard, my father already married to Hera, his sister. My mother said that when I was born, the gods told her I would be a hero and a king, and my legacy would shape the world. Even though they were gods, deep down I knew they were wrong. I'd never be good enough.

Antolios grunted and slid in farther. "That's it," he gasped. Our noses touched, but he sounded far away.

My father never came to see me anymore, and my mother rarely spoke to me. I was puny for a demigod, and weak, and no one liked me. And I wasn't good at this. My self-loathing was made worse by the tears that stung my eyes.

Antolios pulled me onto him until his hips rested against me. His voice was smooth and low, purring in his chest. "Perseus. You feel *so tight and hot.*"

My first instinct was to hide my face, because I was fairly certain that my thoughts hadn't been private, but something in the light of Antolios's eyes held me captive and I couldn't look away. I tried to feel the shame I knew was lurking in my mind, but I couldn't. The knots of tension in my abdomen eased and the pain faded, though the intense pressure was still there. The voices had stopped, and with each breath I felt more centered and sure.

I ran my hands up and down Antolios's arms, assuring him that I was all right.

Antolios shifted his legs behind him so he was lying on top of me, still keeping his cock snug in my ass. As he shifted, my ass gripped him, the new sensations of tight friction encouraging me to believe this wasn't all bad. He slapped his feet on the bed and laughed. "My foot's asleep."

I smiled and let my knees fall out to the side, my heels resting on the bed.

Antolios gathered himself and pulled out, and then pushed in. We both cried out, and I clenched his arms. The next thrust made my back arch, and my erection leaped back with forceful pulses. It was too much, but I didn't want him to stop. Our lips were almost touching, and then Antolios thrust forward and we kissed.

"Thank you." His breath puffed against my lips. *Gods, you're amazing.*

Slowly we moved together, and I gradually met his thrusts, working my stomach and hips. Behind the pressure and razor-like pleasure was a warm sensation uniting everything and making it hard to think again. I couldn't breathe.

Our sweaty skin squeaked as it slid together, and I propped myself up on my elbows, forcing Antolios to rock back his pelvis and dig into me. My head fell back, and he fastened his mouth to the apple of my throat, drawing sloppy circles over it with his tongue.

We went faster as my legs spread up and my body pounded with a hot and dire need. I fell back onto the bed and grabbed hold of my aching cock, stroking it between our stomachs. The energy screamed through my body and balls, and I jerked, the wet heat of my semen splashing between us. Grunting, I blinked away the shards of white in my vision.

Antolios panted and sped up, deeply penetrating me as he strained out a cry. I groaned as he ground us together. Jerking and panting, he pressed his lips into my hair. The side of his head rested against mine, and I wrapped my legs and arms around him.

We trembled there for a time, our hearts racing together, but eventually Antolios pulled away. A hot rush followed in his wake, and I stared at the ceiling, limbs flopped out to the side, and couldn't figure out how to work my body.

Antolios rolled off the bed and ducked into the bathroom. He came back with a cloth and brought it to my chest and rear, and even though the fabric was soft, I winced, feeling raw and vulnerable. With a sigh, he cuddled around me as though it were the most natural thing in the world to touch me, but no one had ever touched me this way.

Lying in his arms, I listened to the wind whipping the curtains and slowly turned my head toward the window. The sky was the color of a bruise. It was warm for the hour, but there wasn't any rain. How had I missed a storm brewing? I quested for my father, but I didn't find him. Was I responsible for this storm? There was something funny about that, but my thoughts slid around and were hard to hold onto.

"Go to sleep," Antolios mumbled in my ear. I tried to keep my eyes open, to figure this all out, but I couldn't.

CHAPTER THREE

THE SUN was just rising, and the tide was at its peak as I stood in the cool, wet sand while the ocean lapped at my feet. Gulls were calling above the roar of the surf, and my hair tossed in the morning wind.

I threw a shell into the waves and swept up another. I would have loved to say that the past weeks had been perfect, but they hadn't been. I had been thinking that when two people got together, things changed. I wasn't sure *why* I thought that, because nothing had changed with my parents. My mother, while regarded highly, was simply Zeus's current-century's lover, and though he did visit her more than he visited me, I had never seen them together as I had seen some other married couples.

Antolios was still… Antolios. We sat together in class, ate together at meals, and he slept in my room, but not much else. I wasn't sure what I had been expecting. I threw another shell into the ocean.

The sex had been good, at first. Antolios made me feel like I had never felt before, and I wanted it to be that simple and perfect, but it wasn't.

I dug my toes into the sand and squinted in the morning sun. I shook my head and kept wandering down the coast, my feet squeezing the moisture from the sand.

I wasn't going to class today.

Even though my mouth still tasted of the figs I had grabbed on my way out the door, my lips were twisted as though I had eaten a lemon. What had happened that morning was…. Gods, I couldn't have left the room fast enough.

I had been penetrating Antolios, something he had been demanding lately. That was all well and good, but I had been trying for the past week or so to figure out what he actually liked.

Because he just lay there. I had tried going fast and hard, gentle and slow, trying other positions… but he just lay there like a dead fish. The thing was, I knew he was having a good time. He fucking came all over the bed—every time.

This morning had been the last straw for me. I was so unnerved that I had practically run out of the room, leaving Antolios covered in his own seed and trying to trick him by thinking about the mess hall being full of pudding. Maybe he'd think I was really hungry or something. Shit.

I didn't want to feel petty, but he was hogging that position, and I didn't even know if he liked it. And the only reason I could think of for him to act so weird was that he was using me for sex. Because that's what demigods did.

He didn't really owe me anything, but I didn't want to be used.

I wandered up the beach and sat in the fine, cold sand. The sun was rising, the air shifting as it heated. Everyone thought that when the sky was clear the air was calm, but they were wrong. It was constantly dancing as if to music, sometimes fast and sometimes slowly. I closed my eyes and let myself get absorbed in the motion.

Up there in the clouds, amid all that potential energy, I felt like a demigod prince. I could create lighting, rain, and wind. If that was my will, then it would happen, because my will was law.

When I opened my eyes again, the sun was almost at its highest point. I rolled to my feet and brushed sand off my legs, then went to get a snack from the kitchens. I wasn't ready to see Antolios yet. I avoided him, meandering the woods and the beach, places where I knew I could be alone. Finally after suppertime I had come to a conclusion.

I could understand how maybe Antolios and I came from different perspectives when it came to sex, and I could even understand how we liked the same thing, but what I couldn't understand was why he felt he had to use me. Maybe sharing was a concept foreign to demigods, but if this was going to work I needed more.

Resolved, I entered the main building and marched up the steps to his room. I turned right toward the dormitories and walked down the long halls. At the end of one of the halls, in the corner, was Antolios's room. I took a breath, stepped up to it, and knocked.

I almost jumped when Antolios opened the door before my knuckles had left the wood. Had he just been standing there? I cleared my throat. "Uh, can we speak?"

He stared at me with those bright white eyes for unnervingly long moments, then finally stepped aside and allowed me to enter his room. It looked the same as the other dorm rooms, except his bed was longer.

I sat on the bed, because there weren't any couches. Antolios closed the door, and shuffled into the middle of the room with his head down. His height made his limbs appear almost too skinny, but they were tight with muscle, and I knew they were strong.

"What's going on?" I said.

He crossed his arms. "What?"

"Don't give me that. I know you better now." I rolled my eyes. "Don't make me spell it out for you."

There was a long pause. Antolios's hair was already tied up for sleeping, and he wasn't wearing sandals. His jaw cut a line when he was thinking, and I wanted to reach up and run my fingers across it.

"Don't you get what you want?" Antolios tripped over his words, rushing them, which was odd considering his voice was usually even.

"I thought things would be different."

"What do you mean?" His eyes searched me, and I squinted from the bright glare.

Suddenly a lump formed in my throat. I wasn't sure where it had come from. "What if I want something more? Something…." I tried to find the word as I stared into his glow.

"Balanced," Antolios said.

I snapped out of it and shot him a look. "I don't want to exchange favors all of the time. We can both like it. Don't you like it?" My voice cracked oddly, and I held my breath.

Antolios sighed and walked over to the end of the bed, sitting down and staring at his feet while he flexed his long pale toes. "I like it." He put his hands on his knees. "Just not in the way you do."

My heart pounded in my chest. "What do you mean?"

He turned his head so I could see the corner of his eye, but I couldn't tell if he was watching me. I had only seen his rainbow irises a few times, mostly when I was looking hard. "Sometimes, when we do certain things, I don't feel it like you do. The storm in your head, the one I shook loose? It helps me." Antolios looked at his hands. "I've had problems with my powers. For whatever reason, listening to the storm in your mind dulls them temporarily—makes me deaf. It stops the background noise."

I blinked. All day I had been dreading what I thought he was going to say, and this wasn't anywhere near what I had expected.

"I can't turn off my powers." His words became more clipped as his northern accent leaked through. "I constantly hear people's thoughts through the walls and the floor and the ceiling." He watched me, and his tone softened. "I usually find it hard to be around people, but I have slept so well with you."

I felt oddly relieved, and with that some of my annoyance crept back into my voice. "Are you just using me to medicate yourself with whatever is in my brain?" The blood pulsed at my temples. Were these last couple of weeks just a lie?

"I do like you!" Antolios said quickly. "And I have a good time—"

"Then what's with the lack of enthusiasm?"

"Well…." Antolios cleared his throat. "I have to concentrate on the storm to listen to it fully, and it's overwhelming. I don't know what to do with my body. Look, I'm sorry, I thought you were getting what you wanted, and I didn't think you'd care—"

"You didn't think I would care?"

Antolios made a strangled noise. "I'm sorry. I didn't know what you wanted from me—you didn't know! This was how everyone does it, and I thought that it would be what you wanted too."

"I guess…." I looked away this time. Wasn't that why I had come here, to talk about what I wanted? My mouth went dry as I tried to figure out what I was going to say.

"If you don't want to anymore, I understand. I know I'm a freak."

I turned to him, his face drawn and shoulders hunched. I wasn't sure how I felt about attracting people with the power in my head, a power I didn't fully understand myself, but was it really that different than me being attracted to the color of his skin or his scent? Demigods. We're all cursed.

"I didn't say that," I said. "I didn't even think it, so shut up a minute." I chewed my lip. "What if we tried something else?"

"Whatever you like."

WE SAT cross-legged on the forest floor a few kilometers from the academy, our knees touching. Holding his hands, I breathed slowly and became more aware of the weight and movement of the air—now I hardly noticed my connection with it unless I was concentrating. I didn't know what Antolios needed exactly, and neither of us knew what we were doing, but that was okay. I had a feeling it was always going to be like that between us.

I closed my eyes and woke the storm.

A cool wind blew my hair, and then it whipped through the trees. As I shifted the hot and cold currents, thunder cracked above. White flashed through my eyelids, but I kept feeding it until I could feel it for kilometers in all directions, pulsing.

My mind was roaring, and a tree branch near us creaked.

Antolios gasped. "Okay, just… hold it in your mind." *Don't….*

Even though I didn't conceptualize my powers in that way, I thought I knew what he was talking about. I stopped trying to create a storm, and simply opened myself up to observing it. My head cleared as I did so, and the weather gradually lightened to a mild breeze.

I wasn't aware of time passing, but the warm air from the day cooled and fell to the ground. I assumed Antolios was getting what he needed, because he hadn't said anything else. Could he share my awareness and awe of the sky when he was inside my head?

I was nudged. When I opened my eyes, I gasped and shivered. Antolios's hair was dripping down his face, and his nipples poked out through the wet fabric of his tunic. It clung to him, lining the rim of his belly button and his cock, shriveled and tight against his body.

We got up creakily and made our way back to the house, Antolios's eyes illuminating our path.

I chuckled through shudders. "Well, that was fun."

He nodded in a distracted way, his arms wrapped around himself, but he didn't say anything. We followed the trail back in silence.

In my room, and after I'd had a bath drawn, Antolios and I stepped into the warmth of the sunken tub, both sighing with ease, and I thanked Sarah and Marta, and dismissed them. We lay up to our necks in the hot water, and I closed my eyes until the heat had soaked through me. When I opened them, Antolios was staring at me, the light seeming softer somehow, but maybe that was just his expression. He was smiling.

"I don't know how to thank you." He smiled the biggest smile I'd ever seen on his face. His teeth were as white as the light from his eyes.

I scooted up a step in the tub and hugged my knees to my chest. "Of course. I didn't know."

"It's not your fault. For all of my abilities, it's no secret that I'm not great with people. Sometimes it's easier to avoid people or use them than to try to make friendships."

"I'd like us to be friends."

He laughed. "We are! No one has ever done anything like this for me before. I think I can hear *my own thoughts.*"

I grinned in celebration, but then my smile slipped. "We don't have to… if you don't want. We could just be friends, and I would like that." I tried to smile again, to show him that I meant it, but my lips jerked as though they were attached to strings.

Antolios grimaced. "I'm sorry I took advantage of you, Perseus. I assumed you wouldn't want to help me without getting something out of it too. For all my abilities, I can be obtuse." He rubbed his forehead. "My mother basically dumped me here when I was ten."

"I remember," I said. "You came in a black carriage pulled by big black horses. When you opened the door to get out, gold spilled to the stones. You had been sitting in it."

He chuckled wryly. "She wanted me as far away from her as possible."

"I'm glad you're here."

"Me too. I'd uh… like to start over if we could?"

I smiled and relaxed for the first time all day, and he smiled warmly back. I sat on the floor of the tub with him, my shoulder against his side. We held hands, twining our fingers together, light and dark.

"I'd like to try something with you," Antolios said. "I have a power that allows me to open up a connection between us, something you can feel too."

My mouth dropped open, and I had to spit the water out before I could answer. "I can read your mind?"

"No. It's an empathic connection, a sharing of feelings, not thoughts."

"Oh. Wait… have you done this before?"

I sort of meant it as a joke, but Antolios stiffened. "Once. With my best friend in Larissa."

I blinked, surprised and maybe a tad jealous that Antolios had had a best friend, but then I felt guilty. I cringed, watching his face for any sign he had heard me, but he didn't change his expression, so I quickly said, "I'll be able to feel your feelings?"

"When we touch," he confirmed. "But it may take a while for you to get used to it."

"Okay. What do I have to do?" I started to cross my legs, getting into the position we were in before.

"Nothing, just be quiet."

I relaxed back against the steps and closed my eyes, trying to detect him in my mind, like I had the first time, but I was alone in my head. Antolios shook me and I opened my eyes. "It's done? That was fast."

He kept his hand on me. "What do you feel?"

"I… uh…." The sky was dark outside, and a cool sea breeze came in through the windows. I was relaxed, and the smell of almond soap and lavender filled the bathroom. Then, almost resembling a pleasant ache, I felt something else. Another easy sensation bloomed in my mind. "I feel you," I whispered.

"And I feel you." He smiled and held my hand.

"Couldn't you do this before?"

"No. I'm not usually empathic. This is a special spell I can do between our minds, linking the two. Normally I only hear thoughts as shouts or whispers." He cleared his throat and muttered, "Which is why you threw me off this morning with your deception. I mean, really? Pudding? Interesting choice, considering what we were doing."

I blushed, and he winked at me.

"Sometimes with people I am close to, I can detect sensations, and if I touch someone it gets easier. Like this." He squeezed my hand. "I like this."

"Me too." A jolt of hot lightning raced up my spine, and it warmed my chest and sank into my balls. My cock filled. Antolios's cock was already hard and floating toward the surface. I smiled and reached for him. "Aye, I like it."

CHAPTER FOUR

A DRY cough resounded through the room, and I glanced up, yanking my finger from my wavy black hair. Professor Scops was at her desk sorting through papers as we students sprawled on cushions, reading. There were young boys and girls along with older students like Antolios and Bortos all crammed into the same class. The library was filled with shelves of scrolls, and even though it was at the bottom floor of the educational annex, it got stuffy in the summer, so we all gathered by the windows near Professor Scops's desk.

Antolios had made it to Reading, and I was relieved. The night before I'd had a hard time sleeping without him, worried that he wasn't feeling well. He hadn't been there for Gymnasium or our midday meal either. This headache had lasted longer than the others he'd had over the past months.

I refocused on my scroll about Loncy, one of our greatest heroes. He was a son of Aphrodite and had traveled the kingdoms of Greece and beyond, and was often considered to be one of the most beautiful and dangerous men to have ever lived. Demigods didn't usually judge one another by their powers but rather by their cunning, skill, and bravery. Loncy was a champion of Athena because of his keenness, but his power was the manipulation of sound and, like Antolios's, had not been seen for many centuries. He had done all sorts of fantastical things, and many great men and women had fallen hopelessly in love with him. He'd vanished at sea long ago, but Poseidon denied that he'd had anything to do with it.

Storm demigods were fairly common, and the last one had been Kia, a daughter of Hermes, but she had died in battle several years before I was born. It was a coincidence that I shared the same power as Zeus, one that Hera wasn't happy with.

Professor Scops cleared her throat. "Students, class is finished for today. Remember that your reports are due after the weekend."

I shuffled out the room with the other students and then waited outside the door for Antolios. He shambled out, his face still gray, and I fell into step beside him. Demigods weren't supposed to suffer from disease, but Antolios suffered from something.

Feeling better? I said in my head, knowing he would "hear" it.

"Much better," he said softly.

I wanted to hold his hand to assure myself that he was feeling better, but Antolios would disapprove of the open display of affection, so we walked downstairs in silence. We were lovers, and we knew it, but no one else did. I didn't understand why Antolios wanted to keep it secret—I wanted to shout it out to the world.

Once we walked outside the open doors, everyone spread out in different directions.

One of the kids behind us shouted, "Hey, Palamedes!"

Palamedes was in front of us and turned, twisting to see who was talking. His blond hair swept across his face as he considered Thea with bright green eyes. He was well muscled and tall, though not as tall as Antolios or Zoticus. No one was.

Thea's voice had a nasty edge, and when I looked over my shoulder at her she was sneering. Her dark hair was piled on her head with combs in it. Even though most of the students wore white casual tunics, she was wearing a green dress. "What's your name?"

The students around us laughed, and Palamedes turned bright red. He made a rude gesture at her, spun around, and cut a path toward the woods.

The group called out his name and taunted him until his blond head disappeared into the trees. He got upset when people thought he was stupid, but it was funny that he couldn't remember his name, even when he seemed to understand when people were talking to him. The professors let him put a circle on his work instead.

I laughed along with everyone because Palamedes was such an ass, but when I turned to Antolios to share the joke, he was scowling. I stopped laughing, worried that he thought I was being a coward because I probably wasn't brave enough to make fun of Palamedes to his face.

What? Heat rose to my cheeks. *He's an ass. Actually, I enjoy ass much more than him.*

Antolios looked disgusted and shook his head. "People shouldn't make fun of him for this."

"He gets what he gives," I said.

Antolios shrugged off my words with no comment and slowed down. Thea and her friends were still laughing as they walked by us. When they had gone, he reached for my fingers, and I would have felt cozy about the gesture, but I knew it was only because he didn't feel up to full strength and wanted to talk privately. I felt the bond open up, and yes, he was weak and tired, and I stifled a yawn, his sleepiness creeping into me.

It's not just his name he forgets, Antolios said in my mind. *One time I walked into the latrines, and he was standing there, looking lost. I gathered that he had forgotten how to pee, but he desperately needed to go. He left, pretending that he had already gone.*

I stopped walking. *What's wrong with him? How do you forget something like that?*

We are encouraged by the gods to not speak of it.

My mouth dropped open. *Of what?*

Antolios shrugged. *This… balance that happens within all of us.* His face was pinched into a frown as he studied me. *I was wondering if you knew what yours was. I supposed I would have seen it by now, but I haven't, and you don't even think about it.*

What do you mean? My what? I uneasily wondered if my suspicions about something being wrong with me were correct and even more horrible than I had originally believed.

All demigods have this, but it is different for all of us. I get headaches, as you know.

That's why you get them? I knew that some… odd things had happened through the years to various students, but I'd assumed it was because we were demigods and complicated. I had no idea that there could be more of an explanation.

Yes, and that's why Palamedes can't remember things, he said. *Zoticus suffers from nightmares, Phoebe from fevers, and Leonidas eats stones. That kind of thing.*

I scratched my head. "I don't think I have one…. I'm short?"

Antolios's voice surged through me, demanding my attention. *That's not what I mean. It's usually something cyclic and related to our powers, but not always. No one has said anything to you? Not your mother, father, or the clerics? It would have been around when you gained full control of your powers, around when I came to Seriphos.*

I opened my mouth and closed it again.

Antolios gazed through me for breathless moments and then looked away. *Weird.*

My brain was a bit foggy, and I blinked, trying to clear the spots from my vision. "Everyone has it?"

Every demigod, he said.

I grunted. "My mother is human, and it's well known who sired me. Hera wouldn't be trying to kill me, otherwise."

I don't know why you don't have one, Antolios said at last, shrugging. His face was still pinched thoughtfully, but his voice in my head wasn't as resonant. The pressure eased from my skull. *I guess it's a good thing. I'd rather not have mine, and I'm sure other demigods would say the same.*

We started walking down the path again, but then I stopped. *Wait, Leonidas eats stones? Why does this happen again?*

Antolios strode ahead of me, his white tunic swishing about his long legs. "There are weirder ones than that."

I ran forward to catch up. "Tell me!"

"Maybe later."

I studied his face to see if he was teasing, but he was still frowning, his pale lips drawn together. He had fixed his gaze toward the setting sun, and the curls around his head glowed, so I reached up to run my hands through the golden strands. "What do you want to do until supper? Are you still tired?"

"Let's go swimming," he said.

I smiled and dropped my hand. Swimming sounded good.

THE NEXT day, the sound of my door opening woke me up. Sarah and Marta came into my room wheeling hot water and rocks for my bath. I blinked in the morning light, and then I turned to look at Antolios, who was watching me. I blinked in his light too.

I waved to my slaves. "Good morning." They bowed their heads and wished me good morning, then disappeared into the bathroom.

Antolios was smiling and studying me, his pointy chin held in his hand, and I got the feeling that he had been doing that for a while. If I admitted it, I'd been staring and grinning a lot lately too.

"And good morning." I dragged him to me. Our skin was warm from sleep, and our breath was heavy and sour, but it was us and fantastic.

Antolios pulled away and held up a finger. "One. Then food and the beach."

"One," I agreed and kissed him again. I inhaled his scent and groaned, grinding my erection against his hip.

He chuckled against my lips. *You liar.*

I snickered and threw the blanket over our heads.

After sex and a bath, we grabbed almond cakes from the kitchen and sprinted down to the beach. We had been getting up early on some days so Antolios could deafen himself with the storm and take the edge off his abilities. It helped him sleep, and really helped him focus during sex. Though he'd still stare off into space at times, my ass was happy.

Antolios told me a joke while we were going down the wooden stairs to the sand, something he'd heard in Page's head, and I laughed so hard I fell down the stairs and landed in a heap. I spit sand from my mouth, still grinning. I'd been a lot clumsier of late too.

We assumed our meditative positions, the morning sun warming our faces. It was hard to track time when I was in the clouds, but by the time Antolios pulled me out of it, I was starving. We raced back to the academy, and in the mess hall I sat at a table, stuffing more almond cakes into my mouth. Antolios poured us tea while I loaded my tray up with stewed grains and fruit. I jammed it all into my mouth at the same time, then bit into an orange with the peel. The mix of flavors didn't bother me, and I kept shoveling it in.

"Uh…," Antolios said. *Are you feeling all right?*

I glanced at him, mouth full, and nodded. Maybe my body ached a little—I probably pulled something during sex. I tried to moisten the mass in my mouth with the bitter tea. It was hard to swallow fast enough and breathe at the same time.

You want to slow down? Antolios peered down the table, and I followed his gaze. Everyone was staring at me. My face flamed. I glared at Nicanor, who was sitting next to me and ogling me with big brown cow eyes.

"What's your problem?" I tried to say, but I sprayed food all over his plate.

The skinny boy flinched away from me.

My face fell a little, and I examined my own plate. There was partially mutilated fruit smeared over it, and I was clutching clumps of barely identifiable cake in my fists. I tried to mumble apologies, but they didn't make it past the bolus in my throat. I swallowed and my knees started to hurt.

Let's go upstairs, Antolios said.

I wanted to, I really did. My face was burning and my body was aching, but I was just so hungry. My chest hurt.

I'll bring food.

I stood up and kept my gaze on the floor, leaving my mess all over the table. I hobbled upstairs, my knees aching more and more with every step. As I crashed into my room, my legs locked awkwardly, and I threw myself on the bed. I moaned and clutched my back as it seized up as well. "Ow, ow, ow!"

Antolios placed his cold hand on my forehead. "What's wrong?"

"I don't know." I panted and ground my teeth together. I couldn't breathe.

He pulled his hands away. "I'm going to get a cleric."

I shook my head. "No! Don't!"

Antolios's face was close, his thick blond hair already tied up for Gymnasium. "Come on, Perseus. Something's wrong!"

"No! They'll tell my mother, and she'll get all… weird." I winced at how petulant that sounded.

"Stop being melodramatic." Antolios slid his hands up my tunic and rubbed my back, and I finally remembered how to breathe, letting the air from my lungs explode out before I sucked it in. Antolios spoke to me in my head, his tone calm and concerned. The bond between us surfaced into my mind, the soothing emotions distinctly different than my own. Sometimes I had a hard time reading him, but it seemed he had amplified his emotions in my brain. He lay down and pulled me alongside him.

I closed my eyes, and the pain pulsed behind my lids while I tried to breathe through it. What if this was the curse, or whatever, that Antolios had been talking about?

"Perseus?"

The shards of pain had turned into dull throbs. "What?"

"Are you taller?"

My eyes flew open. "What!"

"I'm serious…." He spread out and lined me up against him. "Look, the top of your head is now between my clavicle and nipple."

I snickered and glanced up at his chin, then down at our feet, still sandy from the beach. "Holy shit, you're right. I'm almost at your shoulder!" I got super excited, but a stab of pain in my ribs brought me down from my glee.

"You've been eating more for a while now, just not like *that*."

I swallowed. "I don't know what that was about."

"I think you're heavier." He squeezed my arms, tickling me under the armpits.

I giggled and curled up, but that made me wince and suck in air. "It hurts to move!"

Antolios rubbed my back. "Are you going to Gymnasium?"

"I don't think I can." We were supposed to fight with our powers, which at the very least was always interesting. Who didn't like using their powers? Well, Antolios didn't.

"Okay, I'll stay with you. Are we going to call up the clerics?"

"No. I'm fine. I'm just sore," I said.

"And irritable."

I growled and nibbled his nipple through his tunic.

Antolios chuckled and grabbed an almond cake from the chest. "I'm sure you'd rather have this."

I stuffed it into my mouth, chewed, and swallowed. I licked the crumbs off my fingers. "So, do you think I'm going to get taller?"

"I don't know, but the clerics might."

"Seriously, Antolios. No clerics."

"Gods, Perseus, they are there to help. Just because that one time—"

I put my hands over my ears. "Blah blah blah!"

Antolios's dryly amused voice flooded my head. *It was your fault. You shouldn't have demanded that they pull it.*

"Aggghh!" I punched Antolios in the shoulder, and he laughed. I couldn't feel too upset, though—my painful past memories were worth seeing him smile. My chest swelled with happiness, and I forgot about the ache in my knees and back. He held me closer.

Not having a father figure while growing up, and having a mother who insisted that she would not pull teeth, I'd had to go to the clerics when I had a tooth that was stuck. One time I had gone to the infirmary to have them pull a tooth as usual, but they'd said it wasn't ready. I knew it was ready—it was wiggling when I put my tongue to it. I had asked them politely to pull it, so they did.

There was so much blood I'd almost choked on it. They had healed me, but I swore they took their sweet time about it. The rest of my teeth thankfully fell out while I was sleeping.

"Do you think your mother had your father pull the rest out while you were sleeping?" Antolios said.

"What? She did?"

"I don't know," Antolios mused. "I guess I could look into it."

I chuckled ruefully. "He always comes when she calls, but not when I do."

"The gods have no time for the children of their illicit affairs."

We curled up, and I listened to the steady swish and thump of Antolios's heart. The pain in my joints grew, and soon I was sweating and rocking against the throbbing.

Antolios murmured in my hair. "Perseus… I'm sorry."

"It's for a good cause, right?" I laughed deliriously.

He didn't say anything, just petted me. I clung to his tunic, now damp with my sweat.

"Hey, look at me for a second," he said.

I looked up, squinting into his bright eyes. The pain lessened, and my breathing slowed. I stretched my legs, working out the cramps, and yawned in his face. "Sorry," I mumbled.

"I think…," Antolios said.

My muscles became jelly, and my lips were hard to move. "I'm tired."

Antolios shifted under me, and his voice rose. "I'm doing that! How do you feel?"

"Fine… tired." I forced my eyes open and smiled at him.

His face was open, eyebrows high. "I just found the pain in your brain and put a cloud on it."

I laid my head on his shoulder, his words humming through me. "You're so bright and powerful and amazing. My hero. My angel."

"Your angel, eh?" Antolios kissed my head. "I think I made you drunk."

I stuck my lip out. "I'm not drunk, just relaxed and happy. So happy. Can we stay here all day?"

"You'll get hungry."

My eyes drifted closed. "Cross that bridge…." I fell in and out of dreams, but I knew that Antolios was with me the entire time.

I WOKE up. There were voices and shifting lights, and warm hands left my skin.

Antolios seemed to speak from far away. "Thank you. I will. He'll be upset if he sees you."

Another voice muttered something, and the door closed.

Cool hands rubbed my chest. I was… naked. "Angel?" I mumbled.

"Are you okay?" Antolios said.

I opened my eyes, everything too bright and blurry, and yawned. Antolios was hovering over me. "What time is it?" I said.

His face flickered. "Early morning."

Confused, I glanced out the window. Pale morning light came in through the wispy curtains. "How is it…?" I struggled to sit up and Antolios helped me. "Is it the *next day*?"

"Yes… well, there was an accident."

I rubbed my eyes and ran a hand through my hair. Gods, I was hungry. Antolios handed me a roll filled with goat cheese and fig and honey off the chest, and I munched happily for a moment. "Wait—what accident?" I said with my mouth full.

He slumped next to me, his pretty brows pinched with worry. "I was getting fatigued from soothing your pain, so I tried to help you sleep off the worst of it, but I accidentally knocked you so far unconscious you were unresponsive."

I laughed and winked. "Asshole."

His fair skin blushed prettily. "At first I thought you just needed the rest, but this morning I couldn't wake you. I don't know if I was still deafened from yesterday's meditation or what, but I tried for a *half hour*. I had the clerics help me."

"Ah. That's why it smells like old shoe leather, and that incense they burn. Cleric Cyrus was here."

"So you're not mad?" Antolios sighed in relief.

"Naw. I feel better, actually."

Antolios took a breath and eyed me warily. "I have another confession to make. While they were up here I had them look at you, to see why you were in pain."

I groaned and slapped a hand over my face.

His voice rose. "They couldn't tell me if you're growing or not, since the last time you let them look at you was over four years ago, but you are… changing."

"Oh," I mumbled under my hand. "I could have told you that."

He laughed at my joke, even though I delivered it weakly. It was great that I was developing further, but the confirmation brought up more questions as to why I hadn't been. At least it was happening, or finishing up happening. Maybe I'd be as tall as Zeus. No one could call me short if I was as tall as the king of the gods, right? That would be blasphemy, or something.

Antolios's voice became light and teasing. "Now I know your whining is just whining, and you aren't going to explode or something. I'm sure it's happened. Who knows with demigods?"

I enjoyed Antolios worrying about me, but maybe that was something I shouldn't say. He drew designs with his fingers over my chest, and I pulled my hand off my face and finally met his gaze. Antolios seemed relaxed, but I could feel the tension in the way he held his body. He eyed me, a faint smirk on his face.

Rolling onto me in one smooth motion, he pinned me to the mattress. I didn't even know he paid attention during wrestling. He pushed me against the mattress, spreading me out with his strong hands and thighs. Desire flared through the bond, and I groaned. Our lips touched, softly and then harder. He pressed his entire length into me, lifting his tunic and rubbing our cocks together.

I froze. "Uh, can I go to the bathroom first?"

He chuckled and rolled to the side. "Hurry."

I sprang off the bed and got my ass slapped in the move. I hurried.

I WAS in my private history lesson later that day, reclining on the large pillows and trying to pay attention to Professor Enoch, but my head kept rotating toward the window, where I could smell the sea and the trees near this part of the grounds.

"In the beginning, there was only Chaos...." The old man lectured about how some of the gods of the Greek pantheon existed in other cultures' lore with different names, and about the minor gods and what their parts were in creation. My brain was still messed up with all the different origin stories, and I completely zoned out Enoch's droning voice.

It was weird that I hadn't been bothered by Antolios messing with my head earlier that day, or any other day, really.

When I was very young, I had thought that my mother had created the academy so that I would have children to play with. However, I learned that demigods tended to be lone wolves, and even though most of the students seemed to be there to learn from the best, quite a few of them were probably spying for their respective kingdoms. I was also expected to use those around me for my gain. I could tell myself I was using Antolios for sex, and my mentors would understand that very well, but I knew if Ramios saw me with Antolios, he would berate me for leaving myself vulnerable.

Why was it so easy to let Antolios touch me that way?

"Who is Celestian?" Professor Enoch's voice suddenly boomed nearby. The old man was standing above me, his sandaled foot on my floor pillow.

My chin popped out of my hand as I gaped at my professor. His pupils were milky, and his white beard was thinning. "Celestian?" I said. "Another name for Uranus, god of sky and space."

I wasn't fooling Professor Enoch, and he peered at me from under bushy brows. "What do you call a mortal sired under Uranus?"

"Uh...."

"That was a trick question," Enoch sighed. "Perseus, your attention has not been adequate of late."

"I'm sorry, Professor."

"Go." Enoch waved a gnarled hand. "We are done for today."

I smiled and shoved my papers in my shoulder bag.

"Have Antolios explain this all to you. He holds your supreme interest these days."

I kept my gaze on the floor, my face flaming. "I'll do that." I rose from the floor, nearly running toward the door. A dry chuckle echoed after me.

I dashed down the long hall and broke out the open entrance of the annex and into the afternoon. Throwing my bag on the grass and leaning against a stone pillar, I crossed my arms and tried to ignore the feeling that I had just been exposed. Enoch had let me out early, so it would be a little longer before Antolios was out of his history class with the other advanced students.

The sound of steps in the grass near the side of the building alerted me before Palamedes, Leonidas, and Thea strolled around the corner.

Why weren't they in class? I greeted them with a nod as they fanned out in front of me. Both Palamedes and Leonidas were wearing simple white tunics with sandals, but Thea was wearing a dress belted with linked golden rings, and jewelry. She even wore metal sandals. They looked uncomfortable.

"Perseus." Palamedes smiled with all of his teeth, and his green eyes flashed dangerously. The bronze muscles under his tunic stretched as he swaggered up to me. He had a sling in his belt.

I frowned. "What do you want?"

Thea and Leonidas exchanged glances, and Leonidas rolled his shoulders and spread his wings out, the pearly feathers rustling. His hair was black and short. I always thought that was odd. Shouldn't his feathers be the color of his head hair?

"We just wanted to talk to you." Palamedes's smile was overly friendly.

"So talk."

The three of them looked at one another again, and I tensed up. Almost without realizing it, I woke the storm, creating pressure and friction. I wasn't sure if I could take them. If I could get Palamedes down, maybe. Thea shared her brother's power of creating darkness, and I had beaten Bortos soundly in the last match. A powerful enough gust of wind could keep Leonidas grounded. Shit.

A bright light lit the side of my face, and my heart leaped in my throat when Antolios walked into view. My smile froze. His head was bent, and he looked even more withdrawn than usual. He came up and stood an arm's length from me, but it felt like a kilometer.

Palamedes clapped his hands together. "Well, now that we're all here…." Students walked past, and some shot us glances but continued on their way.

"What's this about, *Palamedes*?" Just saying his name made me sick.

A dark look passed over Palamedes's face, and we stared each other down.

Don't, Antolios said. *Let me handle this.*

His words threw me off-balance, and I whipped my head away, crossing my arms. I glared at the sky, and my ears popped, the hair on my arms rising as well. The clouds grew dark and heavy.

"The rumor is that you are very close." Leonidas's voice was full of scorn. I raised a brow at him and almost laughed, but apparently he didn't find the statement as ironic as I did. He stared at Antolios and me disapprovingly.

Antolios *did* laugh, a bold blast that unnerved me more than anything so far. He was standing straight now, looking down on the three of them. "So?" He dropped his bag to the grass.

Thea stepped forward, her brown hair pulled back from her face and a flower in her ear. Clouds of darkness curled from her fingers and toes. "You're not just fucking. You're paired, and don't deny it. We've seen you," she said.

Leonidas's voice cut. "You *hold hands*."

I flushed, and Palamedes flashed another overly charming smile, his teeth white and cheeks pink. He brushed aside his blond bangs. The asshole probably loved this.

"An *exclusive pairing.*" Thea lifted her petite nose into the air.

I glanced back and forth between them. As far as I knew, no one had wanted me before Antolios, so what the fuck was this about? Did Thea want me? Did she want Antolios? *What the fuck?*

Antolios didn't answer me. He smirked and shrugged so casually I knew he was faking it. "Did you want some of this, Palamedes?" Antolios cocked a hip, displaying his ass. "Or maybe you want something else…?"

Palamedes turned an interesting shade of red, his eyes bulging, and I snickered.

"Enough talk. You are demigods, and you should both be shamed for this," Leonidas said. "Just tell us who the girl is, and we'll get on with it."

I reared back. *Girl? It?*

Thea laughed. "It's probably the son of the king of the gods. I'm going to love making him a man."

Leonidas glared at Thea and stabbed a finger at Antolios. "He doesn't fight!"

I winced and looked away. It was true. I wasn't sure why Antolios bothered to compete in the matches—probably because he'd be ridiculed more if he didn't. We never talked about why he didn't enjoy fighting, but now I felt his shame as if it were my own.

"No one is the woman, you pathetic children," Antolios said. "I can carry the bull if I raised the calf."

What? I said, but Antolios wasn't paying attention to me.

Thea and Leonidas quieted and exchange worried glances.

Palamedes made a sound like he was dislodging something vile from his nostrils. "He was a man! They're both men!"

Antolios, what the fuck is going on?

He ignored me again. Leonidas and Thea looked me up and down doubtfully. Palamedes caught their looks and stamped his foot, gesturing to me. "Come on! Even though he's puny, he was a man! He needs to be taught a lesson!"

A blood vessel popped in my eye. "Fuck you!" I whipped my head to Leonidas and Thea. "I don't know what the fuck your problems are, but this is none of your business. You're still children, and I'll forgive you your insolence if you leave now." I didn't wait to see if they followed my orders, and I turned my entire body to Palamedes, letting my hate boil. "But you, asshole. Just fucking *try* me."

Perseus....

Palamedes smirked. "You're the bitch."

"No!" Antolios screamed, but I was already making a path for the lightning from the sky to Palamedes's chest.

Palamedes rolled just as the thin white bolt hit the ground, kicking up clots of dirt. His hands blurred and the sling flashed. Antolios stepped in front of me.

I ducked and rolled, but something stung my head and I cried out, tumbling onto the ground. Getting my legs under me, I struggled to pop back up and fight, but then the entire world was plunged into night. Thea had probably cast darkness on the area.

There were thuds and shouts. When I put my hand against the painful spot on my head, it came back warm and wet, and I smelled blood. I felt the impacts of feet running across the ground, and the beat of wings blew my hair. Pain laced my vision, and the world went silent as I crouched in the grass.

Someone approached, and I threw up my fists, but then I smelled Antolios and slumped. His breath tickled my face, and I thought he said something to me, but I didn't know what it was. The world buzzed and tilted as Antolios picked me up. If Thea was gone, why was it still dark? I kept blinking, trying to see, and then everything else faded.

"Get off me!" I shouted. I was surrounded by the incense smells of the infirmary and the black-and-white robes of the clerics of Zeus. I batted at people's hands, and they gradually parted, revealing the white light of my lover.

"It's okay." Antolios reached for me.

I sat up as Head Cleric Cyrus sniffed at me. "He'll be all right." The robed figures moved off to other business.

One of my eyes was gelled shut, and I had blood in my hair and crusted down the side of my face and tunic. I hopped off the bed and hobbled forward, my head swimming. "Where is he?"

"Easy." Antolios wrapped his hands around my waist. "They can help you feel better if you stay."

Growling, I shrugged him off. "Where is he?"

"Probably still in the grass."

My breath came out in gasps, and my vision blurred. "I'm going to kill him." I'd gotten all the way out of the infirmary and halfway to the back door when Antolios placed his hands on my shoulders and pushed down. My knees buckled, but he supported me before I fell over.

Antolios hauled me back into the center of the house. "Come on. Let's take a bath."

My eyes stung. "Fucking asshole! He's such an asshole."

"I know. Let's talk about it upstairs."

My shoulders fell, and I let him lead me back to my rooms.

CHAPTER FIVE

ANTOLIOS RANG the bell when we got inside my bedroom and then tried to take off my tunic, but my fists were clenched, so he had to wrench my arms up to remove my clothes. He unwound my sandals and pulled me into the bathroom, sitting me on the bench next to the window. My slaves came in, and he asked them to start a bath.

He wet a cloth and washed my face, wringing the bloody water out in the basin. It smelled of iron. When he was done, I got up without a word and trudged into my bedroom. Picking up the heavy metal ball on my shelf, I lay down on the rug and tossed it into the air. Twenty times up with one hand and twenty times up with the other. Twenty and twenty.

"Bath's ready," Antolios said.

In the steaming bathroom, I stomped into the water, the rocks still sizzling at the bottom of the tub. Antolios stepped into the tub to join me, hissing and wincing from the heat. I threw my ball again. Twenty and twenty.

Finally I said, "So, are you going to tell me what that was about?"

Antolios's voice echoed off the tiles of the room. "I think you already know."

I gritted my teeth. "Why do they care?"

"You've lived your entire life with demigods, Perseus. In the outside world, there aren't a lot of us, and the only times we see each other are on the opposite ends of battlefields."

I knew that. I wasn't going to be a general, though. I wasn't really going to get to be a prince, either. My grandfather had exiled me from Argos, and so I would stay in Seriphos to train until it was time for me to take the throne.

"There are some rules for our kind of thing that humankind holds to, and consequently so do other demigods," he said.

"Rules? Our kind of thing?" I sneered. "My father just brought some prince up to Mount Olympus to be his cupbearer. Cupbearer! Like that's a thing. I've heard about the girl-only parties in the dormitories, Leonidas fucks everything, and look at Nicanor!" My heart pounded, and I felt light-headed.

Antolios dragged his hand over his face, the room darkening and then brightening again. "First of all, no one gives a fuck about Nicanor. He's sired by some lesser god, and let's face it, he's more of a social leper than I am. Second, you heard what they said. They don't have a problem that we fuck. They have a problem that we're *paired*."

"None of their business."

"They think so, and so will Greece. You're a son of Zeus and have a prophecy. You're important to the gods."

"What about the gods?" I spat.

"They follow the rules too, and there are rules." Antolios sighed. "Look, I'll give you a point if you can come up with one example of your father being the passive partner to another male."

"What about your father?"

Antolios laughed hollowly. "I'd argue that Apollo is the butt of many jokes on Mount Olympus." His face softened. "Whether you agree or not, the other students judge you more harshly. There probably wasn't anything we could have done to stop them from trying what they did, but what you don't understand is how significant it was that they asked. They were attempting to fit you into their idea of a hero, despite what you think."

I grabbed the bar of soap and scrubbed myself under the water, removing the remains of my fight with Palamedes. Even though Palamedes was sleeping it off in the dirt, I felt as if I'd lost.

I'd be playing dumb if I pretended not to understand some of what Antolios was saying. My father took that prince, a pretty boy, to Mount Olympus, but I had never seen our kind of thing before—close equals—not even in girl-and-boy pairs among demigods. We just didn't do this, and I knew that. I had chosen to pursue a pairing with Antolios anyway because I wanted it, and that was the only thing that should matter to anyone.

Maybe I was acting like a demigod after all.

I broke the surface and sluiced the water from my face with my hand. "Fine. Let's tell them I take it up the ass. I don't care, and Palamedes won't successfully goad me again."

"You can't. Your honor is at stake."

I snatched up my ball again. "I'm going to be a hero as the gods said."

"There's a difference between fame and infamy."

I stalked out of the tub, my body heavy, and dried off with a cloth and tossed it to the floor. With my back to Antolios, I said, "Do you want to stop? Is that what you're saying?"

Antolios splashed out of the water and came up behind me, placing his hand on my shoulder. "No. And we won't have to tell them anything."

My lip quivered, and I blinked back tears. "If you're going to say it, just say it."

"I'm going to erase their memories of us together."

My breath hitched. "Wh—?"

Antolios rushed out, "I've done something similar on a smaller scale, but I think I can manage it. They won't remember this fight or the fact that we're lovers. If I can't do it completely, at least I can confuse them."

I had no doubt he could do it, and his solution seemed perfect. No one would suspect, because he was the only demigod to have his kind of power in centuries, and no one knew what he was capable of. I should have been relieved, but if this was the answer to our problems, then why did I feel ashamed and disappointed? Ignoring Antolios, I collected my ball and plodded to my bed.

"Perseus?"

I flopped down, staring out the window.

"We'll just have to be careful," he said. "Can you do that?"

I turned to Antolios. He was looking down on me, his arms crossed and back stiff. I swallowed. "I don't care about my honor," I whispered. The terrible words echoed in the silence, but I felt a kind of peace at saying them.

Antolios frowned. *Perseus.*

I tossed my ball into the air a few times. "Fine. Then I assume you'll sleep in your room tonight?"

I'd better.

I tensed and chucked the ball at the wall. It flew across the room and landed by the window with a hollow *thunk*, cracks splintering out from the hole in the stucco. The Head Residential was going to be annoyed when he saw that. Flipping onto my stomach, I slammed a pillow over my head.

Perseus.

"Just go away." My voice was already breaking. Antolios walked across the floor and then opened and shut the door. As soon as it closed, I let a sob escape my lips, and rubbed the hot tears from my eyes. I missed him already, and I wasn't sure why I had taken my anger out on him. He hadn't threatened us—Palamedes had.

Palamedes and I were going to have words—I'd grab his balls and fry them with lightning. Then we'd see who the girl was. I punched the bed with my hands and knees, but then my joints ached and I stopped. Wearily, I rang the bell next to my bed and waited for my servants.

When Sarah and Marta came in, I told them I wanted supper in my room, three helpings of everything, and some willow-bark tea.

They looked at me with concern. "Are you ill, sir?"

I shook my head. "I just… pulled something."

"We could massage you." They stepped closer, their lips curving into heated smiles.

"Thank you, but no." I blushed. "That will be all."

They left with identical bows. The twins were my age and had been given to me as a present from King Demetre when I was eight. Dark and curvy, they had always been a bit forward, but it felt more awkward these days. I finally understood the flirting looks they gave me, and I sighed and stared out the window.

I SPENT the weekend in my rooms avoiding everyone, but I knew I couldn't hide forever, so when school recommenced I went downstairs for breakfast. Palamedes didn't look up at me as I walked by. What had Antolios had done to him? I took my tray and found a table away from Antolios and my usual corner.

We were using our powers in Gymnasium, and robed clerics stood outside the practice pens, ready to help when we got injured. Normally I liked these days—it felt good to throw around a little power now and then—but my first pair-up was with Antolios. When I asked Ramios why I was always paired with him, he said that it was good to fight people who were better than me. That really stuck in my craw.

I hopped the fence into our pen and didn't bother to get a weapon. Slapping my hands together, I watched the static crackle between my palms. My body wasn't the only thing that was growing, and I'd noticed that along with my increased connection with the air I had more power and control of storms. My lightning bolts were stronger. I could probably kill someone with them if I really wanted to.

"Ready!" Ramios shouted from the center of the field.

Antolios took position across from me but didn't assume fighting stance.

I glowered at him. *You wouldn't want anyone to think that you favor me, would you?*

He raised his fists and stepped toward me.

"Set!"

We circled each other, and Antolios didn't look mad or sorry or anything. He was the same tall pale man with a blank face and social issues. I kept stoking the storm, the clouds roiling.

"Fight!"

I shot out my hands, and flickering energy flew from my palms. Antolios ducked, and I caught a flash of his white gaze.

I saw black.

I woke up facedown in the dust with my mouth coated in dirt. I stood and spat, my face twisting. Antolios was standing across the pen from me, his back to me.

"What the fuck was that?" I demanded, still spitting. Usually he just ran away.

That's how I got Palamedes down, he said, standing straight. *This is how I fight.*

"Fine!" I spat again and assumed the position. "If that's how you want it."

Ramios ambled up to the cleric standing at our pen and leaned against the wooden frame. He eyed the storm warily. "You can do this, Perseus. Use your will."

I snorted. Use my will? Fucking right, I'll use my will, my will and my power. I slapped my hands together again, the blue-white electricity arcing off my fingers. My hair was floating about my head.

"Again," Ramios commanded over the noise of shouts and grunts.

Antolios didn't turn around. *I'm not going to fight you.*

My mouth dropped open, and I spun to Ramios, gesturing at Antolios. "He's not going to fight me."

Ramios didn't even look at Antolios, just straightened and nodded. "Okay, wait here. I'll grab Corinna from the advanced class." He started to walk away, his cloak trailing in the dirt.

I screamed at Antolios's back. "Fucking fight me, coward!"

Ramios stopped, and the background noise of clanging weapons died down. Antolios's shoulders stiffened.

My lips tasted like dirt, and I spat at Antolios's feet. "You heard me. You're a fucking coward."

Antolios stood there in the silence, but I'd had enough of it.

I created a path from the clouds to my lover's heart, holding my breath as I waited for the bolt to strike. I felt the concussion of the sky splitting, and the hairs on my arms rose with elation. My vision exploded with brightness, but before I got to see if I hit my mark, I lost consciousness.

THIS TIME I woke in the infirmary. Again. I groaned and rolled off the cot. "What the fuck...." My head felt the size of a melon and full of lead.

A robed cleric came over and asked me how I was.

"Fine," I mumbled. "What time is it?"

"Past the midday meal," said the woman. "Are you hungry?"

I cursed and stumbled out of the infirmary to my room, feeling dizzy and groggy. Ramios had probably left me unconscious as punishment for attacking Antolios when he wasn't ready, and I probably deserved it. I took a cold bath and threw my bag over my shoulder, running out the door. The ground wavered—what the fuck had Antolios done to me? With his high-powered bullshit, Antolios should be in the advanced class. Why wasn't he?

I missed Music, so I ran to Reading. Everyone had turned in their report and was on the cushions already. I handed mine to Professor Scops and hurried to pick another scroll from the shelf.

Antolios didn't return my look, and I felt a stab of guilt.

I shouldn't have called him a coward, and Antolios was right, I probably needed to brush up on proper social customs. Eventually I would be king, and there was only so much my mother and professors could teach me. The other students knew what it was like out in the real world. I didn't.

I wandered among the shelves, my eyes flicking over the titles. The scrolls were all piled together, ribbons dangling down the shelves, and I stopped and read a title. *The History of Sex in Greece.* Antolios had said that I needed to understand. I plucked the scroll from the shelf and plodded toward the cushions.

Instead of sitting with Antolios, I plopped down by Zoticus, whose large hands made his scroll look tiny. I smiled at him, but he rolled onto his side, turning his broad back toward me. I slumped on the rug and unraveled my scroll. It had *pictures…*.

It had been over an hour when someone gasped and stood up. "Professor! Antolios is bleeding."

I wrenched my gaze to them.

With a tangle of brown hair over one eye, Phoebe peered at Antolios. She made a face as blood flooded Antolios's nose and ran down his shirt. "I think he's unconscious," she said.

Professor Scops glanced at Antolios, a slight frown on her face. "What? Oh, can someone—thank you, Perseus."

I was already up and moving, and I gathered him into my arms and lifted him up. The light coming off his eyes looked the same, but he didn't respond to the questions I asked in our heads. Keeping his long limbs from bumping into anything, I hurried through the building and ran down the dirt path to the main house.

I swung him into the infirmary, shouting for help. It was my second time there today, and the woman from earlier came over and had me lay him down on a cot. Her eyes glossed over with golden light, and she reached out her hands, touching him on his forehead. Golden light spilled from her palms and worked its way under his skin, illuminating the shadows of his skull. I shivered.

After a minute she pulled her hands away and shook her head. "I healed his nose. However, I can't wake him up except for small moments." She looked at me and said hurriedly, "Don't worry, he's fine, just sleeping very soundly."

I stepped up to him and brushed a strand of blond hair from his face. He looked so peaceful, his jaw soft and lips partially open.

"Usually in these situations we pray to the gods for guidance." She bowed and left to make arrangements.

I rolled my eyes. When didn't they pray to the gods? The gods never listened anyway, and I reasoned that Antolios didn't need to stay there to sleep, so I lifted him again and took him to my room. I cleaned him up, fetched a snack, and even retrieved our bags, but he still wasn't awake when I returned. I lay next to him on my bed and read, nibbling on fruit and nodding off in between.

When I awoke in the morning, he was still sleeping, and I called the clerics in to check on him. I asked them again why he was sleeping, and they shrugged, saying that only the gods knew. They assured me that they would keep praying.

I ate breakfast and was finishing my scroll when Antolios inhaled sharply. Propped up on several pillows, I glanced down at his face. He opened his eyes and blinked rapidly, so I nudged him. "Hey, are you okay?"

He nodded slowly and licked his cracked lips. "I feel weird. What happened?" I told him about passing out in class. He dragged his hands across his face. "I was removing memories. Memory is complicated."

I didn't know if I was angry or feeling sorry for him. "We can still do my plan."

Antolios shook his head, his golden hair frizzy. "It's okay. I think I have most of them, or at least the potentially problematic ones."

I gave myself permission to feel irritated at the situation as I set aside my scroll. "This is cheating, you know. It doesn't solve anything."

"Says you." He sighed. "I don't want to fight."

I scooted alongside him and laid my head on his chest, wrapping my arms around him. "I don't want to fight either." The bond opened, and Antolios's weariness sank through me. "I'm sorry I called you a coward. I didn't mean it."

"Yes you did."

"But—"

Antolios smoothed my hair. "Don't worry about it. It doesn't upset me." And then he said in my head, *I try not to get upset.*

I almost didn't catch that last part. "What do you mean?"

"I try not to lose control. I've hurt people. People I care about."

I felt a rush of pride I was sure he could feel through our bond. "You are insanely powerful, angel."

Antolios sounded sad. "I'm sorry I don't love my powers."

I rubbed his side. "You were right. We can't keep fighting with other students, and you obviously can't keep wiping their memories, so I agree, we have to tone it down, and yes, I was upset about that." My throat closed, and I had to push out the words. "It's just not fair. I've never felt like this before. I… I think I love you."

Antolios laughed, and I gaped up at him. "I know you do." He was smiling warmly. "We've been in love for a while now."

I laughed too. Of course we were in love.

Antolios pulled me to his lips, and we kissed. Heat blazed through me as I rolled over him, straddling his hips. He hooked a long arm under the bed to yank up the jug of olive oil and tipped some into his hand, greasing his penis as I watched. My cock was already sticking out, pointing at him.

I bent and nibbled his chin and cheeks, then kissed his lips and nose. As I worked my tongue into his mouth, I spread my ass and lightly positioned myself over his cock. Holding it for me, he pushed up, the tip sinking into my hole. We didn't speak as we both worked him into me, and when I sat comfortably over him, we held hands, threading our fingers together.

I raised my hips, then lowered them, and we groaned. Leaning forward, I brushed his lips with mine. "I love you." I clenched my ass.

"I love you," Antolios moaned.

Hands locked, I used my legs to glide us together, and Antolios countered my thrusts. I didn't have to say a word. I barely thought, and Antolios was *there*.

There… shorter… smoother.

"Oh my gods, *there*!" I arched my back and cried out. I stared at the ceiling, through the ceiling, the world opening up for me. Antolios's desire bloomed in my mind, melding with my own.

"Antolios," I said helplessly. He crashed his hips into mine, rubbing me relentlessly in that one beautiful spot. The tension built up at the base of my cock, and his fingers popped as I clutched them to my chest.

I love you, he said.

I climbed higher and higher, and just before I went insane from the buildup, I seized up, my legs squeezing his hips. Garbling nonsense, I sprayed him with ribbons of come, my cock thumping with my heartbeat. Finally I fell forward, gasping, and leaned my head against his.

Antolios wrapped his arms around me and kept his burst going. He groaned next to my ear and jerked into my ass, sending another tremor through my body.

"Oh," I sighed.

Dropping his hips and raising his knees, Antolios cradled me. "I love you," he said.

"I know." I smiled against his chest. "I feel like an egg, cracked open with the mess of me everywhere."

Antolios chuckled and shifted so he fell out of my ass, the fluid rushing out of me. "Of me too."

"You know what I mean," I said, still smiling. "I'm exposed with you, and sometimes I think that's a bad thing, but I don't care."

"I'll bet you say that to all the psychics."

I brought his fingers to my lips and soothed them with kisses. "There's no one like you, angel. Can I keep you?"

"I'm yours, but you knew that."

Yes, I did.

CHAPTER SIX

I PUMPED my arms and leaped from the stairs of the trail and into the sand. Sinking into it, I kicked off, tearing down the beach. Footsteps thudded behind me, but I ran faster, my legs nearly blurring. I yanked my tunic off, the wind catching it and ripping it away.

Scaling the rocks of the tide pools, I sprinted to the cliff's edge and hurled myself into the air. I gave myself a boost with the wind currents, soaring higher and spinning. Behind me, Antolios had crested the ledge, gathering himself to jump.

I stuck my tongue out at him and then fell, the cool waves swallowing me and taking my breath away. Sputtering to the surface, I spit the briny water from my mouth and slicked back my long hair. The frothing circle where Antolios had entered the ocean still bubbled, and I searched the depths for his white light. I treaded water, bobbing with the swells while gulls called across the roar of the waves.

"Come and get me!" Antolios shouted behind me.

I grinned and turned, catching his eyes blinking over the swells. As I thrust through the chilled water toward Antolios, my body tingled with a wonderful anticipation. Antolios graduated soon, but I knew deep down that we were going to be together forever.

I glanced up from a stroke and lost sight of him. Scanning the water warily, I waited. A hand grabbed my ankle, and I was sucked under. I kept my eyes closed and felt hands press into the sides of my face, holding me until his lips smashed against mine. We kissed, my mouth full of salt water and tongue, as we floated to the top.

I took a breath of air, and Antolios dragged me to him, his chest hard and slick. We kissed and yanked on each other's cocks, sinking back into the water. Tangled in each other's arms and tumbling with the waves, we washed up down the shore. My beard had been sprouting up over the last months, and it scratched against Antolios's cheeks, deepening the pink of the beard burn he was already sporting.

Sand scratched us everywhere, so we used our mouths, sucking the grit from one another's cocks and rocking with the waves.

Antolios's finger had just found my hole when laughter trickled down from the cliffs above.

We pulled apart and looked up. Bortos and a couple of younger students were giving us decisive thumbs-downs and blowing raspberries from the tops of the cliffs. I grabbed my erection and waved it at them, inspiring another round of laughter. I laughed along, but then Antolios jumped to his feet and sprinted down the beach.

I scrambled to my feet and ran to catch up. "Wait. Come on, angel, wait!"

But he didn't slow down. Antolios's pale back was straight, his hair coming out of its knot and flapping behind him. He flew over the sand like a purebred racer, born for it. His long legs took him far away from me, and I knew I was losing him. My chest tightened as I tried to find another burst of speed, but I couldn't. I was just about to give up when Antolios finally slowed.

I stopped next to him and put my hands on my knees, gasping. Antolios brushed his loose hair from his face.

"They were just teasing," I said when I caught my breath. We had started sleeping together again, and perhaps we had been too lax of late, but I worried we'd go back to sleeping apart after this. "Nothing bad."

"Says you," Antolios said. He was barely breathing hard as he frowned and yanked at his tangled, sand-filled hair.

"It would have been the same no matter who they saw," I said. "Bortos and those students are okay."

"You don't understand." He ripped a snarl out of his hair.

"What don't I understand?"

"People!"

"It can't be that bad," I said.

He threw his hands to his sides and finally looked me in the eye. A chill went down my spine. "Yes, it can. I can't stop it. I can't protect us."

My chin trembled. "What are you saying?"

Antolios blinked and then sighed and reached for my shoulder, squeezing it. "Nothing. I'm sorry." He put his arms around me, smashing me to his sweaty, firm chest. I tasted salt and sand.

I rested my forehead comfortably against his shoulder, taller than I used to be. He kissed my head, and some of my tension eased. "Let's go back," he said. "You're hungry."

"Aye," I sighed. "I am."

THE NEXT day we ate breakfast in silence and sparred in Gymnasium in silence. We weren't fighting, not really. There just wasn't anything left to say that hadn't already been said.

At first, I thought Antolios was being quiet because he was focusing on erasing more memories of our pairing from people's heads, but he admitted to me during our midday meal that he wasn't. He said he wasn't going to do that anymore because he didn't see the point. I agreed, but that was usually my argument, not his.

After our final class for the day, I was supposed to meet Antolios in the clearing in the woods. We had planned to read elvish poetry but would probably get bored halfway through and make love. At least, that had been the plan. I had been waiting for hours, and he still hadn't shown. It was suppertime, but luckily I had brought snacks so I wouldn't starve. The grass was softer here in the woods than by the beach, and I picked the small yellow flowers and listened to the wind.

I picked another flower, twirling it in my fingers. I had known for a while that Antolios wasn't going to show. Anxiety rushed through me, and my heart skipped a beat. Something had happened to Antolios on the beach after those students had found us together.

Admittedly we were not as careful as we once had been, but no one had challenged us in a while. Palamedes and those others didn't even remember the confrontation we'd had, and since I had grown in size and skill, Palamedes had mostly stopped picking on me.

Ramios had even pulled me aside during Gymnasium and told me I was ready to start in the advanced class. I'd be training with an actual demigod hero, Tydides, a son of Ares. Most demigods died in battle long before old age—about two hundred years—but Tydides had lost a leg during a battle against Argos, and King Demetre had forced Tydides to retire. He was a fire demigod, and Corinna had said that he could burn anything, even the ocean.

It was going to be an honor to be his pupil, and getting into the advanced class was something I had always wanted, but this meant I would barely see Antolios during the school day. I found my victory not as great as I had hoped and wondered what that meant. Maybe Antolios was rubbing off on me.

I had been meaning to ask him if he would join me on my adventures to heroism. We could fight evil, go on quests for the gods, and travel the globe. What else was he going to do? He was a prince, but we all were royalty in some form or another, and Antolios wasn't that close in line for Thessaly's throne, his mother a minor noble in Larissa. Apollo had always been less… discerning than the other gods. I was going to ask Antolios to join me the night before, since his graduation was approaching, but he had been upset over the incident at the beach. And now he hadn't shown up.

It was well after supper, and I had given up waiting for him. Just as I was throwing my bag over my shoulder, I heard his voice off in the woods. Another voice answered him, deeper and rumbling through the trees. I ran along the path in the woods and then burst into a sprint when I heard him ahead of me.

Rounding a large pine, I jerked to a stop. Antolios was standing on the path, and Professor Oston was behind him, his man-and-horse frame standing a little taller than Antolios. They had both stopped, and were both staring at me with raised eyebrows.

"Ah, Son of Zeus. Good evening." Oston gazed at me with one blue eye and one brown, his bushy brown beard covering his lips.

"Good evening, Professor," I said reflexively. I looked at Antolios. *Where were you?*

As if I had spoken out loud, Oston answered, "I apologize for keeping Antolios, Son of Zeus, but we were just having supper. Would you care to walk back with us?"

Not knowing what else I was going to do, I nodded stiffly and fell into step beside Antolios as we continued to the school. The professor clomped behind us. What had I been interrupting? Jealousy flared, but then I felt ridiculous and petty. Oston was over five hundred years old. And he smelled like horse, not that that was bad necessarily….

"Have you ever seen the dark, Son of Apollo?" Oston said, his voice mild and deep. Antolios was lighting the path ahead of us with his eyes.

"Please call me Antolios."

"Ah, yes, I forgot. Pardon me, but some traditions are harder to break. It could be said that at my age, I am slightly set in my ways."

"No, I haven't," said Antolios softly. "But I am working on it. I hear it's nice."

Oston let out a deep belly laugh that echoed off the trees. "Indeed it is! I wouldn't be able to sleep without the dark."

I smiled. Sometimes I had to put an arm or a pillow over my face so I could fall asleep, but I usually woke up with Antolios's light blazing into me anyway.

Oston continued to ask questions and make friendly observations. His horse body was smaller than a normal horse's, and his coat was brown with two white patches under his belly. His human torso was deeply tan and strong from teaching dance, and he didn't wear clothes. The dark hair of his tail swished, as dark brown as his head hair.

We just had supper, Antolios said in my head.

Oh, I sent. *Why didn't you tell me?*

It wasn't planned. I skipped class and went for a walk. Oston was hunting in the woods, and he offered to share his meal.

Why did you skip class?

Antolios reached out and touched my hand, giving it a squeeze. *Professor Kayla is dull.*

Are you mad at me? I asked.

No.

Is something wrong?

No. Antolios turned his head to Oston. "Professor, do you know any other centaurs?"

Oston lowered his bushy brown brows and snorted. "I do, but I am not on good terms with any."

"There are herds near Pelion," Antolios said.

"In the great texts it is said that our race was sired on Pelion's highest peak, so I suppose that Thessaly is our homeland, but I was born in Arcadia."

"Why don't you like the other centaurs?" I said.

"We have differing ideas on the definition of basic rights."

When Oston didn't say anything further, I said, "Oh."

Oston spoke of living among the elves in Arcadia, and told us a little of the history of dance in Greece. He said that in the north the dances were energetic and full of leaps, but in the south they were fluid and slow, the way I danced. When we reached his yurt he bid us good evening, and Antolios and I hurried back toward my rooms.

Barely making it through the door, we pawed each other and our mouths met, teeth clashing. "Did you eat rabbit?" I mumbled.

Yes. We fell on the bed, and I pulled off Antolios's tunic, running my hands up his lean sides. We panted and gasped, our skin was so hot.

What are you going to do after you graduate? I asked before I could stop myself. I froze halfway through a kiss, my tongue still in his mouth, and I stared into his white eyes.

Antolios made a surprised sound. *Where did that come from?*

I pulled my mouth away from him, studying his schooled expression for any sign of… anything. "You graduate in a few months," I said. "What are you going to do?"

Antolios smiled, but it was wicked hot with passion, and not warm with intimacy. He wrapped his hand around my cock and fisted me. *Did you want to discuss it? Should I stop?*

"It's nice!" I gasped. My eyes rolled back in my head, and I groaned, thrusting my hips up. "I was just… wondering…."

"Yes?" Antolios laid me down on the bed, rutting against me and tugging on my cock.

I groaned, and my cock pulsed and spilled in mindless pleasure. While I was still breathless and recovering, Antolios rolled me on my stomach, and leaned over and grabbed the oil. The errant drops fell onto my ass as he slicked his penis, and then he pushed into me slowly, his panting breaths stirring my hair. The sensation was sharp and jarring, and I fought the urge to buck him off by lifting into his thrusts instead, working through it.

"Your ass is heaven," Antolios breathed into my ear. "Every time." We both surrendered to our dance, and all of my troubles fled into the night.

Chapter Seven

THE SUN was already making its climb to the top of the sky when I awoke on the floor of my bedroom. Antolios was gone, leaving behind his heady scent and the destruction of my room. I pulled myself up off the rug and shuffled to the bath, yawning. The twins had even made the bed without waking me and were on their way out, gathering up my linens. I smiled and waved as they left. Glancing out the window, I noticed I had risen in plenty of time for breakfast before Gymnasium.

After rinsing off in the basin and dressing, I hummed a tune and tramped downstairs to the mess for breakfast—but I didn't see Antolios at any of the tables. Confused, I bounded upstairs and strode into his room. The door was open, but he wasn't there. All of his belongings were gone.

I sprinted down to the chariot port.

One of the doormen was standing in the shade of the warm morning. "Galen, have you seen Antolios?"

The old man nodded, and my heart leaped. "Yes, Son of Zeus. The son of Apollo left by coach late last night."

"What?" I couldn't even recognize the words coming out of his mouth, and I knew I must have been giving him a strange look, because he flinched and rushed his words.

"He said he was heading back to his family's estate, sir."

I staggered, and my heart turned to ice, dropping into my gut. I stopped breathing and swayed on my feet, feeling pale. Stumbling up to my room, my eyes filled but didn't spill until I made it through my door. I slammed it and slid to the floor.

Rain fell and thunder rolled.

LATER THAT day I wandered the stables, forgetting about meals and class times. I had come back from a run and a swim, thinking that if I ran far enough and swam hard enough I would be so exhausted that I wouldn't be able to feel any pain, but I had been wrong. Now I was depressed and tired instead of just depressed.

I had asked my mother if Antolios had been called away by his mother or his kingdom—since sometimes that happened with the older students—but he hadn't. So I had written him a letter and sent it by bird. It would probably get to Thessaly before Antolios did.

A gray horse stuck its head out of the stalls and stamped and snorted for attention. I tried to smile and went over to him, stroking his black mane. I petted him through the fence, hoping it would soothe the both of us like a magic salve. The horse's neck was warm, the skin thin and incredibly soft. His heart thudded slowly against my hand, and I tried to match its calm rhythm with my own, but my pulse jumped out of my control whenever I thought of Antolios.

We hadn't really been fighting, so why had he left?

I gave the horse another pat and trudged out of the stables toward Oston's yurt. Music class was finishing, and students walked down the path out of the woods. I slipped into the trees so no one would see me, coming up to our lesson area from another path.

Oston was putting away instruments when I stepped into the circle of tree trunks that served as chairs. His bulky horse body moved gracefully around the stumps and picked up lyres and pipes, placing them in woolen bags. His dark human hair was tied into a braid down his back, reaching all to the way to his horse half.

"What did you say to him?" I said softly.

Oston looked up from pulling a cover over a harp and bowed his head. "Hello, Son of Zeus." His voice was rich and deep. He had said that he was five hundred years old, but there was barely any gray in his full beard.

I moved into the inner ring of tree stumps. "What did you and Antolios talk about the night before last?"

The centaur's tail swooshed, and he shifted his weight, the muscles rippling under his shiny coat. "Would you care for some tea?"

I nodded, hoping that his offer meant he would eventually answer my questions. Oston turned his body sharply for one so large and led the way into his wooden yurt. Leather flaps covered the openings, and I pushed through them into a combination kitchen and great room. There was a fire on one wall and a table in the middle of the floor, surrounded by tall stools.

"Have a seat," Oston said.

I walked barefoot across the dirt floor laid with woven reeds, and perched on a stool at the high table. Oston left briefly through the back room, and through the window I watched him gather wood from the side of the house. The animals in back made noises of greeting to him, and he sang softly, his voice resonant. Behind the animals were the latrines we used during class.

Oston came back with the bundle of wood and made a fire with flint, steel, and dry grass, then left again to fill a pot with water. It was the end of spring and almost summer, but even with the fire heating up the yurt, I couldn't get warm. I felt thin and worn.

The centaur finished his chores and clomped up to the table, watching me with his dark brows lowered. "You missed Music, and now you are missing Reading."

"I know," I said dully.

Oston considered me with those eerie mismatched eyes for long moments and finally said, "Why do you wish to know about my conversation with Antolios?"

"He left," I whispered, and saying it made my nose and eyes sting. "Did my mother tell you to say something to him?"

Oston shook his head, his frown deepening. "You misunderstand."

I waited, but the centaur didn't say more. He moved to the cupboard and pulled out two bowl-sized mugs and a few clay jars. The scent of chamomile and lavender and goatweed drifted across the room as he prepared tea bags. The fire snapped, and the water pinged against the side of the copper pot.

Oston filled our mugs with hot water and herbs. "Drink this," he said.

I took the bowl from him, watching the herb sachet sink to the bottom. Soon the water turned a deep red, almost brown. The steam warmed my face, but I felt numb inside. "No one wants me to be happy." My voice came out broken and raw.

Oston put his mug on the table. "That was not the way of it, Perseus. The other day, when I came across Antolios, he was upset. I offered to make him supper, and I mostly talked to him, but he did not say much. Drink your tea."

I took a sip of the hot liquid, sweet and floral. "What did you say to him?"

"You and I both know that you do not need to say much to the son of Apollo."

I glared into my mug and drank more.

Oston put his hands on the table. "I told him he had to decide whether the pain he was feeling was worth the reasons he continued to endure it."

I started to cry despite myself. "You said that?"

"I also said that all pain fades with time, and he had to be patient. Regret is a heavy and lasting burden that not even old centaurs bear well."

"Why would you say that?" I wiped my eyes, and Oston handed me a cloth. I blew my nose.

"Drink your tea." His voice was soft and deep, but I couldn't look up at him. I just stared at his hands, a musician's hands. "I may be old, but I remember being young and in love. I remember losing that."

I thought about the first few arguments Antolios and I had. Him using me, Palamedes, and stupid fights about his annoying mind reading. Over the past few months, our fights had changed… in that we hadn't had any. Not until now.

Antolios had been afraid and hiding it. I gulped down more tea, not realizing how thirsty I had been. Had I drunk anything today?

Oston hands were still on the table, and he hadn't taken a sip of his tea yet.

"What's in this?" I peered into my nearly empty mug.

"Herbs to help you relax."

"I'm a demigod," I said slowly and carefully, pushing the mug away from me. "You can't poison me with these herbs."

Oston's voice never wavered. Even across the table, I could feel his words in my chest. "I'm not trying to poison you, Perseus."

Antolios hadn't thought our love was worth the pain. But I felt that none of my pain was worth the amazing love I'd had. Nothing was… and now it was gone. My chin quivered. I was too tired for this. I hopped down from the table. "I'm going home."

Oston moved closer as if he was going to touch me, his horsey scent warm and sweet. "Would you like me to walk you home?"

I shook my head. "I'm okay."

"You can come back any time."

"Okay."

"Take care of yourself, Perseus."

I left the house through the front flaps and wandered back to the main building, my thoughts vague and far apart. I wasn't hungry, but I made a stop at the pantry, slipping in and taking an entire barrel of wine with me. Hauling it back to my room, I pushed open the door with my foot, stepped in, and kicked it closed.

I WAS just starting to go to class again. It had been two weeks. I was sober, but I didn't do any homework, and sometimes I had to leave class to cry or hit something. I never knew which. My mother hadn't talked to me about skipping class, and students had pretty much left me alone. I probably had heartache written all over my face, and the fact that not even Palamedes wanted to tease me was telling as to how bad I looked.

At the end of my history lesson I wandered the beach. Students were yelling and challenging each other to various contests at the jumping rocks, so I turned the other way. It seemed like yesterday that Antolios and I were jumping those rocks.

The tide came in as I scaled the rocks at the other end of the beach. Small sea creatures clung to life in the shallow pools, and the spray from the ocean misted across my face. At the top of the rocks, I gazed over the vast ocean, the sun setting. I felt small, mortal, and alone, and when I tried to connect with the air, I couldn't open myself up to it. If it were possible, the sky seemed too at peace to endure me and the state I was in. Eventually I climbed down and ambled back to the school, toward Oston's house.

A SPLASH, thumps of hooves, and the swish of the yurt flaps indicated that Oston had finished rinsing himself and had gone back inside the yurt's bedroom.

I gingerly squatted on the floor of the wooden stall and wiped at my mouth, my hands shaking. Taking deep breaths, I clutched my abdomen and waited for the pressure to ease. The evening breeze trickled through the stall door, and my damp body shivered. My bowels moved, and I leaped up and sat on the wooden seat, the muscles of my thighs rippling under my skin.

I grunted and then gripped my knees. They weren't knobby anymore, but surrounded by corded muscles. A line of hair ran down my trunk and ended in a thatch of black. I wiggled my toes, the second digit longer than the big one. They had black hairs on them too. I didn't recognize myself. Even my hands were different, with thick fingers and big palms. The changes hadn't been *that* long ago.

I wiped the sweat from my brow, taking my time. I probably should have listened to Oston, but I had been lonely and hadn't been thinking clearly, and I wasn't certain if I was thinking clearly now either. I finished using the latrines and limped to the yurt, brushing aside the leather flaps.

The water ran down Oston's dark legs and dripped to the floor. He lowered thick brows over his mismatched brown and blue eyes. His human skin was tan and stretched tightly from the sun; his horse hair was short, and now I knew just how soft it was. "Are you well?"

Stepping all the way into the bedroom, I smiled weakly. "Aye." My stomach grumbled, and I knew I wouldn't last the night if I didn't get something to eat. "Do you have any stew left?"

"It's still in the pot." He tossed his thick-haired head toward the kitchen. "Help yourself."

I went into the kitchen and ladled myself another bowlful of stew, then climbed onto a stool. I winced as my ass hit the seat, and I tried to shift my weight, but no matter how I sat I couldn't get comfortable. The stew was still warm, and I scooped up meat and potatoes with a heel of crusty bread.

Oston clomped around the bedroom moving furniture back into place. He came into the kitchen and grabbed the kettle, taking it out back to fill it. I chewed slowly. I was still hungry often, but not as much as I had been, and it seemed more manageable now. Oston came back and put the water on the fire, taking the stew off. "Do you want this? Otherwise I'll give it to the pigs."

"Please." I held up my bowl. "We hardly eat game."

Oston snorted. "Fish doesn't agree with me, so I do most of my own cooking." He handed me another hunk of bread.

Between mouthfuls I said, "I think I may be more comfortable on my back."

His eyes almost comically widened. "You want to see me again?"

I swallowed a bit of venison and carrot. "Aye, why not? I was simply overzealous, and," I chuckled, "it felt like I was ass up under a waterfall."

I was certain that Oston had been expecting to go a lot slower than we had, but when I had let him slide his hands up my tunic, I hadn't wanted to stop at fondling. I rushed us through everything, and I had realized a bit too late that I should have taken it easier.

"What about Antolios?" Crossing his arms, he turned to face me, and his back legs shifted to follow his front.

I pushed my bowl away. "He left. I'm not looking for a… replacement. You said that was okay, right?"

"I would not possess you wholly," Oston agreed, still staring at me incredulously. His thin wide mouth was stretched over blocky teeth. "To limit your freedom would be as grievous as caging a bird. I would prefer to see you regularly, however."

"You're still going to give me voice lessons?"

"I will teach you as I taught Loncy," Oston said. "You shall learn the ways of gods and men."

I flushed with pleasure, though I realized he was flattering me. Oston filled his bowl-sized mugs with tea and handed me one, and I took a sip. It was bittersweet with turmeric and honey, and I smiled to myself.

"Come to me three times per week," Oston said. "We'll spend time together, eat supper, and then proceed with your instruction. Unless you want supper before?"

"Supper after is fine," I said quickly.

The centaur moved closer to me, smelling of sweet grass and fur. "Would you care to stay? Rest with me for a while?"

I released a breath, my shoulders dropping. "That would be nice." I took Oston's hand, and he led me back to the bedroom.

"THIS IS not a discussion," my mother said at her desk. She tapped the top of the table with lacquered nails, and her bangles clinked on the wooden surface.

"But most men don't get married until they're thirty!" I stomped around the office and gestured wildly.

"You are a demigod and a prince! You're certainly not 'most men.'" She rolled her kohl-lined eyes.

"You don't even know if I'll be king!" I said. "We're exiled! I'm pretty sure that means I'm not in line for the throne."

My mother pursed her painted lips. "You are his only male heir, so says the oracle. When he passes, we will simply travel to Argos and you will claim your rights. You are a son of Zeus."

"She's thirteen!" I had already said this, but my mother hadn't been listening the first time. How could she not see how ridiculous this was?

"She's a woman. I sent our clerics to check," my mother said, as though we were talking about a lamb and not a person.

"Ack!" I covered my ears and paced back and forth.

"You won't actually have to marry her for some time yet, but being betrothed will increase your acceptance to the Argives and make the process smoother when it comes time for you to rule."

I turned and faced her with a huff. "Shouldn't she be, I don't know, playing with dolls or swimming or something still?"

My mother smiled at me, and I tried not to cringe. "What's better for a princess than marrying a demigod prince?" I opened my mouth but then thought better of it. "She is of a great house and will provide you with lots of heirs."

"I don't want heirs, *Mitéra*." I rubbed my temples. As usual, this conversation with my mother was going nowhere.

"What you want is not important. Your prophecy says that you will have heirs, and they will be heroes and kings and shape the world." My mother smiled indulgently and rose from her desk, gliding around to grasp my shoulders and gaze into my eyes. I dropped my arms to my sides, and she patted me. "It's okay," she said. "There are always slave boys."

"Ack!" I choked on my tongue. Before I knew it, I was out the door.

My mother called after me. "Perseus? Perseus!"

I burst into a sprint, and her voice faded away to nothing.

I HAD left Seriphos with no intention of ever going back. It was the third day on the coastal road, and my horse, Spirit—as I had named him—wearily plodded along. Despite the sun beating down on us and blowing away all the shadows, gloomy thoughts circled my mind.

When I made camp that night, my nightmares found me at last.

I had left the academy and stolen gold, a horse, and my destiny—becoming a thief.

I could blame my mother and her incessant pestering or my father and his lack of involvement in my life. I could even blame my birthday. I'd just celebrated my nineteenth.

Though most people didn't celebrate their birthdays, on mine we held our routine sacrifices to Hera, in hopes that she would stop trying to kill me. This year we had sacrificed even more bulls and goats than usual. I supposed I could blame Hera too.

But the real reason I had left Seriphos had everything and nothing to do with any of those things.

That night I went to bed on the side of the road, wielding the memory of Antolios like a talisman, but even it couldn't save me from the darkness of my dreams.

I AWOKE slowly, my body heavy from sleep. It was dark, and a storm brewed above. It churned with no wind or rain, but thunder boomed and Spirit shrieked. I quested into the storm and found him.

"Perseus." The voice rumbled through me, elation and terror surging in my veins.

I stood, gaping into the heaving heavens above. "Hail, *Patéras.*"

Flash!

A man stood a short distance away with his back to me. His white hair was long and wavy, and he wore a modest wool chiton with a leather belt and simple sandals. He had a wreath of olive leaves on his head, and his strong arms were crossed behind his back.

Another flash and a crack, and my father turned his head, half of his face lit in the lightning. A piercing sky-blue eye was leveled at me. I hadn't really noticed it before since my father rarely manifested, but his eyes were the same color as mine, a blue so light it almost glowed in the dark.

I knelt.

"Perseus, your mother asked me to speak with you. She believes that you are being rash and wishes you to return home." His voice was still deep but quieter now that he was speaking through humanlike lips.

We were all meant to obey the gods, and I felt that with nearly every fiber of my being—but one. One strong fiber in my core didn't care what he had to say, and I knew that he couldn't force me to obey him.

"She doesn't know what's best for me," I heard myself saying. *You don't know what's best for me. Antolios doesn't know what's best for me.* "I'm not going back." My chest tightened.

"Rise."

I rose. My father had turned to face me fully. My mouth grew dry, and my heart raced. I put my chin out and tried to stand tall. It was then that I realized that my father was still taller than me, and I would never be as tall as the king of the gods.

Zeus crossed his arms over his chest and assessed me. His skin was creamier and pinker than my own, and his white beard curled. "I see." His pale blue eyes drilled into mine.

I glanced away and back again, not sure I had heard him correctly. He saw? He saw what? Was that all he was going to say? My shoulders caved in, and my gaze fell to my bare feet, nestled in gravel and dirt. Did he truly see me?

Fear, hurt, shame, and anger all burned inside of me, but I seized the anger, the only emotion that wasn't threatening to bring me to my knees. My lip curled. What did my father know of it? Where had he been my entire life? The last time I had seen him was in a spring storm as he was passing through months before, but we never spoke. My blood boiled, and I thrust my shoulders back.

"You don't know me!" I said.

His lips quirked, and then his expression clouded over.

"I'm not going to participate in my prophecy. I'm not going to be king. I don't want any of it!" My entire body was taut as a bowstring, and my jaw hurt.

My father tucked his chin and regarded me under lowered white brows.

I searched his face over and over, but found nothing. No anger, no judgment, no sorrow, just the visage of the king of the gods, looking down at one of his subjects.

"As you wish," Zeus said. He disappeared, and so did the storm.

A howl ripped from my throat, and I dropped to my knees. Tears sprang hot from my eyes, and my nose burned. What had I done? I crawled back to my blankets and curled into a ball, hoping that he would strike me down but knowing he wouldn't. He was gone. I had pushed him away.

My body shook with sobs, and the fire died in my breast, replaced by an empty pit that consumed me as the night deepened. With the dawn, Spirit and I continued our way down the coast, looking for a new place to call home.

PART TWO
DELOS

Chapter Eight

Five years later

I SPENT the first years in Delos working on repairs to a farm I bought by the Bay of Scyros, on the southern coast of Epiro and only a couple weeks' ride from Seriphos. It had an old vineyard and olive grove, and I had found locals who knew how to process olives and wine. I replaced chipped tiles, slapped on new stucco, built furniture, repaired fireplaces, and had the latrines in the back dug out. On my farm roamed chickens, goats, two pigs, and a farm cat, and I still had Spirit, my trusty steed.

I was busy during the days, but almost every night I went down to the Salty Pony, a tavern by the docks, to unwind. I had cut my hair to my ears and reduced my full beard to a short chin beard with a mustache, but no one had recognized or come looking for me.

My hands had more calluses on them from my work in the fields, and though my olive oil sold steadily enough, making wine wasn't profitable yet. Heightened senses had given me an excellent palate for my work, but it took time to get in with the elves who dominated the wine business. Every year they came to my house, drank the bulk of my wine, and assured me that it would be better next year.

I had toiled away the entire day building a wine rack for my living room, and at dusk I cleaned up and rode Spirit to the Salty Pony.

Vano and Thom were already at our usual table. Vano stood on his chair pointing a stubby finger at Thom, his boyish face furrowed into a scowl. He wore an embroidered jacket with bronze buttons running in a line down his round middle, and his pink cheeks indicated that the half-empty pint next to him was his. Being half a man's size meant that he didn't have much of a constitution for drink, but he did well enough.

"Your fault!" Vano was saying. "You wouldn't believe what my wife said to me the next morning!"

Thom folded his lanky arms across his chest, visibly trying not to smile. His light eyes danced in merriment, and he fingered the points of his styled mustache. "You were drunk out of your gourd, and no one could tell you anything." He glanced up and saw me approaching. "He was, wasn't he, Percy? There wasn't anything we could say to him. His tiny cock was set on her."

Vano snorted and sat back, and I smiled. Oh yes, the lady who smelled strongly of perfume. I surveyed the tavern and met the eyes of Jordan, the bartender. I raised my thumb for a pint, and he nodded, pulling a mug down from the shelf and filling it from a keg. I sat down. "It's sadly true."

Vano used both of his hands to lift his mug and gulp beer. He flourished a handkerchief from his pocket and dabbed his mouth, then tucked it away. "My wife smelled me before I even walked into the bedroom. She made me sleep on the couch! To top it off, the woman was a complete cocktease and nothing happened between us! I'm going to get you both back for this, you know."

Thom laughed and waved him off.

The bartender dropped off my pint and yanked a rag off his belt, wiping down the circular wooden tables.

I took a sip of my beer. It wasn't very good, but it helped me keep up the appearance of being a normal farmer. As far as anyone knew, I was human. It was easier this way.

Thom was a supervisor at the docks, and Vano had his own tailoring business, so they both had better schedules than our other friends. Kell and Chris were probably still working at the docks.

By the time Kell and Chris arrived, the rest of us were heavily into our cups. Chris stalked up to our usual table, scowling with his aggressive black brows. His hair was black and coarse in tight curls against his scalp, and he was shorter than the average Greek man, with broad shoulders, but he was missing the usual bulky muscle to go with his wide frame. He slouched into one of the chairs.

"Fucking Laconian fleet!" Chris spat. "Dock supervisor made us stay late."

"Aye, but he paid us double our wages for those hours." Walking with a slight limp from a twisted foot, Kell grinned and brushed a strand of shaggy brown hair from his face. He sat and hailed a pint and even ordered bread and goat meat. Kell was skinny as well, but his frame was taller and slender. Both were missing a few teeth. All of my friends were shorter than I, demigods being taller than most of the other races, and I had to admit that I liked that.

Kell and Chris discussed the Laconian fleet in the bay, informing us that it was headed to Arcadia for war. It seemed every decade the island realms made a push for Arcadia's shores, trying to get closer to the supply of artisan glass and wine. None of the attacks on the elves' kingdom were successful, the land being mostly surrounded by mountains and easily defended, but that didn't stop Laconia from trying.

A flood of newcomers entered the bar, and my friends and I stopped and observed them. My jaw dropped when the ugliest dwarf woman I had ever seen stomped in and ordered a pint, sitting at her own table. At least I thought she was a female. She had a wispy beard on her chin. She slurped her mead, ignoring everyone's stares.

Vano shared an owlish expression with us and then fixed his gaze on me. "You have to fuck her, Percy," he whispered. My friend's faces brightened in that way drunken people get when they think they've had a great idea.

My face twisted. "No, she's gross. I can smell her from here."

Kell pointed his finger at me. "You said you'd fuck *anyone.*"

I froze with my mug almost to my lips. The first time my friends had caught me behind the stables, getting plowed by some minor lord, they had been shocked to say the least. I had joked that I would fuck anyone, and they seemed to have accepted it. My performance had earned me the name "Pretty Percy," but I cared more about fitting in than about my god-given name. It was also blissfully normal to have a short name, despite how it came about, and if it disrespected my father... more the better.

"We dare you, and we'll pay you," said Chris, dark eyes steady on mine. "I earned some extra coin today."

Thom protested. "I don't want to see this." The others told him to shut up, giving him meaningful looks, and eventually he raised his hands in surrender.

I pretended I was thinking it over as they haggled with me over the amount, and then I nodded at the deal and chugged my beer. I reached across the table and finished Vano's beer and then made my way to the dwarf.

The dwarf's skin was cracked like gray mud, and bits of something were stuck in her... beard. Her hair was scraggly, and she had browning teeth and the meanest beady eyes. She was thick and short but probably outweighed me. She had two saggy flaps on her chest under her tattered shirt that I guessed were breasts, but considering the situation her sex was probably insignificant.

The odor of sewer, rotting fish, and of something possibly more insidious grew as I got closer. I held my breath—she must work in the bowels of a ship. Mastering my disgust, I stepped up to her and flashed a smile. She slammed her mead down and glared at me.

Leaning across the table, I whispered in her ear, saying the first things that popped into my head and promising her a night to remember. She pulled back with a snort and squinted at me. I flinched, expecting to get hit.

My friends laughed in the background. Assholes.

The dwarf jumped to her feet, but instead of hitting me, she picked me up and threw me over her shoulder as if I were a bag of apples. As she carried me out the door, I flopped against her back, the toes of my boots dragging on the ground. I waved at my friends and gave them a thumbs-up. Their faces were priceless, and Kell waved back uncertainly, unsure if he was saying good-bye for good.

I SHUFFLED in an hour later, blood seeping through my clothes from various wounds. I smiled lopsidedly from the gouges in my face, and limped over to my friends, the arousal that had been dulling my pain earlier completely faded. When I got to our table, I held out my hand expectantly, but no one moved. I raised a brow at my friends.

"Show us proof." Vano crossed his small arms over his chest.

I gestured to my bloody shirt. "What proof do you require?"

They snickered, and Vano coughed delicately into his fist. "Show us the *marks*."

My gaze flickered over each of their smug faces, and then realization hit me. "You all know about this?"

"Everyone knows about Loony Lucy." Thom attempted to muffle his laughter.

My friends couldn't hold it in anymore. "Show 'em, show 'em!" they chanted through chortles.

My face twisted in annoyance as I peeked around to see if anyone was watching. Then I deftly untied the laces on my breeches. Pulling my pants down in the front, I displayed the twin knife wounds in my upper thighs, pivoting so they could see how deep the oozing sores went.

"She sucks cock like Aphrodite," I said.

Averting their eyes after getting confirmation, they said, "Put it away!" They roared, tears on their faces, and Kell snorted beer out of his nose. Vano looked as if he had just run across town, his moon face red and sweaty. I smirked and laced back up, and they readily parted with their money.

"Does she stab and then suck, or suck and then stab?" Chris snickered.

"I wi—I wi—I wish I could have seen your face! When she—" Vano couldn't finish, wheezing in breaths.

I snorted and sat down slowly, and they fed me some beers. One of my eyes was swollen shut, and my entire body was a bruise, but I was in pretty good spirits. Lucinda, as she had told me her name was, was actually kind of fun in a thrilling way, once my nose had overloaded from her gods-awful smell.

Thom gave me a sympathetic look, marred slightly by his smile under his mustache. "Are you going to get healed at the temple?"

I shook my head and reached into my pocket, pulling out a vial of black paste. "The apothecary sold me this. Want to share it with me?"

Thom hesitated, but the rest of them nodded eagerly. "I can't," Thom said. "That stuff knocks me out, and I have to be home before sunrise, or Alala will have my hide."

"Come on," Chris said. "Don't be a woman. We'll make sure you get home." Thom folded his arms over his chest and fingered his mustache.

"I'll make sure you get home," I said.

Thom nodded. "All right."

Chris's eyes grew. "You trust him and not me?"

"In Thom's defense," Vano said, grinning with his big teeth, "the last time you took this stuff we had to chase your naked ass around town to keep you from wagging your dick at the ladies… and gents."

Kell threw his head back and slapped his hands over his eyes, laughing. "I remember that!"

Chris's face turned red. "He shouldn't have known about that, seeing as he was passed out. You all have big mouths."

"Speaking of which," I said, "if you make mention of my doings this night to anyone, I'll relate my encounter to you every day for the rest of your lives. In detail."

"We won't," Kell assured me.

"Okay, then." I got up and winced. "Let's go out back. Jordan hates the smell of poppy." My friends couldn't look at me without laughing, and I started laughing too. At the end of the night, I threw Thom's lanky body over my shoulder and we stumbled back to his house. I headed home late.

My farmhouse was a half-hour ride from town—a small, stucco building with a red-tiled roof. I led Spirit into the barn and groomed and fed him. I was filthy and wanted nothing more than a bath and my bed, so when I entered the main house, I kicked off my boots, and was just entering my bedroom and peeling off my shirt when a hush fell through the house.

All the sound of the world dropped away except for the thud of my beating heart. The ceiling of my bedroom was illuminated by a white glow, and I jerked my head toward the door to the porch.

A shining woman stood in my bedroom, right in between the pillars that flanked the open doorway. She was indescribably beautiful and radiated cool white light. Wearing chainmail down to her toes, she had on a golden helmet with her black, curled hair spilling from it. Her eyes were gray.

My eyes bugged out of my head.

I gaped at my clothes, the remnants of that night's passion suddenly seeming vulgar and horrific in her presence. I smelled fucking awful. I scrambled to Athena's feet and prostrated myself before her, kissing the floor. "Goddess!"

"Perseus." Her voice was piercing—ice on my brain. "You waste your godhead with this life."

"Yes, Goddess." My heart pounded painfully in my chest, and I tasted metal.

"I have a task for you, Son of Zeus."

"A task?" I echoed. I heard… trumpets? I suspected that I had completely lost my sanity.

"Yes. You are my champion." Her voice rang out like swords clanging.

I was thankful I was already on the ground and closed my eyes, trying to calm the racing of my blood. I had never considered myself a particularly clever man, and I wasn't much of a fighter these days. What would Athena want with me?

"Are you sure?" I choked on the last part, not believing that those impertinent words had been my own. I hoped she would take pity on me and make my death a quick one.

"It must be you." Athena spoke in a clear monotone, as if she were reciting a well-known fact.

"Yes, Goddess." Sweat slicked the floor where my forehead pressed against it.

"Champion, you will bring me the head of the gorgon, Medusa. She resides in the forest of the coastal mountains. Let me show you."

I closed my eyes, not sure what to expect, and then the hills of the coast loomed in my mind from far above. As if I were a bird, I dropped out of the sky, the mountains near Mycenae growing until trees became discernable and then a path. I flew along the path until I circled the sides of a cliff, chunks of ruins scattered outside of an opening in the rocks.

"I see it," I said.

"You may rise." As I stood, Athena held out her arms in front of her, and the space between glowed with a circle of light. It dimmed, and she held a silver shield, almost a circular mirror. She presented it to me, and I took it limply. "You will need this to view her. No mortal can look at Medusa's flesh-and-blood visage and survive." Her gray eyes were severe, fully present and also beyond time. "Do not look directly upon her, even when she is dead. Know that as my champion you have my blessing. Godspeed."

Athena left, and the sound of the world crashed back. The roar of the waves rang through my ears. I stood there in disbelief long enough for my stomach to recover from the shock and growl, reminding me loudly that I hadn't eaten in a while.

I ate, packed, and prepared my house for my absence. In the morning when my workers arrived, I made arrangements for them to look after the farm while I was gone. It seemed a good idea to not think the fact that my plans to avoid the gods had gone to shit. I hummed under my breath as I rode Spirit into town, bought supplies, and headed out. Thank the gods for denial.

CHAPTER NINE

IT WAS an evening of the second week of my trek through the coastal mountains toward Mycenae, and I had used up all my ideas for distraction, so there was no avoiding anything anymore. In the weeks of uncomfortable riding, I had spent a pathetic amount of time pining over Antolios and feeling like an ass about it. It had been so long, and I still couldn't get him out of my head.

The only other thing I had to focus on was the fact that I was lost. Well, sort of. I knew where I had *been*, but the god-vision map had been less than reliable, and I should have hit the cave of Medusa already. I was in the general area, but I hadn't seen a cave or ruins.

And I still had no idea why Athena had ordered me on this quest.

I knew the story of Medusa. Everyone did. Centuries ago she had been a beautiful maiden, and Poseidon had taken an interest in her. Medusa had been a pious servant of the gods and had sought refuge from Poseidon's unwanted advances in the temple of Athena, the virginal goddess. However, Poseidon had little concern for the wishes of a mere mortal.

Poseidon had raped Medusa while she was praying for her salvation.

Athena was enraged by the act, but she could not justify punishing one of her fellow Olympians. She took her vengeance on Medusa instead, making her so hideous that when people saw her they died. Medusa had fled the temple and now preyed on heroes stupid enough to loot her legendary treasure.

Why Athena wanted Medusa dead after all these years, I had no clue. I'd guess that she was feeling guilty over punishing the innocent party, but Greece thought that Medusa had gotten what she deserved, and unfortunately the gods probably did as well.

Spirit plodded along the path, snorting every once in a while to remind me that he hadn't eaten since midday and we were passing lots of tasty-looking grass, greener than the grasses of Delos.

I patted his neck. "Don't worry, boy, we'll stop soon." Cracker bread, dry cheese, and olives became less and less appealing as the weeks went by. I hadn't had a warm meal since we had left the roads between towns and started making our way through the coastal mountains.

Light broke through the trees, and a dark crack emerged up ahead in the stone cliff we had been riding around. As I moved closer, the mouth of a cave gaped wide. I had found Medusa's lair.

I dismounted, removing Spirit's bridle and pulling my armor and weapons out of my pack. "Well, boy, have at it." Spirit didn't need to be told twice, and he roamed around the base of the trees, tearing out the green shoots with his teeth.

I hefted my sword. Forged by Hephaestus and given to me as a gift by my father, it was a weapon I hadn't wielded in ages, and it was time to put it to some use. Gripping my shield and sword, I crept to the entrance to the cave, poking my head in before I slipped into the darkness.

I worked my way along the rough, wet wall of the cave, a rug of moss growing along the sides. The footing was uneven, but I edged along smoothly. There was something to be said for divine reflexes.

The light gradually faded and disappeared. My heart raced and my nose flared. The air was stagnant and smelled of mildew. I secured my shield into its harness on my back and kept my hand on the wall, my other hand clutching my sword. I hadn't thought to get a mage light or a torch. I had a striker, but that wouldn't do me much good now.

A sticky web draped across my face, and I flailed at it, dancing in a circle. When I finally gained control over myself, I had no idea which way I was facing in the darkness. I hoped I had picked the right direction when I continued crawling forward.

Eventually there was enough light to see my hand sliding along the stone wall in front of me. Soon I could see my boots shuffling along the broken floor. I pulled my hand away from the wall and reached for my shield. The broken rocks became smooth tile, revealing vague drawings and then elaborate paintings. The corridor opened, ambient noise echoing oddly, but I took my time examining the frescoes.

Paintings of figures riding chariots and of other men-at-arms stretched along the walls. At the top was a woman, shining in bright mail. Her face had been rubbed out. There were also murals of a starlike figure among men with maps and abacuses. The figure's face was also rubbed out.

This used to be Athena's temple. This was where Medusa had been raped and cursed....

Why had Athena not simply killed Medusa herself if she wanted her temple back? Maybe she couldn't get it back? If this temple was desecrated, then it was no longer the goddess's. Perhaps she had lost her presence here.

A shiver went down my spine. The steady *drip, drip, drip* of the water hit the stones from a far-off place in the cavern. The air was oppressively wet and stagnant.

When I rounded a corner, I stopped. In front of me was a large room, stretching almost beyond my sight. I wasn't sure how I had missed this space for the better part of a day. The large temple was collapsed in parts, with broken light coming from the crumbled ceiling. Pillars crossed, half-fallen, holding the remaining parts of the dome.

Despite being run-down, I could tell that the temple had once been grand. There must have been hundreds of clerics and worshippers who visited here, doing Athena's bidding and praying to the goddess.

The middle of the temple sloped down into a large pool of water, where something glinted in the depths. Around the pool were odd lumps of rock. Curious, I walked toward the center of the temple, the lumps of stone becoming larger and more defined. Soon I could see that they weren't just lumps. A crude depiction of a face surfaced out of one stone. A hand. Lumps turned to feet. The faces were screaming.

They were all people.

As I moved farther into the labyrinth of stone people, I eventually found myself surrounded by their contorted and gruesome forms. Examining a particularly intact one, I marveled how detailed the sculptures were. I could almost twine my fingers in their hair. My gaze dropped, and I stopped. Where the… person's groin should be, there was only broken and jagged stone. I turned around and looked at the others. They were all missing chunks between their legs.

I swallowed reflexively.

A voice whispered through the silence. "I can smell you, Son of Zeus."

I started and then quieted, my breath held. My senses quested through the maze…. The air did not vibrate around me, giving away the voice's location, but I gathered energy to me, charging my body, and my hair rose from my head. There was enough of a hole in the ceiling that I could summon weather into this temple, but not enough to pull lightning from the storm above. My summoned bolts would have to do. Neither my sword nor shield reacted to my increasing charge—god-made, both of them.

"Zeus, as depraved as his brother." A dry chuckle ricocheted around the room. "And they call me a monster...." The echo stopped abruptly.

I thrust my shield up and viewed through the reflection to the way I had come, the entrance now dark and far away. A flash of movement glinted across the surface of my shield and then vanished. I spun around.

"You are polluted." The voice was closer now, but I couldn't detect where it was coming from, the hushed, hissing noises oddly distorted.

My gaze searched the shadows through the mirror of my shield.

"Do you want to be saved?" Medusa whispered.

I felt her breath on my neck. Spinning, I snapped my sword and shield into an attack, but my shield hit empty air. I danced around in circles, searching for any movement.

Laughter trickled off the walls and down my spine.

I shivered.

"I'll rip the offense from thine body," she whispered to me. "You can be free...."

The reflection in my shield revealed a hazy figure in brown rags floating toward me with sharp fingers outstretched. I shut my eyes and whirled toward it, stabbing out while my shield blocked my chest. Pain burned my sword arm, and I gasped, curling up and cradling my forearm, as warm blood gushed against my hand.

I risked a glance at my arm. It seemed deep, welling bright red blood, but there wasn't much I could do about it at the moment. Medusa hadn't seemed affected by my electric charge when she raked me with her nails. That could mean she was impervious to lightning too. Great.

I checked the reflection in my shield, but there was no sign of Medusa except for her echoing hissing laughter. My arm burned, but my fingers still worked, and I could still grip my sword, so I readied my stance again, blood trickling down my elbow. A lot of blood.

I could die here.

I crept to a taller stone figure and put my back up against it, using my mirror shield to peek around. My heart was pounding, and if I could hear it, then Medusa probably could too. There was no hiding from her in her domain.

Her voice was far away. "Son of Zeus, were you sent by Athena?"

I hadn't enjoyed our little talk so far, so I said nothing. I searched the surface of my mirror relentlessly, flicking it up and down and to the sides, but found nothing.

Medusa chuckled, her voice closer now. "You are not the first champion she has sent to me. There have been many others, for centuries."

A drop of sweat dripped down my back.

"What makes you think that *you* can kill me?" The reverberation of her voice in the air stopped, and I couldn't hear anything but the thudding of my heart.

A slight movement of the hairs near my right ear made me tense. I felt another stir. Gripping my sword and shutting my eyes, I grimaced and held my breath. I shifted my weight to my toes and dropped my shoulder, placing my sword along my hip.

A rush of movement and sound screamed toward me and nearly blew me back.

I braced and pivoted toward the sound, whipping my blade out in a smooth arc. My sword made contact with something, sliding through to the other side and then swinging over my shoulder.

A small thud was followed by a larger slap against the stones. Then there was quiet. I snapped back into a defensive stance and listened, my eyes still squeezed shut. But there was only the dripping of water, my breath, and my heartbeat. My arm started to burn again.

I peered through my shield and found Medusa in two pieces, her body in a heap and her head covered with coils. Neither piece was moving, so I sheathed my sword and closed my eyes again, grabbing the sackcloth at my belt and kneeling to grope for her head.

First I found her body, emaciated and funky. My hands came away from her stump warm and wet, covered with blood. I tapped the stones around where I remembered the head being, and my fingers found smooth, cold ropes—

Snakes. I pulled my hands back reflexively.

There had been many legends about the ugliness of gorgons, but I had forgotten the rumor that gorgons had snakes for hair. I sat back as my heart rate slowed. Rumor confirmed. I grimaced and brought my hands back to her head, quickly grabbing a handful of nasty serpent skin and shoving all of it into the sack. I cinched it closed and opened my eyes.

Medusa's small body was still on the floor. Perhaps the rags she wore had once been fine, but now they were crusted with filth and torn. It was hard to imagine her beautiful. The curse had destroyed everything she had been known for as a mortal.

I got to my feet and drew my sword again, my mouth in a line.

I had to be sure. Athena hadn't said it directly, but the rumors.... God-seed was divinely potent, and even though it had been centuries since Medusa had been raped, if the legend was true and Poseidon had taken her, then she was with child, no matter how fermented her womb.

As I pointed my weapon toward her abdomen I became surer of my actions. I raised my weapon, but just before I was able to thrust, I was knocked back.

My head cracked against stone and my vision exploded into white lights. The sound of the world dimmed.

Blurrily, I opened my eyes. The world was mute.

There was movement in Medusa's body.

I blinked, and when I opened my eyes again, a figure was growing out of the tatters of Medusa's corpse. Blood was splattered everywhere. I tasted it on my lips. In my lap was a hunk of something red and wet.

I blinked again. The figure was stretched out to the size of a man and continuing to grow. It twisted and struggled to standing, its large form rapidly becoming the height of four men and the width of three.

My head filled with a loud whine.

The giant opened its maw toward the ceiling, body clenched in rage and agony as its muscles grew and bulged. I knew it was screaming.

I was still clutching my sword and shield.

The giant turned its slimy pale head toward me and met my gaze with hard, cavernous eyes. It opened its mouth again, and this time I heard its bloodcurdling roar, spit flying from its lips as it revealed jagged teeth. I felt the roar in my chest.

I jerked and sprang up, scampering around the stone figure I had slammed against. The giant thumped behind me as I zigzagged around the rubble to avoid him. I sprinted toward the water pooled in the middle of the temple. Another bellow of rage and heavy crashes told me that he was smashing through the pillars after me. Great.

I splashed into the icy water, knees high, and ran up a pillar half-fallen in the water. Propelling myself over the crumbled and mossy marble, I aimed to escape through the ceiling, but as I crested the top of the pillar I realized I couldn't make the leap out, so I spun around.

The giant was charging up the incline right behind me, fat hands reaching.

Red flashed in my peripheral vision, and I pulled back my sword and gathered strength in my legs and then leaped over the giant's head. He made a grab for me, but his movements were clumsy and slow. I sailed over his head, my arms wheeling. As I fell past his waist, I thrust my sword back, sticking him in the side.

The giant howled and slapped me away, and I plunged into the water of the pond.

The rush of water filled my ears and flooded into my nose and open mouth. I smacked the bottom, my head cracking against something hard and my armor clanging. I choked and opened my eyes, the water shocking them with cold, but I couldn't see anything, my vision hazy. Tinny sounds hit my ears, and when I pushed off the bottom, rocks slid under my feet and made more surreal echoes of metal sliding against metal. I broke the surface, gasping and coughing up water.

With my chin barely above the surface in the deepest part of the pool, I glanced over just as the giant surged toward me, my sword sticking out of his side.

I dove under the giant's grab, batting at his hands with my shield. He whacked me on the back, sending me skidding and bouncing off the rocks between his legs. I leaped up behind him, my mind bright with pain, and spied my sword within reach.

Grasping the pommel, I yanked it out. The giant spun around, grabbing for me. After ducking under the water again, I jumped up and thrust my sword into his groin. When my blade ground into bone, I let go and swam away.

Popping up to the surface, I watched the giant squirm. Below him, the water was turning red with blood. He clutched his thigh, whimpering. We met gazes and considered each other. Though I had been terrified mere moments before, I felt a pang of guilt. Panting and groaning, the giant hunched farther and farther over until he collapsed into the pond, making waves of blood. The waves hit my face, and I watched until the water was still and calm.

My arm throbbing, I threw my shield on my back and retrieved my sword from the giant's thigh. Turning to trudge out of the pool, I stopped.

Near the edge of the pool was a large white-winged horse, pawing at the stones and curving its neck toward me. The horse reared, spreading its wings as it kicked the air.

I squeezed my hilt.

Pegasus, it telepathically sent to me in a deep voice.

I jerked as if slapped. It reminded me of when Antolios had spoken in my mind…. Before I could speak, the horse cantered off and took flight, flying out of the hole in the ceiling.

I just stood there, thigh-deep in bloody water, clutching my sword.

Eventually my teeth chattered, and I had to get out. Everything hurt, especially my head and back and arm. As I waded out of the water, the glint in the water caught my attention again. I studied the silver shapes on the pool's floor… they were mirror shields. An entire pile of them, identical to my own.

My stomach lurched, and I trembled from weariness. I was drenched and had nothing to dry my sword with, but I sheathed it anyway and hoped for the best. It was forged in a volcano, so it'd probably be fine. My clothing was ripped at the knees and arms, and even the seat of my breeches. Every glimpse of my flesh revealed bright red wounds that burned and itched, and one of my nipples was shredded. Not wearing adequate armor had been careless on my part. My sword arm was a mess of torn skin, but I'd wait to clean it and inspect the damage when I got back to my pack. It throbbed in a sickening way, and another wash of weariness assaulted me.

I picked my way around the cavern, expecting to find hidden treasure. There wasn't anything aside from a few trinkets and that pile of shields on the pond floor, but I already had one of those. My boots squished as I limped back the way I had come in. When I emerged from the cave, the sky was still light, but an early-evening breeze blew through the trees and my thin, wet clothes, making me shiver. I whistled for my horse.

The sound of the birds and the breeze stopped, and a bright figure materialized at the edge of the woods.

I approached her and knelt. "Athena, I have slain the gorgon, Medusa." I presented her with the sack from my belt.

"Thank you, Perseus." She took the sack and placed her hand on me, my body brimming with light and elation. In a rush of warmth, my hurts of the day vanished. I sighed and relaxed, not even realizing until then how tense I had been.

I kept my head down until Athena told me to rise. She carried a large, triangular shield with a golden relief of Medusa on it, the snakes in Medusa's hair spread out and so detailed they looked real—her face open in a soundless scream.

"I will tell Mount Olympus of your deeds. You will be a hero," Athena told me.

I looked away and nodded, scratching at my lower back. I should have felt proud. I was a goddess's champion, and I had successfully completed my task. I had slain a gorgon.

But I knew that I had lost something more important.

"Until we meet again, Champion." Athena disappeared.

My horse, Spirit, came out of the woods, and the world lit up with song again. I prepared for the ride back, stripping, scrubbing my body of blood, and grabbing a fresh shirt and breeches. I wadded my soiled clothes and shoved them into my pack. My breeches could be repaired, but my shirt would have to be made into scraps.

I felt hollow and used. Antolios had been right. I couldn't escape the gods or my destiny. I had been a fool. Everything I had done now seemed childish. Running away, yelling at my parents, trying to pretend I was someone I was not…. What a waste.

I mounted Spirit and headed back to whatever life the gods would allow me to have.

CHAPTER TEN

PANTS AROUND my ankles and knees grinding in the dirt, I moaned as Lord Prastinos swelled inside me, hot and worming. I gave my hand a burst of speed, giving myself that last little boost before I spilled into the scattered straw.

Prastinos gave his last jerk and grunt, but I was still clenching and groaning when he pulled out. The fullness left me in a rush as his hands pushed off from my hips, and I dropped my head into my arms and sighed.

Buckles clicked, cloth rustled, and boots scuffed the dirt behind me.

I opened my eyes and flipped to my rear, knees bent out as far as my pants would allow. I still had my boots on. The stables behind the Salty Pony were littered with straw and horseshit. Not the most private of places, as I knew from experience, but it would do in a pinch.

I snagged a busy, well-manicured hand and kissed it. Russet eyes glared at me, and Prastinos tried to snatch it away, but I held on tighter.

"How about a kiss before you go?" I smiled.

Prastinos snarled. "Get away from me, boy!" He tried again to wrench his hand free but couldn't. A little doubt flicked into those brown eyes.

"Boy?" I chuckled darkly and shook my chin with my other hand. "This didn't grow in yesterday, *sir*." I gave him another sweet smile. "How about that kiss?"

Prastinos squirmed to get out of my grasp. "Unhand me, you filth!" He pulled back his free arm and punched me in the side of the head, but looked confused when I didn't even register the blow. He met my gaze and paled.

"Wrong answer." I yanked on his thumb, hearing it pop, and then released him.

The lord whipped around, screaming and cradling his limb. "You broke my hand! You'll pay for this, fucking whore!" Spittle flew from his lips, and his eyes burned with hatred. He made another strangled cry as he lurched and stumbled around the side of the stables.

One of the horses brayed.

"I'm twenty-four!" I called after him.

Prastinos's curses gradually faded away, and so did my brief satisfaction. I sagged. "Fuck." Sighing, I pushed myself to my feet and pulled up my pants, tying the laces and clenching my jaw. I cursed again and trudged around the side of the tavern to the latrines, using the facilities before I ducked inside.

Lord Prastinos had been passing by in his carriage when I had been handing Spirit's lead to Henrick, the stable boy. I knew the lord was going to be trouble by the way he leered at me, but when he had suggested that we go in the back and "conduct business," I had assured myself that it wouldn't take long. It hadn't, but somehow it always ended up the same with these kinds of men. And yet I did it over and over again.

I found my friends at our usual table and hailed myself a drink.

"Uh-oh." Vano looked me up and down. His button nose flared. "Look at him."

Kell's brown hair frizzed out from his head as he turned to regard me. "Oh shit, Percy. What did you do?"

I winced and plopped down, studying my fingernails. I picked out some dirt I had probably gotten from the fields earlier that day. "Nothing," I mumbled.

"Who did you hurt this time?" Kell frowned.

"Come on, Kell," I said. "That last time was an accident!"

Kell looked away, taking a sip of beer, and I sighed and put my head in my hands. There was something wet in my hair. How had I missed that? I resisted the urge to smell it and quickly wiped it away. Jordan came over with my beer, and I nodded my thanks.

Chris's voice was hard. When I looked up, his black eyes were even harder. "You don't have to fuck 'em in the back of the tavern, you know."

"Fiery dwarf!" Thom whistled and leaned back from the table.

"Aye, I don't need to see that again." Kell elbowed me with a wink, temporarily forgetting his issue with my actions toward that other minor lord a few months before. Demigod strength wasn't always a good thing.

Everyone laughed except for Chris, who was still staring at me. He hawked and spat on the floor. "You just let them fuck you right where everyone can see. It's not safe."

My face heated, and I reexamined my fingernails.

"Fiery dwarf!" Thom chortled.

Chris snapped, "I'm not a dwarf!"

"As you say," Kell said. "I don't know any human who can live off meat and beer. But you can."

"Shut your whore mouth!"

Vano interjected. "The guards are going to be showing up soon. Maybe some of us with less reputable natures should flit out to the back for a smoke?"

Thom got up. "I'm going. Anyone want to join?" He gave me a friendly smile. "We'll catch up when you get back."

I tried to casually wave to them, but my hand flopped on the table. "Aye. I'll see you all in a bit. They won't kill me while they can still get money out of me."

My friends disappeared out the back door, and I gulped my beer down. On top of his tailoring business, Vano smuggled foreign goods through Delos, and Chris and Kell were always one step away from being thrown in jail for fighting at the docks. None of them wanted to be there when the guards showed up.

I swallowed the last of my beer when a group of guards came in wearing gray tunics and sporting cudgels. "Perseus," the fat one said, "come with us."

"Okay." I rolled to my feet and followed them out of the tavern to the guardhouse.

After taking care of business I returned to the Salty Pony, my pockets empty. I was grumbling under my breath and kicking my feet when I sat back down with my friends, who were now red-eyed and smelled like old polecat.

"That bad, huh?" Vano said blandly.

I crossed my arms and growled, "They took everything I had on me! That's twice as much as last time!"

"Well, maybe you shouldn't assault people," Kell said.

I rolled my eyes and surveyed the tavern. Unfortunately there weren't many people, but maybe some would trickle in later. It was fairly early; the sun hadn't even set yet. Chris still wasn't looking in my direction.

"We still have some hashish. Want some?" Thom said.

"That sounds great." I smiled. "I got the next batch."

"It's okay, Percy, I got this. You always get the next batch." Thom pulled out his pouch.

"That's because he smokes most of it," Kell complained.

I shrugged and reached for my pipe. We stayed up fairly late, smoking and drinking, but the bar never got crowded. I hadn't found someone to go home with, so when my friends got up to take Kell home, I joined them.

Kell was weaving and swinging his arms as we walked toward the docks where he and Chris lived. After we dropped off Vano and Thom in the nicer part of town, I'd head to Penelope's, the local whorehouse. It was late enough, and Prastinos really hadn't done it for me—he'd merely whetted my appetite.

"It wasn't funny because she was ugly, Kell. It was funny because each of her breasts was twice the size of Vano's head," Thom explained patiently.

Vano let out a high-pitched giggle and then slapped a hand over his mouth.

Kell leered at him, his arms out wide for a hug. "Come here, darling!"

Squealing, Vano ran around, Kell tottering after him. The halfling ducked under my legs, and Kell almost barreled into me. I held my hand out and pushed him to the side, and then Vano ducked back through my legs.

"I just want a hug!" Kell grinned.

"Stay away from me, you pervert!" Vano laughed.

I pretended to stumble around drunk, and Vano danced in and out of my legs. Together we kept the inebriated Kell from getting his paws on Vano. Thom was laughing, but Chris stalked ahead, a scowl on his face. He hadn't said much all night.

I didn't know what I could say to Chris, but I knew that I was too old to play this game much longer. Prastinos had thought I was a boy, and some of the other men I had been with had thought the same, but this wasn't something I was going to shrug off when I got older, and I wasn't interested in joining the other men of Greece with their love of boys. I wasn't sure what I was going to do, but I couldn't keep affording the rates I had paid earlier.

A group of men meandered down the street from the other direction. One of them was Stanos. The dwarf's face was a mess of scar tissue and was missing an eye, and if what Kell and Chris said was true, then he was as cruel as he was ugly. He was a supervisor who had a reputation of favoritism, and if you weren't one of his favorites, you found yourself hurt on the job.

Our groups passed, and Stanos said something under his breath. His friends laughed, but I pretended I hadn't heard what they had said, still keeping an eye on stumbling Kell.

Chris stopped in his tracks, head tilted and fists balled.

Before I could stop him, Chris had spun around and charged Stanos, yelling with a bright red face.

"Wait!" I said.

Thom and Vano gaped as Chris leaped onto Stanos's back. Stanos's friends hollered and came after Chris, punching him and trying to pull him off. Everything seemed to be happening too fast.

Then one man pulled a club from his belt, and I rushed into the fight. I hit the man with the club on the elbow, my aim slightly off, but he fell back onto his ass without a sound.

Vano screeched and grabbed Stanos's leg, biting into his thigh. Chris strangled Stanos as the dwarf punched his head. With fire in his eyes and veins bulging out of his neck, Chris held on, and all three of them fell onto the street in a heap.

Thom had rolled his sleeves up and was taking sloppy swings at one of the other men, and fortunately his opponent seemed equally drunk and wasn't landing any of his return punches. I wasn't as sober as I wanted to be either, my body heavy and the world swimming at the edges.

Kell had wandered into the fight, his inebriation giving him a more pronounced limp from his twisted foot than usual. "What the fuck is happening?"

Chris had Stanos on his back, straddling him, and punched him in the face. "He called Percy a wide-ass!"

Kell shook a finger at Stanos. "That's not nice! Only we call him that." Kell put his hands on his hips, expecting everyone to drop the fight now that he had straightened it out with logic.

Vano stopped biting Stanos's ankles. "Aye! Only we're allowed to call him that!"

I strode over to the other man on Stanos's team who looked too drunk to do much of anything. I kicked him in the stomach before he could decide to do something stupid, and he crumpled to the ground. I caught the gaze of Thom's opponent. The man gawked at his companion at my feet and took off the other way, running.

"Aye, asshole, run!" Thom breathed heavily and stumbled. "You're a fucking burden to the earth… and shit."

Now there was only Stanos. And he still looked conscious. *I'll give it to the dwarves, they are tough.* Chris struggled to get his hand free from Stanos's grip so he could deck him again.

"Chris, stop." I reached for him.

Movement at the edge of the street caught my attention, and I turned as three men stepped out of the shadows. I vaguely recognized one of them as Lord Prastinos's driver. The other two were swinging metal balls on the ends of ropes as they approached us. They released the weapons.

The projectiles whistled through the air, and Kell and Thom fell to the ground. Thom let out a squawk, but Kell couldn't figure out how he was suddenly prone and just lay there.

Before I could get over there to help, the three men rushed me. Organized. I ducked, spun, and tried to get a burst going, but my feet were awkwardly placed and I made their work easier for them by almost falling on my ass. I was definitely more intoxicated than I'd thought. The men pinned me in a few moves.

Lights and pain went off in my head. One of them had punched me in the face. I bucked and kicked, managing to get one of them off me, and wrenched my arm, hitting something solid with my fist. Just as I wrestled loose, they converged on me again, trapping my arms and legs. Someone hit me in the groin, and my entire body exploded in pain. I huffed and crumpled and then got hit in the back of the head.

I groaned, pain swelling into my gut. I wanted to curl up in a ball, but they were forcing me to the ground, spreading me out. My face squished into the street and two people sat on me, further mashing my crotch.

I gurgled and thought I was going to be sick, but then the weight on my back lifted, and Kell yelled something above me. I fought wildly and threw the last two men off, rolling to standing. I kicked a revenge hit to one of the men's groins. Fuckers. The man fell over, out cold before he hit the ground.

Glancing up, I caught the shine of a blade just before it entered Kell's gut.

"No!" I screamed.

Kell blinked and grasped the hilt as he slowly sat down in the street.

"No!" I thrust my arm out, shooting lightning from my fingers and hitting the grinning thug in the chest. The man spun and fell to the earth, smoking.

The last thug reconsidered, his eyes wide, and ran the other way, ducking into the shadows behind the stucco buildings.

I limped over to Kell, who was breathing shallowly and holding his bleeding stomach. His eyes were closed, and his face was already sweaty and pale, his frizzy hair now damp and plastered to his head.

"Kell? Kell!" I pulled him into my arms and stood, suddenly feeling dead sober. I looked at my friends, all staring at me, mouths open.

"I'll be back." I burst into a sprint toward the temple, clutching Kell to me so he didn't get jostled too badly, as the wind whistled by my face.

In what seemed like forever and no time at all, we came to the temple of Apollo on the edge of the docks. Lamps were lit along the stone steps, and I flew up them, barreling into the reception hall where a stunned cleric was waiting at a desk.

"He needs help," I panted.

The cleric, in the yellow robes of Apollo, mutely pointed across the temple to where the beds were lined up, her eyes wide.

I strode to the other side of the temple and laid Kell down on the first open bed available, just as other clerics came rushing in and I was shoved aside.

The clerics surrounded Kell in a yellow wave, and one of them put their hands on his face while another yanked the dagger out. Light emanated from the cleric's hands and traveled through Kell's skin and down his belly, glowing through his shirt and then fading.

Kell gasped and shot up in bed. He took a deep breath and then retched and vomited blood all down the yellow robes of the cleric in front of him. His eyes watered, and he wiped his mouth with the back of his hand.

The cleric's face fell. "I hate working nights." He trudged away, the bloody dagger he had pulled from Kell still in his grip.

One of the other clerics handed Kell a basin and a cloth. Kell took it woodenly and mopped at his face, then noticed me standing at the edge of the curtains. "What the fuck just happened?" he said. "Did I just see you fucking shoot a man with *lightning*?"

I stepped closer to him. "How are you?"

Kell took the water the cleric offered and rinsed out his mouth. "I just got stabbed in the gut, so… actually not bad, considering." He looked down at his shirt. "Shit, this was new."

The cleric helped Kell clean up and then gave him some wafers and thin soup. I didn't have money to give to the temple because of paying the city guards earlier, and I didn't wear jewelry. I promised the cleric I would come back later and donate, but she just rolled her eyes at me and left.

Kell staggered to his feet. "Let's get outta here. I hate clerics."

Kell and I limped down the steps of the temple to the street. "Ugh," he said. "I feel hungover already. Don't get high and drunk and then get stabbed." He looked over at me. "Why didn't you get healed?"

I gently probed my swollen lip and ear. "I'm not fond of clerics either."

Kell laughed. "Sanctimonious pricks."

We walked in quiet for a time, but I knew it wouldn't last long. Kell had that look on his face, as if he was reeling in a big fish of a thought. Finally he said, "You throw lightning around, but you're not a cleric. And you're not a mage. I mean, as far as I know they can't do lightning. Wait, are you a mage?"

"No," I sighed. "I'm a demigod."

"You're a…." Kell frowned. "But you're a farmer."

I shrugged. "Aye."

Kell scratched his head. "Well, that's nice, then, right? Why didn't you say something?"

The rush of shame made me weary. "Long story. I don't really talk about it."

"Oh." Kell's frown deepened.

Thom and Chris and Vano were waiting for us in a tight circle, whispering with one another. When they saw us, they looked grateful to see Kell but completely ignored me. Stanos and the other men who had littered the street were gone.

"Hey!" Kell waved. "Guess what? Percy is a demigod!"

I winced.

"We worked it out, thanks." Chris was scowling so hard I could barely see his black eyes.

"Oh." Kell's face fell. "Well, I thought that was interesting."

"Come on, Kell." Thom held his arm out. "We'll take you home."

Kell looked at me with wide brown eyes, his hair starting to frizz again from his head. "You coming too?"

Chris answered for me. "No. Percy has to get back to his double life. Don't you?"

"Hey—" I started.

"Save it," Chris said. They all turned around and left. I could still hear them talking as they walked off.

"Why are we mad at him?" Kell said.

"Because he lied," Chris said.

"But he doesn't talk about it," said Kell. "You don't talk about being part dwarf."

"Shut up."

"He could have stopped all of this before it started, Kell," Thom said. "This whole thing could have been avoided. Now Stanos is going to have it in for you."

"Oh. Well, that's shitty."

That about summed it up. I spun around and stalked back to the Salty Pony.

"THANK YOU for coming on such short notice, sir," Magistrate Dexius said. We were sitting at his wooden desk on the second floor of the civic building. The windows and the doors to the veranda were open, looking at the sunset over the Bay of Scyros.

I smiled. I had waited a week to respond to the magistrate's summons. After the fight on the street, word had gotten around that I was the hero who had slain the gorgon Medusa. My friends still hadn't talked to me, but I went to the tavern every night anyway to see if they showed up, just in case they changed their minds.

The magistrate's aide, Polos, filled my wine glass with his strong arm and lifted his brow at me. He was in his forties with short curls on his head and a thick, gray-streaked black beard. I turned my smile to him.

"That was the good wine, yes, Polos?" The magistrate looked worriedly at my cup.

"Yes, sir," Polos said in his deep voice, both his dark brows climbing. From the time I had first been greeted as royalty by the magistrate, Polos had not stopped searching my face. He retreated into a corner, his broad shoulders and tapered waist swaying. He turned and crossed his arms and legs, leaning against the wall in the shadows and watching me with hooded eyes.

The magistrate was sweating and also ceaselessly inspecting me, his gaze darting from my clothes to my face. He coughed politely. "I hope you understand, I did not intend offense, but I sent a message to Seriphos to confirm the rumors that a demigod was actually living in my city. I had no idea that he was you. A son of Zeus, no less."

Polos stirred and made a noise, and the magistrate shot him a warning look.

I stiffened and gripped the arms of my chair, the wood groaning disconcertingly. "You did *what*?"

The magistrate jumped a little. "Everyone knows that Danae's Academy in Seriphos trains demigod youth. Please understand. If you had come to me when you first arrived here, I would have accepted your claims without question, but—"

"I have made no claims." My teeth clenched. "I have asked nothing of your office."

"Of course, sir." The magistrate gave a nervous laugh.

"My business is my own, Magistrate Dexius. If I had cared to make claims, my word should have been satisfactory for you." I lowered my voice. "Being a man of faith, as I am sure you are, you know that the gods deal harshly with those who falsely declare to be their children."

The magistrate's heart rate jumped, and he stammered. "My sincerest apologies, sir. I meant no disrespect. I had to know in order to better serve you! Having a son of Zeus in Delos, well, that truly is an honor."

I took a sip of wine but didn't taste it. "What did my mother say?"

The magistrate gave another polite cough. "Princess Danae implied that it would be wise of me to respect the authority you hold...." He hurriedly gulped some wine.

I sat back. "I do not wish to participate in Delos's government, if that is what you are worried about. No one else needs to know of my presence. In fact, the less things change the better."

The magistrate carefully put down his cup and raised a quivering finger. "About Lord Prastinos—"

"I don't care about him. Keep the money." I scowled.

The magistrate rushed his words in a relieved sigh. "It won't happen again."

"Fine." I hoped my face wasn't as red as it felt.

The magistrate swallowed more wine and gestured for Polos to fill his cup. The magistrate's fingers jumped as if everything he touched was hot. "If we should require your service...."

I lifted a brow. "For?"

"If there was an attack or a beast.... We would compensate you," the magistrate said.

"Fine. Are we finished?" I got up.

Magistrate Dexius hopped to his feet and said that his assistant would contact me if anything came up, and I gave Polos one last look before I walked out of the offices and into the evening. I left the marble arches of the civics building and descended the stone stairs toward the street. Guards were making rounds, lighting the torches for the night.

I sauntered around the side of the building and lit a pipe, leaning against one of the pillars and inhaling the smoke. Prastinos probably hadn't gone into detail about the assault, but he'd said enough. With my past transgressions and what had happened with Stanos, it appeared as if I had a reputation. I could be safer and visit Penelope's… but that didn't have the same appeal.

I sighed. Maybe I wouldn't have to worry about it anymore. Soon, the entire town would know I was a demigod. Perhaps strong men would be throwing themselves at my feet. I chuckled and took another drag, watching the blue smoke twist from my lips. Unlikely.

The sky was clear, the stars twinkling, and I closed my eyes and finished my pipe. Reaching into the bag at my belt, I pulled out my bag of hashish and my striker, a weird, dwarven-made handheld flint-and-steel thing. I filled the bowl and squeezed the prongs of the striker to the point where I got a spark. The ridges of the steel were rubbing off… I'd have to get Chris to look at it.

I sighed when I remembered that my friends weren't talking to me, and puffed furiously until I got my pipe roiling. The last of the families had left for the night, and those who came out during the dark flooded the streets in droves, laughing and wandering toward the public places where they would carouse with their friends.

I was tapping out my pipe when Magistrate Dexius bustled out of the civic building. Not long after that, I picked up the slow, sure steps of Polos before he appeared at the bottom of the stairs. I strode from the shadows, getting his attention as he stepped off the last step.

He started at the sight of me, almost dropping the parchment in his arms, and began to bow his head.

"Oh, please don't do that." I flushed.

Polos stood hesitantly, his usually solid brow quivering. "Son of Zeus," he said carefully.

I waved my hand and walked up to him, really close. He smelled musky, and his heartbeat drummed. "Come on, don't do that either. It's just Perseus."

"All right, Perseus. How can I help you?" Holding a stack of scrolls, he shifted his stance, his tunic showing off his muscled legs.

"I was hoping we could spend some time together this evening." I searched his face. "Unless you're having a girl over," I added quickly.

Polos bowed his head too late to cover his expression. His mouth was tight, jaw flexed, and his eyes were hard with hurt. "I don't think that would be a good idea," he said.

I didn't know what I had expected him to say, but I didn't anticipate the gut-wrenching ache of loneliness I felt. I stepped back and cleared my throat. "Okay, it's no problem."

Polos lifted his gaze to mine. "Unless you have business to speak of, Perseus?"

Business. I shook my head and backed up farther. "No. Forget it."

"Good night." I didn't wait to see him go. I stomped into the street, wanting to smash something. I still had an erection to bat a ball with as I paced toward the Salty Pony, so I tried to tuck it into my waistband. The crows take my cock.

When I entered the tavern, there were plenty of people in it. Men were throwing knives at the wall and drinking, and a haze of hashish filled the air. Jordan gave me a wave and an eyebrow lift, but I shook my head. My friends weren't there. I left and headed back toward Penelope's for dice, drinking, and maybe nailing a man or three.

I ground my teeth and kicked rocks across the street, sending them clinking off the sides of buildings. I had lost my anonymity, my friends, and the closest thing I'd had to a lover in years, all in a couple of weeks. Because of fucking prophecy. I had thought I could outrun it or make it bend to my terms, but I had been destined to lose this silly game I had tried to play with the Fates.

Maybe Athena was using me for her own schemes and it had nothing to do with my destiny. Maybe this whole hero thing would fade away and everyone would forget about it. Maybe I could still have friends and find love, and maybe I'd sprout wings like Leonidas and could fucking fly to another continent.

I slunk by a busy tavern and clung to the shadows, keeping out of the cheerful light and noise. As I was leaving the ruckus behind me, a group of four rambled toward me on the street. Through the darkness I saw them before they saw me, and I was tempted to duck behind a building. Instead, I stopped and waited for them to come closer.

Vano noticed me first, and his little legs slowed. Everyone looked at me.

"Perseus." Chris frowned and shoved his hands into his ratty pockets. "Prince Perseus," he amended.

"I believe it is most proper to refer to him as a son of Zeus, that being his higher title." Thom watched me under his bushy brows. "Of course, we'll address our liege however he requires."

I sighed and strode into the street, my hands open at my sides. "I only want to be Percy to you."

Everyone scuffed their shoes against the stones and looked embarrassed. Everyone but Chris, who glared at me. "You want to be our friend, even though you're some kind of fucking divine hero?"

I nodded and stopped before him, getting close so he could see the truth in my eyes. "I'm sorry about Kell getting hurt, and I should have stepped in sooner. I won't hide things from you any longer. Peace?"

Chris clenched his fists, and I knew he was going to hit me a second before he did. He slammed me in the jaw, and even though I saw it coming, my head whipped to the side from the blow. I stumbled and cupped my cheek, my face throbbing.

He smirked. "Aye, I suppose we can be friends again."

I ran a tongue along my teeth just to make sure they were all there and then tasted blood and spat. I chuckled and worked my jaw. It was already getting stiff. "Gods, Chris. You hit like a fucking dwarf."

Chris winced and shook his hand. "What's your skull made out of? Bricks?"

"Aye," Vano said. "Divine bricks."

"Where are you headed, Percy?" Thom said, grinning.

I stopped laughing. "Uh… Penelope's."

My friends shared a look and a chuckle, and then Chris turned around and marched toward the whorehouse. "Come on. I'll buy you some time with Geoff."

I shook my head vigorously. "Forget the whorehouse. Let's have a beer. I'll tell you what you want to know. I'm really sorry."

Thom nodded and strode after Chris. "I'll pitch in too."

I felt myself blushing. "Look, it doesn't really work that way with Geoff…."

"I know Penelope," Vano said. His small hand gripped mine, and he tugged me along.

"Of course you do," I muttered.

"Why not?" said Kell. "Wenching sounds good, and Percy can probably get us into the gold room now that he's famous."

I allowed myself to be herded by my friends. We all joked and laughed, and no one called me "Prince" or "Son of Zeus." Kell ribbed me about all the vulgar and degrading things he was going to have Geoff do to me, and even though the acts were disgusting and meant to humiliate me, I couldn't help but smile.

Chapter Eleven

A few nights later, I was twisted in my white linens when I awoke to a faint prickling across my skin. The linens crumbled at the end of the bed danced in the breeze from the open door, and pale moonlight flooded the room.

I pushed myself to sitting, throwing my legs over the side of the bed and listening: the sound of the ocean, the breeze through the olive trees, the creak of the bed, and my breath and heartbeat.

I ambled down the main hall to the latrines and shouldered out the back door, the farm relatively quiet. A quarter of a kilometer from the house, the goats snored in the barn.

The latrine was a two-seater, made of wood. I pulled open the door. When I finished pissing, I threw some ashes down the hole and shut the lid, then stepped back outside and listened some more. Nothing seemed out of place, but I couldn't shake the feeling that I was being watched. I entered the house and padded through the bedroom to the veranda, my feet slapping against the tiles, and grasped the wooden rail at the edge of the patio. I gazed out and into the wall of black, considering drinking more wine. Maybe from the year before. That had been my first good year, or so said the elves. If they were right, this year could be better.

The ocean was dark, a wall of black in the distance. My gaze fell onto a spot of white light at the shoreline—a moonbeam, or not....

Pulling myself from the rail, I set off through the olive trees toward the beach.

As the figure came into focus, my easy stroll became an eager lope. When I reached Antolios, we were both smiling ear to ear. I threw my arms around him, surrounded by his wonderful dirty scent.

The bond opened up between us, and I couldn't stop the tears from sliding down my cheeks. His presence in my mind grew, strong and solid. It had been so long I had almost forgotten how good it felt to be this close to someone. His love for me consumed me, and I basked in it.

I hadn't realized I was falling until Antolios sat my butt in the sand, and held my hand. My head was swimming—I couldn't figure out whose emotions were whose, and it was all too much. I was tangled in our bond, weary, sick, and elated, but eventually I pulled myself out of my stupor. I came to, blinking rapidly, and watched the moon light the caps of the waves before they crashed against the shore.

Antolios was wearing a long white shirt with silver embroidery, and dark leather pants that stretched along the long muscles of his legs. His pale toes dug into the sand, and he had one arm wrapped around his knees, his back curved. My gaze traveled up his hunched chest to his long neck and angular jaw. His beautiful curled hair was pulled behind his head in the Thessalian knot.

Without thinking, I reached up and untied his hair, letting it fall thick across his back and running my fingers through its soft, springy tresses. It felt better than silk. I blinked into those white eyes, my tears blurring them into stars. We leaned into each other and kissed, sighing when our lips locked, and then sighing again when we pulled apart. I couldn't rip my gaze away from him, and I was still dizzy, so he lifted me into his arms and carried me back to my bedroom.

In my bedroom I undressed him slowly, running my hands down pale skin that seemed so familiar but also new from the passage of time. The white static from my fingertips licked his flesh. Dropping to my knees, I pulled his pants down and dug my face into his fragrant pubic hair. He lifted his feet out of his breeches, and his arousal bobbed in front of my face. I ran my cheek along it while staring up into his white glow. Brushing my tongue against his cock, I teased it into my mouth, encircling it with my lips.

Antolios breathed deep, his eyes closing as I sucked him. I slurped down and then pulled up, twisting my tongue around the tip. I was just getting into it when Antolios said, "Come here."

Antolios crawled onto the bed and reclined in the middle, his flesh almost blending into the color of the blankets. I rummaged in a nightstand drawer, carried the oil to his side, and slid on top of him. Our pubic hair was a perfect contrast, gold and black. I rubbed our cocks together, his porcelain and pink and mine dark and dusky.

Bending down, I kissed him, our noses breathing into each other. With my eyes closed, I opened the bottle of oil and slicked a heavy coating onto his cock. I stoppered the bottle and tossed it aside. Using the remaining oil, I stuck my fingers against my ass and quickly squeezed a few in, keeping Antolios's lips pressed to mine.

I lined his cock up with my hole and slowly sat, watching his face. His eyes were closed, the glow muted, and his delicate eyebrows were slanted in pleasure.

My body knew his as it knew itself, and I rode him hard and fast.

Arousal expanded deep inside me, and Antolios's long hands gripped my sides, steadying us as we burst into our last moments before orgasm. A single line appeared above his brow, and his mouth opened in a soft cry. I groaned, and our voices melded into one as I ejaculated all over his chest and the bed.

I sat heavily on his penis, trapping it inside of me.

Antolios slid his hands up my chest to my neck and then cupped my face. He put his thumb in my mouth, and I sucked it.

"I love you, angel," I said around his thumb.

I love you too.

Hearing his voice that way for the first time in years sent a shiver down my spine, and his love for me through the bond added to the heavy feeling of satisfaction throughout my entire body. I rocked my hips, riding his softening cock, hoping we could keep going forever, but knowing we would have to stop eventually.

Antolios's face fell.

Sighing and slumping forward, I released his cock from my ass in a warm rush. I buried my face in his neck and snatched up one of his hands up to my mouth, kissing it.

"What have you been doing all these years?" I whispered into his neck.

"I'm a general of Pelion's armies."

"You're a general? I thought it was a rumor. I heard you killed Corinna in some battle."

"I didn't want to kill her, but you know how it is," Antolios said. "After I won, the battle was called off. Her death spared thousands."

Antolios's fingers trickled up and down my spine, but despite this I was starting to feel uneasy. My mouth put it together before my brain did. I blurted, "What else do you do in Pelion?"

"You know, things. Perseus, I—"

I thrust myself up onto my arms and looked right into his bright eyes. "Come live with me."

Antolios closed his eyes. "I can't."

I nudged him, and he opened them again. "Then I'll come and live with you!"

"You can't." He shifted under me.

"Why not? Don't you still love me?"

"Yes."

I barely noticed it at first, but as I stared at Antolios's pained and weary face, I grew more aware of the sky and woke the sleeping storm. Trembling, I rolled off him and knelt on the bed. It began to rain a light mist.

"Then why did you leave?" I said. "You left without saying good-bye."

Antolios propped himself up on his elbows. "You're serving the gods and fulfilling your prophecy. There is no room for me in your life."

"That's not true. You're a hero too! You killed the fastest woman alive!"

Antolios made a sound in his throat. "I don't have a life's plan protected by the gods as you do."

Rain blew into my bedroom, and Antolios eyed it warily, but I felt a powerful rush. Thunder rumbled off the coast, and the sky pulsed with the beat of my heart. "It hasn't affected my life," I said. "Not really."

Antolios sat up and held his knees. "You're going to have a legacy, a family. Where would I fit into that?"

"I don't have to stay at home, for fuck's sake! I'll have monsters to kill and people to meet. Royalty." My voice rose, and a flash of lightning blinded the room. A split second later the sky boomed.

Antolios glanced out the window and then back at me.

"What?" I said. "Come on."

His shoulders sagged. "I can't."

"Why not?" Another flash and crack. The branches of the olive trees whipped about, and the floor near the porch entry was flooded with water.

Antolios's head hung, and his voice was quiet. "Perseus, I'm married."

"What?" I couldn't have heard him right. I silenced the clouds, letting the storm blow and pour instead.

He lifted his gaze to mine, the white light searing through me. *I'm married.*

Arms over my head and fingers gripping my hair, I groaned, my voice hoarse and broken. "You can't. I waited."

"My mother arranged it," Antolios said. "To Cora, daughter of King Niklaus and heir apparent to the throne of Thessaly."

"You're going to be a king?" I was crying, but I wasn't sure how long I had been. The wet grooves down my cheeks seemed well traveled by tears.

"A crown prince," he said.

The air danced vibrantly around me, rocking me, but it was hardly a comfort. "Do you love her?"

Yes, Antolios said.

Air had no weight in my lungs, and I fell to the bed, spinning and spinning.

Antolios smoothed the covers by him. "Come here," he said. When he crawled toward me and reached out a hand, I recoiled.

"Don't touch me," I said, my vision blurry. The storm kicked up again, and thunder swelled and throbbed in my head. Rain pelted the stucco walls.

Some of my connection with the storm was lost, and I became drowsy. Even though he wasn't touching me, I knew Antolios was soothing me somehow. It was as if a blanket was being drawn over my thoughts and senses. I tried to roll off the bed, but I couldn't move.

Antolios gathered me into his lap, and a tear from his face rolled down my arm and was absorbed in the skin at my wrist. His chest shook. "I love you, Perseus. I'm sorry for not saying good-bye. Gods, I can't bear this."

My lips fell open, and I drooled.

He sobbed, clutching me to him. I was smashed into his neck, so I couldn't see his face, but his body shuddered under me. "I'm sorry I'm here, but I couldn't help it. I needed to see you. I can't be without you, but I can't be with you. I'm sorry." He kissed my head, and I listened to his sobs for a long time. I had never heard him cry, and even if I had wanted to say something, I'm not sure I would have been able to.

Eventually he snuffled and managed to speak. "Do you want to sleep now?"

I'd barely even nodded my head when the world blissfully dropped away.

I OPENED my eyes to the late-morning sun. The clouds had yet to burn off completely from the night storm. Antolios slept against my back. Where our skin touched was a slick of sweat, and my ass was glued to his crotch. His hair was draped over us, smelling of almonds and neroli. I ran my hands through it, the light spinning the ringlets to gold.

Antolios was snoring slightly through his straight nose, and I frowned with sadness, the expression pulling at the skin of my puffy eyes. He had never snored before. I lay there until I heard my workers down in the fields talking and laughing.

Antolios woke, and I almost gasped from the sudden rush of blood through my body. His hand crept down toward my erection. I gazed over my shoulder at him, his eyes still hooded from sleep. A smile grew on his face, the brightness of it blowing away my unhappy thoughts.

"Good morning," he said, voice husky. He stroked me.

I leaned back into him and closed my eyes. "Good morning."

SOMETIME LATER I went to gather eggs from the chickens and met with a strange horse in my stables. I approached the powerful black work horse, hooves the size of plates. He tossed his head at me and accepted a pat on the nose. I saw to Spirit and the black's hay and water, fed the rest of the animals, and then gathered what I could from the garden. My workers were already in the fields, bending over grapevines.

When I stepped back into the kitchen, Antolios was naked and drinking tea and reading a scroll at the table. His wet hair fell down his back, and he bobbed a leg on his knee.

"Is that your horse?" I said.

"His name is Thunder." He smiled slyly.

Grinning, I brought my bounty to the kitchen counters and prepared our meal, serving Antolios warm juice and goat's milk. "So you have kids." I tried to keep my tone light.

"Etiaya, Lilyos, and Vora. A fourth on the way."

"How's that?" I said with my back to him. I cracked eggs and threw them in a bowl with the chopped vegetables. Usually I had stewed grains, day-old bread, or whatever fruit I had ripe for my morning meal, but this was special.

"Good. I think you'd enjoy it." I didn't say anything, so Antolios said, "They're fun and sweet, and being a father is interesting."

"Why do you have to leave tomorrow?" I poured the mixture into the pan over the fire. It sizzled and popped, and the smell of eggs and vegetables filled the kitchen.

"Cora is due soon, and we discovered that I have certain talents for helping her through labor. If I'm not at her side in time, I'm seriously a dead man. We're visiting King Demetre, even though she was insane to travel this pregnant, and the only reason I was allowed this small adventure was because I promised to stop and pay my respects to your mother."

I turned the eggs.

"Don't be like that," he said.

"Be like what?"

"Sulky."

"I miss you, and I haven't seen you in years." I couldn't keep the petulance out of my voice. Antolios stripped me of everything I had tried to build into myself these last years. I banged the pan onto the counter and scraped the contents onto two plates, tossing goat cheese and herbs on top and shoving them onto the table.

Antolios, infuriatingly calm, picked up his fork and speared a bite, blowing on it. "Well, maybe next time you can come up and see me, and then we'll have more time."

"Really? I can come up to Pelion?"

Antolios chewed and swallowed. "Sure, why not? This is really good, by the way."

"Won't Cora be upset?" I played with my cup of juice.

"You are the heir apparent to Argos and a demigod hero. She would be honored to host you. As for other things…. I love you too. I always will." He stuffed his face.

I stared at the wine cabinet on the far wall and slowly drained my juice, then started in on my eggs. "What do you want to do today?"

Antolios cleaned up his plate and reached for his milk. "We have all day, right? You don't have to be anywhere? Help out with any farm things…."

"We just finished up the season, and my workers can get on without me."

"We could… find something to keep us busy." Antolios grinned.

I laughed. "First, I suppose I should prep our meals for the day…. Fish okay?"

"Fish is wonderful." Antolios leaned back and took me in. "I am impressed with you. Look at you. Look at this." He gestured around. "You cook, clean, and make and grow things."

Frowning, I slowly put down my fork.

Antolios hissed. "I'm sorry. That was careless of me."

I shook my head. "Enjoy the time we have, right?"

"Right." Antolios's face bloomed into an almost comical grin, something he learned for his children perhaps. "How can I help?"

"Do you cook?" I lifted a brow.

"No."

I pointed to a pile of pails in the corner. "There's a well up the hill from the barn. Fill those, and I'll start on the bread."

Antolios rose and kissed my head. "Should I put on clothes first?"

"I forbid it. You're just going to have to deal with my men ogling you." I grinned, because I knew they would. Who wouldn't ogle a man over two meters tall with moonlight coming from his eyes? Naked or not, he was striking.

Antolios chuckled and grabbed the pails. I watched his tight ass disappear down the hallway and then shook myself. Time to make the biggest batch of bread known to mortals.

THE NEXT morning I slowly prepared and packed food for Antolios's trip. He was sitting at the table in his travel clothes, hair bound up and boots on, finishing his morning meal. I hadn't pretended to be hungry.

"Will you write?" I shoved a couple of large loaves of bread in a sack.

"Yes."

I wrapped cheese in cloth and dumped it in the sack as well.

"Perseus," Antolios said hesitantly, "be careful of King Demetre. He's been spying on you."

Turning halfway toward him, I raised a brow.

"The slaves you had when we were at the academy… they told him things. I'm sorry I didn't catch it, but I don't think they knew they were spies. He's still getting information about you, but I'm not sure how. And he thinks of you often."

"What does he want?"

Antolios looked troubled. "I don't know. Be careful… just be careful."

I nodded and put my hands on the counter, looking out the window to the olive orchard. King Demetre was my divine half brother, and I was the heir apparent to the kingdom next to his, so I supposed it made sense that he would be curious about me. I'd probably never figure out who was spying on me, though, I met so many people…. I couldn't even remember their names after the night was over, and even their faces started to blur together. So many.

"You're not a whore," Antolios said.

I stiffened and stared at the gulls settling in the olive trees. A few nights before, when my friends had paid for that hour with Geoff, the whore had said something to me as we were putting our clothes back on.

Geoff had been tying that ridiculous scarf at his throat and buttoning his heavy jacket when he smiled at me with those perfect plump lips and told me he had truly enjoyed our time together.

I had grinned, throwing on my boots and saying the same, striding to the door.

"I felt very relaxed around you," Geoff had said, "like we were two whores fucking around."

I had paused. After we had been introduced and left alone, I had asked him to be familiar with me, claiming I got off on it or something, but really I just didn't want to deal with being called "sir" and other bullshit now that it was known I was a demigod.

Geoff had caught me off guard, but I had smiled and nodded, taking it for the compliment I thought he meant. I hadn't known what to say to him.

I knew what to say to Antolios. "That's none of your business."

"I'm worried about you," Antolios said.

I ran my thumbs along the tiles of my counter, tiles I had lain with my bare hands. I had built the table too, and the large wine rack at the other end of the great room. Copper pots and pans hung from the ceiling by the fire, and a wooden chest leaned up against the wall between two large windows. I had painted the tiles royal blue and egg yolk yellow....

"Perseus."

I cleared my throat. "I miss you."

"I've missed you too. You know you can see me again."

Crossing my arms, I spun around to face him. "When?"

Antolios's white lights bored into me. "Next summer."

"Next summer! A whole year!"

"Less than a year. The snow will clear in spring."

"I don't care!" I said. "I'll fucking climb the mountains if I have to! Or I'll sail the coast!"

"Perseus."

"Why do you get to decide!" I brushed away the tears I was ashamed to cry, and my nose stuffed up. I took a few deep breaths out of my mouth.

"Don't do this." Antolios straightened, unfolding his long limbs. He tucked in his gray shirt.

"No!" I pointed a finger at him. "The time we had is gone, and this is what I'm left with when you leave. I don't understand what you did, and you may think I act like a child, but you don't get to tell me I'm overreacting." Tears fell down my face, and I turned away. So much for not being dramatic. I gasped. "I feel like I'm dying."

"I'm sorry," he said.

"As you say." I threw the rest of his food into his travel sack and handed it over, looking up at him. "Tell me you love me and go. At least I deserve that much."

Antolios took the bag from me and bent to whisper in my ear. "I do, you know. I love you."

I tilted my head up and pressed my lips to his. We kissed, our cheeks wet with my snot and tears, but too soon he pulled away and strode out the door to Thunder, who was hitched up at the post in the drive. Antolios swung up onto his massive horse.

I love you, he said, and then he rode away.

I stared after him, waiting and waiting, until he was well out of sight, until the fire grew in my gut. Everything I had worked for… was for nothing. Running away from the gods, making a home for Antolios and me…. Nothing.

I snapped, squeezing my fists and screaming at the top of my lungs. The air cracked around me, and my hair stood on end. I beat my hands into my thighs, and thunder exploded in the sky.

My gaze fell on the table where he had eaten. In two strides I was there, slamming my hands down, shattering the table and sending spoons, forks, and cups sailing into the air and clattering onto the floor.

My chest was tight, painful. I couldn't breathe. I strode across the room and snatched up pillows from the couches, ripping them apart and watching the feathers fly. Furniture snapped under my swift kicks, and I tore up the rugs with my bare hands and teeth.

My mouth still tasting of wool, I stood in front of my wine rack, an entire wall of wood and glass and wine. I had built it with my own sweat and blood.

I shot my hand out toward it, and lightning lanced into the shelf. It groaned and caved, glass popping and shattering. A river of wine spread from it across the tiled floor.

My will be done.

Several of the bottles survived the fall, and one rolled to a stop at my foot. The handwritten date on the label said it was of the year before, a good year. I stalked into the bedroom and threw open the trunk at the end of my oversized bed. I shredded the wrappings from my sword, shiny as if it were new, and tested the blade with my thumb. I had never needed to sharpen it.

I held an intact bottle of wine before me, and in a quick motion, I sliced off the top of the wine bottle with my sword, right through the wax and cork and glass.

"A god-blade fit for Perseus, Son of Zeus." I drank right out of the top of the broken bottle until it was gone. I sputtered, wiping my chin with my arm. "Yes," I choked out. "A good year."

I stalked into the living room and searched for another intact bottle.

RED LIGHT pulsed outside my closed eyelids. I groaned and threw an arm over my face.

"Perseus? You all right?"

I grimaced. "Franko, just let me sleep." I was slurring, my words muffled under my arm. I tried to pull my blankets over my head, but I couldn't find them.

Laughter barked above me, and I tore my arm from my face and blinked rapidly in the light, my eyes smarting. What the fuck were my workers doing in my room? I had the beginnings of a headache as I rocked with the odd swaying motions of the bed. The fuzzy forms of the workers came into focus above me. Franko bent his head over me, his straw hat casting a shadow over his face. His skin was leathery and dark from years of working in the sun.

I was outside, in the middle of my orchard, lying in the dirt. And I was still drunk.

"Ugh," I said.

My workers laughed, and Franko held out a hand. I reached for it and missed. Franko gripped me by the elbow, yanking me up. I found myself face-to-face with everyone and their floppy hats and grins. My stomach roiled, and my heart battered against my ribs.

As my mouth filled with saliva, I pulled away from Franko, but he threw an arm over my shoulder to stabilize me. Panicking, I turned and retched. He released me and everyone shuffled back, but not before I threw up all over Donovan's boots. My vomit tasted of alcohol and fish I didn't remember eating.

"I'm sorry, I'm sorry, I'm sorry," I mumbled. I wiped my mouth but only managed to smear it across my beard. The men around me laughed, but it was halting.

Donovan wiped his boots in the grassy dirt.

"I'm sorry, Donovan."

Donovan scowled down at his feet. "Don't worry about it. Let's get you back to the house. You done now?"

I hung my head. "I think so."

Two people flanked me and took hold of my shoulders, and we stumbled back to the house. I had passed out in the middle of the property, right where the olive grove met the vineyard, so we had a way to go. I tripped on rocks and sticks and nearly fell, but my workers had me. The familiar smell of warming trees and the salty tang of the ocean followed us. I put one foot in front of the other and pretended that the insects and birds were singing us along.

My stomach flipped again, and I lurched to a stop. "I'm gonna throw up again." My voice was small and sad, but instead of laughing, the men scattered.

My stomach lurched, and I tried to lean over on my knees, but they were out of my control and squirming. During my first retch, I thudded to the earth. "Oh gods." I groaned and heaved again, not bringing anything up.

Franko chuckled nervously off to the side. "Shit, Perseus, how much did you have?"

I made another effort to empty my stomach, my eyes bulging out of my sockets and body clenching. "Enough," I said at last, coughing.

Franko muttered his agreement.

My lips were cold and wet, and my eyelids drooped as I yawned. I spit a few times in the dirt and rolled over, curling up, but then a quick thud of boots came toward me.

"Aw, don't do that. Come on, let's get you home," they said.

My eyes welled. "But I'm so tired…. I'm just going to close my eyes for a minute."

More laughter, and then I was grabbed and yanked up.

"Come on. We need to get you inside," Franko said.

I wanted to cause a scene, demand that they let me go, but I didn't have the energy. If I thought too much about what was going on, or struggled too hard, then I'd break into a place of understanding that I didn't want to be in. An unpleasant feeling ticked in the back of my mind, but I pushed it aside. The gnarled trees threw patches of shade, and I squinted and focused on moving my legs.

My porch came into sight. I stopped again, and the men stepped back warily.

"I have to piss," I said. Snickers followed me over to the stucco wall of my house—the latrines and my bedroom seemed too far away. I fumbled at the laces of my pants and finally aimed and released. Tottering, I tried to get my other hand up to hold me steady, but my face and shoulder smashed against the rough siding anyway.

I peed for an eternity, and my eyes drifted closed again. My face scratched down the wall, and jolted awake and finished up, trying to ignore the fact that I had pissed on my boots. Crawling with my hands along the wall toward my bedroom door, I finally made it into my room. Reaching my arms out for my bed, I was eager to welcome oblivion, but then my workers took hold of my shoulders and bustled me into the great room.

And there in the wreck of my living room, proud and radiant, was Athena.

All the men dropped to their knees, and because I wasn't supported anymore, I slumped to the floor. A piece of glass was a hairsbreadth from my eye, swimming in and out of my vision, and I struggled to get myself up on my elbows.

Athena's voice pierced my brain. "Thank you," she said to the others. "Your service is appreciated. Know that my eye will be on you and yours and their safety. Leave us."

I stared at the dark red floor as the boots of my workers stomped out of earshot.

"Hail, Goddess," I said to the blackened tiles. Athena didn't say anything for a time, no doubt regretting her choice in a champion. I couldn't say I blamed her. I tried to ignore the feeling of being tossed about on a boat, swallowing and praying I wouldn't get sick again.

"Champion," Athena said. "I have another task for you. King Cepheus and Queen Cassiopeia have offended Poseidon. Poseidon will demand that the king place his youngest daughter on a rock by the sea, and Cetus, the great sea serpent, will come for her. You will rescue the princess."

I grunted.

"You will find her along the coast of King Cepheus's castle, near Owl's Lookout."

I tried to speak without slurring. "Owl's Lookout is a week's ride. Won't I be too late?"

"Poseidon has not told the king yet of his demands, but you will leave before nightfall."

I inwardly groaned. "Yes, Goddess."

"I will aid your return journey once you have completed your task. Look to the skies near Owl's Lookout and pray to me."

"Yes, Goddess. Thank you." I frowned. "Goddess?"

"Yes, Champion?"

"What blessing did you give me?"

If it was possible, Athena's voice softened in amusement. "I blessed you with the aura of intelligence. You will appear cleverer than you are, but only to those who do not know you well."

"Very wise." I nodded exaggeratedly.

"I know," Athena said, her voice light. "Godspeed, Son of Zeus." She was gone. I hadn't noticed that the birds had been silent until their song came back in full force, harshly cheery.

I called out to Franko, who I could still hear shuffling on the porch. He hustled in and stepped around the mess of broken furniture and spilled wine. I pulled my eyelids open with everything I had, but my head was sagging toward the floor and my knees were trembling from trying to keep me from falling over.

"You're Athena's champion?" Franko's voice was soft and reverent. "An angel—"

"Franko. Wake me up in a few hours? I'm going to be gone." The floor rushed up to meet me.

"Yes, sir. Don't worry about anything, Perseus. We'll take care of it."

"Thanks," I mumbled. Before Franko could tell me not to, I passed out.

Chapter Twelve

Andromeda

ANDROMEDA'S WRISTS were rubbed raw from her struggles to break free of the chains that fixed her to the large rock. The tide was coming in. Based on the waterline on the cliff behind her, she'd be long dead when it reached its apex. Drowned. Or eaten.

Things had just been getting good in Andromeda's life. She was a princess and considered one of the fairest maidens on the southern coast. She had been so close to finding a wonderful husband, marrying him, and living happily ever after.

The clerics had taken Andromeda in the morning, before she had fully awoken. Servants Andromeda had known since before she could remember had chained her and left her here, alone and nearly naked. Before they had departed, the clerics explained to her why she was being sacrificed, which was more than her parents had told her.

Andromeda's mother's face had been wet, and her father had looked pained, but that was all. Her parents were simply obeying Poseidon, but at that moment their piety meant nothing to Andromeda. They were her parents, and this was how she was going to remember them in the Underworld for eternity. If she remembered anything of her life.

King Cepheus and Queen Cassiopeia were proud of Andromeda, with her unusual auburn hair and creamy skin, and in their search for the perfect husband, they had boasted about her beauty, claiming that she was lovelier than the sea nymphs. If this had happened just once, perhaps Poseidon would not have minded, for mortals were silly, flawed, and required much forgiveness. Despite warnings by the clerics, though, her mother and father had rejected suitor after suitor, and continued to make their claims.

Andromeda had been told that Poseidon was sending Cetus, the great sea serpent, to devour her. The rocks cut into her feet as the water licked at her toes. Shadows shifted below the surface of the waves but vanished before she could be certain of what caused them. Earlier she had been banging her manacles in earnest, but no one had come to her aid, and now that she had seen the darkness in the water, she tried to keep her chains from scraping against the rocks.

A flash of gray scales broke the surface, and below the waves, fiery eyes watched her. Cetus had come.

Andromeda's heart beat fast, panic settling into her heaving chest. She had already screamed herself raw, but she tried to cry out again, only managing a small mewl. She flung herself from one side to the other of the rock, as far as her bonds would allow.

Someone coughed behind her.

Andromeda jumped and spun toward the source. She stared.

A man crouched like a panther on the rocks, observing her with startling pale blue eyes. His face lit with a kind smile. "Hello. I'm Perseus."

Dark from the sun, he had short jet-black hair. His sort of boyish look was enhanced by high cheekbones and soft pink lips, but he wasn't a boy. He had shed all the fat of his childhood and had a short black mustache and chin beard. He wore simple armor over his riding clothes and held a brilliant round shield on one arm and a large steel sword in his other hand. Through his airy white shirt, she could tell that he was strong and fit....

"My name is Andromeda," she finally stammered. The cold ocean water licked her calves. Her eyes widened, and she darted a glance at the sea. "You have to get out of here. This place is dangerous. There's a monster!"

Perseus seemed amused and regarded her for a moment. "I know," he said. "I'm here to rescue you. I was sent by Athena."

Andromeda stared, dumbfounded, as Perseus rose smoothly and stepped over the rocks toward the edge of the water, inspecting its depths. She didn't know why, but she laughed. It was fantastic that he was here, but she had seen hints of the enormity that waited for her. "Well, Perseus, it's nice to meet you, and thank you for coming. You seem nice, but I guess we may die together?"

Perseus looked at her with an arched brow. "Die?"

A long dark form burst forth from the water, screeching so loudly that Andromeda brought her manacled hands up to her ears in pain and terror, and she squeezed her eyes shut.

The scream was suddenly cut short, and when Andromeda recovered, Perseus was diving into the water, armor and all. The frothing waves swallowed him, and the scaly gray monster followed right behind. Andromeda shrank back into the rock, her heart racing.

An age seemed to pass without any movement in the water. Then Cetus exploded from the waves again and darted its small head side to side, scanning the surface with lava red eyes. The fringe on its neck and back stood up, and it gripped the rocks in front of Andromeda with small lizard hands. It raised its long neck high into the air and then struck down into the water.

Andromeda screamed.

The monster's jagged maw came up empty.

Andromeda spotted Perseus. He had latched onto the serpent's long neck with one hand and was climbing his way up the fringes. Each heave of his muscled arm pulled him closer and closer to Cetus's head. The serpent squealed, and Andromeda once again cowered against the rock, the shrill noise grating against her nerves.

Perseus drew back his sword, and Cetus whipped about. Andromeda gasped as he was thrown off, but he twisted quickly and plunged feetfirst into the waves with Cetus chasing after him. Andromeda found herself screaming once again, her voice hoarse.

The roiling water wiped away their struggle below the surface. She held her breath, but when she could hold it no longer, Perseus still hadn't surfaced. She leaned toward the edge of the rock, the waves now up to her thighs, but couldn't see any sign of either man or monster. Andromeda started crying, but the only wetness on her cheeks was from the ocean's spray.

The water seethed—Cetus's head exploded out of the waves, mouth open in a soundless gape. Perseus straddled its fringe once again. His face dripped blood, white teeth bared, as he reached around Cetus's neck and dragged his blade across the scaly flesh.

Cetus floundered, tossing spasmodically from side to side. Bucked off, Perseus barreled into the swells and disappeared. Blood ran from Cetus's neck, and its eyes darted around in disbelief. It tried to scream, but all that came out was a disturbing gurgle.

Andromeda watched as the serpent sank into the waves. Soon, there were no movements besides the churn of the red ocean. She waded to the edge again, searching for Perseus. The tide was now up to her waist, the waves splashing her chest. She was watching the water in front of her when Perseus scrambled onto the rocks, farther down the ledge.

He stood, dripping with blood and water, his muscles rippling beneath his clinging clothing. Andromeda looked down at her own wet shift and modestly turned away, eyeing Perseus over her shoulder.

Blood ran down his face from a large gash on his forehead, and he wiped at it with his sleeve. He waded toward her, legs churning through the water as he secured his shield. His beauty took Andromeda's breath away.

"Look away," Perseus told her gently when he reached her.

She turned her head and leaned away from him.

A harsh vibration stung her wrists, and she winced and closed her eyes as the next blow struck.

After it was over, Perseus soothed her hurts away with his strong hands, and much to her shock, he wrapped his arms around her and told her that it was going to be okay. The weight of the entire morning suddenly hit Andromeda. She cried as he held her, and tears came this time, mixing with the salt on her face.

Andromeda felt his voice through his chest as Perseus spoke. "Shall we go?"

She smiled and nodded, trying in vain to dry her face.

ANDROMEDA DIDN'T want to go home. "Let my parents think me dead. They deserve it." She knew she was being rash for wanting to punish them for their actions, but she also knew that she could not go back to the way things had been. She couldn't pretend that they hadn't done this to her.

Perseus sighed, suddenly appearing older than she thought he was. "You should be careful with these kinds of decisions."

"Can't I live with you? I can work for you, cooking and cleaning," she said.

"You want to live with me?" he said. "I'm a simple farmer…. Aren't you a princess?"

Andromeda scowled. "Just because I was raised a princess doesn't mean I can't learn to work on a farm!"

Perseus blinked at her and then stepped back and gave a surprisingly graceful and formal bow. "I am honored, and I accept your service."

Andromeda flushed and relaxed.

Perseus peeled off his armor and shirt and then wrung out his bloody top and handed it to her. She gratefully slid the shirt over her shift, and together, the two garments weren't as see-through. As he shoved his armor in a large pack and threw it over his broad shoulders, Andromeda noticed the scattered black hair on his chest. A fine line of it trailed down his body, right over his belly button, and all the way into his waistband.

She tried not to stare.

Perseus and Andromeda had to climb rocks before they reached the sandy beach, and he helped her across a wide gap by lifting her and lightly tossing her to the other side. Her feet bled, and when she got sand in her wounds they ached fiercely, but she didn't limp or complain.

They hiked up the shore until they reached the grassy plateaus above. Perseus said that his horse was along the top of the cliff back the way they had come, so they hiked above the ocean on the breezy bluffs. Perseus's gray horse was munching on the grass when they arrived.

"Sit on the grass," Perseus said.

Andromeda sat, and Perseus dug in his pack and pulled out a flask. He knelt in front of her and washed her feet, a faint line of concern on his brow as he inspected her wounds. His touch was soft, and he was so close she could smell his black hair. Almond… and something deeper. He reached into his pack again and took out bandages and ointment, rubbing the salve on her feet and wrapping them in linen. Picking her up easily, he placed her onto the riding pad on the back of the horse. The horse flicked its ears and tore at the grass.

"There's no saddle," Andromeda said.

"I never trained him to wear one." Perseus frowned at her. "Spirit is trained to wear a harness and pull a cart."

Perseus looked slightly offended, so Andromeda quickly said, "I just meant that I don't normally see riders without saddles, except soldiers." But Perseus wasn't wearing a tunic, just leather pants and boots, and he wasn't displaying the colors of any kingdom.

Tipping water from his flask into his hand, Perseus washed his face of blood, exposing the deep, pink gash that ran along his hairline down to his ear. He tended to his wounds, wincing, and then hopped onto the horse, settling in behind her. His arms came loosely around her sides, and he took up the lead.

They headed along the coastal road, and Andromeda informed Perseus of her parents' boasts, and how they had angered Poseidon. The shirt that Perseus had given her wasn't much drier or thicker than her shift, but the sun was strong, and soon she stopped shivering. Perseus's hips rocked against her with the movement of the stallion, and occasionally she dozed. The burned smell of an evergreen pricked at her nose in a faint and pleasant way—she realized it was him.

Toward evening, they had arrived at Owl's Lookout, but before they went into town, Perseus dismounted and helped Andromeda down.

"Are we staying in the town for the night?" she asked.

He smiled slyly. "We're waiting for our next ride." She didn't understand, but he would say no more about it. Perseus fussed with the straps of Spirit's riding pad and then watched the sky, waiting. At first Andromeda wasn't sure what they were waiting for, but when she saw them she knew.

Three gigantic snowy owls flew toward them, each easily the size of a house.

Perseus took Andromeda's hand and grinned as the birds got closer. His blue eyes glowed youthfully, and yet again she wondered how old he was.

Andromeda knew she should feel fear or anticipation or at least a little interest, but it took too much energy to bring up any emotions. She was too exhausted to worry about three giant owls with sharp beaks and talons getting ready to grab her.

Spirit screamed in terror as a large owl swooped down and picked him up, and Andromeda covered her ears reflexively, the sound reminding her of Cetus. The wings of the owl flapped Andromeda's hair about her face, and then she was carefully cradled in large talons and lifted off the ground. She held on to the thick, smooth claw and curled on her side, watching the world slip away.

They flew past sunset, and in the dark landscape she spied the white dots of farmhouses. When the moon had risen near the top of the sky, the owls spiraled down toward one of the red-roofed, stucco farmhouses. Old olive trees swept down the slopes to the ocean.

Perseus and Andromeda were released near the house, but Spirit was set down in the grove. He screamed again and bucked. Perseus waved farewell to the owls as they flapped away. He retrieved Spirit to settle him down, and then the two disappeared into the stables. When Perseus came out, he took Andromeda into the main house.

Dropping his gear at the door, he turned to her. "I'll heat water for a bath and prepare you something to eat, if you'd like."

Andromeda nodded. She felt a little out of place, but she was very hungry. Her servants hadn't given her a meal, and Perseus had only brought olives, hard cheese, and crackers that they had shared riding to Owl's Lookout. She remembered the way his cheeks had hollowed as he spit the olive pits off to the side.

The room they were in was large, with cream-colored stucco walls and dark wood beams in a vaulted ceiling. Some chairs and a small table were cluttered in a corner, but other than that the room was mostly empty.

Perseus caught her staring. "I… uh… am in the middle of getting new furnishings." He smiled. "Would you help me pick them out?" He strode to the end of the room with the fireplace and kitchen.

Andromeda's face flushed with pleasure. "I would love to."

Perseus went about preparing supper and fetching and heating water for her bath. When Andromeda tried to step in, he waved her down into a chair near the tiny table and many bottles of wine standing together. While they were riding, he had said he was a vintner, which she thought to be a higher class than the farmer he had originally claimed to be. He hadn't mentioned a wife, and there didn't seem to be anyone else in the house. With the ease that he performed house chores, he was most likely a bachelor. His name was vaguely familiar, but she couldn't quite finger why.

Perseus had forgotten to put on another shirt once he got home, so she watched him pace about his chores half-naked. He gave her some wine, and it wasn't even watered down. She drank the wine, even though her parents hadn't thought it proper for young ladies to do so. If she was old enough to get sacrificed to a serpent, then she was old enough to drink.

He served her cheese, smoked fish, bread, and figs and set them on the small makeshift table. She tried to eat but managed only a few swallows before she felt so stuffed she thought she would be sick. Perseus joined her in a chair, his bites precise and quick. He ate fast and glanced up at her.

"Are you finished?" he said.

Andromeda nodded and began to stand to help him with the dishes, but he got up briskly and laid a hand gently on her shoulder, imploring her to remain seated. She was pleased but a bit confused by this treatment. He was possibly pampering her today because she'd had such a shock. Tomorrow she would learn how to properly tend to the house.

Perseus finished cleaning and lifted the heavy pot of hot water to the bathroom with ease. After returning for a few large rocks that had been sitting in the fire, he led Andromeda out of the great room to a long hall. The second door down was ajar, and she could see into the bathroom, which had a sunken turquoise tub in the floor.

He closed the door behind her and waited until she cracked it open, handing him his shirt and her fragile garment for washing. He informed her through the door that he had a blanket on a bench for her when she finished.

Andromeda thanked him and then sat at the edge of the tiled bath. Her wrists were red, swollen, and would probably bruise. She unwound the linen on her feet—the cuts were not as bad as she'd thought, merely scratches. She found a container for cloth waste and set the soiled bandages in there. Her feet were still sore, and she carefully stepped down into the hot water.

She spent a long time in the tub, washing her dark red hair and ivory skin with the almond soap she found. Her unique features had been one of the reasons she was seen as beautiful, and one of the reasons she had been sent to her death. She had thought that they would guarantee her a future with a prince and a family, but instead she would be a vintner's servant. At least the gods' plans for her apparently didn't include being sacrificed.

Andromeda dried herself and peeked into chests until she came across some large jars of olive oil. After rubbing herself down, she wrapped herself in the blanket Perseus had provided and glanced out the second door. Stepping into a bedroom, she took in the dominating white four-poster bed, with its delicate cream drapes and copious pillows.

Andromeda gazed out a columned doorway that led to an outdoor veranda. Outside, Perseus turned and caught her eye. He watched her watch him. Those blue eyes, that glowing skin… there was something about him. Why was a champion of Athena a farmer? Andromeda had so many questions.

Perseus smiled, and her heart fluttered.

He beckoned her out, and she approached, seeing that he had more wine set up for them at a table. She sat as he poured, and she adjusted her "dress" so it wouldn't slip down. The black hair under his arms flashed under the sure movements of his shoulders, and she found the sight oddly alluring.

They made small talk for a while. Andromeda loved how Perseus looked at her, steady and open, as though he was considering her. Even though she was an adult, she was the youngest daughter in her family, and no one at the palace had taken her seriously. Eventually Perseus went inside and checked on her shift. He came back with it and handed it to her, still warm from the fire, and she ducked inside to change.

When Andromeda finished changing and opened the bathroom door, Perseus was kneeling on the porch in front of a shining woman in full mail with a sword and shield. The woman was magnificently beautiful and ethereal…. Timeless.

The woman looked up from Perseus, meeting Andromeda's gaze with steel gray eyes. "Greetings, Andromeda." Her voice rang pure in Andromeda's ears.

Recognizing the goddess, Andromeda hurriedly knelt beside Perseus. "*Mitéra.*"

"I sent my champion to you today for two reasons. The first was to right a wrong by Poseidon, for he can be vain and too quick to anger, and the second was because of prophecy. Perseus is a son of Zeus and will be a great hero."

Andromeda barely stifled a gasp and glanced at Perseus. He was crouched, his gaze on the floor, with a blush on his hard cheeks. She remembered where she had heard the name "Perseus" before; an adventurer had stopped by for supper at her parents' palace and relayed the news that a demigod had slain Medusa in the hills to the east. Perseus, the hero, had saved her.

Athena said, "His sons will be great kings, and they will produce even greater heroes. Andromeda, you share this legacy. You will be immortalized in the stars."

Blood rushed to Andromeda's face, and she was so astonished that she didn't realize that Athena was telling them both to rise until she felt Perseus's hand at her elbow, helping her up. She barely heard Athena when she instructed them to hold hands, said the holy words, and then had them agree to be man and wife.

Before she could fully process what was happening, Athena had left, and the world woke up with sound as if from a dream.

Andromeda felt a little faint. She turned to Perseus. "Is that it?"

Perseus gave a half smile and stared at the sky. "Gods. They are brief." Was he being facetious? Perseus seemed far away, but then he recovered from his musings and plucked his wine from the table. He raised his cup to her and winked. "Wife."

With his toast, she realized that she couldn't have been dreaming. She was married to a god-blood. She laughed, and he chuckled with her. They sat back down and toasted each other again.

By the time they'd finished the bottle of wine, Andromeda was dizzy and happy. She had started off the morning being fed to a serpent, and now she had been married to a demigod by a god. She felt like running on the beach, even though she should be exhausted.

It was probably early morning, and a breeze from the ocean had kicked up. She tried to sneak glances at her new husband in the light from the lamps. Something had been tickling her mind. "Perseus, you're a son of a god, so why do you live on a farm?"

Immediately, Andromeda knew she had made a mistake. Perseus's face darkened, and he paused, the silence heavy. She was about to apologize, when he said, "My family and I have differing opinions on some things. I am in *self-imposed* exile."

Andromeda's eyes widened. "How are you going to have a royal legacy if you don't acknowledge your own royalty?" Athena had said that their sons would be kings.

He regarded her, expression blank, and shrugged a shoulder. "I don't know."

It occurred to her that she was going to have children with him. She flushed.

Perseus was still watching her. "More wine?" he said.

"No, thank you." Trying to think was already frustrating, and she felt foolish.

Perseus nodded and took their dishes inside. She followed him into the bedroom but stayed behind when he went through the hall to the kitchen. Dishes clinked together.

Andromeda stared at the tall bed. Not every woman was married to a god-blood. She would have thought that Athena had been mistaken about her, but the gods were never wrong. Fingertips numb and clumsy, she threw off her shift and strode toward the bed. The mattress was lined with blankets, so it didn't crackle when she hopped onto it and lay back on the pillows, and arranged her hair artfully around her shoulders.

Her heart beat furiously in her breast, but she didn't have time to be nervous long.

Perseus came through the bedroom door, and stopped when he saw her. His eyes grew wide, and he glanced outside where they had been sitting, as though maybe he was imagining her on his bed, and if he looked back at the porch, she would really be there.

He directed his gaze to her again, his eyes warming. She tried not to tremble. He took a slow breath and stepped forward, every movement liquid and powerful and deliberate.

Andromeda relaxed back and smiled.

CHAPTER THIRTEEN

ANDROMEDA AND I barely left the bedroom the first few weeks, and I was realizing that having someone around all the time was nice. We couldn't talk about religion, obviously, and she looked at me funny sometimes, like I wasn't real, or I was *too* real, or something. But other than that, things were easy.

At the same time, I knew I was being used by the gods, and Andromeda and I were supposed to have a legacy full of kings and heroes. Was I ready for that? Was I ready to give up my dreams? Dreams I had held on to for so long and so desperately. Dreams that had seemed bigger than me, bigger than destiny. Well, I guessed they weren't bigger than destiny after all.

Andromeda kissed the tears away from my face, and we made love again. I got lost in our sex and told myself that everything was natural.

The next weeks I took Andromeda to Delos, to the market, and even to the Salty Pony, showing her off to my friends early in the evening before they all got drunk. I bought her new dresses, let her redesign the house, and purchased a horse for her. When I wasn't working, I taught Andromeda how to cook, clean, and everything I knew about animal husbandry. Franko's wife and daughter often came to the house and helped her while the men and I labored in the fields. I seriously considered money for the first time ever and even expanded my business, hiring people to travel to outside cities to sell my wares. I even admitted to being "that demigod who had slain Medusa." My fame protected her, protected us.

Things were going well until Andromeda got sick.

Demigods didn't suffer from most of the diseases of mortals. I had been sick before, but not *sick*, not infected with something. Andromeda was *sick*. And I had no idea what to do. Her illness spread from nighttime to the day, and after a week of her being absolutely miserable, she finally agreed to let me take her to the temple. I couldn't blame her for resisting at first. I hated clerics too.

I packed us up the afternoon Andromeda agreed to go, and we left. We had to stop several times on the way so she could heave in the sand. Her eyes were smeared with darkness, and she looked so far away, I'd never be able to reach her.

When we got to the temple, Andromeda didn't insist I join her, so when they took her, I waited out in the pristine halls, pacing back and forth. The other guests didn't go near me or greet me, even though some of them recognized me.

When the clerics led Andromeda back to the foyer, what seemed like hours later, I tried to stand still as she approached me. My fingers twitched.

Andromeda gazed up at me, her large brown eyes watering. "I'm pregnant."

I jerked as if slapped, feeling relieved and foolish and the gods knew what else. She was going to be all right.

I almost danced Andromeda into the air, but she wasn't feeling well, so I gave her a gentle hug instead, my chest buzzing with energy. I kissed her hair, and we held each other and cried happy tears.

Maybe we'd both be all right.

WE SAT at the table for supper. Suppers were the one meal Andromeda seemed to be able to tolerate for a few hours, before she'd be awake all night throwing it back up. She slept little these days and ate less.

She served me and sat down. "When do the elves visit again?" she asked.

"Not until spring." I picked around my plate. Andromeda had seen elves for the first time when they had come to my farm. They weren't as rare as demigods by any stretch of the imagination, but most of them lived in Arcadia, the elves' home kingdom, or in the northern parts of Greece. They preferred trees to sand.

"What did they say?"

"What they say all the time. More rain, less rain. I had to take out a lot of plants when I bought this place, and the ones I planted in their stead are going to bear harvestable fruit next year. They said that because the plants are young, I should sing to them." I chuckled, and Andromeda joined me.

"I enjoy your singing," she said.

"Hopefully the plants will too." I smiled.

Andromeda finished cleaning her plate and then glanced at mine. "Aren't you hungry?"

I played with my fork. "Not really." I had been feeling a bit off lately. I had yelled at my workers the other day, and since then I couldn't shake the irritability. I hadn't been sleeping, and I couldn't remember when I had last eaten a full meal.

Andromeda's eyes brimmed with tears. "Don't you like it?"

I didn't answer right away, still noting my various symptoms.

She sighed. "It's terrible, isn't it?"

That snapped me out of my contemplation. "What? No! It's delicious!"

She looked at me expectantly, but I knew that if I put one forkful in my mouth, I would vomit. I frowned. Demigods didn't get food poisoning….

Andromeda's chin trembled.

"I'm not feeling well," I said out of desperation. I immediately regretted it.

She blinked the tears from her eyes and regarded me. "What do you mean? I thought demigods didn't get sick?"

I hedged. "I'm sure there are other things that could cause me to feel ill besides disease."

Andromeda reached across the table and took my hand, smiling in sympathy. "Do you want to go to the temple?"

I shook my head vigorously. "I may just be tired." But that wasn't the right thing to say either.

Andromeda's face fell, and she rose and collected my plate, dumping the leftovers into the pail for the pigs.

I cursed to myself. "It's not your fault. That… doesn't even bother me." I knew I slept at least a little. Andromeda hadn't been feeling well enough for sex, and in order to avoid waking up to a mess, I wore a *perizoma* to bed. Luckily Andromeda hadn't found it odd. Apparently loincloths were popular among the higher class, even on the coasts. I hoped for the rest of Greece's sake that they didn't need them for the same reason I did. Could a surge in my libido make me irritable and restless?

I scolded myself. That line of reasoning wasn't going to take me anywhere good. Having constant erections didn't make anyone sick. But what was with the loss of sleep and appetite?

On her way out of the kitchen to slop the pigs, Andromeda kissed me on the head. I caught a whiff of her flowery scent, and my cock pulsed and grew thicker as she shut the front door behind her.

"Shit." I pinched my nose. Blood pounded in my head too, and I knew I had another bad headache coming on.

I could nap with Andromeda and see if that would help. Being half-god, you'd think I'd only need half the amount of sleep of a human, but that wasn't the case. Sure, sometimes I burned the candle at both ends, but then I'd have a marathon sleeping session a few nights later. That's what I needed, a few nights of solid sleep. Then things would be okay again.

But by the week's end I wasn't better. In fact, I had another alarming symptom.

I had finished bathing and grabbed my knife and oil to shave. Studying myself in the mirror, I couldn't find the blue of my eyes. The dark gray swirl of the storm stared back at me, and my head pounded with it.

ANDROMEDA SIZED me up after we woke up from our nap. "Perseus! You've lost weight."

I rolled out of bed and shrugged.

She frowned, but her dark eyes were soft. "You said that you would go to the temple if things got worse. How about tomorrow? I'm worried."

Clerics. I swallowed the pit growing in my throat. "Uh, all right."

Andromeda nodded and put her hand on my leg, smiling. I smiled back at her, my penis stirring. She moved her hand quickly and got up, turning away and tying her hair up onto her head.

I sighed and dressed for the rest of my workday.

The following morning, I rode Spirit to Delos. We clopped along the streets until we came to the temple to Apollo, the white stone looming above all of the stucco buildings.

There was another reason to fear this particular visit besides my aversion to clerics.

It was true that demigods didn't suffer from most of the diseases of mortals. But they did suffer from some things, things that were dark and incurable, such as madness. I hadn't wanted Andromeda to come with me because I was afraid I might be mad.

I tethered Spirit to one of the hitching posts and trudged up the stairs. A lesser cleric wearing yellow robes met me in the reception hall. She smiled at me and asked what I needed. She even kissed my cheeks—did I know her? Had I slept with her? I couldn't remember.

I told her I was there to see a healer, and she asked me how Andromeda was. Of course. I felt stupid. I had been coming in with Andromeda lately. The cleric must know me from that. Not everything was about my cock.

I was still mentally kicking myself when I was led to the rows of beds and told to have a seat on one of them. The curtains were drawn around me, and I sat and fidgeted with the edge of the coarse linens. People whispered in other areas of the temple, and I listened with half attention. I didn't have to wait long. An old woman with a shaved head and wearing the sun-inspired robes of Apollo pushed through the curtains.

She strode right up to me. "I'm Cleric Agathe. I'm told that you are Perseus?"

"That's me," I said.

The cleric's eyes shone with golden light, scanning me. "Interesting," she said when the glow had faded. She peered at me over a beaklike nose. "They said you were a local hero, but they didn't mention you were a demigod. You don't appear to be bleeding or half-dead, so what brings you to the temple of Apollo today, Perseus?"

I coughed. "My wife made me come here."

"I see." No smile. Not even a twinkle in her aged blue eyes. "Let's start off simpler, shall we? I'm just going to feel my way around."

I nodded my consent, but she was already groping my neck with her cool fingers. Waves of warm energy flowed through me, and she frowned and moved her hands up and down the back of my head. After a minute she stepped away and crossed her arms. "What are your symptoms?"

I shrugged. "I can't sleep, I have no appetite, and I'm getting headaches. I feel tense all the time, almost jittery."

The cleric nodded. "Is that color, or whatever, normal for you?" She pointed at my eyes.

I winced. "Normally my eyes are blue."

"I see. Take off your clothes and let me have a look at you." Her stare gave me the idea that every second I wasn't already naked was wasting her time.

"Okay…." My hands fumbled around the hem of my shirt, but I finally pulled it over my head. I kicked off my boots and then took a breath and slowly undid the laces of my breeches, sliding them down to my ankles. I sat on the cot but didn't know what to do with my arms, so I crossed them over my chest.

I found a fly on the high ceiling and stared very hard at it. There were two flies.

Cleric Agathe inhaled sharply. "How long have you had that?"

I cringed and briefly glanced at her face. "Maybe a couple of weeks?"

She was scrutinizing my groin. "When you say 'a couple of weeks,' do you mean to say that you've had this for the entire duration? Or are there breaks?" She was hunched over and examining my penis.

"Uh… I guess it goes down sometimes." For some odd reason, the cleric's reaction was actually comforting. I turned my full attention back to her. She was staring at it in a detached and scientific way, like it was a thing.

"Does it hurt?"

"A little." Okay, maybe more than a little. I really hoped she didn't want to touch it, and then I hoped she would. *Please, touch it….*

Agathe nodded and stood up. "Well, Perseus, I have no idea what's wrong with you. I'm not specialized in demigods, and frankly I don't know who is, besides a god. We could arrange a prayer for you?"

I tried not to slump in the heavy blend of disappointment and relief. "That won't be necessary."

Agathe pointed at my penis. "What I can tell you is that if you don't do something about that soon, you're going to lose it."

"What!" I jerked and resisted the urge to clutch my penis.

The cleric nodded. "You see that bluish tinge you have down there? That's not a good sign, and I'm actually surprised it's not worse, but you're a demigod, so maybe you have that going for you. As it is, we have two options. We can either bleed you with a minor surgical procedure, or you can try some manual stimulation to see if you can get the blood to go down. Have you tried that yet?" She searched my expression for a few moments. "I thought all men intuitively knew how to masturbate?"

I had broken into a cold sweat at the mention of "surgery" and had to startle myself out of my nightmare before I could respond. "No, I haven't tried that yet."

"So what will it be?"

I made my next words painstakingly clear. "I'll try the *latter* option, thank you."

"I thought you might." Was that a small smile tugging at the corner of her lips? "I'll check back with you in a little while?"

I shrugged, and the cleric left. Putting my elbows on my knees and my sweaty head in my hands, I sighed. Why hadn't I thought of masturbation? I could have avoided all of this humiliation. I guessed it'd never been that interesting—I'd tried it a few times in school when I was younger—but when someone else was with me, it changed the game completely. I'd never had a problem finding someone else.

But I didn't want to be my father. I was married, and I didn't want to find someone else. I needed to figure this shit out, and masturbation seemed to be a good alternative. Maybe that was what men did when their wives were pregnant and miserable. Once I gave it some thought, it made a certain amount of sense. I felt a rush of relief. I was a normal person, and this was a normal person's problem. I almost laughed.

Satisfied that I had my cure well in hand, I reached over to grab some cloths from the chest.

WHEN I got home, Andromeda asked me how my visit had gone.

"Fine." I handed her the Rod of Asclepius charm that I had begged off Cleric Agathe to prove to my wife that I had actually gone. "There isn't anything wrong with me, but she recommends that I get more rest, go for walks, and eat plenty of fiber."

Andromeda rubbed my arm. "Did she say why you're losing weight or why your eyes are cloudy all of the time?"

"No, but she seemed to think it'll clear up on its own. Are my eyes still cloudy?" I hurried into the hall and gazed into the mirror. Yes, they were, and I still had a headache. Now that I had a moment to think about it, I still felt on edge, as though I had shocked myself with electricity or drunk too much tea.

I had practically filled the waste receptacle at the temple with cloths… but maybe I needed to do it some more. Make up for lost time, or something. It might help me sleep.

"Yes, but I'm glad there isn't anything seriously wrong with you." Andromeda kissed the back of my neck and then went to do some chores before her nap.

I soaked in the tub for a while and went for a walk until suppertime, but I still slept poorly. After the third day of masturbating, I thought maybe I could help my problem if I did a better job of satisfying myself. With Andromeda out of the picture, I'd have to get creative.

I finally took action when I woke up in the kitchen the next day with the pronged end of a fork up my ass.

Later that same day, I strolled through my orchard and vineyard until I reached the processing building. I stepped inside the dark warehouse and passed the wooden presses to walk down the stairs to the basement. I held the mirror from the hall on one arm, and I held a lamp with the other.

There was probably enough light to see by, but as I passed the rows and rows of oak barrels I noticed a spiderweb or two, and I was glad I had the light so I could avoid them. The closet was in the back corner. Light from the lantern flickered over the rough wooden door, and when I pulled it open, it revealed a tiny room with no windows. A mop and bucket sat on the floor.

The weather was responding to my angst, getting harder for me to control, and was a constant reminder that I'd go mad if I couldn't calm down. I set the mirror against the wall and shut the door behind me.

In that space there were no boundaries, but I took no lasting pleasure from what I was doing. In ways it made it worse, making me even more tired and edgy, but I didn't know what else to do, so I kept at it. I bought inventive objects to try and satiate my desire, but they didn't help. The dark energy of the sky—of me—grew.

IT HAD been over three months since I married Andromeda. I didn't sleep or eat, and my eyes had changed from a pleasant light gray to dark, churning slate. I felt every shift in the air through my brain and body, but I couldn't calm it. There hadn't been a sunny day in over a week.

Even though I was miserable, Andromeda was doing better. I hoped that maybe we could resume our affections, but instead of sickness, she complained of various aches and pains and was still sleeping a lot. That was okay, really. I had forgotten what it was to be any other way. In fact, the worse my cock hurt, the easier it was to ignore the fact that I wanted to shove it into anything and get off. I was pretty sure this wasn't normal anymore. I was pretty sure I was mad.

Andromeda had asked me to go to the temple again, but I refused. She complained that I bit my nails down to nubs, but I didn't care. She tried to feed me, and I'd walk out the door; she'd ask me to sleep with her and then groused that I wiggled too much.

I sat at the table during supper. It made Andromeda happy. This was the only time we got to be together. That was probably my fault, but it was hard to be with her in the same room sometimes. She smelled so good, and her skin was nearly luminescent. Her breasts were huge.

Andromeda's voice was loud and painful, and every syllable was a knife to my skull. White flashes flicked at the rim of my vision, and my gut cramped like I was going to be sick, but I knew better. I was holding on until I could go back to my cellar room and be alone for the rest of the night.

"Obviously the clerics didn't catch whatever you have the first time, but maybe now that your symptoms are worse?" Andromeda said.

I put my fists into my ears and ground my teeth in pain.

"Perseus, did you hear me?"

I held my breath and bore down, trying to squeeze away the pulsing in my head.

"I wish you would go to the temple. I've been praying for you."

I screamed.

I felt the word "fuck" fly from my lips, but I wasn't sure what else I said. I slammed my hand down on the table, and a crack sang throughout the house.

I snapped back to reality.

Andromeda's chair scraped, and she stumbled away from me, her mouth opening in a soundless scream. I didn't even trust myself to comfort her, but instead ran out the front door and rode Spirit hard and fast to town.

It was storming, black clouds spreading across the sky.

I was soaking wet by the time I stumbled into the Salty Pony. I smelled my friends and blindly sat down at their table. They greeted me, and I grunted, chewing my nails.

"No, no, no!" Vano leaped out of his chair. Small hands pawed at my clothes and poked me in the sides and the middle. "You lost more weight. You said you wouldn't! Now I have to take in all your clothes again." Vano tsked and tutted, his hands patting me down.

A drink was put into my hand. I brought it to my lips, sputtering as I choked down the hard alcohol. My legs bounced—my skin was crawling.

Chris chuckled. "Doesn't your wife feed you?"

"They've been too busy to eat, I reckon," Kell said. Chris gave a rough laugh.

"Oh my gods, where are your shoulders? And your ass!" Vano moaned. Kell and Chris bantered back and forth about my ass and Vano's obsession with it.

Vano spoke in my ear. "Andromeda is due in the summer, right?"

I scratched my unkempt beard and then tucked my shirt back in. The storm outside howled with wind and thunder, bashing against the sides of the tavern.

"So… how's married life?" Kell said.

I nodded while I finished my drink. Dancing in my seat, I pulled out my shirt again.

"If he gets any skinnier, he'll look like Chris." Vano hopped up into his chair.

"Hey!"

"Seriously, for a dwarf, you're scrawny," Kell said.

"I'm not a dwarf!" said Chris.

"Probably half, but at least a quarter," Vano said.

"I'm just short."

"Well, we can settle this once and for all. We'll take you down to the temple, and they'll tell us. They should be able to detect dwarfiness," Kell said. "You should also send a message to that orphanage in Thessaly."

"There weren't any records," Chris said. He nudged me on the shoulder. "Tell them I don't smell dwarfy, Percy."

I reached for my cup, but it was empty.

"Percy!"

I jumped, and my knees hit the table. Everyone's cups leaped into the air, then clattered to the floor and broke. Vano was yelling, Chris and Kell were yelling, and Jordan was grumping at me behind the bar. I couldn't breathe.

Vano threw his hands up. "What's going on? You look like shit, Percy. And you're acting…."

"Squirrelly," Chris said. His broad shoulders were back, and he watched me carefully, chewing on a stick of calamus root.

I glanced down at my crotch. My pants and shirt couldn't hide it. Next to our table sat a man, maybe forty, definitely fat, who smelled married with children. At the bar was a youth, maybe fifteen, with pink cheeks and a broad grin. An old widow with long hair was by one of the only windows, watching the storm through a crack in the panels. A male, part halfling, tossed knives at a board. Jordan, Vano, Chris, Kell…. Where was Thom?

"Percy!"

I jerked my gaze to my friends with their raised eyebrows.

"What's going on?" Vano said.

Just thinking about my cock made my eyes roll up in the back of my head. I wanted to touch myself, but I knew my hand wasn't the answer, and I was sick of it and myself. I knew what I wanted, what I needed. I licked my lips.

My friends' faces blanched, and Chris edged back in his chair.

I glared, and with as much dignity as I could muster, I rose and stalked out the door.

I OPENED my eyes. The sun was in my face and seagulls called overhead. I was naked, and I smelled horseshit. I was outside the stables of the Salty Pony.

I winced when I moved to get up. Every nerve ending was alight, and my body pounded with pain. Deeply. I checked myself for wounds but didn't find any, not even a scratch. Eventually, I managed to drag myself to my feet and limp around the stables to get Spirit. I was so tired, I wasn't even sure why I had woken up.

My breeches were hanging over the rail of Spirit's stall, but I didn't remember putting them there. My purse was attached to the belt, and full. I frowned as I slipped on my pants. I didn't remember anything after leaving the tavern the night before. Where were my boots and shirt?

Henrick ran out from the back of the stables, asking if I was okay. I nodded, but truthfully I was unsure. He helped me get Spirit ready, informing me how Spirit had eaten well and seemed to miss me. I had no idea why he was telling me all of this, but I gave him a generous tip since he seemed to really care about my horse.

During my uncomfortable ride home, I tried to be grumpy about being awake and sore, but I was so tired I could barely keep my eyes open. I almost fell off several times, catching myself right before I tipped over. When I finally got home, I stabled Spirit and hobbled inside.

Andromeda came out of the bedroom and rushed up to me. "Where have you been?" Her face was frantic, both relieved and angry. Andromeda, angry?

I tried to tell her I had been at the tavern, but I didn't think she heard me. I barely heard my own voice. The room blurred in and out of focus, and I stumbled past her to the bedroom.

"You've been gone for three days!" she wailed at me.

I stripped off my pants and crawled into bed. *Three days?* My head hit the pillow, and I fell asleep.

WHEN I opened my eyes again, Andromeda was lying next to me on the bed, watching me. Her auburn hair was in a bun on her head, strands falling down the sides of her face. "Perseus?" she said.

"Aye?" My mouth was sticky and horrid tasting.

She sat up, her brown eyes wide. "Thank the gods." It looked early, but that didn't seem right. "How are you feeling?" she said.

I blinked, and I moved around a bit, my body aching. I tried to sit up, but my arms were weak and my vision blurred. "What time is it?"

"It's morning," she said.

I tried to sit up again. "Oh."

Andromeda was looking at me expectantly, and when I didn't say anything, her lip trembled. "Where have you been? You've been gone for three days."

My heart sank. The tiredness, the deep aching… everywhere. I wasn't sure, but I had a good idea where I'd been. "I'm sorry, honey."

"You're sorry? I'm pregnant and you left me for three days without a word! I don't know how to get to your money, so what exactly did you expect me to do?"

"I swear to the gods, Andromeda, I didn't mean to be gone that long. The last thing I remember is leaving the house to spend time with my friends at the tavern."

Andromeda looked away. "I sent for the clerics while you were sleeping."

"They came here?" My nose flared, trying to scent anything unusual. "What did they say?"

Her lips twisted as though the words were bitter in her mouth. "That you were malnourished and sleep deprived."

"That's it?" My mind raced.

"That's it." She crossed her arms over her breasts and looked at me, tears in her eyes. "What's going on?"

"Honestly, honey, I don't know. I woke up at the Salty Pony, feeling as if I had a round with Atlas. My friends were gone. I don't remember anything else."

"You stormed out." Her voice was so small and wretched it broke my heart.

I sighed. "I remember that. I'm sorry. I promise I'm not going anywhere." I was an ass, and I knew I was even worse than that for what I was about to say. "I just… got scared."

"Scared?"

"Aye," I said with more conviction, reaching for her hand. She let me take it, and I rubbed my thumb along her soft skin. "Of being a father. I love the gods, but trust me when I say they aren't the best parents. I don't want to be like that."

"You're not going to be a bad father, Perseus."

I felt another stab of guilt. "I don't know…."

When Andromeda smiled, it pulled up her upper lip, showing the slight gap in her front teeth. It was cute. "Is that the reason you've been acting so odd?"

"I want to be a good father."

"You will be." She wiped her eyes and squeezed my hand. "This is all new for me too, you know. I want to be a good mother."

I smiled at her. "I know you will be."

She breathed a sigh. I almost felt good again. She looked me up and down, her forehead creased with worry. "How are you feeling?"

I shrugged, still holding her hand and smiling. "I'm a little hungry."

Her eyes widened, and she nearly ran to the kitchen. I propped myself up with some pillows, the blood thudding in my ears. My vision darkened at the corners, and my heart pattered. I almost fell asleep again, but Andromeda came back and handed me warm juice, making sure I could hold the cup before she left again.

I drank it in a few swallows. Setting the cup aside, I sat up a bit further and waited for the waves of dizziness to pass. Even feeling exhausted and sore, I knew something was different. I felt better than I had in months, clearer and more focused.

I set my bare feet on the floor. They were filthy. Shakily, I made my way down the hall, using the wall as a guide. I passed the side hallway where I was making a nursery for our child, then stepped out of the back door.

After using the latrines, an experience that was unnervingly unpleasant, I shuffled back down the hall toward the bathroom, my feet sliding against the cool tiles. I shuddered as I approached the mirror, dreading what I would see. Grasping the edge of the basin, I raised my eyes and gazed at my reflection.

Two sky blue eyes stared back at me. No dark storm. No headache.

And then I knew without a doubt that I'd done something. My entire body ached with the memory, even if my mind couldn't recall it. Even if I had said no—and I couldn't even remember if I had or what I'd done—did saying no really count if I wanted it? Needed it?

And I did need it. I knew that now too. This was my curse.

Antolios had always suggested that a demigod's curse was some kind of side effect or balancer to our power, representing the various facets of the Olympic gods and their domains. It was carried in our blood.

Ichor. God-blood.

Beating in our hearts was the gift of the gods but also their curse. I knew why they didn't want to discuss these phenomena. Our curses weren't the result of human weakness. They were manifestations of the gods' own imperfections, *their* weaknesses.

The gods were fallible, and they cursed their children and then denied responsibility for it. They made us think we were flawed. They made us hide it for them.

Until now I hadn't known what my curse was. Not even Antolios had known. I had been avoiding this reality for months, but my blue eyes wouldn't let me avoid it any longer. I knew what was wrong with me and which god's curse I had.

Zeus had always been known for his lust.

My father had contrived many schemes to seduce women, youth, men, and other gods. Legend told of him disguising himself as objects, animals, and even the opposite sex to get what he wanted. My own mother had been overcome when Zeus had come to her as a shower of gold.

I still had so many questions but no one to ask—no one but the one person I couldn't ask.

I checked myself again for the bruises I felt all over but didn't find a mark. I met my clear and blue eyes, my chest tightening and lips curling into a sneer. Holding my breath, I tried to squeeze it down, to compress the rage that threatened to bleed out of me.

"Filthy whore," I growled through clenched teeth.

I spat at my reflection. The spit scattered across the mirror, splintering my image.

Why did it have to be this?

All of those things I had done… with all of those people, for years and years. It didn't matter if there was a reason. I did it. I did all of it. I had begged for it. It was probably a good thing that I couldn't remember what had happened to me. It didn't matter that I had been out of my mind. I had probably begged for it too, and I deserved what I got. A sore body and a memory gap of a few days seemed the least of my problems.

My eyes filled with tears that I blinked away. With a shaky hand, I took a rag and wet it in the basin. I carefully wiped the mirror so Andromeda wouldn't see the mess. She couldn't carry this burden as well.

More lies…. *So be it.*

I moved back to the bed, every sensation too harsh, as if I was newly born. I was trembling when I tucked myself back into the sheets, already exhausted again.

Andromeda came in with a plate full of eggs, cheese, and dried fish. She watched me as I ate. When I finished that, she came back with bread and fruit and then goat's milk. I ate all of it.

"Thank you. I'm tired." I sank into the mountains of pillows, and my vision tunneled on her.

She looked pleased. "Go to sleep. I'll be here."

CHAPTER FOURTEEN

Four years later

SPIRIT AND I arrived home from our trip to Pelion in the evening. I could hear my oldest child screaming at the door before I was in the drive.

"Mama! Let me out! Baba's home!"

The door to the farmhouse opened, and out crashed Perses, my son, with his flame red hair and pale skin. He hurried over to me, his smile and blue eyes lighting up his face, and I hopped off Spirit and held my arms open wide for him.

As he ran into my arms, my heart almost broke with happiness. His sweet young smell surrounded me as I kissed him all over his freckled face and in the curls of his red hair. He was laughing madly, barely able to keep still, and I picked him up and threw him above my head.

As I was throwing him, his squeals getting louder and louder, Andromeda shuffled out the door with my daughter gripping her leg. Gorgophone was two years old, with straight, short black hair and the same light blue eyes as my son. My eyes.

Andromeda worriedly eyed me tossing our son about, but I wouldn't drop him. Her belly was large, due in a couple of months with our third child. We hadn't had problems becoming pregnant, but that didn't mean things had been easy. I had almost lost Perses and Andromeda.

"Baba home." Gorgophone smiled at me.

I had to put Perses down to gather her in my arms and kiss her head. She gave me a sloppy kiss on the cheek that was basically licking my face. Hopefully she didn't keep doing that as she got older, because that would be hard to explain to strangers.

"Welcome home, Perseus. Was it all boring, or did you do some fun things too?" Andromeda said.

I gave my daughter another squeeze. "We traveled and visited a wood elf clan in Thessaly. Cora and Antolios have six kids." I laughed.

"Why is that funny?" Andromeda smiled.

"Six daughters! I mean, what are the odds? I would need an abacus." I gave my daughter another kiss, trying to teach her to kiss with her mouth closed. "Slayer, were you good for Mama?"

Perses answered for her. "She was, Baba. I was too."

Andromeda winked at me to let me know that yes, they had been good.

"I guess you deserve the presents I brought you." I smiled and took them over to Spirit, who had wandered a few meters away and was picking at weeds. I set Gorgophone down and dug into my bags, pulling out a cloak, child-sized but styled after a soldier's. Perses wiggled excitedly as I clipped it to his tunic. I also gave him two wooden figurines I had carved.

"Is it a king and a queen?" His freckled face grinned ear to ear. I confirmed that they were. "Thank you, Baba. I need a princess. My hero has to rescue her."

"Okay, little buddy, one princess coming soon," I promised. I dug inside my packs again and pulled out a cloth doll, handing it to Gorgophone. The doll was dressed in the fashion of the women of the north and even had real hair done up in a knot on its head.

Gorgophone took the doll gravely and examined it. She was so engrossed she didn't notice me kiss her on the head and walk away with Spirit as Perses capered around in his cloak. When I came out of the barn after stabling Spirit, Andromeda and the kids were already inside, and it was getting dark.

I threw my bags down at the door and asked if everyone had eaten. Perses was trying to teach Gorgophone how to role-play with his wooden figurines, but she wasn't grasping the concept and kept bashing the toys on the floor.

Andromeda was on the couch holding her big belly. She told me they had eaten earlier, so I found some leftovers and helped myself. By then Andromeda had fallen asleep. I warmed goat's milk for Gorgophone in the dying embers of the kitchen fire and helped her drink from the cup without spilling. I took her to the latrines and then put her to bed in the nursery, giving her a kiss on the head. I sang her a song that my mother had sung to me when I was little. Gorgophone fell asleep before I was even halfway through the second verse. I gave her another kiss on the head and walked out into the hallway.

When I had bought the farm, this side hall had been designed for servants. I had started to divide the remaining rooms into smaller ones, so that each of our kids would have their own space. It wasn't anything as nice as the way I grew up, but I'd have Gorgophone's room done by the time our baby was born, and then the baby would take the nursery.

I let Perses stay up later than usual while I held Andromeda on the couch as she dozed. I played with her long auburn hair. Her cheeks were flushed. She was always radiant when she was pregnant. Well, after those first few months, at least. Eventually Perses wandered to his room and put himself to bed, and I carried Andromeda to ours. She didn't wake as I moved her, and I snuggled up to her and tried to sleep.

I tossed, restless.

My visit with Antolios had been complicated. With the timing around my family and business, I hadn't been able to see him since he had visited Delos. He had renovated an old hunting lodge so we could spend time alone together. It almost reminded me of when we had been in school and had the weekends to ourselves.

It was nice… but something had hung between us. Hermes had visited me on my way to Thessaly. The god had just shown up, floating upside down in the air and greeting me with a booming, "Hello, traveler!" He had been wearing a tunic, which oddly had not fallen open in his inverted position, and winged sandals and a hat. His beard was coarse and black, and his brown eyes were lit with mischief. And desire.

We had struck a bargain. I would spend a few days with him, and he'd give me a lift to Pelion to cut down my time in the saddle. Only gods don't play by the rules.

Hermes took me to a sacred grove, and from there my recall was hazy. There was a bed that was a living part of a tree, and there was a river and a waterfall. Nymphs sang in the trees, and every sensation was erotic and I was satisfied beyond measure.

When I walked out of the grove, my horse was waiting for me, and I was a day's ride from Pelion. I didn't find out until I reached the capitol that I had been gone for well over a week, but he had taken me farther than I had expected, so I supposed our bargain had been met.

Those sorts of dalliances with the gods were normal, and I should have felt honored to have such favor of Hermes. I also shouldn't have felt compelled to hide my relationship with him from anyone, but I had decided that I wouldn't bring it up to Antolios. Only no one could hide anything from him.

Antolios had been waiting for me at the doors to the palace. I had my arms out but hadn't even fully approached him when he collapsed into a heap on the ground, unconscious. I had been detained, guards and clerics and mayhem all over, until it had been sorted out. He had been taken away to "rest awhile," but he met me again at supper and he seemed fine.

Antolios hadn't mentioned why he had collapsed, and we didn't talk about Hermes—what was there to say? We both knew that it wouldn't be my last visit with the god, and it wasn't. Hermes had approached me again on my way back to Delos.

It had been over a week since then, but after all these years, I was learning that a week was too long.

Nevertheless, I thrashed in bed for another hour, sweating and keyed up, trying to find some control. Eventually I threw on clean breeches and a shirt. Spirit was probably tired from our travels, so I figured I'd walk to the Salty Pony.

Just as I was leaving the dirt drive, the front door to the house opened, and Andromeda stepped out in her nightgown, holding her large belly.

Her auburn hair fell around her shoulders. "Where are you going?"

I smiled and turned around. "I'm just going to spend time with my friends."

"You could spend time with me."

I grew still, and a slow, sick feeling worked its way through my body. "It's okay. You're tired, honey." I gave her a reassuring smile and walked backward a few steps toward the road. "We'll talk in the morning."

I didn't wait to see her face. I turned around and walked on.

THE NEXT morning I was in the warehouse. This was our busiest time of year, harvesting the grapes, then pressing and processing them into barrels. The wooden presses were large, and it took two men to operate one of them. Two men, or just me.

I was working one press while two of my workers worked another, and the entire warehouse smelled of grape juice and yeast. As I pressed, my men lined up and filled oak drums branded with "Driftwood Barrels."

I heard Perses screaming before he reached the warehouse. "Baba! Mama's sick! Baba!"

My blood ran cold as I raced out. I thought I'd have to calm Perses first, but his face wasn't panicked.

"Baba!" he said, almost vibrating with excitement. "We rescue Mama?"

I didn't ask what had happened. I picked him up, smashing him to my chest, and burst into a sprint toward the house. Perses giggled into my shirt as the wind took his curls from between my fingers and whipped them around.

Andromeda wasn't on the bedroom veranda, so I ran around the side of the house under the awning to the front. There she was, sitting in a chair, hunched over. I set Perses down and ran to her. Her face was pinched in pain and she was clutching her middle. She was wearing her favorite violet housedress with her hair pulled back in a ponytail.

I didn't even ask what was wrong before I placed my hands on her face and healed her. The spell rushed through me and into her—just like Apollo said it would—and she gasped as the light from my palms had settled into her skin.

Then she glared, and her hands balled.

She was going to hit me.

"Take me to the temple," she said through clenched teeth.

"Are you okay?" I asked.

Her jaw was tight, and she wouldn't meet my gaze.

I got the cart ready and hooked it up to Spirit. Gorgophone was playing in the grass, and I scooped her up and placed her in the cart.

"Come on, Perses. Keep a watch on your sister." I offered to help Andromeda into the cart, but she shoved away from me and got in on her own, her knees shaking.

I could hear her grunting with pain in the back, and I'd glance at her over my shoulder as I drove. She seemed so far away and sad.

When we got to the temple, Andromeda got out and hobbled up the stairs, cradling the bottom of her belly. My heart was racing. I gathered up the kids, one on each hip, and hurried after her.

In the reception hall, the clerics were helping Andromeda to a room, and she glared at me again. "Stay here with the kids."

I opened my mouth and then closed it again. Why did she keep pushing me away? The kids squirmed out of my arms and ran over to the toys in the corner. I stood there, gazing to where Andromeda had disappeared behind a curtain, not able to move or think.

Then I heard her. "Perseus! Perseus!"

In a moment I was across the temple and through the curtains, and in the next I was holding her hand. Her dress was hiked up, and Andromeda's eyes were wild as she babbled to the clerics about it not being time yet.

The head cleric was already between Andromeda's legs, and other clerics were touching Andromeda's belly, the golden light sinking into her skin.

Head Cleric Agathe leveled a look at Andromeda. "You're going to have this baby now."

Andromeda got quiet and turned her head toward me, tears streaming down her face.

There was no place to sit, so I came in closer and held her to me, our hearts pounding together. The prayers of the clerics droned as Andromeda's body tightened to its own unstoppable rhythm.

She pulled her face away from my shoulder and grabbed her abdomen. Her normally pale skin was red and blotchy, her hair was plastered to her head, and sweat rolled down her neck. She curled her toes, and her face grew tight, focused.

I whispered in her ear. "You're doing so well, honey. I love you. It's going to be okay." But it wasn't supposed to be time yet, and the clerics were so busy helping that they hadn't told me what was wrong.

The clerics all converged between Andromeda's legs, and Andromeda cried out.

Purple, wet, and small, the smallest of our children, our newborn was raised to the light. A boy. The golden light from the cleric's hands worked through his skin.

He scrunched up his face, opened his mouth, and squalled.

Andromeda laughed and then cried, huge tears rolling down her face.

The clerics handed Andromeda our son, and she pulled down her shirt and offered him her breast. He was fussy, still screaming, but eventually he latched on. Andromeda cooed at him and wiped some of the slime off his face and hair with her dress.

The clerics bustled in and out, but I only had eyes for my son. I touched his skull, small and hot and wet. He had the beginnings of black hair on his head. His fingers and toes were small and spidery.

Andromeda looked up at me, tears still in her eyes. "What's his name?"

I smiled at our child, and my voice oddly resonated off the walls. "Electryon."

ANDROMEDA AND Electryon were going to have to stay in the temple for at least a week. Electryon was healthy, but they wanted to make sure that he and Andromeda would be strong enough to travel back to the house.

After his birth, Andromeda drew away from me again. At first I thought it was because she was focused on the baby, but then I noticed she wouldn't meet my gaze.

While she was napping one day, I packed the kids up and took them into the nice part of town. We stopped at a small house with a small yard. All the buildings leaned up against each other, tall with white stucco and red-tiled roofs. Thom and Alala had lived in the city for many years and didn't own livestock. Their son was already grown and had left the house.

I knocked at the red door. Alala opened it, her face wrinkling into a smile when she saw me. Usually when I saw her she was sleeping while I snuck in and dropped unconscious Thom off in their bed so he wouldn't get in trouble.

"Perseus," she said. "Hello." Her graying hair was tied back in a bun. She was older than Thom, but her hair was a reminder that not all my friends were going to be around as long as I would.

"Hello, Alala." The kids had escaped the cart and ran to my feet.

Alala smiled at them, her face lighting up. Perses held out his hand, and she shook it. Gorgophone hid her hands behind her back and put her face into my leg.

Alala laughed. "Hello, young ones! Come inside." She gestured us all in.

The house had a living space, a kitchen with a fire, and a bedroom upstairs. They shared an outdoor latrine with the neighbor.

Alala went into a separate room and came back with a crate of toys. The kids ran to it and immediately dug in. She smiled down on them and then looked at me. "Can I get you some tea? I could start the midday meal."

"No, thank you. I have a favor to ask." I cleared my throat.

She raised her brows at me. "Thom won't be home until evening."

"That's not… I mean… I was wondering if the kids could stay with you for a week." I quickly said, "I'd swing by during the day and take them out for a bit. Andromeda had the baby early and… I wasn't expecting…." I looked at my feet and shifted.

Alala gasped. "Are they all right?"

I sighed. "Yes, they're all right. I just… need to spend some time with her." I finally looked up. I wasn't sure why this was so hard for me.

She gave me a grandmotherly smile and nodded. "I would love to have them stay. It's been so long since I've had children here. I keep hoping that Duncan will have some, but he hasn't. He's too busy, I suppose."

Relief flooded through me, and we watched my kids play with the old toys. Alala asked me what their schedules were, and we discussed particulars. I took my leave before she started the midday meal.

Back at the temple, I left Spirit and the cart at the stables, then trudged up the stone steps. My own wife wouldn't talk to me, and I knew I had created this distance and distrust between us. I knew I needed help, and not just with the kids. My parents were out of the question. If they didn't have anything to say to me, then I had nothing to say to them. But maybe it was time to call on Queen Cassiopeia and King Cepheus. They should know their daughter was still alive.

I was crossing the temple, heading for Andromeda's partitioned-off room, when I heard her speaking with her friend Soussanna. Soussanna was an older woman in Andromeda's circle of friends. She didn't have any children of her own, but she often spent time with the other women and their children. I wasn't surprised that Soussanna knew Andromeda was at the temple. She seemed to know everything.

I stopped outside the room and waited for them to finish, just happy that Andromeda had someone visit her.

"Why didn't you tell me?" Andromeda's voice came from the other side of the curtain. She was whispering, but I could tell she was stuffed up as though she had been crying.

I froze.

Soussanna made a sharp noise. "Hush, child. Why would I tell you that? And why would you pray to Hera? Fool girl!"

I drew a sharp breath and held it.

"She is the goddess of marriage," Andromeda warbled.

"You're lucky you're still alive."

Andromeda started sobbing. I looked around and then snuck into an adjacent room, carefully pulling the curtains closed. I stood still, listening to them speak.

"Hush. He is your husband. Did no one teach you anything? It isn't your place to question him. And he's a demigod." Soussanna made a noise because Electryon started crying. There was shuffling and more sobbing, and the entire time she was murmuring, "Hush, hush."

Finally Soussanna said, "Your baby will be fine. You're lucky. You have beautiful children, blessed. They shine. Any woman would kill to be you."

Andromeda cried, "I know, I know."

"But what made you think that Hera would help you? He's the bastard son of Zeus! You're lucky she spared you. Here," she said. "Let me take him. That's it. Now eat something. Your hero won't want you anymore if you're too skinny."

Andromeda's voice was thick with grief. "The tramp he was with had no hips. She was as flat as a boy!"

The baby started crying again.

"Hush, hush," Soussanna said.

I couldn't take any more, my face hot and stomach sick. I ducked out of the curtains and hurried toward the back of the temple toward the docks. I rushed by clerics and other worshippers, running out the back door and onto the wooden planks. I jogged down the pier, my mind scattered.

I stood at the edge, staring at the sea. There weren't many ships moored on this side of the wharf, and the gulls circled overhead.

I had been with a woman last night, and Andromeda had seen. I wasn't sure how she knew, but she did. I hadn't thought she would be able to sneak up on me. I could smell her a kilometer away....

Hera. My jaw clenched.

The goddess had almost killed our first child and Andromeda in the process. If Apollo hadn't shown up, I would have lost her and Perses. Apollo had named me one of his champions and given me his blessing of healing powers, so that I could help him during the birth.

And now Hera was doing it again, and there was nothing I could do about it. I couldn't fight her—she was a goddess—and I couldn't blame her, because this was my fault. I could tell Andromeda the truth, but what could I say? I wanted to be normal. I deserved as much. *We* deserved as much.

I could stop.... I dropped my gaze to my boots. The dock was crusted with bird shit, and it reeked of fish. The sun beat down on my neck. I stared at the ocean for a long time, long enough to have a few gulls try to land on me and for one to shit on my shoulder. I scowled and brushed it off, then went back inside.

I WAS sleeping in the chair next to Andromeda's bed when the baby mewled. Andromeda lifted Electryon from his blankets on the bed.

In the dark, I watched her through my brows with my chin tucked to my chest, my hands folded over my stomach, and my legs kicked out. I didn't move or make a sound as Electryon nursed. He was still small but no longer purple. He had blue eyes too. The eyes of the line of Zeus. Did my father even care that he had grandchildren? Maybe our lives were too short for him.

Andromeda finished feeding Electryon and laid him back in the nest of blankets next to her. Her back was to me but she said, "Where are the kids?"

I started. "At Alala and Thom's house, until you and Electryon can come home."

Andromeda nodded, but she didn't say anything for a while. Then, in a voice that was so small I almost didn't hear her, she said, "Do you love me?"

"Of course I do." Heat of shame and guilt washed through me. In the quiet of the temple, I could hear both of their breaths and heartbeats. Electryon's was fast and strong—he would be fine. I wasn't so sure about my wife. "Andromeda, are we okay?"

She shrugged a shoulder, still curled around our son as he slept. "It's not my place to say such things," she whispered.

"What do you mean?"

"It's not a woman's place."

"Demigods don't do things that way, honey."

Her voice became hard. "I'm not a demigod."

I drew a breath and let it out slowly. "You are the mother of my divine children."

She rolled over and faced me, lying on her side. A flame of pride flickered in her eyes.

"You carried them to life," I said. "We were both chosen by the gods."

Electryon fussed, and I rose. At the other side of the bed, I reached in and picked him up. I cradled him to my chest, his tiny chin against my shoulder, and rocked him. Eventually, he fell asleep, the little exhalations through his nose precious.

"Do you have a short name for him yet?" Andromeda asked me.

"No."

"You usually do."

I kissed Electryon on the head gently so I wouldn't wake him. He smelled amazing, sweet as milk. "It'll come to me."

"Maybe you won't give him one because you named him."

I glanced at her. She was smirking.

Apollo had named Perses, and Andromeda had named Gorgophone. Andromeda had known how I felt about naming children after the father and his greatest deeds, but she had done it anyway, to honor me.

I grinned at her and looked back at my son. "Maybe I won't."

PART THREE
DESTINY

CHAPTER FIFTEEN

Six years later
Andromeda

ANDROMEDA WOKE around midnight, her bladder nearly overflowing. Glancing to the side, she noted that Perseus was gone. Frowning, she worked her way over to the chamber pot, not wanting to walk all the way to the latrines, and idly rubbed her belly, swelling with their sixth child.

Andromeda and Perseus had certainly been fruitful, as the goddess had said, and their children were prophesied to become great kings. She had no doubt of it. In the same manner as their father, the children walked on air. Perseus couldn't see it—it was normal for him—but Andromeda did. Their family was envied by everyone.

She and Perseus were rumored to be the most beautiful couple on the southern coast. When Andromeda went into Delos, there was hardly anyone who did not know who she was. People knocked at the door, wanting to serve them, and since their needs had grown with their family, Perseus had let some of them stay.

Andromeda was living every girl's dream, and once it had been her dream too. If only she had known that a girl's dream came at a woman's price.

She told herself that she had stopped making her marriage only about the two of them years ago, but who was she fooling? Her gaze still got stuck on his body and face. She still had to rip herself away from him. He made love to her completely, like it was the first time, and for moments she wouldn't know who she was.

It was enough, wasn't it?

Andromeda used the chamber pot and waddled out of the bathroom, glancing outside.

Perseus wasn't at the tavern but, in fact, on the porch. He was naked and leaning with his forearms against the rail. He stared at the sky, so still that Andromeda blinked a few times in the darkness just to be sure she wasn't imagining him there. She joined him on the veranda, waiting for him to notice her.

Perseus didn't see her at first, but when she took another step he slowly rotated his head toward her, gazing through her with those eyes, gray and roiling. She stood still as he slowly came back from wherever he had been, gray clearing to blue. Perseus took a breath and said her name, and the air vibrated with his voice.

Andromeda walked up beside him and slid an arm around his warm and naked back. "What were you thinking?"

Perseus took another deep breath and glanced at the sky. "I have to tell you something." He hesitated. "I'll be leaving tomorrow, but I'm not sure for how long."

"Has Athena sent you on another quest?" Andromeda said.

Perseus shook his head. "Not Athena, but maybe someone else? It's hard to explain. I don't know why, but I know I must travel north. Perhaps I will be guided from there."

Andromeda fought confusion and growing alarm. The gods had always been clear with what they wanted of him. "When will you be back?"

Perseus shook his head. "I don't know."

Andromeda searched his big blue eyes, strong brows, and the set of his full lips but didn't find any answers. "What about me and the children?"

Perseus held out his palms to the sides, pleading with her. Andromeda's heart thumped. "The children will be fine. You are the best mother."

"What about us?" She hugged her belly, not being able to imagine a birth without him.

Perseus placed a hand on her abdomen. "You are strong. I'll try to be home soon, I promise."

If the gods had asked for Perseus's sword, then he must go. She bowed her head. "Of course. I'll pack you some food."

Perseus kissed her head and thanked her and then strode to his trunk to collect his weapons and armor.

Andromeda was still preparing food for his travels when Perseus marched out to ready Spirit. The sky was just lightening, but even in the dark he didn't need a candle. She rested her shaky hands on the counter, and since his keen ears couldn't hear her from the stables, she allowed a few tears to fall from her face. She couldn't put her finger on why she was so concerned, but there had been something unsettling in his eyes when he told her. He was confused, yes, but there was anticipation in them she hadn't seen before.

She hurriedly dried her face and finished packing.

"Mama!" Alcaeus started to cry from the nursery, and Andromeda wiped her hands on her apron and hastened down to the first bedroom off the main hallway. He stopped crying long before she opened the door. He grinned and bounced excitedly in the crib, forgotten tears glistening in his eyes.

Alcaeus put his little arms in the air, getting ready to be picked up. "Mama!" Big pale blue eyes stared up at her. They all had their father's eyes. Andromeda joked with Perseus that that's how he knew they were his; otherwise, who would believe that flame-haired Perses and their other fair children came from him?

Andromeda gathered Alcaeus into her arms, gave him kisses all over his face, and patted his behind. "Good boy, Alcaeus. You're such a big boy. Let's go to the potty." She set him down, and he took off running down the hall and out the back door.

"Mama, I pee!" Before she could catch up with him, he was already outside with his diaper down, peeing on a bush. "I pee!"

Andromeda chuckled. Well, at least she didn't have to wash soiled linen. When he was finished, she tried to give him a new pair of "padded shorts" to wear, but he refused to take them. "Come on, baby, you can't poo outside."

Alcaeus drew his fine blond eyebrows into a frown and pointed at the dirt. "Goats poo."

She stifled a laugh. He meant that the goats went to the bathroom outside. "The goats poo where they're supposed to, and people poo where they are supposed to."

Alcaeus glared at the ground, pouting. "Brothers and sister no wear pants."

Andromeda put her hands on her hips. "They use the potty like big boys and girls."

"I use the potty."

"You promise?" She tried to hide a smile.

"Yes."

"You'll tell Mama and let Mama help you?"

"I can do myself." He stamped a foot impatiently and took the tunic, not the shorts, from her hands, wiggling into it.

"Alcaeus...."

He crossed his arms indignantly. His tunic was backward.

She sighed. "Okay, but what if Mama has to use the potty too? Can you at least ask her if she does before you go? That would be gentlemanly."

He nodded and beamed up at her, a stray strand of straight blond hair over one eye, and Andromeda couldn't hide her smile any longer.

Later that day, Perseus gathered all the children up in a group hug and talked to them softly. He kissed their heads, and some had tears in their eyes. Perses was standing apart from them with his skinny arms over his chest. He was ten and thought he had to be brave.

Perseus pulled himself away, his face wet. Striding over to Andromeda, he wrapped her in his arms, kissing her. He lingered, pressing one hand against her back with the other on her belly.

When she was breathless from kisses, Perseus stepped back, and with a final smile he left. He mounted Spirit, his trusty old gray, and rode slowly down the dirt road. The children ran along, calling out to him until he left the farm.

CHAPTER SIXTEEN

I WANDERED through towns and cities, making my slow way north around the coast. I was rudderless, or so I thought at first. Sometimes I seemed to choose which road to take or which inn to stay at without a second thought.

I had no idea who had called to me in Delos.

Antolios wouldn't have been able to affect the weather, so it must have been a god. But then why the secrecy? They had always been forthright before, uncomfortably so at times.

One day went into the next, but I didn't get any more messages, no further guidance.

As I rode through the city of Sidon I came across the Hungry Hydra. It was still early evening, and if I pushed harder I could make the next small city by nightfall, but I stopped and had Spirit stabled. I floated through the motions of getting a room and cleaning up, and found myself in the tavern at a table with a beer and a fine meal. And three lovely ladies.

Their dresses were well-worn, with bodices cramped with lace and embroidery. Two of the girls were dark and had long black hair tied up in ribbons, and they smelled as if they used the same soap. The other girl was taller and had long blonde hair that she let fall over her shoulders in ringlets.

They gazed at me as I ate the artichoke and chicken and drank the warm beer they had bought me, making sure I had plenty of fuel. I knew the strategy. I had used it before, myself. With my first sip of the offered ale, I had basically signed a contract, and we all knew how this night was going to end.

Someone cleared their throat loudly from across the room, and I swiveled around, my mouth still full of chicken.

The man was short and thick, wearing dirty but sturdy clothing, and his face was leathery and tan. He stood on the table and waved his hand. "Hey, listen up!" His voice was gruff.

The tavern grew quiet, and a few chairs groaned.

"My caravan is looking for help crossing the Goat Hills to Copper Cairns. As you know, the roads are run by brigands and monsters, and we'd appreciate assistance in scouting and defense. Standard day shift, plus every few nights a rotation at watch. Along with fire and food, we'll provide one gold piece upon safe arrival. I'll be here for another hour if anyone wants to join. Thanks for your ears." He jumped off the table with a thud that rattled the wooden cutlery.

Before I knew what I was doing, I was up and striding over to him. I extended my hand and he took it. "My name is Perseus. I'd be happy to help with the escort."

The man sized me up and grinned, showing brown and broken teeth under his bristly mustache. He pumped my hand twice and let go. "We'd welcome your help, Perseus. My name is Berne." He gestured to the wall by the back door. "That's our guide, Sabu. We'll mostly need you for front guard during the day, so you'll get sleep. We have a good cook too."

I nodded absently and scrutinized the figure in the dark corner. I hadn't noticed him earlier and was a bit taken aback to see a wood elf this far south. Smaller and darker than high elves, wood elves were not usually seen in big cities. The elf crossed his arms over dusty firs and stared back at me with incredible green eyes, as green as the first shoots of spring. His ears barely poked out of the mop of dark brown hair on his head, dreadlocked and dirty.

Berne and I finished up business. I was meeting the caravan in the center of town in the morning. I shook Berne's hand again and nodded at the elf, but the elf ducked out the back door.

When I turned around, the girls were staring at me with worried expressions. I plodded back to the table, and one of the girls—Cara, if I remembered her name correctly—leaned across the table as I sat down to finish my meal. "Are you leaving Sidon, Perseus?"

"At first light." The girls let out a sigh, and I covered a smile with another draught of ale. They watched me eagerly, and I grew hard. I cleared my throat and worked on my artichoke.

The past years had given me a lot of time to think about my curse. I hadn't talked about it to anyone, not even Antolios. He could read my mind, so what was the point in talking about it? Besides, when we were together it was never really an issue. He made me feel as if I didn't have a curse.

I dragged each leaf of the artichoke across my teeth, chewing the meaty flesh and swallowing. As I spooned the hair off the heart, I watched the women, their lips pink and parted. The ebb and flow of my desire coursed through my veins and pulsed in my skull, and the storm had probably ducked out of the recesses of my brain and darkened my eyes, but no one seemed to notice.

This wasn't what I really wanted, but the man I wanted wasn't willing to commit. On top of that, I had a wife and children. I couldn't let them see this side of me. Sex was just sex, right? It didn't make a man. Did it? My heart and loins were rarely on the same page.

I dipped half of the heart in olive oil. My mind roared, and a flush crept up my face. I could smell them. Vanilla and cinnamon and flowers....

I finished my meal and stood, my cock throbbing. As if they were attached to me by strings, the women followed me up to my room.

So easy.

It was so easy to lead them to my room, to take off their clothes and let them take off mine. To lay them on my bed. It was so easy to use my hands, my mouth, and my cock to please them.

"Perseus," they said. "Our hero." Their cries drowned out the storm and my doubt. I danced with them. One feeling, sweaty and pure.

I ended it by draping each breast with a strand of my pearly come.

We curled together, a tangled ball of spent sex. The storm was quiet. I had my release from it. For now.

So easy.

The women fell asleep, but I couldn't. I stared at the ceiling and then felt the air vibrating *through* the ceiling and into the sky. I let my body drop away as though this had all happened to someone else and that person lying in bed with those women wasn't me. If I got too close to being that person again, I'd see that though my cock was satisfied, my breast was empty and aching. I didn't want to feel that yet. I'd have to eventually, but not yet.

Soon the ghosts of the sleeping women would be added to the sea of ghosts in my dreams, becoming nameless and faceless. I'd already forgotten one of their names.

When I finally fell asleep, my dreams were lighter than my thoughts. I dreamed of playing in the ocean with my children, and of Andromeda, swollen with child and sitting in the shallow water, laughing as I tossed the kids into the waves.

I SAT in the grass off the side of the road as Sabu and Korvo tended to my bleeding arms. We hadn't slain the gryphons that attacked us, and we'd lost sight of them as they flew away. Spirit was relaxed and chopping at the grass as if nothing had ever happened, so we were probably fine for now. The caravan was still huddled down the road with the rest of the guards surrounding them, waiting for the all clear.

"All I'm saying is that we should have had a discussion on who does what before everyone rushed into it," Korvo said. The tall dark huntsman cleaned my wounds.

I grimaced. "Sorry."

Sabu chewed up some of the herbs he had grabbed out of a satchel. He yanked the green wad out of his mouth and slapped it on my bleeding flesh. I blinked but didn't say anything.

Korvo pulled white linen strips from his pack and wound them around my arms, keeping all the goo in place. "Well, it would have been useful to know that you're a bloody battle cleric!"

I made a noncommittal grunt.

It was easier this way. During the birth of Perses, Apollo had granted me the blessing of battle healing, a simple healing spell that could knit others' flesh, but not my own. I had healed Sabu and Korvo after our fight with the gryphons, but I hadn't healed myself. Because of that, and the fact that I had thrown a lightning bolt or two, Korvo had assumed that I was a battle cleric of Zeus. He didn't need to know the truth.

Korvo peered at Sabu. "I don't know what you are."

I didn't know what the elf was either. Spirit had spooked and whinnied just before a gryphon charged out of the foliage at us. As I was dealing with that beast, another one had swooped out of the sky, and the elf had shifted into a huge bear and mauled the second gryphon.

Of the magical practitioners, mages manipulated the arcane and the elements, and battle clerics could harness a blessing from their god along with the battle healing spell. Healing clerics had many medically related spells, but none of them turned people into animals. Some demigods throughout history had been able to change into animals, but elves weren't usually capable of that—they didn't express god-blood the same as humans. And wood elves, unlike high elves, weren't even partly divine.

Sabu was possibly a demon or worshipper of other gods besides the Greek pantheon, and as an angel or champion of the Olympians, it was my duty to protect the Greeks against him. Was this why I was summoned, to keep an eye on Sabu? The compulsions that had been driving me had basically stopped since I met the dark-skinned elf.

"I'm Sabu," Sabu said as if in explanation and walked away.

I would have to watch him closely.

Korvo rolled his eyes and secured my bandages. "Right. Now that we have that out of the way, we'll know what to bloody expect. Shit, it's like you two haven't adventured before." I stared back at him, and Korvo swore.

"The beasts were after my horse," I said. "There wasn't a lot of time for a discussion."

"At least I know you two are going to rush in headfirst." He continued to grumble as he packed up his things.

I stood and signaled the caravan that we were ready to continue down the road, and we kept an eye to the sky just in case the gryphons showed back up.

THAT EVENING we made camp, and I leaned against my pack, resting solidly against a tree stump near the fire. The cool night had fallen in the Goat Hills, colder than on the southern coasts, and I wore a vest that Vano had made for me over my thin white shirt. I'd just finished a supper of stew and hard bread and had kicked my feet out toward the fire, the warmth licking through my boots.

Korvo was dicing with some of the guards, and the rest of the caravan was either bustling about the fires or erecting a large tent where they would all sleep for the night. Sabu had slipped into the woods next to camp after supper, but I couldn't see or hear him.

I was full and cozy, but my foot bobbed restlessly. Almost without my notice, I took measure of everyone in the camp. My gaze fell on one of the laboring men.

Actually, he was a dwarf. He pounded the stakes into the ground, puffing and grunting with every heave of his mallet. The cords of his muscles danced. Heat flooded my groin, and I rolled to my feet.

The dwarf's light brown hair was plastered to his skull, and sweat dripped down his face as he bent to fasten a rope of the tent to each stake he hammered into the ground. I strode over and assumed where the next set of stakes ought to go, and grabbed a hammer from the pile of tools. I pounded the stake into the ground effortlessly, and then did another. I finished a few more stakes before I allowed myself a peek to the side.

The laborer was watching me, eyebrows raised. His shirt was off-white from sweat, and he had patches on his wool pants.

I winked at him.

We finished up with the tent, and the women took over, bringing in bedrolls and blankets from the wagons surrounding the camp. The men ambled toward the cook fires for supper, and my new friend gave me a warm glance with his brown eyes before he headed over with the rest.

Quickly walking up to him, I slapped the dwarf on his dense shoulder. "Hello." I offered him my most guileless smile. "I'm Perseus."

The dwarf smiled back. He was about as tall as my shoulder, but wide. "I'm Achim."

"So, are you looking for work in Copper Cairns?" I said.

We stopped walking and faced each other. "Aye," he said. "I'm going to work in the mines."

I asked him a few more friendly questions. Achim had a family, but he hadn't seen them in months because he traveled, looking for work. In that moment I felt a twinge of guilt. Dwarves were… possibly not as into the whole man-and-boy thing as other Greeks. And I hadn't been approached by random men who thought I was a boy in many years. Also, this particular dwarf had a family.

But that wasn't going to stop me.

I continued to murmur to him as the storm dropped down from my brain and clouded my vision. Achim stared into my eyes, and his answers came slower. I pulled on the storm some more, the intensity behind my eyes growing. My will squeezed my skull. It felt so good.

"Would you care to head off to one of the carts," I whispered, "maybe get to know each other better?" I wasn't very good with words. I never really needed to be.

Achim gazed at me, part wonder and part confusion. "Aye."

I grinned, taking him by the shoulder and leading him across the camp to my wagon. I snagged my pack as we went, and when we reached the wagon I hopped in, my boots clomping across the wood. I threw my pack into the corner, unbuttoned my vest, and pulled my shirt over my head, throwing everything into a pile. A light breeze brushed through the dusting of hair I had on my chest, and my arms were still wrapped with the bandages from earlier.

I turned to the entrance of the wagon. Achim stood in the grass, unsure what to do, but something desperate and wild flickered across his features. I dropped to my knees in front of him.

Eyes to eyes, I grabbed his face with both of my hands and pulled his lips to mine. Our beards touched, and I ground our faces together for the incredible feel of it. As our kiss intensified and lips moved apart, I slipped my tongue into his mouth.

Achim exhaled, his breath whooshing by my face as he slapped a meaty paw on my shoulder and squeezed. I pulled back a little, taking in Achim's glazed eyes and flushed neck. I smiled and tugged him into the wagon with me.

He steadied himself on my shoulders as I yanked down his pants, my face brushing along his stout cock. He watched me almost shyly, chewing his bottom lip, and moved his hands to my head, where he worked his thick fingers through my hair.

I gave him a grin and took a breath, diving onto his cock. Achim gasped and then groaned, the noise grumbling through his chest as I stretched my lips over him. I sucked and pulled him in and out of my mouth, and his grip on my hair grew stronger.

Releasing him, I hurriedly pulled off my boots and breeches, kicking them to the side as Achim did the same. I was almost panting as I placed my hands and knees on the floor of the wagon.

I peeked back at Achim, momentarily wondering if this was going to work, but he was already coming up behind me, reaching a hand toward my hip with the other hand on the base of his cock. His pupils were blown; mouth slack.

Achim's cock was still somewhat wet as he pushed it against my anus, but it stuck a bit and I held my breath and closed my eyes as he worked his thickness in. I groaned loudly and broke into a sweat despite the cool air. My fingers gripped the floor of the wagon. From the pulsing of the pain and ecstasy, I raked my nails across the wood, digging small grooves into the boards.

After he pushed up against my ass, we balanced ourselves for a moment, the small movements piercing pleasure through my lower abdomen and shooting down my cock. Achim clutched my hips and with halting and shaky breaths moved in and out of me.

I clenched my eyes shut. "Oh gods," I groaned. "Oh my fucking gods."

He leaned into me, pushing me down until we were almost completely touching. My head hung loosely between my shoulders, his hot breath on my neck. He nibbled my ear while shortening his thrusts, grunting alongside my face. I pushed against him, and at the tender touch of his lips to my cheek, I let out a small helpless noise.

Achim's hair rubbed against my back, our bodies slick with sweat. My forearms knotted with the weight and rhythm. My anus burned with fiery pleasure, and I groaned again with a growing need. I clenched my anus and then jerked from the intensity.

Achim gasped in my ear and emitted a low groan. His breath quickened, and his thrusts became more urgent and forceful.

My mouth flooded with the desire to consume him. I pulled away, his cock plopping out of my ass. Spinning around, I retook his cock with my hands and stretched my lips as wide as I could, encasing him in my mouth.

He grabbed my hair, nearly ripping it from my scalp, and threw back his head, howling. I growled, and Achim grunted and stiffened.

A spurt of warmth went down my gullet when I heard the screams.

Chapter Seventeen

The entire camp erupted into shouts. I pulled Achim's cock out of my mouth, whipping my head toward the commotion. Korvo rushed off into the dark, and Sabu raced out of the woods to chase after him.

A few strong waves of semen hit my face as I dropped Achim's pulsing cock and lunged for my weapons. He retook his cock and slowly stroked it out, oblivious to the growing alarm. I grabbed my weapons and vaulted the side of the wagon. Still swiping the semen from my burning eyes, I dashed into the dark.

My arms and legs pumped furiously with my burst of speed, and soon I was caught up with Korvo and the others. Something moved in the dark, and I called for the storm and sprinted toward the unknown. The heady awareness of the power of the air filled my mind.

The light from the moon illuminated my target. It was a deathly creature, with bones visible through its jerky skin, and milky luminescent eyes. Once, it could have been a woman with its long, stringy hair and bony hips. Now it was undead.

Despite its pallor, its mouth was red and gaping open—a limos, commonly called a hunger demon because its mouth looked like a hungry baby's: red, toothless, and yearning. Limos beat their victims to unconsciousness and then sucked their souls through the victims' mouths.

The limos shambled toward me wearing rags and carrying a large wooden club wrapped with steel rings. It swung at me with its eerie and yearning grin.

The club connected solidly with my side and sent me tumbling back a meter. An arrow shot out from behind me and landed in the monster's thigh, not even slowing it down. I created a path for the lightning to follow, the jagged flash searing through the demon's flesh. The resulting acrid smell burned away the strong odor of rot, and a clap of thunder shook the camp.

The creature flew a few arm lengths away and fell to the dirt, the glow in its eyes fading. More shouts alerted me to two additional hunger demons shambling toward camp. Arrows flew toward them and landed in their breasts, and a giant bear clawed at one. While bear-Sabu had his back turned, another limos raked its dirty nails down his side.

Sabu roared and swung a powerful paw at it.

I charged in, bringing my sword over my shoulder and swinging through the nearest demon's body, rending it like paper. As I turned toward the last limos standing, it took a few arrows in the head. Then Sabu mauled it to the ground.

The limos dead, Sabu shrank, fur becoming clothes and brown skin. His eyes never changed color from that spring green, and his side was still a mess of bloody ribbons.

I sheathed my sword and knelt at his side. "Do you want a heal?"

He clenched his eyes shut but nodded. I gripped his exposed dark flesh, the light from my hands fading into his body and glowing where his back was torn. As the glow faded, his back knit and became whole again. Sabu sighed and opened his eyes, giving me a nod and standing up.

A whip of wind reminded me I was naked… and my cock was half-hard. My mouth also tasted of my ass, and from the tightness on my face, I must have missed a few spots where Achim had sprayed me with semen. Sabu didn't seem to mind, but I stepped back and covered my crotch with my shield.

Korvo said he could follow the tracks if we wanted to pursue the source of the hunger demons, but we all agreed that we should do it in the morning when it was light. Guards dragged the bodies away and burned them. The smell of their burning, rotting flesh drifted into camp, and I grimaced and shuddered.

I had a bruise spreading along my rib cage, but I couldn't feel the pain yet. My blood still pumped strong, blushing my body. People surreptitiously watched me, but I couldn't bring myself to care. My soul sang songs of victory.

Sabu retreated back into the woods, and most of the guards had already left to clean up the bodies. The caravan slowly wound down, and people conversed in soft voices. Korvo sauntered away, his barking laughter fading as he searched for another dicing game.

I returned to my wagon.

Achim was still naked and hanging off the side, his eyes wide. "What the Zeus was that?"

I threw my gear over the side of the wagon and ambled to the entrance, idly rubbing my erection. "Undead. Three of them. We'll figure it out tomorrow." I smiled and then glanced meaningfully at my cock.

Achim took a breath, and I could see the wheels in his head turning. He had just seen me throwing around bolts and shredding up monsters. That image wasn't meshing with what he wanted to do with me.

"What do you want?" he asked softly.

I crawled into the wagon, not breaking eye contact. "I want it like before." His eyebrows rose as I reached for him. "Just like before." I pressed my lips to his, and we fell to the boards with a thump.

AFTER ACHIM had nodded off, we lay next to each other on the floor of the wagon, my blankets over us and my pack under my head. He snored softly.

Guilt trickled through me. My motives hadn't been in Achim's best interests, but he'd had a good time, maybe even a great one, and I started to feel better.

The stars twinkled above. I traced the constellations with my finger and then froze. The constellations…. My arm dropped. Andromeda and I were going to be up there someday, so Athena had said.

Andromeda and I.

She knew that I slept with women, but I was pretty sure she still didn't know about my couplings with men. Years ago, she had asked me to show her how to take me into her mouth.

I had stopped, my blood freezing, and I'd looked at her. Did she know who she was asking? I searched her face over and over for any sign… but all I saw was genuine naiveté. All I saw was a wife who wanted to pleasure her husband.

I'd thought that discovering her ignorance would fill me with relief, but it hadn't. Instead I had felt insurmountable bitterness.

I had shown her. I had shown her how to suck cock like a champion, but there was a difference between her talents and mine. She was using hers to please her husband, and I was using mine to please half of fucking Greece.

Knowing who I really was would destroy her. Her not knowing was destroying me.

I thought myself into circles and then yawned. Achim and I put out a lot of heat, and the light breeze across my face was a perfect combination with our scorching flesh. I shut my eyes.

I dreamed of a terrible storm that relentlessly pursued me. I could feel it, alive and churning, trying to consume me in its chaos. I ran and ran. The gods were coming. My father was coming. The hairs on my arms stood up in excitement, but my belly was a pit of fear and despair.

IT WAS late afternoon on the third day from Goat Hill Quarry, and the caravan rolled slowly behind Korvo, Sabu, and me. Sabu drifted in and out of the woods, and Korvo was equally stealthy on the other side of the road, bow in hand. I strolled with Spirit and sang songs, trying to attract the attention of anything that wanted to take a shot at us.

Bird-Sabu flew up out of the trees and then swooped down, landing in front of me and morphing to an elf. "Smoke ahead," he said.

I peered where he was pointing and could just make out the curl of black smoke in the distance. Turning, I put my fingers in my mouth and whistled three blasts.

The caravan stopped and formed a ring.

Korvo jogged out of the trees. "What's going on?"

"Smoke," I said. I imagined I could smell it now. I figured Spirit would be safe here, but just in case I whistled again and pointed to my cart. One of the guards came up to grab my horse, and Korvo and Sabu and I set off down the road to investigate the source of the smoke.

Getting closer, I detected the smell of burned flesh. My skin crawled. Even closer, we found the burning remains of a caravan. We wandered around the carnage and discovered several dead high elves badly gored and charred. Hoofprints dotted the ground, but the horses had either run off or had been taken. Sabu poked at the bodies, commenting casually that the injuries seemed to be consistent with blunt objects and spears.

Korvo picked through the pockets of the dead, collecting valuables. He caught me watching him. "What? They don't need this stuff anymore." He stopped and cocked his head, his gaze following a trail of hooves into the woods off the road.

Sabu was drawn to the same spot, and the two of them shared a glance. "Centaurs," they said at the same time. Their voices were laced with trepidation.

I frowned. Oston had not said good things about other centaurs, and Antolios believed they were barbarous people. While smaller than a large horse, I knew that centaurs were powerful and intelligent. They weren't a magical race such as elves or humans, so if we met up with them we wouldn't have to worry about clerics or mages.

As if he was reading my mind, Sabu said, "Let's follow."

I nodded. "There may be survivors."

We followed the tracks for a while. Sabu shifted into a cat and silently padded around the trees, and both Korvo and I watched our steps while we snuck through the brush. Trees mostly blocked my view, but soon I heard talking, gruff and deep like Oston's voice. We stopped at the edge of a clearing, and I snaked my head around a tree trunk while Korvo did the same.

Centaurs. A small herd.

I strained my neck from one side of the tree to the other, my gaze flicking across the clearing. Bonfires were set up, with elves tied to stakes around them. A female high elf lay in a heap close to where we were standing, her eyes glassy, and her body naked and caked with blood and dirt. She had just been left there, discarded. I tensed as anger washed through me.

None of the tied-up elves looked alive either. The farthest one was smaller, and my gut soured with horror—it must be a child, but it was hard to tell from the way it was slumped over. I fingered the pommel of my sword.

There weren't any shelters, and a couple of centaurs were napping on their sides at the bonfire nearest me. Two centaurs were setting up the spits of elves. One was throwing branches on the central bonfire, two were fighting, and a male and female were copulating on the far side of the clearing, almost in the trees.

Nine centaurs and three of us.

I didn't favor our odds, and there could be more around that I hadn't seen. Korvo shared a nervous look with me. "Where's Sabu?" I mouthed to him.

As if on cue, the elf stretched up from the ground in front of us. Korvo nearly jumped out of his boots and hit his head on a tree branch, and I glanced to see if the centaurs had heard us. None had.

"I can take out the two on the other side. Wait for my signal," Sabu said quietly and disappeared again.

I nodded, but Sabu had already gone.

Korvo mouthed, "What did he say?"

"Wait for his signal," I whispered. Korvo's eyes widened, and he readied his bow. We crept closer to the sleeping centaurs. They were light brown, with long black human hair and horse tails. Flies buzzed around the piles of horse shit.

The two copulating centaurs separated, and I worried that they would move off, but instead they grappled and the male mounted the female again, pulling her hair back with his hands.

I raked my gaze across the field. I'd get the two napping in the front, then the ones with the weapons, and then the ones trussing up the elves. I pulled on the storm, and the sky darkened.

Something moved on the other side of the clearing, and bright green eyes flashed. In one amazingly smooth and powerful motion, Sabu leaped onto the two centaurs and brought them to the ground.

I burst from behind the trees and yanked on the hair of the sleeping centaurs, exposing their necks and slitting their throats. Shouts rang out, and arrows whizzed by my head.

The centaurs who had been fighting moved toward me, and I created a path in the sky for the lightning to strike them. One bolt found its target, but the other landed off to the side. I shifted as the centaur swept its club at me, and then I slashed my blade along its flank.

The centaur's guts protruded—wet and purple—as it groaned and fell over. Rolling to my feet, I stabbed through its back, cutting off its grunts.

When I looked up, Sabu had shredded the last standing centaur, and Korvo was retrieving his arrows. I sheathed my sword and ran among the fallen elves, touching and trying to heal them. Their skin was cold, and no glow went through their bodies when I performed my spell. The female elves were unspeakably mutilated, and the males were bludgeoned to death, hardly recognizable. I fought to keep my gorge from rising.

I hurried to the spits and did the same with the elves tied to the stakes, no hope left in my heart. As I approached the last elf, the child, I realized he wasn't a child. He wasn't even an elf. He was a human… an adolescent. His clothes were scraps of dirty leather, and blood matted his greasy brown hair. I laid my hands on him, fearing the worst.

The spell lit up the kid's skin, sinking into his flesh with a glow. The gash on his head sealed, and he jerked and gasped, his eyes flying open and rolling in his head. He screamed at me, big brown eyes sightless in terror.

"Whoa! Whoa!" I held up my hands. "We're here to help."

The kid stopped screaming, but his breaths were too fast.

"It's okay," I said. "You're safe now." I put a hand on his shoulder, trying to settle him down. As soon as I touched him, his face crumpled and he cried. Afraid to hold him, and not really knowing what to do, I took out my knife and cut him from the stake. Korvo and Sabu just stood there, looking at him blankly. Released, the kid fell to the ground in a ball, sobbing.

He suddenly quieted, and his eyes popped open. He jerked up and ran from body to body, searching them.

I cleared my throat gently. "They're all dead."

The kid didn't stop, his jaw set. He stumbled over one of the fallen centaurs, and then his face lit up. He picked up a curious axe. The haft was pale leather, and the blade was dark as midnight. His eyes dilated to only a thin ring of muddy brown when he touched it, and his lips moved as if he were whispering to someone. I got a chill even looking at the axe. Pale leather….

The kid fondled it and slipped it into his belt. He turned to us and sketched a bow. "Thank you for saving me. My name is Nero." His voice was clear and surprisingly deep and calm.

I strode over and held out my hand. "Nice to meet you. I'm Perseus." I pointed to my companions. "That's Sabu, and that's Korvo." Everyone murmured pleasantries.

Nero cleared his throat. "This was a royal envoy from Arcadia to Ilium. We were heading to the palace when we were interrupted by several earthquakes."

"I'm sorry for your loss," I said.

Nero nodded his thanks at me.

"We also felt several earthquakes in Goat Hill Quarry," Korvo said.

"We got a message from Arcadia to investigate the source of the quakes," Nero said, "so we turned around and were heading to the Spine of the Gods." He hung his head. "I guess I have to go back. I'm simply an elemental mage. Only the clerics were able to track the magics responsible for the quakes. And now they're all dead."

I froze. The Spine of the Gods. Copper Cairns was at its base. At the base of Mount Olympus.

"You're a mage?" Korvo looked doubtful. "What are you, twelve?"

"I'm eighteen." Nero's eyes narrowed. "Fully trained."

"Okay, sorry." Korvo held up his hands and sauntered around the bodies.

"I'm a cleric," I lied. "I'll help you with your research." Everyone gaped at me. I was shocked too. The words just rushed out of my mouth, lies and all. "Surely your masters wouldn't want you to return empty-handed?"

"Easy there, charmer!" Korvo said. He pocketed something he had looted. "I signed up to go to Copper Cairns. No farther. I'm not hiking up the Spine for some kid's science project. Especially for no pay!"

Nero's voice cut through the air. "I'm not a slave."

Korvo blinked. "What?"

Nero was looking at me, his hand clenched around the axe. "They are not my masters. I am not a slave."

"I didn't mean it that way," I said quickly. "My apologies."

"They are my mentors." Nero looked around. "Were." That last part he said so softly I was probably the only one who heard him.

"I want to get paid, take another job, and get paid for that. That's how I work. I don't have time for this babysitting shit." Korvo crossed his arms.

I smiled at Nero. "So, what do you say? We have to pass through Copper Cairns anyway. How about we gear up while we're there, and Spirit and I'll take you up the mountain pass? Wherever you need to go. You can look around and then report your findings to Arcadia."

"I will come," said Sabu.

Korvo raised his eyebrows at him. "Are you serious?" He snorted. "Elves and their weird shit." Sabu didn't seem offended by the comment, his face bland. We watched Nero.

Nero nodded, and I clasped my hand on his shoulder. "Let's get you a meal, a bath, and a bed," I said. "Sound good?" We walked off, and Sabu followed.

"I'm not coming on this stupid mountain-climbing trip. I'm not!" Korvo said. "Do you hear me?"

Chapter Eighteen

Sabu flew out of the sky and landed near the wagon.

We had arrived at Copper Cairns the night before and headed out to Mount Olympus in the morning. After the caravan had paid us, Korvo had decided to come too.

Sabu turned into an elf again and was holding a raw fish. He nearly yelled at the back of the cart where Korvo and Nero were huddled under blankets. "Anyone want some herring?"

Korvo and Nero groaned, and I could have sworn I heard one of them gag. We had caroused until late, most of us happy to have a hot meal, a bed, and plenty of dwarvish women and whisky, but in the morning those two were the worse for wear. I wasn't really okay either, but for different reasons. I hadn't slept due to a nightmare.

In my dream I had been on my knees in a billowing snowstorm. Though I couldn't see him, I felt my father in the storm, calling to me. I knew where I was going.

Mount Olympus, the tallest mountain in Greece, at the end of the Spine of the Gods. The throne of the twelve Olympians. No one had questioned me when I said we needed to go to Mount Olympus for Nero's answers, and I hadn't wanted to explain my experience.

We were well into our first day on the pass. It was steep but wide enough for Spirit to walk with the cart. By midday, snow had accumulated on the path, and I couldn't feel my nose or fingers even though I had bought warm gear in Copper Cairns. The gear had cost me almost all my earnings from escorting the caravan to Copper Cairns, but I didn't need the money.

A storm had kicked up—one I had no control over. I had tried to tinker with it as it got colder, but I couldn't. It seemed to be fixed in the sky.

Sabu turned into a giant bear to handle the cold better, and when we stopped for a meal, Nero and Korvo pulled themselves out of the back of the cart and ate something. They were pasty and smelled of sweat soured by alcohol.

We moved on, the swirling wall of snow obscuring the path ahead. On one side of the path was the cliff; the other was a drop into white nothing. The wind blew into the cliff face and bit into my cheeks.

Pebbles rolling down the face of the rocks were my only warning.

Swirling white forms dropped onto us, and I quickly realized they weren't wind funnels. They blew toward Spirit, and he pierced the air with his cry, rearing and kicking at the whirls. The echo bounced off the mountainside, eerie and haunting. I yelled out an alarm and pulled my sword free, sprinting toward the blurs attacking my horse.

They were so fast.

By the time I got there, sprinting with a burst, they had already latched onto Spirit. Ribbons of blood painted the snow, and three forms with white wings and hag-like faces were hunched over him. Their hair was gray and tatty, and they used long curved talons to rip off chunks of Spirit's flesh.

Harpies. Supposedly part of Zeus's domain, but when I commanded them to stop, they didn't hear me.

Spirit had stopped screaming.

I was tearing into a harpy with my sword when the gaze of another met mine. Their eyes were gray storms. Like my own. The harpy I attacked shrieked and convulsed at the end of my weapon. I ripped it out of her chest as the other two winged monsters rose from the gore and tried to take flight. They snapped at me with sharp, bloody beaks, the wrinkled skin folding around their mouths.

I widened my stance and met their stares with bared teeth and the tip of my blade.

A bolt of fire exploded into one of them, knocking it out of the sky. Bear-Sabu attacked the other, mauling it down on the path. I strode over to the harpy Nero had felled with fire and dragged my sword across its leathery throat, finishing it.

More magic seared at my peripherals, and I spun around to the last harpy, raked with long gashes. Her talons were up in defense, but her eyes were glazed. Sabu had ripped out her throat with his maw.

I sheathed my sword and trudged over to Spirit's body. He was suspended in a kind of gross mockery of life, his dark hair flared against the snow and his tongue lolled out. The open cavity of his chest steamed, the snow melting around his spilled intestines. His eyes were already freezing over. I had to look away.

A weight settled over me. I knew I wouldn't be able to properly bury my friend, my most trusted companion. I couldn't imagine traveling without him, but he was gone. I was among those I didn't trust, those with secrets possibly worse than my own, and heading to the gods knew what.

OVER THE next week we ate little and slept less. The food was cold and required too much spit to chew and swallow. Our water had to be thawed at night, but it would freeze by midday if we didn't keep our flasks close to our bodies. Sometimes we would make camp in the late afternoon, before nightfall, because we had found a shelter and didn't know if there would be one farther up the path.

The snow was relentless, getting into every nook and cranny and searing my skin with ice. I'd never be warm again. We shared blankets at night, but on nights that we didn't have a fire, no one could keep warm. Not even bear-Sabu was comfortable.

At the end of the first week, in the morning, we packed up and moved on. We had come to a fork in the road with a giant cliff in front of us. One way would take us around the mountain, and the other would let us climb straight to the top. We pulled out our hiking gear. Sabu couldn't fly up since the winds were too strong, so he climbed with us.

Nero had asked me if I was sure we were going the right way. I was. I had never been so certain of anything in my life. I was surprised they couldn't feel it. The storm seemed to be pushing us.

At midday, when we reached a large ledge, I wasn't shocked to see the bell-shaped temple etched into the side near the mountain's summit. We still couldn't see the peak of the mountain through the clouds and snow. A path led up to the entrance of the temple, lined with statues of heroes past. One of the statues was of a man holding his hands to his mouth, as if yelling. My courage was roused by the sight of my hero, Loncy, among the revered of Mount Olympus, but he was a small comfort.

I was here. Now what?

At the end of the street was a set of metal doors leading into the mountainside. It was engraved with bronze figures, each holding an object: scepters, tridents, bows, a lyre, and a lightning bolt. Everyone stared at the engravings a long time.

"Is this what I think it is?" Korvo asked.

I didn't answer.

Korvo went to push on the doors, and my gaze was drawn to the odd stacks of boulders at the sides. They didn't have any snow on them. I was just about to mention this to the team, but just then Korvo got the doors opened, and we stepped into a large atrium.

We shut the doors behind us, cutting off the wind. The inner hall was made of unblemished marble, pillars stretching up to the tall ceiling. In the middle of the floor were gigantic black marble statues depicting various scenes of creation. I hadn't thought much about my lessons since the academy.

As I dusted snow off my clothes, I wandered past the statues.

Chaos was the beginning, the abyss of nothing and magic that spawned the first gods.

Uranus and Gaia, heaven and earth.

The two gave life to the first Titans, Kronos and his brothers and sisters. Foreseeing wickedness, Uranus punished his children, and Kronos rebelled and overthrew his father, creating the first pantheon of twelve gods.

The Titans gave birth to Zeus and his brothers and sisters, and created the wood elves to worship them. In prophecy, Kronos saw his children rise up against him, so he ate them to preserve his power. Zeus escaped, made a deal with the elves to release them from bondage, and rescued his siblings.

The Titanomachy: gods against gods. Zeus was victorious and created the second pantheon of the gods, the twelve Olympians.

As the new rulers, the Olympians created the humans in their image, and then Hephaestus, jealous of the other gods, created the dwarves and halflings in his image.

A winged sandal poked out from behind the dark statue dedicated to the nymphs and demigods.

"No!" I burst into a sprint around the corner of the statue.

Golden ichor splattered the sides of the black marble and pooled at the base. The winged sandal was all that was identifiable; everything else was an explosion of golden fluid. I dropped to my knees and picked up the sandal, the feathers torn. It still hummed faintly with power.

The echoes of steps pattered toward me, and I threw the sandal back into the blood and wiped my fingers on my breeches. I stood shakily as everyone gathered around the remains, and I tried to bury the memories I had with the god.

"What's this?" Korvo reached for the sandal.

"Don't," I said. My throat felt thick and scratchy, and my voice echoed harshly in the temple. "That fluid is ichor, god-blood. It's poisonous." I swallowed. "This was a god. Hermes."

Korvo frowned. "The gods can't die."

My jaw tightened, and I turned away. "Some of them may have before."

In two more puddles, we found long golden strands of hair and a helmet, but the only other traces of what could have happened were odd piles of sand. The sand was present in each of the puddles, and no one knew what that meant.

The only exit from the atrium, aside from the front doors, was a hall that spiraled upward. We wound our way up the gold and marble ramp. The frescoes on the ceiling depicted the birth of the second generation of Olympians.

It took us a while to wind up the open hallway. Once we were at the top, the atrium looked small below us, but I could still see the glittering splashes of gold where the gods had died. We reached a bronze door at the end of the hall, and the storm raged outside. I felt it through the door. We decided to crack it open and see where it led.

Korvo lifted the lever, meaning to only crack the door, but the wind blew it into us. I was standing close enough that I threw my body against it until I had it braced part way shut.

Korvo ducked his head through and then pulled it back in. "There's a person out there on a platform," he said. We pushed the door closed. "Should we talk to him? Or kill him?"

"Did he see you?" said Nero.

Korvo shook his head and then stopped and shrugged. "Maybe?"

Nero's gaze darted to the door, and he fondled his axe haft.

"I vote to kill him," I said. "He's probably responsible for this attack." Nero murmured agreement, and Sabu watched us.

"We aren't sure what's happening," Korvo said. "What if the gods are at war with each other? What if killing this man forces us to choose a side of a battle? And who are we to interfere with the gods' affairs? Also, the man hasn't attacked us yet… and he probably saw me."

Nero and I frowned, but Sabu shrugged.

Korvo leered at me. "Perseus can go talk to him. He's more *sociable*."

I had been chewing deer jerky for a week, and I could feel the knot in my jaw as I clenched my teeth. I didn't trust any of the words that might come out of my mouth, so I nodded my acceptance of his plan.

As I was taking off my pack and pulling off my coat, Korvo slapped my shoulder and whispered in my ear, "Watch yourself, charmer. This one looks weird."

My lip curled, and I grabbed the cool handle of the door. I opened it and stepped through, my hair blowing in the gusts of wind. The sounds of the three of them grunting and trying to close the door were cut off as it shut.

I strode onto the large circular terrace. It looked out from the side of the mountain, and a staircase along the edge continued up. The view was the swirling storm. Large flakes of snow blew into the cave and clung to my eyelashes.

Under the overhang, a dark man stood facing the storm. I saw what Korvo was talking about. Weird indeed. He was wearing a tunic with an odd, heavily beaded necklace. He had tattoos up his neck and a dark shaved scalp. As he turned his face to me, I took note of his thick eye-makeup and pointed chin beard. I put on my best smile and tried to appear relaxed as I strolled up to him.

The man smiled benevolently and swept his hand around him. "Welcome to Mount Olympus." His voice was mellow and smooth. "I am Cronius."

As I held out my hand, I took in the stick-and-crescent style tattoos and his flat sandals. Cronius did not hesitate in clasping my hand, and we let go after exactly the appropriate amount of time. His skin was almost glowing, and the heavy kohl around his eyes made him look feline.

I had to raise my voice over the rush of the wind. "I am Perseus."

"Perseus," Cronius said slowly, as if tasting my name. "What brings you to Mount Olympus on this rather foul day?"

"I could ask you the same," I said. I kept my hands visible, but I was highly aware of where my sword was.

"So you could." The top of Cronius's lip twitched, and he drew back slightly. "Let me reintroduce myself. I am Cronius, son of Epimetheus and Pandora. I am a cleric of Kronos." His eyes took on a cold fire.

I growled. "Demon."

He sneered, then dropped it and turned away, watching the storm. "The Olympians and Titans may not get along, but this does not have to end in blood spilled between us, Perseus. Go, and I will spare you."

Cronius chuckled darkly. "Sons should not be punished for the sins of their fathers."

I gripped my pommel. "What have you done?"

Cronius smirked. "I would think it obvious. *We* are here to free Kronos and usher in a new dawn for mankind."

"Impossible and mad." But I had seen what they were capable of. God-slayers.

"As we speak, the last of the Olympians lies dying, and Kronos will be freed. It is inevitable."

Horror swelled in my throat. "The gods can't die—"

"Rubbish. Everything has a beginning and an end." Cronius laughed. "There is no such thing as eternity."

Growling, I whipped my sword from its scabbard and grabbed the round shield from my back. I lunged, but Cronius smoothly spun away from me and flashed twin daggers that he whisked from his tunic. He snapped them at me, and I bent at the waist and flipped into the air. Landing in front of him, I slashed at his face and called a bolt of lightning from the sky.

Cronius dodged my attacks but didn't notice the arrow coming at him from the side. The arrow hit his arm with a *thunk*, and Cronius snarled. A second later a bolt of ice blasted into his other shoulder.

My party had joined the battle, and now he was outnumbered.

I spun my sword in an arc, but before I could bring it down on him, I was grabbed and hauled off my feet. Struggling and kicking, I tried to break free from whatever had me. I glanced behind me—a towering stack of boulders was crushing me.

Before the rocks folded me into them and closed me off from the world, I spied bear-Sabu swipe at Cronius's face with a roar. I tried to yell, but my scream was muffled by the rocks, and I tasted the cold grit of stone. The rocks squeezed me, but squirming was useless and only made it harder to breathe.

I called on the power of the sky to smite the rocks. I even electrified my body and tried to push them back with wind, to no avail. I struck the elemental over and over again and flexed my arms, trying to break free. Lights barbed through my darkening vision as the stones continued to thump and fold around me.

The crack of my fingers breaking against the hilt of my sword overwhelmed me with pain. I tried to scream, but I had no breath. My heart slapped against my ribs in agony, and I twisted in mindless fear.

Heavy weariness crept over me, and soon dulling black flashes replaced the painful white ones in my vision. I sagged. Sometimes it was easier to give up than to fight. Fighting had never really gotten me anywhere. And honestly, once I got past the pain, dying didn't seem so bad. I was so tired. It seemed like such a waste—everything.

I shot my awareness to the sky as I drifted into unconsciousness. I had one last thing to say before I left this world and joined the stars. *Patéras, I'm sorry.*

My body convulsed in its last efforts to live, but I had already let go.

The sky split as my body and mind lit with a pain and ecstasy I had never known. A solid core of lightning burned out of the sky to hit me and the elemental. Nothing had felt so powerful and raw. The world exploded.

I opened my eyes. I was staring at Korvo's boots. Breathless and jittery, I rolled to my feet.

I choked in a few breaths. My clothes and hair were seared. My sword was on the ground, and I stumbled over to pick it up, but my right hand was maimed. I carefully strapped my shield to my back and picked up my sword with my left hand. Swinging it, I tested my grip.

Korvo gaped at me. Sabu and Cronius fought at the edge of the terrace, and I winked at Korvo, and then ran to rejoin the melee action.

When Cronius saw that I had won against his elemental, his eyes widened. The terrace began to shake and crumble at the edges, turning to sand and rolling off the mountainside.

Cronius let the falling sand take him away, but as the ground disappeared under our feet, Sabu and I broke for the stairs leading up the side of the mountain. Korvo and Nero were already perched on the staircase, reaching their hands out to us. We made the steps just as the last of the terrace dropped away.

My knees hit solid stone.

There was now a giant dent in the side of the mountain where the platform had been. Our packs were on the other side, still in the atrium hallway. The wind blew my hair, and I put my head between my knees, crashing from the rush and struggling just to breathe.

"Perseus!"

I snapped back. "What?"

"Are you hurt?" Korvo said.

I held up my hand. "I think my fingers are broken." My last few fingers were swollen, and my leather gauntlet was mashed into my flesh. The result was a purple pulp.

Korvo made a face. Nero was crouched in the corner, looking small and drawn.

"Don't move," Sabu said. He had a blood-caked slice along his hairline all the way to his dark, pointed ear, his skin hanging. When he gently touched my fingers, I used the contact to heal him. Sabu's face slowly glowed, and his gash healed, but the elf didn't seem to notice. "Look away," he said.

I looked down and winced as he peeled my gauntlet away from my flesh. Sabu's breath was next to my ear, and I could smell him. Sweet spring. There was a pop, and the pain hit me a moment later. I hollered and invented curses, but then something was stuffed into my mouth. Tears leaked down my cheeks as I whipped about. Harsh voices told me to be quiet.

Fuck that.

Sabu didn't grind my pinky into place so much as smear it, it was smashed so badly. I tried to scream, but no sound came out from under the gag. Something gripped me on all sides, and blinding white panic seized me. I couldn't think and thrashed against my bonds.

I was forced into that place again, dark and quiet, at the edge of my sanity. I whimpered, but I couldn't curl up, because the bonds of air held me upright. I told myself I was okay—finally relaxing against Nero's magic. When I was still, he released me to the steps. I slumped, groaning softly, and shivered from the chill.

Someone stuffed mulch in my mouth, and I recognized the bitter taste. Willow bark. My eyes fluttered open, and I mechanically chewed the pieces. It was over.

"Sorry," I said at last. My voice was harsh and raspy.

Korvo was farther up the stairs, peering over the edge of the wall. "No one is coming. The storm is too loud."

I felt light-headed and hazarded a look at my hand. It was wrapped in a glove of linen, just the thumb and forefinger sticking out. That green paste Sabu had probably slapped on it oozed out on all sides. My hand throbbed with the rapid beat of my heart, and I was sick to my stomach.

I waited until I could get my legs back under me, then stood and carefully hooked my shield to my right arm. Sabu helped me secure it so I didn't have to hold the grip, and when I was all situated he gave me something else. I didn't even ask what it was. I chewed and swallowed the herbs, and then sucked down some of the icy water he handed me. I explained what was going on in the temple, still chewing bits of bark from in between my teeth.

Sabu hadn't reacted to the bit about the Titans, nor had he said anything about not wanting to fight against them, so I guessed he wasn't a Titan-worshipping demon. There was that, at least.

"Another Titanomachy?" Korvo shook his head. "Just what the apocalypse ordered."

"We have to see if there are any gods left to save," I said. *My father.*

The storm was still bad, blowing snow into us. We climbed the icy stairs along the edge of the mountain. When we crested the top, we gazed down into the marble-lined bowl of the summit. Rows of tall fluted columns ran around the edge of the large sunken platform. Down the marble steps, in the middle of the stage, stood bejeweled men and more elementals.

Cronius was there. He had somehow survived the fall and appeared unharmed. I knew he was a demigod, and from what I'd seen, it seemed his power involved some sort of manipulation of the earth. He could make quicksand.

He posed in the middle of the platform, holding a shimmering scythe and bellowing as his fellow clerics gestured wildly, apparently in some kind of trance. Cronius pointed the scythe down at a prone and radiant white-haired man at his feet. The old man had sand all over him and an olive-leaf crown on his head. He slowly turned his soft blue eyes to me.

My heart skipped a beat. "*Patéras!*" I ran toward him without thinking.

Cronius lifted the scythe to bring it down on Zeus.

I sprinted down the steps, but panther-Sabu leaped over my head and landed at the bottom of the stairs, raking through one of the clerics with his claws.

I knelt at my father's side, and he gazed at me, his mouth opening as if he were about to speak, but then his eyes rolled back into his head. His veins glowed under his skin, and he looked… old. He'd always had white hair, but he looked weaker, sick.

I reached out to touch him, but before I could heal him, he disappeared. I glanced around and then my father popped back into existence next to Nero. Zeus was unconscious, but the kid gave me a thumbs-up. I nodded my thanks just before one of the elementals smashed into me.

I ducked under the grasping rock arms and stabbed at the chinks between the stacks of boulders of its body. My sword sliced through the rocks like air, and I must have been doing some damage to it, but then I realized that the elemental was turning its body to sand so that my blade slid through without harm. I bashed into it with my shield and got better results, breaking the elemental up into chunks.

Fire and ice sang through the air, and arrows peppered the floor. Nero shot magic at the clerics, and Sabu was now a bear and bashing into the elementals much as I had done. We had a couple of the elementals down and only a few clerics left, including Cronius.

I stalked over to get the demigod's attention.

As I was moving toward Cronius, I caught a glimmer out of the corner of my eye, where my father had been lying. I turned just as the blur of Nero's axe sliced into my father's chest.

"Noooooo!" My screams of anguish blended with Nero's cries of elation.

Zeus's body shimmered and blew up in a shower of golden light and ichor, knocking us all back and throwing Cronius and me into each other.

I ripped my gaze away from the gore as I was forced into combat with Cronius, who laughed disbelievingly, his teeth white and perfect. He swung at me, and I blocked the scythe with my shield—

The scythe sliced through my shield as if it were made of butter. A third of my shield slid to the side and clanged to the floor. That shield was god-made….

Not wanting to see what would happen if any other part of me connected with the scythe, I ducked another swing and ran—but Cronius's legs flashed up from under his tunic, and my breath was knocked away by his kick as I flew up and crashed at the bottom of a steep white staircase, my neck snapping back to smack on the steps. Everything dimmed for a moment and then brightened again. Growls, blows, and the fluting of arrows assaulted my ears.

I lifted my head just as bear-Sabu jumped on Cronius and took the scythe in his meaty shoulder. Cronius dragged the blade down to the bear's core. Sabu whined, then turned back into an elf and groaned as Cronius yanked the blade from his body. He picked Sabu up and stalked over to the edge of the mountain, tossing him over.

I only managed a strangled cry, watching in helpless horror as the bloody elf sailed through the air. Space folded again, and Sabu appeared next to Nero, who was still sitting in the wreck of Zeus's body with a sick smile on his face. The ichor had not harmed him.

I tore at the straps on my ruined shield with my teeth and tossed it to the side. A dark crack in the stair drew my attention. When my eyes focused, I realized it wasn't a crack but a wooden staff, jagged as a lightning bolt. I sheathed my sword and picked it up with my good hand. It buzzed with familiarity.

I stood up and hefted it, balancing it perfectly. Without thought, I whipped my arm back and hurled it at Cronius.

The staff sparked to life in the air as it sizzled toward the demigod. Cronius turned toward me just in time for the white-hot bolt to hit him squarely in the chest. He growled and lifted his scythe, gathering himself to charge.

The staff materialized in my hand once again, and I almost dropped it from shock. Korvo flitted across my vision and stabbed Cronius in the back, his blade poking out the demigod's chest.

I tried to yell a warning at Korvo, to tell him to run, but before I could, Cronius spun and impaled him through the heart with his scythe. Korvo sagged at the end of the weapon.

My cry became howling and indistinct.

I hurled the staff again, and it flew from my hand to its mark. The electricity seared into Cronius, striking him in the back of the skull and exiting his forehead. His scythe still impaling Korvo, the demigod hunched over, and after a moment they both toppled, unmoving.

The staff returned once again to my hand.

Down the stairs, several elementals were tearing into the pristine marble of the center platform. Sabu was off to the side, and Nero was burying his axe into the last cleric. The kid shuddered as if in the throes of orgasm as he pulled the blade from the cultist's chest, his mouth open in rapture.

I jumped down the stairs toward Sabu. His eyes were closed, and he was holding his guts in with clenched fingers. I sank down next to him and set my staff aside, laying my hands on him. The glow from my spell sank into his body, and the flesh of his stomach knit slowly together.

When it was done, Sabu's dark brown lids flew open, his pupils springing to pinpoints. He glanced around with green eyes, but his head stopped in the direction of the platform. "Oh shit."

The elementals had torn down the last of the mountaintop, opening a deep cave to the atrium in the center of the mountain. An odd bright blue light glowed from the hole, and Nero shouted, but I couldn't understand him through the wind that howled from the opening. He pointed upward, and both Sabu and I swung our heads to the sky. A meteor of compacted boulders spun slowly through the air, dropping toward the hole.

My eyes narrowed. I stood, launching my staff over and over again at the meteor, and then hit it with the lightning and wind of the storm. They did nothing. It was closer now, and Sabu sprang up and shouted at me. He even pulled my arm, but I hollered in denial.

The meteor was directly above us, seconds from impact.

Arms encircled my waist, and I struggled and then yelped when the arms turned scaly and black and red. I lashed out and electrified my skin, but the lizard arms ignored the shocks, lifting and stuffing me into a dark gaping maw.

The world went black.

I sat in the belly of some sort of demon, slime pouring into my nose and mouth. I tried to get my sword free and summon my staff, but the cocoon held me too tightly. I gagged on the mucus, and my disgust turned to outrage. I thrashed back and forth.

After what felt like hours, the jostling and shaking stopped and the cocoon stilled. My head pounded. The bottom of the cocoon seized me and thrust me back out through an opening into white light.

I was disgorged unceremoniously into the snow. Slime webbed my limbs, and I coughed and sneezed up globs of mucus.

I sat in the dust and rubble of what had been Mount Olympus. The ground shook slightly, and rocks were still settling. A dust of fresh snow coated everything, and it was coming down hard.

Just as I thought. There was Nero, looking sheepish and unscathed, his face losing the last of the demon scales as he shrank back down to size. Sabu crouched off to the side, watching us both.

I rose slowly, flexing every muscle in my body until my bones snapped. "You fucking demon! Do you know what you just did? Do you know who that was?" I tried in vain to wipe my hands off on my sticky shirt, and snarled.

Nero's hair was matted to his forehead, his eyes lined with darkness. "I didn't mean it."

"The crows take you!" I spat. "That was the king of the gods! He could have helped us. He could have helped everyone. He could have saved Korvo." My fists clenched with the urge to smash his face in.

"I couldn't help it," Nero said. He was sitting in the snow, the axe next to him. He stroked it with a finger.

My face twisted. "He was my father." The storm crashed at the back of my mind and all around me, and my hair whipped about.

Nero bowed his head, but he didn't look surprised. "The axe was thirsty...."

Before he could say another word, I summoned my father's staff into my hand and launched it at the axe—the two blew apart in a shower of otherworldly wailing.

I held my hand out for my staff's return, but it didn't come back. I tried again. Nothing.

I growled and spun away, pacing and muttering in the debris and snow. Grinding my teeth, I gasped in breaths in time with the pounding of my heart.

Zeus had been a god, and Nero was just a kid, a street urchin of a mage.

It got harder and harder to breathe. Chest hurting, red flashed as I held my breath. I bore down, squeezing with everything I had, holding it all in.

A ball burned in my breast. Everything went gray.

Air exploded out of my lungs, and I woke as if from a nightmare. Taking a breath, I relaxed and straightened.

I had no idea what had just happened, but suddenly I felt wonderful. I stretched my arms to the sky, reveling in an intense sense of well-being. Checking my body for bumps and bruises, I whistled. Despite the broken hand and some soreness around my ribs, I seemed to be okay.

The storm pulsed above, and my blood sang to its rhythm. The storm felt great, I felt great, and there was only one thing that was missing from my bliss.

Nero....

Maybe there were two things missing from my bliss. I smiled lazily and chuckled. Palamedes had said something interesting to me once.

I slowly turned, as if dancing, and regarded the raggedy misfit. Maybe he could be good for something. That wonderful glow I had been feeling was now everywhere—pounding. It was intoxicating. Loose-jointed and grinning, I sauntered over to Nero.

A flash of fear entered those cow eyes of his, and he trembled. The battering of his heart was melodious, and I put my lips together and hummed along. Nero smelled sweet and sharp, and I closed my eyes and took it all in.

"Mmmm." I flicked my eyes open. "Nero?"

Nero curled up, shaking his head.

"Are you ready to be skull-fucked?"

CHAPTER NINETEEN

I TOOK two steps toward Nero and belted the wimpy kid over the eye with my good hand. The crack of the flesh-on-flesh contact sent electricity through me.

"Nero, you've been a bad boy." I grabbed his ratty shirt and hit him again. Blood ran down his face, and his eyes rolled uselessly in their sockets. I punched him once more, and bones cracked. I licked my lips. "And bad boys should be punished."

Nero's head flopped to the side, and there were bits of teeth in the blood that ran down his face. His nose was a pulp and welling red. Under his swollen eye, the skin was split to the bone. Even unconscious, the little sissy looked sad and put out.

Kneeling beside him, I undid the laces of my breeches with my left hand. I was glad Sabu hadn't said anything, because I didn't want to deal with him and ruin this moment. The first time was always the best. My cock sprang from my pants, and I stroked myself, purring. I was so hard.

Taking Nero's head by the hair, I lined him up right at the tip of my beautiful cock. Now *this* was divine justice. I pressed myself against Nero's eyelid, warm and soft. Flexing my thighs, I prepared to thrust.

"Oh, Nero, you're going to be useful after all."

I took a breath, tensed, and then… frowned.

Blinking, I looked down at myself kneeling in the snow, my penis getting flaccid and cold.

Nero was bloody, broken, and unconscious. I stared and stared at him. He was breathing. I jerked from his side, tucking myself back into my pants and striding through the snow to the edge of the rocky ledge. I swallowed back bile and took deep breaths. Sabu murmured to Nero, trying to rouse him, but he wasn't responding.

The snow was falling harder now. I still couldn't stop it. Deep regret washed through me. Why had my father called me here? For this? We had destroyed the mountain, the home of the Olympians. The entire top of it had collapsed, and the landslide had rolled all the way down to the foothills, trees buried in its path. At the center of the crater, a chill wind blew from the depths. The meteor was down there, pounding at the earth.

It wasn't over. We weren't done.

I shut my eyes and swallowed. Nero still hadn't responded. Sabu glanced at me as I approached, and watched me bend and place my hand on Nero's face. I briefly saw the holy light glow through his skin, but before I could see if he was okay or not, I turned and strode away again, still fearing my holy dark.

Nero groaned.

"Are you okay?" Sabu asked. His tone was gentle, and I felt another surge of guilt.

Nero coughed weakly. "I'm sorry." He whimpered as he spoke. "I couldn't stop it. I don't know why my mentor had that axe, but once I discovered it and touched it, I couldn't get away from its voice."

Nero sniffed loudly. There was some rustling, and he blew his nose. Sabu must have given him something, because Nero thanked him. "The axe promised to show me ancient magic and made me do terrible things," Nero said. "It said it needed the blood of the powerful…."

I knew the storm had retreated back to the depths of my brain for now, but I dared not turn around yet. Crossing my arms over my wet clothes, I shivered. I still smelled of gut juice.

"You know what's funny?" I said to no one and everyone. "I think my father summoned me here to stop this. I've always been a bit of a disappointment."

No one said anything, but what was there to say? I turned back to Nero and Sabu. Nero was looking at his boots, and Sabu had turned into a bear, staring at me with those green eyes.

"I'm going to investigate the hole in the center of the crater. You ready?" I said.

Nero barely nodded, still not looking at me, and Sabu just growled. We hiked toward the crater, the shaking and pounding sounding louder as we approached. The rocks were slick, so we carefully climbed to the center of the rubble where we could look down the dark icy shaft the meteor had been creating. Frigid wind blew from the tunnel, and I squinted and shivered. Fuck, it was cold.

"And this will release a Titan?" Nero said. His voice was quiet, and he flinched when I glanced at him. He reminded me of when we first met, when he had been strapped to that stake. He seemed the scared kid again. The axe had killed a god, a weakened god, but still a god. And it had given him powers that no ordinary mage would have. I briefly entertained the possibility that Nero hadn't been lying about the axe controlling him.

"Giant spears of ice tether the Titans through their hearts and keep them from leaving Tartarus," I said. Throughout Gaia, Zeus had staked the Titans with spears of ice through the crust of the earth—all the way to Tartarus. A pillar that ran all the way from the top of Mount Olympus imprisoned Kronos. "I can only assume that the meteor will keep pushing through this spear of ice until it reaches Kronos and frees him, and then Kronos will free the other Titans." I shielded my eyes with my hand and peered down the shaft. The meteor beat against the bottom. How far did it have to go until it reached the Underworld?

Sabu jumped down the hole and turned into a bird, using the currents of air to drift down.

I turned to Nero. "Looks like it's just you and me."

He gulped. The edges of the ice shaft were smooth, but every few feet there were chips and small ledges we could hold on to. We didn't have our climbing gear, so it would have to do. Worst case, I could possibly buffer our descent with wind if one of us fell, but I wasn't feeling very charitable. I had no desire to help Nero, but I knew I'd probably need him to fight that meteor or ball of elementals—whatever it was.

We made our way down together. If I gripped him too tightly when I lowered him to the ledges or pressed him too hard against the sides of the shaft, what of it?

It didn't take us as long to descend as I had expected. Nero was surprisingly agile. Where had the elves picked him up, anyway? They loved youth and power, and Nero was powerful. He probably wouldn't be able to return to Arcadia when this was over—the elves wouldn't accept him after they discovered he was a god-slayer. Not that I cared, and odds weren't good that we'd live through this. Two demon worshippers and me in the middle of a Titanomachy? Right.

When we dropped to the last icy shelf, the meteor was right below us, still pounding away. Rock elementals formed the meteor, packed together, and they reached out their rock arms to tear into the ice at the bottom of the shaft. The ice around us was ripe with divine magic. It hummed around me.

The storm was still raging, and I pulled on its power, creating a path for the lightning to follow. I hit the meteor over and over again. Sabu turned into a bear and swiped at the meteor, trying to dislodge some of the rocks. Nero was standing with his hand out, muttering to himself.

"I think I can blast the meteor apart," Nero said. We glanced at him, and he dropped his gaze to the ground, his cheeks reddening. "I'll need a catalyst."

Bear-Sabu looked at me, and I looked at him. Neither of us had much.

Nero coughed and then cringed. "Uh, I'll need something living. Something divine."

I clenched my jaw. If I hadn't liked Nero before, I really didn't like him now. He was asking for my blood. Why did it have to be blood magic? What were the elves training him for? If only my father had summoned me sooner, if only he had told me what was going on, and if only I had let Nero die on that stake. None of this would have happened. If only. Now I was at the mercy of a god-slaying, previously demon-possessed, blood-magic-casting mage.

And the Fates. We were out of options. Maybe it was a good time to practice the faith… so I sent a prayer to the Fates, to my father, and to the dead Olympians as I pulled a knife from my belt.

Nero took that as my agreement to his plan and began to etch the ice around us with runes carved by his pocketknife. He gave me a nod when he was finished.

"Fuck it." I tore into the underbelly of my forearm, blood welling through the stinging wound and onto the runes below.

As the blood hit the grooves, it lit up the ice. Once the last sector was lit, Nero signaled me to stanch the blood flow. I used a bit of boiled cloth from the pouch at my belt and pressed it to my wound. Now my right arm was broken *and* bleeding. I crouched against the wall next to Sabu and hoped to the gods that Nero wasn't fucking with me. But then this quest had been fucked from the start, so what did it matter?

Nero whispered furiously, waving his arms. During the crescendo, he raised his voice and swung his hands, and a great rush of red-tinged power rose up from the runes and sailed toward the meteor.

The meteor exploded into rocky bits. Pebbles clinked off the ice, and I had to duck under a few flying chunks. Steam rose from where the meteor had been hit, and a shallow depression formed in the ice shaft, with water pooling in the deeper areas.

Stirring in the rubble, small rocks rolled together to form tiny elementals. They began pounding at the bottom of the shaft again.

I rose and gazed down on them all, drawing my sword. Sabu growled. We gave each other a glance and both jumped, hitting the floor with a splash.

The small elementals weren't hard to break up—a good bash with my shoulder or sword blew them apart—but when we did kill one, the pieces would form up with another elemental. We couldn't think of anything else to do, so we kept at it until we had two giant elementals left. They were even bigger than the ones we had seen on the summit of Mount Olympus.

I charged one of the elementals, but I bounced off and fell down hard on my ass. I drew on the storm and smote the pile of rocks with lightning, but fucking dirt can't be electrified. Wind wouldn't work down in the shaft either; at best, I'd just bash us all against the walls.

Bear-Sabu had blood on his fur as he roared and swung at the other elemental. It turned parts of its body to sand so that when Sabu swiped, his paws went through the rocks. Nero rained down ice and fire, but that didn't seem to be working against the big ones. They were just too big, the size of giants. I had no idea how we were going to do this.

I lured the elemental I was working on over to the other and fought them both, signaling Sabu to get behind them and search for weaknesses in their defense.

I was tiring. I hadn't been able to burst for a while, and the next time one of the elementals threw a punch at me with their boulder fists, I took it in the shoulder and spun to the ground. As one elemental pulled back a fist to deck me again, a light poked through the boulders.

I rolled and stabbed through the opening. My sword twisted in the rocks, and I sawed my arm back and forth, trying to break it apart. Sabu shoved the elemental from behind, and the elemental collapsed, falling to rubble all over me.

The boulders pinned my legs but then shifted and rolled together. Now there was only one, and the resulting elemental loomed over me, bigger than a giant. I tried to back away from it, get my bearings, but the elemental finished pulling itself together and ironed me in the face with a horse-sized fist.

Sprawling, my chin hit the ice. The giant came in for another whack, and I rolled on my back and threw up my arms to shield my head with the last of my strength. My limbs felt heavy as I was clobbered again and again.

The last thing I knew was the incredible pressure in my head.

CHAPTER TWENTY

Sabu

WHEN SABU saw Perseus fall, he lifted his head and roared at the sky, praying to Gaia. He never asked for more than he needed, and as her champion, he knew she would heed his prayers.

He was nonetheless taken aback when a giant raven descended on the elemental and pecked at its head. Sabu shifted form and strode to his fallen companion.

Sabu had grown up in the wild, alone. He had no use for the fleeting whims of the lesser gods or the wanton desires of men. He could not understand what Perseus found in the company of others that would cause him to deviate from the single-minded course of hunter and prey. It was much easier to understand the summer drought or the winter slumber of bears. He did, however, know that they were a pack and warriors of the hunt.

In this, they were brothers, called to the same purpose.

Perseus's face was broken and bloody, and his hands were shattered. Bits of bone and teeth stuck out from his skull. The complete stillness did not unnerve Sabu, for he had seen death many times before. It was part of the natural order. It was Gaia.

Sabu lifted his arms to the air and soundlessly called to her, the natural force. When his hands began feeling as if he had stuck them in warm pots of mud, he slammed them onto Perseus's chest.

CHAPTER TWENTY-ONE

MY EYES flew open, and my body convulsed. I gasped and reflexively curled around my aching chest. Waves upon painful waves of burning energy coursed up and down my spine. I patted my face, my arms, my legs. My hand was healed, and my forearm was as well.

Sabu was standing above me in elf form, but after he met my eyes, he turned into a bear again and bounded toward the elemental. There was a… large black bird fighting the elemental as well.

I shook my head and jumped to my feet, feeling only slightly uncomfortable because I was hungry and had to piss and crap. I took up my fallen sword, in my main hand this time, and charged into battle.

We chipped away at the elemental, and finally Nero used some kind of heat spell that partially melted it. I stabbed at its center, and when it died, it exploded into sand everywhere. I blinked the grit from my eyes and spat it from my mouth.

The raven left with a caw, and bear-Sabu followed its flight.

We stood there for a long time, half expecting something else to emerge and challenge us, but nothing came. The ice eventually started to grow back along the shaft, and Nero suggested that we get out of there.

Sabu flew out, and Nero started the climb back up. I didn't feel like climbing.

I shifted the pressures in the sky, and my ears popped. My cyclones were sloppy and sometimes useless, but I pulled one down on my head anyway. I wobbled up and down the currents of wind until I steadied myself, then rose up into the sky. As I passed Nero, he clung to the sides of the ice tunnel, getting nearly smashed into it. I couldn't feel sorry for him.

At the top of the hole, at what used to be the summit of Mount Olympus, I tried to make a smooth landing, but instead I was blown out of the cyclone and hit the ground with a disheartening thud. It was slightly less painful than it could have been because of the fresh powder on the ground.

When Nero finally climbed up to the top, I had healed Sabu, and we were sharing a bit of hard bread that the elf had squirreled away in one of his pockets.

"The storm is too intense for me to fly far, so we'll all have to go on foot," Sabu said. "We are about a week away from Copper Cairns, maybe more."

"We don't have any supplies," I said. "Or warm clothes." We'd have to take the long road back to Copper Cairns, since all of our climbing equipment had been lost. It was probably going to take us longer than a week. Would we all make it? Sabu probably would. He could live out here, but Nero? Not likely. The kid wasn't wearing anything but his leathers, and I was still damp and wearing a vest, a torn-up shirt, and breeches. I had no hat or gloves.

I shivered and tried again to calm the storm, but my efforts were wasted. It would dissipate when it ran itself out.

We stared at each other for a moment—man, elf, and demigod—and then climbed over the rubble and back toward the road that led to Copper Cairns. When we got to the trail, Sabu offered to carry Nero.

I was exhausted too, but I nodded. "That would be for the best."

Nero didn't hear us, and when Sabu turned into a three-hundred-kilogram buck, I had to place the kid on his back.

We didn't want to make camp above the timberline, and since both Sabu and I could see well in the low light, we hiked until late, reaching the trees well past dark. Nero was still dazed, and I stuffed both of our shirts with brush. It didn't make me feel much warmer, and Nero's lips were blue.

We found a hollow under a tree to spend the night. The branches were heavy with snow, but that seemed to keep the wind out. Sabu turned into a bear and further sheltered us from the elements. I was starving, but I was too cold and exhausted to do anything about it. I didn't sleep well, but I think I got a few hours in before sunrise.

When I awoke in the morning, Sabu was gone. I left Nero sleeping and wandered into the woods to relieve myself. On the way, I passed the elf coming back with several hares.

With my ass still cold and chafed from frozen leaves, I came back into camp, where Sabu had started a fire and was cleaning the hares. Nero was sitting up, his short dark hair a mess and his expression vacant. I helped Sabu with the hares, and we cooked and ate them. They were burned on the edges, raw in the middle, and incredibly greasy, but they were still the best thing I'd ever put into my mouth… well, almost.

I melted some snow and drank it, and then jogged next to Sabu while Nero sat on his back. I was worn out, but the jogging helped keep my toes and hands warm. I didn't think I'd be able to burst to save my life, so hopefully it wouldn't come to that. We took a break at midday, and Nero still hadn't relieved himself or had anything to drink. He had barely eaten that morning. I asked him if he was all right, but he only nodded and wouldn't say anything.

When we continued on, my legs were as heavy as stones. I was tired, hungry, and stank to high heaven. I had tried to clean my shirt in snow that morning, but it hadn't helped the old-piss smell from Nero's demon gut. I was going to have to burn these clothes.

I heard a *thunk* and turned around. Sabu was in elf form again and kneeling next to Nero. "He collapsed off my back," Sabu said. He touched his slender dark fingers to Nero's face. "He's cold."

His skin was cold and clammy when I put my hands on him. I healed him, draining the rest of my energy, but it didn't improve his condition. He didn't wake up. I glanced at the sun as Sabu tried again to rouse him. It wasn't evening yet, but we were going to have to stop and make a fire. I followed Sabu around, holding Nero to my chest, as he found a hollow tree for camp and started a fire. I finished building the fire as he hunted, and then I laid Nero next to the flames, got behind him, and must have nodded off, because the next thing I knew, Sabu had returned with some sparrows.

Nero hadn't woken up, so Sabu and I cooked the sparrows, the smell of roasting meat rising up from the roaring fire. The sparrows were terrible, but I was so tired, I didn't care that I'd probably be picking feathers out of my teeth for weeks. Sabu obviously didn't cook much. Why would he, when he could eat in one of his animal forms?

"So," I said, "how do you keep your clothes on when you shift in and out of forms?"

"Magic." The elf smiled mysteriously.

I raised an eyebrow. "Who's your god?"

Sabu leveled a gaze at me. "Gaia."

It didn't really matter who he worshipped at this point, considering all we had been through together, but it made me feel better that he was a champion of Gaia. Technically she wasn't one of the twelve Olympians, but worshipping her wasn't considered profane. She was the Mother and wasn't supposed to take sides.

I had thought that with all the Olympic gods dead, there would be a shift of power, and the lesser gods would come to claim the fallen throne. But no one had. The sun still rose, the animals acted normally, and the dead hadn't risen.… Maybe Gaia had something to do with that?

We both watched Nero. "We'll put him in between us," Sabu said. "You by the fire and me on the other side." I nodded, and we settled in for the night. At least I'd get some sleep.

I KNEW I was dreaming, because masturbating had never felt this good.

I was covered in honey, and I was smearing it all over my cock and balls. I used both hands, pumping up and down my shaft, and when I came, I scooped up the honey laced with semen and ate it, sucking it off my fingers. I tried to lick it off my cock, but even in my dreams I couldn't do it. That was disappointing.

"Perseus."

I flicked my eyes open as someone pushed my shoulder. Yawning and lifting my arms up, something squirmed out from under me. Nero ran into the trees, sobbing.

"Uh, what?" I mumbled and blinked.

Sabu was kneeling next to me, more hares in his hands. His expression was part amusement, part worry.

I smelled Nero on my clothes, and the warm spot he vacated against me was cooling. I looked down. I had a giant erection. "Oh fuck," I said.

Sabu's mouth twitched.

I groaned and rolled to my feet. Pulling some pine needles from my hair, I sighed. "I'll be back." I hiked into the woods and relieved myself, then came back to camp. Sabu had started a fire, but Nero was still missing.

I cleared my throat. "Uh… did I do anything?"

Sabu shook his head slowly. "As far as I can tell, you were just groping him. Inarticulately."

"Great." I rolled my eyes. "I'll go find him." I followed Nero's footsteps in the snow and eventually caught up to the kid. He was huddled under some branches, hugging his knees to his chest.

"If you're going to kill me, just kill me," he rasped.

"I'm not going to kill you, Nero."

Nero's lip trembled. "Are you going to hurt me?"

"I'm not trying to hurt you either." I sighed. "I'm sorry about this morning. It won't happen again."

Nero peeked through the branches at me, his big brown eyes watering. "Just because I lived with elves doesn't mean I'm into that kind of thing."

"I know." Despite myself, I felt the beginnings of a smile at the corners of my mouth. I relaxed my stance and sighed loudly, putting my hand on my hip and cocking it. I winked at him. "You aren't really my type."

Nero's mouth dropped open.

I laughed and shrugged. "I like my men a little… sturdier."

Nero's eyes bugged out of his head, and he sputtered.

I crossed my arms. "I am in control, but do not test my patience."

He nodded dumbly.

I wanted to believe I wouldn't hurt the kid, but how long would it take for me to not be in control anymore? Weeks or days? I hoped we'd get to Copper Cairns soon. "Are you ready to get out of here, or do you want to freeze to death?" I said.

He crawled out from under the branches. "I'm ready."

"Good." We walked back together.

After a longer hike that day to make up the lost time, we sat at the fire that night. Sabu had turned into a cat and was licking his ass and balls. I watched, breathless and imagining things I probably shouldn't. His tongue was so big…. I swallowed before I drooled all over myself.

Cat-Sabu's ears flicked, and he gathered himself up and slunk into the woods.

Nero was watching me, a faint smile on his face. "Is he your type?"

I exhaled forcefully. "Oh yes. He just doesn't know it yet."

Nero's nose crinkled. "I think his type is furrier."

"I can be furry."

"Can you grow a tail? Because I think he would be into that," Nero said.

We both laughed. The gods might be dead, and we might die before we got to Copper Cairns, but at that moment things weren't so bad. I prayed I didn't screw it up.

IT TOOK us a full week to get to Copper Cairns.

We had stopped talking to each other, and I had tried not to think. The last few days had been rough, and I put one foot in front of the other and nothing else. I hadn't been able to break up the storm yet, and I'd have given anything for the heat of the southern coasts.

We had hiked along the landslide, which ended right before the town. Some of the farms we passed had been obliterated, but otherwise every building was standing.

When we traveled through the city gates, I couldn't help but shudder at my stench. Nero stank too, but his smell was becoming more and more appealing. I had managed to keep my paws off him, thank the gods, but I was aware that I was dangerously close to doing something irrational. Again.

Smelling this strongly bothered me enough that, instead of making for the nearest whorehouse, I made my way to the public bathhouse. We hadn't discussed departure plans, but Sabu and Nero decided to join me. We paid the dwarf at the desk and then walked inside, the heat hitting me and making me sweat instantly. In the middle of the building was a giant pool of steaming water and an area to rinse off before you took the plunge. I breathed in the warm moisture and ambled over to the cubbies.

Nero and Sabu quickly undressed and hovered over to the wooden tub, scrubbing themselves with brushes and soap. I peeled off my clothes, starting with my shirt and dirty vest, and then fingered the laces to my breeches. As I pulled my pants down, my erection sprang loose, purple and throbbing with veins. I sighed, shoved my clothes into a cubby, and slowly turned around.

Ducking my head and keeping my arms in, I tried to appear as small as possible. I picked up a bar of soap and a brush, and began to chip at my layers of grime. The smell of my ass and crotch were overpowering.

Nero hastily left and jumped into the large pool, quickly making his way to the opposite side. Sabu hopped in after him.

I focused on washing my filth away, the river of brown water rolling down the drain in the stone floor. When I was clean enough, I tossed my brush into a corner and stood. I held my penis surreptitiously to the side until I got into the pool. The hot water burned my toes, fingers, and face as I submerged myself. Using the pads of my fingertips, I scrubbed every nook and cranny.

When I broke through the surface, I smoothed back my hair. My beard and other parts had grown bushy. Maybe now that I resembled a black bear Sabu would be interested? I leaned back against the side of the pool.

The hour was sometime between breakfast and midday. There weren't a lot of patrons, and they were mostly dwarves. I was glanced at, but nothing lingering. There were several small groups of two or three, and most of them were discussing the fall of the mountain. The clerics of the town had been telling everyone the gods were dead, but some didn't believe that, because then wouldn't it be the end of the world? And why did the clerics still have their powers, given to them by the gods? But it was true that no one had been able to contact any of the gods, lesser or otherwise.

My groin hurt, but it was easier to deal with when it hurt. It still wasn't wise to think too hard about it, because I knew no one here would want to leave with me. I climbed out of the pool, ready for a different scene. After I walked back to the cubbies, I frowned at my clothes. I had been so concerned about getting clean that I hadn't thought to buy new clothes first, but I was too restless and exhausted to wait for someone to launder them. I sighed. I'd buy clothes next, clean up at an inn, and then go to the whorehouse. Two baths probably wouldn't hurt anyway.

Outside the bathhouse, Sabu and Nero and I said good-bye. I didn't ask them what they were going to do, and they didn't ask me. The less we saw of each other from now on, the better. I didn't want to be reminded of any of this.

At one of the shops, I picked out a few more shirts, breeches, a coat, and some new laces for my boots. At least I still had my coin purse. I was having a hard time contemplating the thickness of several pairs of socks, when the door of the shop flew open and the bell attached to the door rang.

An odd white light behind me cast a shadow of my hands holding the socks. Before I could turn toward the source, strong arms wrapped around me, squeezing the air from my lungs.

The smell of the person hit me. Neroli.

Antolios smelled better than heaven. I threw my arms around him as he crushed me to his chest. "How are you here?" I breathed. "Am I dreaming?"

Antolios kissed the top of my head. "I came looking for you."

I didn't wonder about that, and I didn't care. I knew I was safe and I was loved, and I let myself fall apart in his arms.

I SLOWLY came back from being lost in the clouds. I was in Antolios's arms, sitting in a warm bath at an inn. He was behind me, his pale knees sticking up by my ears. He lifted my chin with his finger and took a knife to my throat.

Scrape, scrape, scrape.

Antolios fastidiously shaved me, all the while complaining about dwarven-style tubs and how he'd had a sunken tub installed in the Pelion palace. King Niklaus had died, and now Cora was queen. Antolios was a crown prince. It had all happened the way he'd said it would.

"Cora nagged and nagged me about the renovation that had to be done because of the tub, but she stopped complaining when she got into it for the first time. It's as big as a pool. We have a mage heat the water day and night. It's really quite beautiful. Instead of tiles, we had it lined with river rock."

Scrape, scrape, scrape.

I had a cup of whisky in my hand, and my mouth tasted of the smoky liquor. My penis strained toward the surface of the water. The bond was open between us, but I only got a vague sense of what Antolios was feeling, a shallow comfort. He was better at hiding his feelings than I was, and sometimes a lack of emotions coming through the bond spoke louder than strong ones.

Antolios was worried.

Scrape, scrape, scrape. Antolios flicked the blade into the water. The black stubble from my face floated on the surface along with the bubbles.

"Hammish is putting together a spread for us in the great room. I asked him to include as many fruits and vegetables as he could find. Doesn't that sound nice?"

I couldn't remember a time Antolios had talked so much. I made a noise of agreement, or at least I intended to.

"I'm lucky to have my manservant with me," he said. "I got a vague message from my father in the middle of the night, and I didn't tell anyone that I was leaving for Delos. I felt weird, as if I were in a trance or being compelled. Hammish just happened to be up and near the stables when I was headed toward them. I suppose I could have called for someone, but I didn't think of it at the time. I was confused, and at first I thought I was dreaming. I'm glad he was there.

"We packed and hitched four horses to the carriage, but while we were leaving the grounds, six monstrous swans flew out of the sky and started hauling the coach into the air. Hammish just about had a heart attack, but luckily he had the presence of mind to release the horses. It took us forever to fly there, and I have to say, relieving yourself out the window of a flying coach has its thrills."

I meant to laugh, but it came out as a sigh. "Were you there? For the end?"

Antolios ran his hands through my wet hair, massaging my scalp. "Yes. The sea was rolling, and the sky was dark as night. They died well, fighting back to back, arrows singing. I killed as many of Kronos's clerics as I could, but I arrived too late. Artemis and Apollo were already covered in the sands of eternity. There wasn't anything I could do. We held each other and said good-bye."

Are they really gone? I sent.

"I don't know. Many of the gods have the sight, so I wonder how they didn't see this coming. And why now? Where did the clerics get such powerful artifacts and weapons?" Antolios shrugged against me. "I thought that maybe I was summoned to help the gods, but when I got there it felt as if I was watching a play, like maybe they knew they were going to die, and no one could stop it. They told me to not be afraid and that they loved me…."

Scrape, scrape, scrape. Antolios set aside the knife and rubbed my face down with oil.

"I'm sorry," I said softly. I dragged my arms over the side of the tub and stood up heavily. The water dripped down my stomach. "How did you get here so fast? The swans?"

"No. They aren't sentient. When Apollo died, they left. I begged a favor from Athena's owls, and we flew. I'm certain that if I were not divine, Hammish would have already strangled me in my sleep."

I stepped out of the tub and walked over to the basin, looking at Antolios's reflection in the mirror as he stood. I had forgotten how tall he was, and pale. He stepped out of the tub, his long legs flexing, and his eyes lit the stone floor in front of him. "Will you come to Seriphos with me? I have to tell my mother."

Antolios's white light hit the mirror and momentarily blinded me. "Yes."

I set my glass of whisky down and grabbed a soft towel. Antolios had cut my beard just the way I did, a short chin beard and a mustache that barely connected at the corners of my lips. My reflection looked oddly slack, as if it were made of clay and not flesh. I tried to smile at myself, but I couldn't.

A tooth stick was placed into my hand. I chewed it mechanically, watching my cheek bulge in the mirror, the spice stinging my tongue. I was handed a salt-and-herb rinse and swished it around my mouth before spitting into the basin. My spit swirled on the surface of the water just like clouds in the sky.

Antolios clasped me on the shoulder and led me out the door. The great room held heavy furniture and a dominating fireplace. There were skins and antlers and even an assortment of stuffed creatures everywhere. At the dining table was the colorful spread of food Hammish had laid out for us. I could hear the servant in one of the back rooms moving things around. Antolios gently pushed me to a seat, spooned fruits and vegetables onto a plate, and handed the plate to me along with heavy cutlery.

Outside, people were praying and conversing about the disaster of the fall of the mountain, the fall of the gods. Many were going to make a trip to see the ruins and pray. Because none of the buildings in Copper Cairns had collapsed from any of the earthquakes in the past weeks, the dwarves were boasting about superior dwarven craftsmanship.

Some thought the gods were punishing them, or had died, or had moved on to a better place, leaving the world to perish. Some said there was a battle and we won, and some said we lost. There were fights, which guards and civilians broke up.

The storm that had been raging had finally broken, and I felt drained. I could barely put food into my mouth. I glanced at Antolios, who was staring at me with those glowing eyes. "Aren't you hungry?" I said.

"I'm okay." His knee bobbed.

"Are you going to eat?"

Antolios swallowed. "Maybe."

I pushed my plate aside. "I'm done."

Antolios stood. His penis pointed up, and his balls were tight against his long shaft. "Are you sure?" It wasn't really a question because he was already pulling me toward the bedroom.

He pushed me onto the soft bed, and his lips pressed against mine. We kissed and Antolios rubbed against me, sliding our cocks together. He groaned and was already breathing heavily. His lust surged through the bond.

I had been thinking about this all week, but I was afraid to let go, worried that if I did, I'd lose control. The monster would take over, and I might hurt him, hurt us.

Antolios moved from my lips down to my neck and chest, then licked a trail to my pubis.

"Don't—" I started to say. *Don't touch it.*

"I know," Antolios said. He bit my thighs.

I closed my eyes and searched the inside of my eyelids, my arms thrown out to the side. He moved my legs apart, and I tried to relax, to keep myself in check. Antolios was going to eat my hole.

Usually called "elf play," these kinds of activities were supposedly more common among elves. But while I'd never met an elf who didn't enjoy this kind of attention, I also hadn't met any who would readily give it.

My mouth twitched. Any second now, Antolios would chastise me and order me to focus. I waited, but he didn't say anything. He just nuzzled my crotch and tickled the area between my balls and ass.

The anticipation was killing me, but I still had so many questions. If the gods saw this coming, why did they let it? Why had they been overpowered by a bunch of mortals, and where had all those weapons come from? Why had my father called on me? Why not... someone else who could have saved him?

I felt a rush of guilt. Antolios had also watched his father die, and he wasn't having a crisis about it. Then again, he had been able to say good-bye.

Was that what my father had been trying to do? Say good-bye to me? Then why had he sent me such a cryptic message if that was what he wanted? Why not just tell me? I would have gone to him if he had asked. Instead, I had watched him die.

Antolios panted between my legs and rubbed himself against the mattress. He lapped at my belly button.

I smiled. "I'm ready."

He dove onto my asshole, spreading my cheeks and working his tongue into me. I held my knees and watched, my neck craning and stomach muscles bulging. He opened his eyes and gazed at me, the white light searing away all thought.

"Oh fuck," I said in a breathy whine. A fire burned in my gut, and I groaned from the rush to my balls and cock.

Antolios writhed on the bed, working his tongue in deeper.

I gasped, my mounting ecstasy consuming me. I wasn't going to last, but I didn't care. I wanted it this way. I flexed my legs around Antolios's head, and dug my hands into his soft curls.

My body began to pulse. It wasn't... unpleasant, exactly. It throbbed achingly—strange but sort of nice. My heart pounded, and sweat poured through my open pores. I didn't feel right, but at the same time I felt *so* right.

"Gods!" I squeezed Antolios's face into my ass. He made sexy wet moans, his head flushed between my legs. The feeling intensified, getting hotter and hotter. The heat spread all the way to the roots of my hair. I dripped sweat and rocked into Antolios's face. I couldn't even feel him in our bond, I was so overwhelmed. Grunts came out of my mouth that I didn't recognize as my own, and I couldn't take it anymore.

Waves of pleasure and pain crashed into my body as if I were coming, but I wasn't. I climbed even higher. I strained out a noise from my depths as my body seized. Even my teeth buzzed, and my back popped.

Finally I crashed and came, my pulse thudding in my ears. Semen sprayed my hair. I tried to laugh but choked. Wave after wave of ejaculate splattered my chin and chest. My cock kept jerking, and tears leaked down my face.

Boneless, I flopped back. Antolios was still slurping at my crack and balls. I closed my eyes and breathed. "Holy fuck, what was that? I love you," I whispered. I was still feeling that weird ache sending waves of heat through my body. I shivered from lying in the humid sheets.

Antolios hurriedly got off the bed and grabbed a jar of oil from his pack. He rubbed it on his stiff cock, hands almost shaking, and I spread my legs wider. He crushed me with his weight and shoved his cock into me. He was burning up.

I groaned as my body shook with sympathetic waves of pleasure. Those waves hit me again, becoming even more intense. Antolios ravaged me, thrusting deep and hard and fast. I lifted my pelvis up to take him and wrapped my legs around his waist, bucking him into me.

Antolios grunted and jerked, filling me. I cried out, and my cock grew hot and heavy. He slumped over me, and we both panted, him from spent pleasure and me from growing desire. We smelled musky and briny.

"How do you stand it?" Antolios licked my chin clean of come.

I sighed and rubbed his sweaty back. "I try not to let it get this bad."

Antolios pulled himself up on shaky elbows and kissed me hard on the lips, his mouth smearing me with the almost too sweet smell of my ass. "I love you."

I smiled. "I love you too."

Antolios glanced between our bodies. "You're still hard."

I pulled him closer. "We can go again when you're ready." I was still in control, not letting the hunger get to me. Things had always been easier with Antolios. Being with him, I almost forgot I had a curse.

"Shh, shh," Antolios said. He pulled back and ran his hand along my cheek. "Let me take care of you." He reached down and gripped me tightly.

My back arched, and I thrust into his hand, growling. "No, no, no," I groaned.

Antolios straddled me and picked up the bottle of oil, spilling some of it into his palm. He met my gaze. "You can't hurt me."

I thrust my cock into his wet hand.

"Let me take care of you." He slid onto me, and the heat from his ass set my gut and cock on fire. I couldn't speak as our love blazed through me.

We came as the stars exploded, hot and wild and forever.

CHAPTER TWENTY-TWO

I GAZED out the window of the coach. We hit another hole in the road, and I rocked into the wall, my head nearly striking the edge of the window. Antolios's hand was motionless on my thigh, and his emotions through the bond were steady and peaceful.

I watched the coastal farms roll by. Everything looked the same. I couldn't believe it. With the Olympians dead, I expected something to break. But the sun rose, the crops grew, and the people went about their world as they always had. None of the other gods had taken up the throne, so how was everything the same? How could the world be godless and still turn?

Antolios slid his hand up my thigh, and I turned from the window to smile at him.

"I'm okay," I said.

His eyes shone into mine, the light attempting to chase away all the shadows of my thoughts. He bent his head, and our lips brushed. I lifted my arms, tangling my fingers in his hair. I clung to him, but I knew it couldn't last. Pulling him closer, I mashed our mouths together.

Maybe the world hadn't ended, but this would. It always did.

IT WAS weeks later in the evening when we finally rolled into Seriphos, the columned buildings tall and white and familiar, and turned down the road toward Danae's Academy. We sat in our sweaty tunics in the heat. Whatever my father had done with the weather had impacted the entire continent, perhaps the entire world. It may take some time for the weather to balance.

I popped my knuckles and bobbed my foot. My mother's balcony came into view as well as the path I had taken to the beach every day when I was young, where I had spent most of my time playing. On that field just before the stairs down to the beach, my father used to meet me and lift me into the storms when I was a child. I had lived for those moments.

I didn't see Galen when I stepped out, but he had been old when I had lived here. I was soggy and travel worn when I asked the doorman if he would have Princess Danae summoned for me.

The doorman flicked his gaze up and down my outfit, no sandals and a simple linen tunic, and sneered. "May I ask who is calling?"

"Tell her it's Perseus, Son of Zeus." That last bit probably hadn't been necessary, but it certainly made the doorman's eyes protrude nicely and sent him scrambling on his way.

Antolios and I waited in the large reception hall. A throng of children ran through the main doors and back halls, heading straight for the mess. It was time for the midday meal. In the sea of sweat and dirt odors, I caught a whiff of jasmine and pomegranate.

My mother glided down the hall from the back. Her hair was streaked with gray, and she had wrinkles around her kohl-lined dark brown eyes. She was still beautiful.

I shifted as she got closer. "*Mitéra—*"

Before I could get the rest of my words out, she had me in a fierce hug, wrapping her slender arms around me. She pressed her head to my shoulder, and I slowly put my arms around her waist. I tried to remember the last time she had hugged me, but I couldn't. We stayed in our embrace for a long time, her hands patting me as though she didn't know whether I was real or whether I'd leave again if she let me go.

Finally she pulled away, her eyes wet. She wiped them hastily. "Perseus, I'm so glad to see you. How long are you going to stay?"

I can stay for a while, Antolios said in my head.

"A couple of weeks," I said to her.

She beamed up at me and stood on her toes, kissing both of my cheeks. Then she seemed to notice Antolios for the first time and bowed to him. "Prince Antolios, it's wonderful to see you."

Antolios bowed. "And you as well, Princess Danae."

She smiled and reached out her hands, pulling him toward her and kissing him on his cheeks. He had to bend nearly in half. Her eyes filled again. "Would an early supper be all right with you both?"

"That would be fine." I shifted my weight from side to side, and tried to take comfort in the familiarity, but nothing felt right.

She dabbed her eyes. "Your rooms are just as you left them, Perseus. I'll see you at supper. Please excuse me." My mother gave me a last smile and turned away, hurrying toward her apartment.

My rooms were exactly as I remembered them, all my clothes still scattered about, though the bed linens had been changed and there wasn't a speck of dust. How long had my mother been having servants clean my room? I picked my armor up off the floor. For fun I tried it on, but the chest piece wouldn't close. I idly put things away, the way I would in my own home, but I felt out of place. Antolios had not followed me to my rooms, and even though he had probably been attempting to give me some space, I felt like we were students again, hiding from everyone.

I had my travel clothes laundered, but I found some older chitons and a cape. They seemed to fit well enough. Sitting on my bed, I fingered a golden princely circlet. After a time, I placed it on my head and went down for supper.

Antolios was already on the terrace, drinking wine and eating olives. I sat next to him and brushed his leg with mine. He smiled at me, encouraging, and I tried to smile back. This conversation was going to be unpleasant, and I was glad that he was with me.

The sun was at the west, lowering over the horizon, but it was still hot. I had thought that after Mount Olympus, I'd never stop shivering, but now I'd never stop sweating. We were served iced water with lemons. The ice was cut in chunks. The old mage I had known as a child must not work for my mother anymore. I missed the shapes she used to make.

My mother came onto the balcony, wearing light linen instead of her satin or silks. We had a pleasant supper, chatting about inane things such as the weather and who still worked at the academy.

I held a spoon over a bowl of frozen fruit dessert and cleared my throat. "Mitéra, there is something I have to tell you." My mother's face fell, and I knew that she knew. "Zeus, and possibly all the gods, have been slain."

"I know," she said quietly. "I'm glad that you are alive and well. I was worried." My mother gazed out over the ocean. "Over a month ago a few of our older students were called away due to mysterious family affairs. Not unheard of, but it was strange that they happened all at once. Then the temple at Delos crumbled, and part of the coastal region fell into the sea. Laconia flooded, and Mount Olympus collapsed." Her voice became soft. "Your father would not answer my prayers, and the clerics lost touch with the gods. Many heroes were reported dead or missing. I feared for you."

She stood suddenly and reached over, pulling me into her arms. I held her, still shocked that she would hug me in front of company. She cradled my head. "I'm sorry, Perseus. I know your father wasn't the most attentive, but he did love you. He would tell me so."

My heart clenched.

Eyes bright with tears, she kissed my cheek. "Will you say something at the funeral?"

I nodded. My mother smiled and then excused herself again. Antolios and I stood, but she was already gone.

IN THE morning, Antolios and I cleaned up and met my mother for a private breakfast. She seemed much recovered, smiling with her salt-streaked hair neatly pulled back into a bun, and wearing a rainbow of jewels. We discussed business and preparations for the funeral, and when a servant handed my mother scrolls to order supplies, she passed the forms to me to complete. She told me that King Acrisius was old, and she wasn't certain how much longer he would live.

I had given this some consideration. We talked about me taking a princelier role now that Hera wasn't trying to make my life miserable or kill me. All three of us conveniently avoided the real reason why I had put myself in exile, and in a way I was grateful, but I was also disappointed. It made everything I had done seem meaningless. But wasn't it? I had acted as a child and run away when I could have stayed or could have even chased Antolios down and made him be with me. I knew he loved me now, but I guess I hadn't known if he truly loved me then. He had left.

Antolios jerked and glanced away, and my cheeks grew warm. He wasn't often bothered by the randomness in my head, but he wasn't immune to feelings. I wanted to hold his hand; however, I knew he wouldn't let me.

When I turned my attention back to my mother, she was watching me, her brow furrowed. My gaze darted toward the exits, but there was no easy way out, so I crossed my arms over my chest and hunched in my seat.

Her lips quirked at the corner and she turned away. "Antolios, how are your children?"

I almost sighed with relief. Better him than me.

"I have nine now. All girls."

I chuckled, and my mother's eyes opened wide. "Nine!" she said. She peppered him with questions about their ages and hobbies, but her gaze kept flicking back to me, and I shifted uncomfortably.

She turned to me expectantly. "And you, Perseus? Are you alone in Delos?"

"Mitéra... I rescued a Cretan princess over ten years ago and married her."

My mother carefully mentioned that she had heard the tale but urged me to continue.

"I have five children, a sixth on the way. Four boys and one girl."

My mother's face bloomed with happiness, and then fell. She put a hand over her eyes, and I tried to go to her, but she waved me back down. She smeared her kohl as she dabbed her face with a napkin. Her voice cracked with emotion. "May I see them?"

"Of course," I said. Unfortunately she cried harder, but we made plans to go to Delos after the funeral. Even though she had cried more in the last day than I had ever seen in my entire life, she was still handling this better than Andromeda's parents had, when she and I had finally traveled back to their palace to let them know she was still alive and well.

The rest of breakfast progressed smoothly enough. Then Antolios and I slipped away and went swimming, finding all of our old favorite spots and making new memories in them.

AFTER ZEUS'S funeral, and the night before my mother and I traveled to Delos, Antolios and I made love until dawn, until we could barely lift a finger. When it was time for him to leave, we held each other in the chariot port, his black coach ready to take him to Pelion.

I stood on my toes and whispered in his ear. "I want to go with you."

"You have to go back to your family, and I have to go back to mine."

"I can move us to Thessaly. Maybe we can marry Perses to one of your daughters."

Antolios smoothed my hair, and I smashed my face into his chest. "I liked your hair longer," he said.

I breathed in the scent of him and sighed. "I'll grow it out."

"You know, betrothing Perses to one of my girls is a good idea. Why didn't I think of that?" He kissed my head. "The next time you come up to Thessaly, bring him along, and we'll see if any of them fancy him. He's your son, so knowing my luck they'll *all* fancy him."

I kissed Antolios's chin, tears falling down my face.

"Shh." He brushed away my tears. "Soon you will be a king in Argos, and we'll practically be neighbors. We'll have so many reasons to be close."

I nodded and squeezed Antolios with another hug. This was what we had. I gazed after him as he rolled away and then turned back to the house.

My mother was watching me from her balcony.

ANDROMEDA LAY on the bed with our baby, Mestor, in her arms. Born the night before, he was my sixth child. I stood at the foot of the bed, while my mother sat in a plush chair, pushed right up to the side. She had stayed in Delos for over a month so she could be around for this, but she had to leave soon.

Mestor gurgled, and my mother and wife laughed.

Andromeda rocked him. "He came out with only two pushes. We didn't even need a cleric or a midwife." She blushed. "We have become experts at having babies."

My mother beamed. "Good. Having babies should be a labor of love, but that doesn't mean it should be hard." She smoothed the downy hair on Mestor's head. "As you've probably heard, I was an only child, and when my father consulted an oracle to see if he would ever have a male heir to take his throne, the oracle told him he would, but his heir would kill him."

Andromeda smiled, her brown eyes wide and reflecting the weak morning sun from the windows. Of course she had heard this story before—it was legend. I frowned and blew away the rest of the fog of the morning so that it would be warm enough in the room. Just a little change, nothing that would unbalance the weather.

My mother sighed. "He locked me in a bronze tower with one of my handmaidens so I would never have a child. I was there for months, with nothing to do but read. The only opening was an oculus in the ceiling."

"How awful," Andromeda murmured.

My mother nodded but then smiled. "And then one night Zeus came to me, the king of the gods." She trailed off and stared at the wall.

Andromeda winked, and I shifted uncomfortably. Did I look like that when I thought of Hermes? Probably not.

Shaking herself, my mother laughed. "And nine months later, Perseus was born. I labored for hours and hours, and finally Zeus arrived for his delivery. In a shower of light, he whisked him up and handed him to me. Perseus's eyes were stormy gray when he came out, but Zeus put his hand on his head, and they turned sky blue."

Andromeda smiled and shifted Mestor in her arms.

My mother shrugged. "Then my father saw that I had a son, and the next day he banished us to Seriphos."

"That sounds horrible," Andromeda said.

"Such is the way of mortals and gods," my mother said.

Andromeda yawned, and I stirred and walked to the side of the bed. "Mitéra, why don't we go for a walk? My wife and infant are tired." I gave Andromeda and the baby loving pecks and then strode into the orchard from the patio.

My mother joined me through the gnarled olive trees. The wind made the branches tremble and sigh as the white gulls called and the ocean crashed. I could sense that when winter came it was going to hit all at once.

"You know," my mother said, "when you and Antolios showed up at the house together, I thought you were a couple. You were very cute when you were children."

"What?" I peered at her, but she just smiled. "We were men, Mitéra, very manly, and not really that cute."

"Right, right, that's what I meant. Manly. Antolios is so much taller than you, and you held hands everywhere. After seeing you with each other, I thought… well, I don't know what I thought."

"Antolios is taller than *everybody*, Mitéra." I tried to grin, but she stared at me, unsmiling, and eventually I dropped it and shook my head. "I love my family, Mitéra."

"I know." My mother halted. "I wish you would call me Mama, as your children call their mother."

To further my shock, she pulled my head down to her lips, kissing me on the hairline. I was baffled, but I slowly put my arms around her slender waist. "Don't misunderstand, but what is the cause of this?"

My mother pulled back, smiling sadly. "Something I learned while you were away. Your father always asked that I not mother you too much and to treat you as a man so that you would become great and strong. Who was I to argue with him?" My mother clucked. "I should have been listening to my gut. When you left all those years ago, I found myself truly alone, with only my worry and regret for company.

"This," she gestured all around her, "is more than I could have hoped for. I know your father didn't speak to you often, but he told me that he was proud of you. I just want you to know that whatever you choose, I'll be proud of you too." She gave me a kiss on the chin and then continued down the grove.

I stared after her for a long minute and then jogged to catch up.

Chapter Twenty-Three

"Baba! Baba!"

I set the last barrel of wine into a client's cart and squinted up, wiping a sweaty lock of hair from my eyes.

Gorgophone ran toward me. Behind her trailed my other children. She reached me first, and breathlessly said, "There are soldiers, Baba, who want to speak with you."

I gave my clients a final handshake and thanked them for coming. I signaled Franko to finish up, and he nodded at me under a wide-brimmed hat. I turned back to my daughter. "Well, Slayer, let's not keep them waiting."

I jogged through the orchard with my children, and they laughed and ran in and out through the olive trees. When we got to the house, I strode through the back door but didn't hear it shut behind me. Glancing over my shoulder, I could see four heads peeking through the crack. I mouthed, "Go play," and the door closed.

I came out of the hall and into the great room. Andromeda was serving goat cheese and bread to a group of silver-armored men. They wore the silver-and-blue tabards of Epiro draped over their cuirasses. A man with a bit of a belly and a bushy brown beard stepped forward. "Hail, Perseus, Son of Zeus."

I shook his hand. "Welcome to my home."

"I am Bakios, a son of King Demetre, and this is my brother Dynios," he said.

I shook everyone's hands, my eyebrows climbing. Bakios and Dynios were two of the king's favored sons. King Demetre, another son of Zeus, was 120 years old and had been ruling for longer than most could remember, except the elves. He had never married, and while there had been stability with him on the throne, his death would undoubtedly lead to a civil war. His bastard children—over a hundred of them—had divided into factions, and it was unheard of to see two of them working this closely together.

But here they were.

Andromeda handed me a cool glass of tea, and I drank and waited patiently. Dynios stood by Bakios's side, glowering and silent.

Bakios coughed. "Perseus, we need to speak to you." His eyes darted to Andromeda. "Perhaps there is somewhere more private that we could discuss business?"

I had a retort on my tongue, but Andromeda announced that she was leaving, sparing me. She left the pitcher out and pattered away. I poured myself another cup.

"There have been rumors that you were there for the fall of Mount Olympus. Is this true?" Bakios said.

"It is." My words were followed by the sounds of armor shifting.

"Then you know that the gods are dead," Bakios said. "There has been an unsettling of the peace among the kingdoms. The gods are no longer taking sides, and there will be war."

I nodded.

Bakios seemed a little surprised at my nonchalant response, and he cleared his throat again. I almost suggested that one of my clerics look at that cough for him. "Epiro would be in your debt if you lead one of its armies in the struggle to defend our borders. As we speak, Kings Titos and Butades send their ships to our shores. The White Queen of Thessaly seeks to cut a path through Argos to Epiro."

The room quieted as I stared at them.

Bakios cleared his throat and hurriedly said, "It is known that you are the sole heir to the throne of Argos, but the king will not hold that against you. This is as much your land as it is ours. We consider you an Epirote by soul if not by birth."

I covered my expression by drinking more tea.

He was starting to sweat. "We will, of course, compensate you throughout your service. You will have your own army and be answerable only to the king, and we will provide you with your own staff, supplemented with horses and chariots. Lastly, if you join this war, your legend will become greater than it already is, told forever to children as a bedtime story. This war will be remembered throughout history."

All the men stood a little taller, and Bakios clapped his hands. Two of the men hustled out the front door and came back lugging a chest. They threw it open, displaying gold and jewels.

"This is a token of the king's appreciation for simply hearing us out today. There will be many more riches if you decide to fight for us. We will pay you seasonally, plus whatever you capture as your spoils. Treasure, as well as other treasures." Bakios chuckled, and the other men laughed.

Bakios searched my face but apparently didn't see the reaction he'd been looking for. He frowned slightly. "The king is not insensitive to the fact that you are an Argive by birth, and I am told to say that he will not ask you to fight against them. We would place you along the southern coasts to defend our shores, your home, against any ships that get past our fleet. For any other assurances and terms, the king has asked you to see him personally in Ilium."

I set down my glass, feeling overwhelmed. I had guessed that there would be a power struggle, but so soon? And involving all of Greece? Well, the entire world would probably reel from the loss of the gods. "I request a night to consider," I said.

We agreed that I would meet them at Delos's docks at noon the next day with my decision. I kicked the chest closed, sat on the lid, and put my chin in my fist. Alive, the gods had incited war, and in death they did as well. There was no escape.

Truthfully, I didn't give a shit about fighting against Argos. I was exiled and had never seen my grandfather or touched Argive soil. When I visited Thessaly, I had to ride through the mountains of Arcadia to avoid entering Argos. I didn't even want to be king, but the excuse might get me out of fighting in the north—where Antolios would be.

I could refuse. I had come home with the expectation of being a farmer again, no gods to tell me otherwise. But Epiro's shores were threatened. Ships would come, with their red-and-gold, and black-and-white sails. Elean and Laconian soldiers would invade my farm. I shivered as I imagined them stalking up to my house, murdering my sons, and taking my wife and daughter.

I didn't really have a choice. I rose to find Andromeda.

IN THE dark of morning, we arrived by ship at the port of Ilium. I had passed through it before, but I had forgotten how large it was. The city by the port stretched all the way to the capital. We took coaches and slowly rode throughout the day and night until it became dark morning again.

The palace sat atop a hill with a ring of ornate pillars that flashed golden in the torch light. The gates were staffed by stiff soldiers who scrutinized each one of us before they allowed the coaches pass. I was led along with my officers through the large gilded main doors and an opulent vestibule. Gold lightning-bolt accents were everywhere, even on the door handles. We were deposited into a waiting room and told to refresh ourselves.

Thom and Kell helped themselves to the snacks on a table. I had appointed them as my lesser officers when they had expressed interest in joining the war, but I had been surprised to learn Thom had been in the army before, on another continent. He had left Galway because he hated it and had hopped a ship to Greece, but he reasoned that fighting for me would be better than working at the docks and he could help me keep an eye on Kell. Vano would kill me if anything happened to either of them.

I stood next to Kell and Thom as they shoved olives and fruit onto their plates. "Why didn't Chris join? Where is he?" I said. "Joining the army seems like the kind of harebrained thing he would do."

Kell grinned, his mouth mostly full of figs. "Chris found a girl."

My eyes widened. "I was only gone for a few months! Wait… a real girl, or did he finally get one of his automatons to suck his cock?"

Kell swallowed his mouthful and smirked. "She's nobility."

"And a dwarf." Thom fingered his mustache. "She convinced him to look up his parentage, and apparently we were right. He's half-dwarf *and* from a noble family in Thessaly."

I gaped. "No shit?"

"Aye, apparently his clan was nearly wiped out by giants when he was a baby, and he was sent to live with his human relatives in Thessaly. They died of some kind of disease, except Chris, and he was put into an orphanage. This girl happens to be of the family who knew his dwarven ancestors, and they're going to get married."

"I wasn't gone that long!"

"Well, the end of the world will do that to people," Kell said.

Just as Thom opened his mouth, a guard marched through the door. "Perseus, Son of Zeus, please follow me."

I shrugged at my friends and strode after the guard, following him back into the vestibule and up a large carpeted staircase. At the end of another hall, we pushed through a set of grand double doors. Our sandals slapped against the marble floor, and torches flickered light off the white walls, illuminating frescoes and the busts of deities.

When we neared another set of double doors, the guard put his finger to his lips, signaling me to be quiet. Inside was another series of halls, and finally I was guided into a waiting area. At this point I was so turned around, I didn't think I could get myself back.

"The king will be with you shortly," the guard whispered. I nodded my thanks, but he gave me an odd look and then scurried away with his head down.

I wandered the large room, mostly empty aside from art and chairs. I walked aimlessly, pausing in front of paintings but not seeing them. King Demetre's power was metal manipulation. He had created the famous golden dome and the encircling pillars of the palace, and I assumed he had done most of the metalwork inside as well. He was one of the longest-lived demigods, but that wasn't saying much for our kind. Most of us died young in battle.

I paused. The sound of moaning reached me from a few doors down… moans punctuated with the occasional scream and slap. I cleaned my nails to the rising dissonance.

The voices died to whimpers, and a door opened and shut down the hall. I stood up straighter and faced the door where the footsteps approached.

King Demetre surged through, smiling. "Perseus, my boy!"

It struck me how much he looked like our father, with his blue eyes and pinker complexion, except that he was wirier, and his hair was more salt-and-pepper, not white. The hair on his chin was gray.

I dropped to my knee and bowed my head. "My king."

Footsteps came closer, and a bejeweled hand came into view. I paused and grew flustered. Demetre had not washed his hands… after. Had someone with lesser senses done this, I would have discounted it, but Demetre was a demigod. He knew I could smell them.

I kissed my brother's hand.

Demetre made a soft, pleased sound deep in his throat and then moved away. "Come, Perseus."

I rose and followed him, my brain unhelpfully sorting through all the scent information.

Demetre led us into another hallway and through a set of carved doors. Plush furniture and small tables dotted the room. The king took the biggest, softest chair and motioned for me to sit next to him. Servants rushed in and set a platter between us. He held out a hand, and a drink was placed into it. I was handed a stiff drink as well, even though it was early morning. The smell of dwarven whisky burned away the smell of sex in my nose.

We drank in silence for a bit and then were set up with a hot breakfast. Demetre plowed through meats, eggs, fish, and fruit, belying his thin figure. I picked at my breakfast. He asked me how the trip had gone, and I inquired about some of the art in the palace.

Demetre finished his breakfast and lit a pipe. "Did you know, little brother, that I have been following your exploits with interest for quite some time?"

I became uneasy, remembering what Antolios had told me. "Yes?"

"I have. Unfortunately, your mother never wanted us to meet." The king chuckled. "Did you get my presents?"

I frowned. "Presents?"

"As sons of Zeus we have certain appetites."

"Ah, those presents," I said. "I did. Thank you, sir."

Demetre had given me two bed slaves, Aiden and Ava. Apparently they didn't appreciate the term "slave" and insisted that I refer to them as "courtesans," but from what I could understand it was the same thing. It was an unusual gift, but then again, he had given me Sarah and Marta when I was a boy. And these courtesans were probably also his spies.

"I have another present for you," Demetre said.

I raised my brow as he clapped his hands, and a stand was rolled in. It had a canvas over it, and when the servants pulled it away, it revealed a beautiful set of armor.

Demetre was grinning. "I made it myself."

My jaw dropped, and I stood and ran my fingers over the seamless engravings. There were silver lightning bolts sewn into the leather flaps flaring from the cuirass and along the trim. A storm was embossed on the front, the jewels sparkling through the clouds. The metals *swirled* together. "You made this…."

Demetre chuckled, clearly pleased with my reaction. "I enjoy building things with my power."

"The details are incredible." I smiled at him. "Thank you, sir."

"As my brother, you deserve it." The king took a puff of his pipe. "Perseus, a son of Zeus and grandson to King Acrisius. Acrisius is a fool for casting you aside. Perhaps he would be dead by now, but no one is certain with prophecy. And now you're mine." He waved a hand at me. "Yes, yes. I understand you don't wish to march on Argos, and I have no problems with that. My armies are spread wide. I command demigods that you haven't met yet, not to mention my sons and daughters. I will not need you in the north, and you will be plenty busy in the south.

"I do have a request for a bit of information, if you have it. Queen Cora rules Thessaly, and I know she has major plans for Argos. Whether her plans stray into Epiro, I am not certain. Her consort is the general of her armies, a son of Apollo. Those who have seen him fight say that he does not lift a finger, and men simply fall before him." The king flashed his gaze to me. "Have you heard anything?"

I covered my gulp with a swig of whisky and almost coughed as the burning liquid went down my throat. This was a test. Hadn't Antolios warned me about this, years ago? I took another drink, pretending that I was trying to recall some unimportant detail. I shrugged. "I attended the academy with a son of Apollo, but I didn't think him remarkable in any way."

Demetre sat back and pursed his lips.

I gave him a lecherous grin. "I fucked him, of course."

Demetre's face split into a smile.

"But he was a loner and a misfit. Weird eyes."

Demetre laughed but then scowled, flopping back into his chair. "By Zeus's beard, he remains an enigma! I can't abide not knowing what I'm up against, and my sources have been less than reliable with him…."

"I guess we'll find out," I said.

"I suppose you're right." He blew out a few perfect smoke rings. "If the Thessalians do make it to Epiro, then I will summon you to fight."

Sweat prickled under my arms and at my nape.

Demetre asked me more questions about my old schoolmates, especially Zoticus and Palamedes. I told him what he already knew, that Palamedes was gifted with the knowledge of weaponry, and Zoticus was strong as a giant.

"Laconia and Elis have warred for centuries," Demetre said. "They have sunk enough ships that you can walk from one island to the other without getting your feet wet. Despite this, my sources tell me that the two heroes lead their armies *together*."

I laughed. "Zoticus and Palamedes? Laconia and Elis? I don't believe it."

Demetre shrugged. "That is what I am told."

"No offense, sir, but your sources are gathering rumors, and bad ones at that. I know the both of them, and if given the opportunity they would kill each other. They were never friendly at the academy, and Palamedes does not play well with others," I said.

"As you say." He cocked a brow. "I heard what happened at Mount Olympus. I saw the damage myself."

I took another swig of my drink. "I'm sorry about our father."

Demetre shook his head. "I'm not blaming you for his death. The gods destroyed themselves." He chuckled. "Bringing the whole top of the mountain down? Well, that's one way to stop the Titans."

"I'm here to help defend Epiro for the Epirotes," I said, perhaps too harshly. "I will fight, sir, but I am not a tool of destruction. I do not wish to bring down another mountain."

The king's chuckle rolled into booming laughter. "We are all tools of destruction, Perseus. Why do you think the gods bred with humans?"

I STOOD in the sands on the coast of Mycenae, facing the ocean and the Elean army. It was cold, my breath coming out in puffs of white, and my fingers and toes were numb.

We waited for the horns and drums to begin.

The Epirotes had already spread out in a wave of light blue tabards. I had been told that I would be fighting Apasia, a daughter of Atlas. She was known for manipulating water and was a favorite of the Eleans. My primary job was to eliminate her.

I glanced at Kell, who looked as if he was going to shake apart, pasty and sweating. Thom was eyeing him worriedly too and slipped a flask into Kell's quaking hands. Kell smiled haltingly and drank hard, spilling some down his chin, before handing it back to Thom, who passed it on to the next soldier.

"Kell?" Thom said.

Kell moped up the sweat that was leaking from under his leather helm. "Aye?"

"If you're going to vomit, you better do it now. It's messier when you do it into sloppy corpse cavities." He grinned and fingered his mustache.

Kell turned green and swallowed.

"Hey, Kell." I handed him my helm. "You can wear this or vomit in it. I don't care. It's yours."

Kell took it from me, his brown eyes lighting up. "Don't you want it?"

"I hate wearing helms."

"That doesn't sound safe, but I suppose your head is made of bricks." He pulled his off, pushed the golden horse-haired one on, and gave Thom a thumbs-up. "How do I look?"

Thom smiled.

"So," I said, "are you all ready?"

Kell nodded, holding his spear, and Thom gripped his sword.

I stoked the storm, the darkness covering the beach. The Eleans were waiting for us near the water, and somewhere in that throng of red and gold was Apasia.

A breeze kicked up, and I created friction. Thunder rolled.

The drums and horns sounded, and all the troops yelled and marched out.

Taking the lead, I sprinted toward the Elean force, down the dunes to the sea. Soon the two armies collided with clashes, bangs, and the whistles of arrows and spells, and the ranks crumbled. There was no sign of Apasia, but the ocean boiled as if someone had filled it with snakes.

I dropped a cyclone on my head and had it lift me into the air. My hair and tunic whipped wildly about, and I lost one sandal that hadn't been properly fastened. Anyone who got too near the base of the cyclone was tossed aside, and when I moved into the middle of the Elean army, I rained down lightning into their ranks, hoping to bring Apasia out to play.

Through the whipping winds, the screams reached me as the first bolts hit. Arrows couldn't touch me, and neither could fire or ice bolts from the mages, but arcane shots were getting through. I had to dodge those. I should have had a group of mages and clerics following me, despelling these kinds of attacks, but I had taken off without warning, so it didn't surprise me that they hadn't caught up yet.

A large globe of water shot toward me from the ground, and my twister ate the water and sprayed me with it. The water was sucked away again, and then I saw her. The figure was wearing armor and the red and gold of Elis. Not a mage. Apasia was standing with a spear in her hand, and balls of water orbited her.

I threw a bolt at her and then shot lightning from the sky for good measure. She somersaulted around my bolts and stretched her heavy globes of water around herself as a shield, protecting her from the electricity. Somehow, the water's duality and her power were deterring the path of my attacks.

Damn inconvenient. I lowered myself to the ground and drew my sword. Spells flashed back and forth, the bright flares blinking across the beach, but most soldiers were watching the two of us, spreading into a widening circle.

I hit the dirt and released the cyclone. I called down another bolt from the sky, directing it at Apasia. She quickly manipulated another thick shield of water before her and ducked.

Now that I was close enough, I could see how young she was. She was dark tan, and as with all demigods, her skin nearly glowed with vitality and strength. Helmless, her dark brown hair spilled over her shoulders, her simple cuirass did not stretch completely over her breasts, and her arm bands and leg braces were flashy but too small, making her outfit more of a short dress than anything useful in battle.

Did she want to die?

She tossed a volley of water at me as she flipped and landed, but I swept my arm and blew it away with a great blast of wind. We sized each other up and then charged, and before I could blink, our weapons rang together.

Apasia thrust her spear at my head, but I parried it and punched her with my other hand. She staggered back, blood dripping from her perfect nose, and pulled the water around her. I stabbed through it with my sword, but the water surged and wrapped around my blade, almost yanking it out of my hands.

I kicked up the wind, hot and cold swirling around me as my ears popped. I pushed. Water blew away from Apasia as the force gained momentum, and she jabbed her spear into the ground but stumbled. She slipped backward in the dirt, eyes wide, and kept trying to anchor herself, but she soon fell to her knees and tumbled back.

I ran after her, partly sucked forward by my own current.

Digging gouges in the earth with her hands and feet, she attempted to slow her slide. Her dark gaze flicked around as she tried to get her bearings.

I ran down the slopes toward the ocean. A lone tree stood flapping in the gale, and Apasia hit it and wrapped around the trunk. Her muscles knotted as she struggled to stand.

I gained on her, raising my sword, and dropped the winds. She slumped, momentarily registering relief, and then gathered herself for action. Before she could rise, I hacked my blade down through her skull, splitting her face. Her hair was tangled and crusted with sand, and it was hard to see her eyes, but I sensed her go deathly still. I heard her last breath.

Darkness loomed above, and I recognized the roar of the ocean, only it was too close. I heard cries from the beach as sprinkles of water dropped on my head, and glanced up as I pulled the sword from her skull.

A large wall of water crashed upon me.

The impact smashed me into the sand and scraped my face raw. The wave dragged me out to sea as I struggled with the tide, trying to anchor myself. At first it did nothing, but I gradually slowed and then took a great breath. I couldn't scramble to my feet before the cold water came rushing back.

Another wave hit me and spun me about. I held on to my blade, my arms burning, but I had lost the shield off my back. My armor was heavy and ungainly. As the wave flowed back to sea again, I planted my feet under me and charged toward the shore.

Breathless, sandy, and sore, I stumbled to the beach and watched as the Elean ships bobbed in the swells. Some had capsized. My face burned where the sand had scraped me, and I needed a heal, but my team of clerics were on the other side of the battlefield, and the Eleans were still fighting even though Apasia had been slain.

I set my mouth into a grim line and stalked back into combat.

It was our first battle, so the fighting lasted well into the night. When the Eleans had finally backed down, both sides piled up the looted bodies and retrieved their dead to burn. I had a piece of an arrow removed from my calf, and my sword arm despelled of frost from an ice bolt.

Carts of dirtied dead Epirotes rolled past me to the tents. We burned them, and the men honored the dead and our victory with their song. Kell seemed greatly recovered, painted in blood and grinning. Thom slapped his shoulder companionably every few minutes and told me how well he had done.

Thom palmed Kell's messy brown hair and pulled Kell up to his face, suddenly serious in the way that only drunks can get. "But, Kell," he said, "you don't need to stab a man thirty times to kill him. Remember that."

Kell nodded, and Thom laughed and slapped him on the shoulder again, quaffing back more mead. We were running out of mead sooner than I had thought, and I was going to have to put a limit on how much the men could drink, but this was the first battle, so I let them all have their fun.

In the morning we were called to battle again by the Eleans, who had regrouped. Without a demigod to fight for them, our forces tore through their ranks. We stopped warring sooner that day, people less eager to fight and more eager to eat supper.

At the end of the week, our death toll was far less than the Eleans', and I sent a letter to the king informing him of our progress.

Part Four
Fate

CHAPTER TWENTY-FOUR

Seven years later

MY SWORD slid through the kid's neck. The demigod didn't break eye contact with me, and he didn't cry out. His boyish face went slack, and he was gone, his hands dropping from my blade.

All at once the bees and ants and birds stopped biting at me and mostly scattered. I threw my weapons to the ground and stripped, dancing and slapping at my skin. Shrieking, I kicked at a mangy skunk that wasn't moving away fast enough for my liking.

I was covered in angry red marks, from pecks on my skull to scratches on my legs. But the bites on my crotch were the worst. Still cursing and gyrating, I didn't notice my team of clerics and mages until they came out from the trees and approached me. They giggled, and I glared, but eventually they healed me of my wounds and poisons.

I sagged from relief and then eyed my clothes. I considered not putting them on, but we had to chase the Eleans out of the woods, and so before I donned the uniform again, I inspected each piece carefully. Someone looted the kid, and we headed out. I missed my own children, and here I was, slaying other people's.

I had gotten to see my children, but not often. I hadn't even met my eighth child, Sthenelus. Andromeda assured me that his birth had been easy—he had nearly fallen out as she was getting out of bed to summon the midwife. I had a second daughter, too, but I hadn't been there for her birth either.

The Eleans retreated, and I rode a cyclone back to camp as our dead were gathered to be burned.

Reports had been coming in that the situation in Argos was dire. King Acrisius might lose the coastline, and if he didn't pull out of the fight soon, he was going to lose the capital. Thessaly had blazed its way south along the coast of Argos as Epiro worked north, but both Laconia and Elis had well-defended ports and prevented anyone from gaining ground. Every new soldier headed to the Trench, as everyone was calling it.

I lay awake at night, fearing what I knew was to come. *Soon.*

I RECEIVED the summons I had been dreading from the king. I took over half my army, everyone I could spare, and left a few of my officers behind, including Thom and Kell. Argos had officially pulled out of the Trench, and since the elves had mostly stayed out of the fighting, King Rumdal of Arcadia had signed a peace treaty with Argos.

My army and I first marched to Delos. Before catching a ship from there, I spent a night with my family. I hardly recognized the house and farm. Andromeda had to tell Autokthe who I was, and my heart felt heavy with lead.

That night I made love to my wife. She wanted another baby. I went along with it, but part of me wanted to spill my seed on the floor. I didn't want to be a stranger to my children, and as long as I fought in this war I would be.

I left on a ship to Ilium the next day, and several days later the king and I stood in a room with a map of Greece on a table and an enlarged map of the Trench on another.

Demetre wasted no time. "Do you see that?" He pointed to the map, his finger aimed at the Trench. Colored flags of all the kingdoms dotted the vellum.

"Yes, sir," I said.

"I want you there. Argos has officially given up that territory," he said. "Queen Cora wants my balls, but so far she is kept in check by the two hounds of Laconia and Elis." Demetre slapped me on the ass, and I tried to keep my eyebrows firmly in place. "You have done well with our coasts, and my numbers are the best I could expect. I have held to my end of the agreement, and now I want you to get me that land." He stabbed his finger at the map again, his eyes shining in lust.

"Yes, sir," I said.

NEAR NIGHTFALL, in a large tent in the Epirote camp, I met with General Akis. The general had taken off his helmet, revealing gray-streaked black hair. His eyes were hard and almost black. He handed some of his armor and weapons to his servants and then shook my hand.

"Welcome to the Trench, Son of Zeus," Akis said.

"Perseus, please."

He nodded once, strode toward the maps in the tent, and spread his hands. "Here is what we are up against." He pointed to the shores. "Here are the Laconian and Elean ports. They fight as one. I would caution you against fighting the two hounds of Laconia and Elis. The demigod Zoticus is gigantic, and getting in the way of his fist hammers is not something I'd recommend. Palamedes, who fights at his side, is quick to kill with almost anything."

I shook my head, still not believing the war between Laconia and Elis could be over after all these centuries.

Akis pushed his finger up to the north. "This is the Thessalian camp. The crown prince of Thessaly can knock you out with a thought, so ranged attacks are best, but he's often in a chariot." He scratched his beard. "What we really need is for you to help General Bryan kill Bortos of Thessaly or the shape-shifter. We know Bortos's general position because he blankets the area in darkness, but he has been hard to kill. Bryan has been trying for years. If you can kill those two, it will greatly weaken the Thessalian ranks. We have lost so many demigods." He sighed. "Frankly, it's a miracle that we have what we have. I'm glad you're here, and the troops will be relieved when they see the reinforcements."

The troops trickled in, looking pale and worn. Leading them was a man in heavy silver plate and a full salt-and-pepper beard.

"Bryan," Akis said, "this is Perseus, the general from the lower coastal region and a son of Zeus."

Bryan shook my hand with a warm firm grip and smiled at me, his brown eyes soft. He was a son of Dionysus and had been serving King Demetre for eighty years, the oldest of the king's servants.

Another general came in from the field, Kelios, the most favored son of Demetre. He had the irises of the line of Zeus, pale blue like my own. Kelios ordered us sit and demanded reports from all the generals as we were served supper. Being a demigod, Bryan technically outranked him, but Bryan sat back and did as Kelios ordered. I wondered about that as we discussed troop placement and ate, and then I opened a barrel of wine to share.

That night I was sleeping warm and comfortable in Ava's and Aiden's arms when I woke, groggy and confused.

The flaps of my tent opened, and I bolted up in bed, summoning a storm.

However, instead of an enemy intruder, I faced Antolios. He was wearing all black, his thick flaxen hair bound to his head.

I rushed him, kissing him full on the mouth. The bond opened up between us, and my body surged with heat and desire. We frantically stripped him of his clothes and kicked the unconscious courtesans off the bed. I scrambled onto my back, and I was caught in his white glare when he entered me.

We made love fast, then slow, and then fast again. I smashed him into me. Maybe this time we could be together forever…. But I knew he had other plans before he even opened his mouth.

"I want you to help me with something," Antolios said.

"Mmmm?" I nuzzled his neck.

"I want peace."

I gazed up at him and licked his chin. "What do you need from me?"

Antolios kissed my lips, breathing into me. "Your charm."

"It's yours." I rolled on top of him.

We made love one more time, but then I had to let him go back to his camp. He gathered up his long black binding from the floor and began to wrap his thick golden hair. Ava and Aiden were still tangled together, asleep on the ground. He had knocked them out. I pulled them back onto the bed, and sat cross-legged as I watched him.

Antolios was about to step outside.

"Wait," I said to him.

Dressed as a shadow, he regarded me, his face drawn in hard lines.

"Will we ever be together?" My chest ached.

Antolios took a breath. "After."

I frowned. "After when?"

"When we are done with our destinies and our families no longer need us." Antolios ducked through the tent flap. His long strides quickly faded away.

If I survive the war.

I WAS on the march again, heading with Bryan and the Epirote armies back to Ilium. After many months of deliberation, the kingdoms of Greece had finally disarmed. All except one. While all the other rulers had planned to meet in Argos for formal peace talks, Demetre hadn't. He hadn't responded to any of our missives. Bryan and I had been sent by the other kingdoms to convince him to sign the treaty in Argos, but we didn't have high hopes. Then again, Bryan was Demetre's oldest general and perhaps his only friend, and I was his half brother. If anyone had a chance, we did.

It took nearly a month to get to the golden capital, and when we entered the gates to the city, I was handed a wonderful but concerning letter from Andromeda. She had given birth to Cynurus, our ninth child, but that would have made his birth at least a month earlier than expected. I reread the letter. She wrote that she was fine, the baby was fine, and that my mother had traveled from Seriphos to help out.

I folded the letter and placed it in my satchel. Either I was going to convince Demetre of peace—really, who could afford war anymore?—or I would quit the army.

Bryan accompanied me up the steps of the palace, and we were led to the throne room, where King Demetre was already waiting to receive us. I wore the armor he had made for me and put on my best smile, but I was already sweating.

Demetre sat on the throne in full armor. The plates of metal on his chest piece seemed to shift as islands over water when he moved. Globes of liquid metal floated above a scepter he held in his hand. The crown he wore was a wreath of daggers, each tip pointing up and painted red.

Bryan and I knelt before the throne. "Hail, King Demetre!"

Not even a cough was heard in the room.

"I've been informed that you've failed to secure the coast of Argos," the king said tightly. I stared at the marble flooring, my heart rate increasing. "My sons also tell me that you have both been conspiring for peace."

It was true. Antolios had whispered in my head, using my voice and face to convince the other kingdoms of peace, and we had. Except Epiro. I had thought we would have sway with Demetre if Bryan and I banded together. I had been a fool.

"What say you, traitors?" Demetre's voice boomed through the throne room.

I took a breath. "King Demetre, we've admittedly not secured the Argive coast for Epiro, but we have done better. The coast will be neutral ground for travel and trade, and no more blood will be spilled. King Acrisius has agreed to it. We could have lasting peace, better than when the gods were alive. This could be a new dawn for mankind."

"Enough!" Demetre's voice cracked off the walls. "I will have your heads for treason." His staff rapped the ground, and something stung my neck. My fingers twitched up to the site of pain, but then my vision bleached to white.

I WOKE up on a cot in a dark cell of stone and heavy bars. Feeling muzzy and wearing only a simple linen tunic, I sat up and tried to wake the storm.

Immediately my head swam, my heart pattered, and I fell back onto the bed. Holding my breath and lying perfectly still, I tried to connect with the air, to feel something. Nothing. The storm still churned in the recesses of my brain, but I couldn't touch it. The air was stagnant and dead, and I forced myself to breathe it in and out. I choked and fought the bile rising in the back of my throat. Clutching my head, I tried not to panic, but I knew I was already panicking.

"Help," I croaked. I thrashed in the sheets of the cot and tried to sit up, but I kept falling back, my vision spinning. I quieted when I heard someone move in a room adjacent to mine.

A voice groaned.

"Bryan," I said.

I heard him get noisily sick on the stones. He spit a few times and then let out a string of impressive curses. "Fairy bells!" I thought that to be another one of his colorful curses, but then he coughed and said it again. "They gave us bleeding fairy bells."

"What?"

"It's a flower," Bryan grumbled. "Blocks magic from mages. The elves discovered it can also take away a demigod's strength and powers— just the ones we consciously express." Bryan spit again. "It isn't too friendly on the gut or heart. If they give us too much, we could die."

"Great." I gritted my teeth and tried not to think about the air. Everything felt so heavy and stifling and dead. Oh gods, I was being smothered. "I can't breathe," I gasped.

"It's okay," Bryan said. "Take deep breaths. In and out." He started talking about his wife, an elf he had met forty years before. He told me about his three sons and then laughed. "You'd think I'd have more, right? Turns out elf females are fertile only once a decade. Apparently they have special ceremonies around that time, and calling them orgies doesn't do them justice. Ha! May the best seed win!" Bryan laughed to himself for a bit, then cleared his throat. "Well, those ceremonies are for the unwedded ladies and gents, of course."

Bryan was easy to listen to, and soon I found myself breathing normally. I inspected my cell while he talked, taking in the thick walls and bars. The bed was solid stone with a wool pad and a thin blanket, and there was a small basin for water and a wooden chamber pot in the corner. No mirrors, no windows, and the torches that served as light were on the other side of the hall, on a wall too far away to reach.

I was weak as a baby, and we weren't going anywhere. Except to our deaths.

The door at the end of the hall opened. It was closest to me, and if I leaned across my cot I could see it. I stood slowly, still dizzy.

King Demetre walked through. The door banged closed behind him. His salt-and-pepper hair was down to his shoulders, his beard trim. He was alone, weaponless, and only wearing a fine red chiton, but then again, what did he have to fear from us? He sauntered past my cell, not even acknowledging me, and stood in front of Bryan's.

I shuffled to the bars so I could watch him.

Demetre grabbed the bars of Bryan's cell, leaning against them and glaring. "What happened to you?" His voice was angry, but also hurt.

"Maybe I'm getting old. I'm done fighting." Bryan sounded tired.

"So you're going to stand by this child?" the king said. "He's killed you."

Bryan's tone was surprisingly soft and warm. "Maybe. I wouldn't expect you to understand."

Demetre snorted. "You're right. I don't." He stood, and then moved back down to my cell. Leaning against the far wall by the torches, he crossed his arms and stared at me with cool blue eyes, the color of my own.

"Hello, brother," Demetre said at last.

I flicked my chin at him and held on to the bars for support.

The king examined his nails. "I saw your sword. Father give it to you?"

I laughed. "You want to make this about who got what from our father? You're wasting your time. He didn't give me shit."

Demetre leveled his gaze at me. "Is that what you think?" A cruel smile grew on his face. "I heard about your… little problem when you were younger. Don't you think that was interesting?"

I huffed. "I have no idea what you are talking about."

"Sure you don't." He licked his lips. "I also heard about what happened with you and Eros."

My heart pounded, and I knew it wasn't from the drugs. "If you have something to say, then fucking say it."

"You're a fool if you deny that father favored you. At the end of his life, who did he summon to his side?"

"Did you want to be there for that waste of time? If I'd known, I would have traded places with you." My stomach somersaulted, and I swallowed thickly.

Demetre waved his hand in front of his face, swatting away my words. "Zeus was a shitty father, but we are brothers, more alike than you know. In time I can forgive you for this pathetic treason. I can make you stronger." Demetre pushed off the wall, so close I could reach out and touch him. His breath smelled of whisky and smoke. "I've been thinking about you… and Eros."

"I don't know what you're talking about."

Demetre scowled. "Don't play coy."

"Don't fucking flatter yourself."

"You and he were together for three days," he stated flatly.

"I'd remember getting fucked by Eros." I was pissed that my brother seemed to know something I didn't. Could this be related to those three days I couldn't remember, when I had discovered my curse? "You shouldn't listen to rumors. They are often wrong."

Demetre studied me, his jaw tight. "We'll see. Maybe you need some time." He stalked out.

I slumped back onto my cot. An interminable amount of time later, we were given supper, but I was too exhausted with questions to be able to eat. I fell into a restless sleep.

I had thought we would be executed immediately, but we weren't. After a few weeks I knew that I was in real trouble. There were worse things than death.

CHAPTER TWENTY-FIVE

BY BRYAN'S reckoning it had been months, but it felt like years. I was itchy and hot and achy, and had lost interest in food and sleeping. Doing the best I could to ignore my growing desire, I spoke with Bryan, and sometimes we sang together, but lately he hadn't initiated any conversations. My head pounded, and I amused myself by ripping my knuckles open against the stone wall.

I stroked myself in the mornings when I woke up so it was easier to take a piss, but that morning I kept going. It was a mistake that I'd unfortunately made before, and regretted every time, but it was easy to fall prey to. I only stopped when I became so exhausted and simultaneously wound up that I retched. I lay there gasping, jittery and sick, until I nodded off for a bit.

That night, as I was lying on my cot, Demetre made another appearance. There were dark circles under his eyes as he gripped the bars of my cell and leered. "How are you feeling?"

He knew about my curse. I didn't know how, but he did. I hooked an arm under my head and grabbed my cock with my other hand, squeezing under the tip until it fattened and purpled. "Gonna suck me? If not, piss off."

Demetre laughed. "So, have you reconsidered?"

"What? Being your bitch?" I hawked and spat on the floor.

Demetre's expression darkened, and he stepped away from the bars. "I killed the king of Crete, and all of the descendants of that royal line. Save a few. Hunted them down like dogs." He picked at his silks.

"Excuse me?" I sat up.

Demetre shrugged. "I hated that they were allowed on my land without paying taxes. It was disrespectful. However... I had my men stop in Delos to pick up your family on the way back. I suppose your wife and children are now the only descendants of that stupid sunken island."

My heart pounded. "You have my family? Here?"

"Around. I am willing to treat them well if you comply with my wishes."

I rushed to the bars. "I'll do anything. Please, don't hurt them."

"You'll do what?" Demetre met my eyes with his, heavy-lidded and listless.

"I'll be your bitch, suck your cock, lick your balls, give you my ass, and whatever else you want to do with me. Please don't hurt them!"

Demetre straightened, looking down his nose at me. "Who says I ever wanted your weak ass?"

He strode out, and I opened my mouth and screamed.

"BRYAN! BRYAN! Seriously, you have to see this." I furiously stroked my shaft. I couldn't burst with my hand because of the fairy bells, but that didn't matter. This wasn't going to take long.

"Go back to your cot," Bryan said from his cell.

"No! No, come here. Hurry." The urge seized and shook me, and I watched through half-closed eyes as spurt after milky spurt of my ejaculate hit the wall across the hall and dribbled down to the floor. It never really felt as good by myself as it did with someone else, but at least I felt something. "Bryan? Did you see that?" I said. "Wow, that's far. I've never seen anyone go farther, except maybe a centaur. Bryan? Bryan!"

He sounded tired. "Yes, I saw. Go lie down. Get some sleep. They'll dart you again."

"You didn't look. I can't even see you." I muttered and went to go punch my wall. I wasn't as strong as I was used to, but I could possibly chip a bone if I tried hard enough.

The guards came in around midday, as far as we could tell, and delivered our meal. My knuckles dripped blood onto the floor. Several of the guards gave me a withering look when they saw the wall sprayed with my cold seed, and I gave them a thumbs-up and a friendly smile. They tossed a tray in front of my cage and Bryan's.

I was in the habit of ignoring my meals, or at least giving them to Bryan, but something potent and foul wafted from the plate they set down. "What's this?" I asked.

The guard with the weird mole by his lip looked at me with a raised brow. Funky smells cloyed at my nose, and my throat tightened as I fled to the back of my cage. "Take that with you." I pointed accusingly at the tray, but they moved past, ignoring me. I covered my nose with an arm and walked over to it, toed it. "It smells like your mother's underwear."

"Give it to me," Bryan said.

I ignored him and reached down, grabbed the slop, and lifted it. Using both hands, I passed the tray to myself until I had to it the height I wanted. All the guards were clustered at the door to get out. I reached my arm back, cocked my hip, and then let the tray fly straight into their backs.

Food spiraled everywhere, and pieces of it slapped against the side of my face. The tray whacked the tall guard on the back of his head. He fell soundlessly into the others, and they all went down in a pile.

I jumped into the air, twisting this way and that. "Yes!" And then I dropped to the floor, rolled, and skittered around the cage as darts pinged off the stones. I flung my wooden chamber pot at the bars and roared with laughter as it split to pieces and splashed piss onto the guards.

"Perseus! Stop!" Bryan yelled.

"Shut up, old man!" I felt a familiar prick in my side and crumpled to the floor. I was out before my head hit.

I woke up in my own mess again, thighs greased. I made a noise of irritation when my fingers came back gloppy, the skirt of my tunic cold and wet. The clerics had healed my hands again—how annoying.

Bryan mentioned something about Demetre coming down and talking to him, but I wasn't listening. I chewed the nails of one hand and stroked myself off with the other, and then ambled over to the stones that were painted with my blood. I ripped my knuckles on them for a while, and when I was able I used the new chamber pot without spilling a drop. Being darted was only fun the first twenty times.

My head ached and my cock throbbed, but after another series of strikes with my fist, my hand hurt worse than anything else. I grit my teeth and threw another punch at the wall.

The guards brought a strange man to my cage after supper.

I slunk between the flickering shadows, watching him, until the guard with the mole on his face called me up to cuff me. Sliding my trembling bloodstained hands through the bars, I wondered at that odd keening noise, barely registering that I was the source. The man they let into my cage was robust, oiled, and shaved. I danced from foot to foot and pulled on the chains until they locked us in together and released my hands.

I couldn't breathe. We faced each other, and the man looked me up and down, his lip curled. He was dark and tattooed with bold shapes, and had meaty balls, but his cock was tiny and shriveled. Oh well.

The man flexed and glared at me.

A small part of my brain screamed, but I batted it away. I managed to choke out, "Assume a position, or I will *assist* you." The slave's eyes flicked doubt, and then I saw red.

The rest of the night was a blur, but I swore that I heard someone laughing in the background, "You're just like me! You're just like me!"

I laughed along.

WHEN I opened my eyes, I was lying on the cold floor, no idea how I had gotten there. I felt languid and content, even though my knees burned, and I had a crick in my neck.

The guards came in, startling me. Had I slept in? They set down... not breakfast. Midday meal? I was starving and shakily crawled over and took my... mat. They had placed my food on a mat instead of a tray, but there was a lot of food.

The events of the night before partially coalesced in my mind, and I just sat there, staring at my soup and bread. I had fucked a man, and King Demetre had been there? He knew about my curse. My memories were hazy, but before I had lost it, Demetre had also said something interesting about our father and when I was younger, something Zeus had done for me that Demetre had been jealous of, and he hadn't meant the sword.

I pulled my mat through the bars. They didn't give us utensils, so I scooped the soup up with bread. I couldn't see Bryan's face, but his hands reached for his bowl and bread.

"You said that Demetre came down to see you?" I said.

Bryan didn't say anything. Maybe I had been mistaken or he hadn't heard me. I was going to repeat myself, but then he said, "Don't talk to me, Perseus. Just give me three nights without you yelling or hitting things or whatever, okay? Three nights of peace and quiet."

"Okay." I went back to my stew, my cheeks flaming.

After I ate, I used the washing supplies they had left me and replaced the blanket on my bed with a new one. My mustache was finally at the point where I could spread it to the sides, but my balls were wrapped in thick dark fur. Gods.

The doors opened again, and the guards came leading a man in chains, the same slave as the night before, with the dark skin and tattoos. He was covered in deep scratches and bruises, and his eyes were swollen shut.

They hadn't healed him. I swallowed.

The tall guard stopped in front of my cell. "Present your hands."

I rose and stuck my hands through the bars, and he cuffed me. The door opened, and the guards pushed the slave in. He was limping, his eyes downcast and his shoulders hunched. Horror grew heavy in my gut as they shut the door and removed my bonds.

The man knelt on the ground, his head touching the stone floor.

I swallowed again. This was another one of Demetre's grotesque games, but this time I was equally to blame. I wondered if he was watching now, and I wondered what he would do if I didn't fuck the slave. Would he punish me again? Would he punish the slave?

Walking over to the man, I touched his shoulder. He flinched. I could see his body better now. He had bite marks on his neck and deep gouges along his sides. I didn't want to look further.

"Get up," I said gently. "Get on the bed."

The slave scurried over to the bed and curled up on his side, breathing heavily.

The bed wasn't wide enough for us to both lie on our backs, and as I slid next to the slave, I had to straighten him out on his side so we could both fit. He trembled under my touch. I really wasn't in the mood, but I had a horrible idea of what would happen if I refused the slave. I pulled the thin blanket over us, and the slave shook harder.

"Shh." I spat into my hand and coated the head of my penis with it. My cock was hard, and I hated myself for that. My body never cared how I felt. I slid my cock in between the slave's thighs. "Shift over a bit. Flex your legs. That's it."

It didn't take long, and when I was done I rolled off the bed and shuffled to the corner farthest away from the slave. I crossed my arms, bent my head, and almost laughed. Stripped bare, this is what I was. And despite the cruelty of circumstance, this was what I should have been doing ages ago.

Better to bed a slave or whore than half of fucking Greece.

The slave shuffled around, and then the guards clomped in and ordered me to present my hands. They took the slave, unbound me, and left.

What about Andromeda and the kids? Were they safe? Had Demetre hurt them? Cold terror washed down my spine, and I shivered. I lay down on my bed, the sheets damp, and rolled into a ball. I had run away from my destiny of becoming a husband and a father, but faced with the possibility that I could lose my entire family, I wanted to see them again, more than anything. I still wanted Antolios, but I'd been destroying my life over something I could never have for far too long.

I prayed. It seemed easier now that the gods were dead. I vowed to be a better husband and father. No more philandering. No more pining after a dream that would probably never come to be. I already felt the loss, and I started to cry. Trying to keep it soft, I smashed my face into the musty mattress.

"Perseus?" Bryan said.

I cried harder.

"Perseus, come on. I'm sorry for getting angry with you. I'm not normally like that."

And of course that made it worse. Snot flooded out of my nose, and my eyes were already swollen and aching with tears.

"Look, I understand now. It's not your fault," he said.

I didn't even recognize my voice, it sounded so wretched. "But I hurt that man."

"He'll be okay."

"I don't like hurting people." I bit my tongue.

Bryan sighed. "I don't like it either."

I stopped crying for a moment.

"I'm good at killing people—we all are—but I don't enjoy it. I wanted to be a scholar when I was younger, but that wasn't to be." Bryan paused a moment. "This isn't your fault. Demetre is an ass, and he always has been."

"I'm a monster," I whispered to the world.

"If you are, then we all are. What happened to Demetre as a boy was regretful, and I can understand how that would change a man."

I mopped my face with my blanket and rolled over. "As a boy?"

"Isn't that when it happened to you? When you got your balancer?"

Balancer…. It took me a moment to understand what he was saying, and then I winced. "Gods, no."

I had always wondered why my curse had come later than the others'. That was part of the reason why, when I did find out what it was, I had been in such denial. It hit most demigods around eight years old, when we gained full control over our powers. I had thought that maybe I'd simply been a late bloomer, but what if my father had done something to me? I should have known better, because nothing was ever simple with being a demigod.

"Really?" Bryan said. "I'm sorry, I didn't mean to assume. What is your balancer, if I may ask? It's not as if we can offend the gods anymore for discussing it."

Balancer…. What a mild name for it. "No, that's okay. Uh, yes, *that* is my balancer."

"So you have the same balancer as your brother," Bryan said. "Interesting. What are the odds of that?"

"I am starting to doubt the randomness of our curses and powers," I said.

"Don't call them that," Bryan said. "They aren't curses. They are only a way for our human bodies to release excess divine energy. It's perfectly natural."

I grunted. It was divine certainly, but it was anything but natural.

"I may not have your balancer, but mine hasn't always been a blessing. I get tremors, and once I dropped my infant son. He turned out all right, but I felt terrible. I'm curious. How late did you get yours?"

"I didn't notice it until I was in my midtwenties."

Bryan made a noise of surprise. "Why so late?"

I didn't answer, my mind racing.

Bryan coughed. "I apologize if I'm making you uncomfortable. I have to admit, I'm extremely interested in this topic, but it has been hard to discuss without offending the gods or other demigods. I'd study it if I could, talk to our youth and help them through it so they wouldn't have to suffer like we did." Bryan paused. "I approved of what you said at the peace conference at the Trench, that the gods were gone, and it was 'time to tell demigod propriety to fuck off.' I believe those were your words, were they not?"

I sighed. "Yes, those were my words." Antolios hadn't even fed that line to me. "I don't know why my balancer came so late, but my father may have had something to do with it."

"Fascinating."

"I guess. I think it may have stunted my growth or something. I didn't start growing until I was eighteen...." I blinked and then started laughing. I couldn't stop.

Bryan laughed along for a bit, but then he asked, "Not that I mind this change of mood, but what's so funny?"

"I—" I was laughing so hard I had to gasp in breath. "I think Antolios literally made me a man."

ANOTHER WEEK had passed. Bryan actually seemed to be enjoying prison—he seemed to have forgotten that we were only alive because Demetre hadn't executed us yet. I was still presented the same slave every night, but now instead of being afraid of me, the slave was sulky. He didn't exactly make it easy. Once he "accidentally" kneed me in the balls, but I figured I deserved that.

It was after supper, and the guards had just come and gathered our dishes. Bryan thanked the guards, and they smiled at him. I thanked them, and they glared. The tall one spit on the floor in front of my cell. Before the door was closed and barred, I heard a scuffle, and I went up to the bars to look. There was another odd shuffle, and then the doorway cracked open—unguarded.

Antolios stepped through, his face a beacon of light.

My eyes watered and burned from the brightness. "Antolios!"

He approached my cell, wearing silver armor. He pulled off a cowl he had draped over his head and secured his staff onto his back. Shining and white—my angel.

"Are you both okay?" Antolios said. He looked me up and down as he used a set of keys to unlock my cell. After opening my cell, he strode to Bryan's.

I stared at the open door in a haze of unreality for a moment. It was hard to believe that I could walk out and not be shot with darts. I moved slowly and stepped over the threshold, feeling oddly exposed. Then I saw Bryan's face and laughed.

Bryan's beard was incredibly bushy, and his normally short hair frizzed out.

"There is a need for haste," Antolios said. He pointed to the wall. "Both of you, sit." I raised an eyebrow but sat on the stone floor. He pulled two vials from his robes and held them up side by side, scrutinizing them. "There is fighting in the capital, and soon it will spill into the palace grounds." He handed us each a vial. "Drink this. All of it."

I tossed the bitter liquid back. Immediately, my heart raced, and my vision blackened. I was glad I was against the wall, because I slumped into it, my chin hitting my chest. My breaths came out ragged and shallow, but I didn't lose consciousness. Eventually the feeling passed, and I blinked the spots away from my vision.

The air came alive around me, and I sighed with relief and reached for the storm.

It boiled to life in the heavens far above, connecting me with everything. I woke it for kilometers around and breathed the fresh, pulsing energy into my lungs, forcing out the stagnant air that had sat there. Minor vibrations in the floor and walls indicated that Bryan was also testing his powers.

"Feel better?" Antolios said to me. I nodded and took his hands, pulling him down for a kiss. His mouth was warm and firm, and he wrapped his arms around me, surrounding me in his dirty smell. I clung to him and drank his lips like mead.

Guess what I found out? I thought. Rocking my pelvis, I sucked on his lower lip.

Antolios tore away from me. *Later.* "Your breath is terrible." He wrinkled his nose.

"The only thing I had to clean my teeth was the corner of my blanket!"

"What's happening?" Bryan rolled to his feet. "Do we have to fight our way out?"

"No," Antolios said. "Most of the guards were called to the perimeter for the fight. We have to find the king. He won't sign the peace treaty, and all the kingdoms have agreed to overthrow him. He must be removed."

Bryan and I gave each other a look.

We jogged out of the dungeons, and Antolios informed us of the king's children and how they had come out of the woodwork, swarming Ilium. Antolios had just now been able to break into the palace. A team of rogues were searching for the king, and the armies were close to breaking down the palace gates.

Antolios led us through the dark halls of stone and then up a couple of winding metal staircases. He ducked into a supply closet and tossed us heavy bags. When I opened mine, it had my armor and weapons in it. "Get dressed," he said.

"We can't wear metal," Brian said. "Demetre manipulates it."

Antolios pulled off his silver breastplate, and went hunting for a leather chest piece. I threw on my tunic and sandals but kept my sword. "If Demetre wants to stab me with it," I said, "then so be it." I said that, but it was god-made, and if it had been useful to him he would have kept it.

Bryan fished around the armory for a club, and Antolios pulled his staff from his back. We didn't have to say anything else, and left together.

I raged the storm and changed the polarity of the air, creating friction. Condensing the moisture inside the palace, I created a light fog, and the haze followed us as we moved through the halls.

Antolios led the way and dropped guards as we neared them. Bryan shook the archers off-balance, giving me time to strike them with lightning from my hands. I relished the nearly unpleasant tingling around my skin. Shouts and cries were louder now that we were upstairs, and I could hear the panic of voices outside the walls.

With every footfall, I connected more solidly with the earth. My awareness of my body was heightened, my reflexes primed and ready. Smells, sounds, and my vision opened up. All of my preternatural senses were returning. I hadn't realized how weak the poison had made me.

We ran around a corner and stopped at the closed throne room doors. Dark-clothed figures popped out of hiding, and Antolios whispered with them as they converged. The rogues reported the king had been seen on the roof earlier, but they thought the king was holed up in the throne room, considering they had checked the entire palace and it was mostly empty. However, they had not seen him in the flesh.

We lined up at the doors. "We go in and find him?" I said.

"I'll find him," Antolios said.

Bryan rolled his shoulders. "Respite is over."

I lifted my arm toward the doors and manifested lightning. The doors blew to bits, and through the settling dust rows and rows of soldiers emerged. With a team of rogues guarding our backs, we demigods ran in, a puddle of fog up to our knees.

Bryan pointed to the throne and swung his club at the group of approaching soldiers. On the throne was a man in metal plate, but a sea of armed guards stood in our way. I stabbed my blade into chests and necks.

Antolios gazed toward the throne as he spun his staff, narrowing his eyes. He flinched, and I ran toward him. "That's not him!" he said.

I slid my blade into an armpit, the soldier's warm blood gushing from the wound and over my hand. He let out a grunt of surprise before I pushed him away and he fell to the floor. I spun, slicing my blade across another's throat. "Where is he, then?" I shouted.

Bryan stomped his foot, shaking the ground. The soldiers who wore heavy plate fell easily, clattering to the floor on their knees. Bryan clubbed them over their heads while they were down. He glanced around, checking behind him. When he looked toward the door, he gasped.

I parried a few swords and spears and then hazarded a look over my shoulder.

The rogues were dead on the floor, impaled by their own knives. I gulped.

Cries shot up through the entire rank of armored soldiers in front of us, and I spun and danced away from several swings, nicking the unarmored backs of several soldiers' knees as I did so. Moans echoed off the walls.

I shot my hand out and lanced lightning into the ranks in front of me, watching it spark from one suit of armor to the next. Rows fell and I grinned.

"I can't find him! There's too much interference!" Antolios said.

The fallen soldiers in front of me stood up as a mass. "What the fuck," I whispered.

As if they were of one mind, the soldiers approached us, putting one foot and then the other in front of them in a ghastly synchronized dance.

I swiped at the soldiers coming toward me, but even when I slit their throats they didn't fall. Most had wide eyes, and some were screaming soundlessly. Over their heads, I could see Antolios trying to bat them down with his staff, but they weren't knocked over.

"He's killed them!" Bryan said.

I recoiled in horror. No… they weren't all dead. I kicked out, trying to knock one of them over. The soldier's face was a rictus of misery. He whispered, "Please, no. Please, no."

He wasn't begging me to spare him. He was begging me to kill him.

The soldiers advanced on us in eerie uniformity—trapped in their suits of armor.

I swallowed rapidly and stepped back. What kind of man would hurt his own men? "He stabbed them with their own armor!"

Antolios leaped back from his group of soldiers, his brow creased in confusion and worry. His white light glared off the walls and pillars as he scanned the throne room for the king. I quickly maneuvered across the room, knocking dead and dying soldiers out of the way, only to see them get up again.

I reached Antolios and stood with him, back to back.

The blasted throne room doors were now sealed again with a sheet of metal. I couldn't see Demetre anywhere, and Antolios wasn't having any luck either. The floor shook, but the soldiers moved on, pinning us into corners. Bryan was now on the opposite side of the room.

Bryan yelled and stomped the ground, almost shaking me from my feet, and then ran through a line of soldiers, sprinting to our location. By the time he got to us, only a few rows of soldiers stood in between us and him, so he vaulted over their heads.

The soldiers stopped in unison.

A volley of metal spikes shot from the ranks toward us. The projectiles were the size of a spear but fairly slow, so Antolios and I dodged them easily. But Bryan was in the middle of a jump, so he couldn't move out of the way.

Several spears impaled him, and he came crashing down in front of us, gasping and grabbing his side. He had three sticking into him: one through the shoulder, one through his leg, and one right through his middle.

Some of the soldiers clanged to the ground, but the rest pushed toward us again.

Antolios clutched me to him. "Put your sword away," he said into my ear.

That got me hard. Fuck. With his hot breath on my face, I sheathed my sword.

After I did, he looked down at Bryan, his eyes illuminating Bryan's sweaty and pinched face. "We're ready," he said.

I was about to ask what we were ready for, but then Bryan closed his eyes and the entire room began to shake. I gripped Antolios as he lowered us to the ground. Bryan was unmoving but breathing, and the floor started to fold around us, blocking the soldiers from view.

"Hold on," Bryan panted.

With a few more jolts and shifts of rock, we were encased in a stone sphere, and then the true shaking began. The earth heaved.

Antolios's eyes lit the inside of the sphere as I was tossed about. Bryan was somehow anchored to the floor, stone wrapped around him, and Antolios was holding on to the sides of the sphere, perched there like a white spider. But not me.

I bashed my face into the sides of our prison and tasted blood. I was smashed against the rocks for many minutes, and by the time I discovered how Antolios was holding on to the rock handles sticking out from the sides of our sphere, the shaking had stopped. Groans of shifting rock still wracked the room.

Bryan moaned, and I crawled to his side. He was half-buried in rock. "Bryan, are you all right?" He shifted slightly, and his eyelids fluttered. I put my hands on him and healed him, carefully working the spears out of his shoulder and thigh, the glow sealing his wounds.

Bryan's eyes flew open. He jerked and then clutched at his middle again, and the rock fell from him as dust. I put my hand on the spear through his torso, pulling him toward me and rolling him to the side. The metal tip poked out his back. It could have gone through organs, and I wasn't sure I could pull it out and heal him at the same time without him losing a lot of blood.

I didn't have a choice. He was going to die if I did nothing. I grabbed the spear, preparing to pull it, but Bryan put his hand over mine. I looked into his eyes, deep brown and calm.

"Go find him," Bryan said.

"But—" I started.

"You have to stop him." Bryan smiled at me and then closed his eyes. His heart was still beating, but faintly. The earth shifted, and a tunnel appeared in our rock sphere. It angled out into the fading daylight. I smelled dust, the haze of it drifting over the exit. Antolios and I crawled to the opening together, sticking our heads out of the hole.

Coughing and sneezing from the settling dust, I squinted and scanned what was left of the throne room. The entire roof had collapsed—now there were only a few pillars standing up. The walls had crumbled. Everything was buried in rock.

A pile of rock along with what had been a wall shifted and became a growing mound.

"That's him," Antolios said.

I crawled out of the hole, pulled my sword from its sheath, and glanced back at Antolios, his face already grim because he knew what I was going to say.

"Stay with Bryan. Find a healer." I turned and ran down the rocks toward the shifting rubble.

I love you, Antolios said in my head. I ran faster.

As I got close, a ball of metal emerged from the rocks. It melted away and revealed Demetre, coughing from the dust. He had no crown, his salted-black hair was tangled, and his fine silk tunic was filthy. He held out his hand and recreated his staff from the metal swirling around him, and then he saw me.

Demetre glared and threw his staff on the ground, creating a disk. He stepped onto it and sailed up and over the crumbled throne room walls.

I called a cyclone from the sky and swirled myself into the air, kicking up more dust. Grit got into my eyes, and I squinted as I tore after Demetre. He sailed across the sunken rooftops of the palace. Bryan had brought the entire building down, and only parts of the roof were still intact. The bell-shaped golden central dome had fallen on its side.

I rained down lightning on Demetre, but he easily dodged the bolts. In answer to my onslaught, he sent pellets of metal at me, and I twisted and bent to avoid them.

While he was breezing over a part of the tiled roof that was still intact, I managed to hit the side of his metal flying disk with lightning, and Demetre wavered on his craft and then pitched forward onto the roof. He rolled and sprang up.

When I reached the edge of the roof, I dropped my cyclone and hit the tiles running. Demetre was waiting for me and threw more projectiles from his disk, then formed the rest of it back into his metal staff. I parried some of the metal balls with my sword and ducked as the rest whistled past my ears.

Demetre's molten armor surged around him, his lips tight and his fingers bloodlessly clutching his staff. The liquid metal at the top pulsed.

I threw out my free hand and launched lightning from it, but he formed a sheet of metal from the glob over his staff and blocked it. I rained down a few more bolts, more powerful ones from the sky, but he expanded his metal net in a large arch and sent spikes into the ground all around him. Maybe I singed him a bit, but the majority of the electricity sizzled out into the roof. Gone.

How many demigods could thwart my power? Gritting my teeth, I dropped the pressure where Demetre stood, sending waves of wind. His eyebrows shot up as the wind howled toward him and grew in force. Those metal shields of his weren't going to help him now. My hair whipped my face, and I created a countercurrent of air so I wouldn't get sucked in after him.

Demetre's sandals slid on the tiles. "You're weak," he said from behind his moving shields. A flash of his white teeth shown through. He was grinning, blue eyes lit. The wind continued to push him back, and I readied lightning for the moment there was another opening.

He chuckled. "You will lose."

I wasn't sure what he found so funny. From where I was standing, I was winning. I tensed and held my breath, creating friction in the sky. My ears popped hard, and the sky grumbled and sparked. As soon as he fell off the edge, I was going to hit him with a bolt so big there would be nothing of him left but ash.

Demetre's foot was almost at the edge, and I knew I had him.

Sharp pain exploded in my torso, and I gasped. I looked down.

Several spots of blood bloomed on my chest. I dropped to my knees as the blood rolled down the inside of my tunic, dripping into my navel and sliding down the groove of my thigh. The wind stopped, and the energy in the sky broke apart and fizzled out.

Demetre dropped the shield partway so I could see his gloating face again. "See? You already lost." He walked over to me and spun a kick at my hand, knocking my sword away. I helplessly watched it spiral out of reach.

I shot my hand out and manifested a weak string of lightning from my fingers at Demetre, but he laughed and threw up his metal shield, blocking it. I didn't know what he was doing exactly, but that shit was fucking annoying.

"Now, now." He shook a finger. The metal floated around him as he folded his hands in front of himself and looked down on me, waiting for me to say something.

I felt my lungs fill with blood and struggled to breathe.

"And here we are," he said at last. "We could have been together." He waited again.

My head swam, and I hunched down, barely able to hold my head up enough to see him through my sweaty black hair.

"Don't you have something to say?" Demetre smiled.

I coughed, pain searing my chest, and tasted blood. "I don't talk to evil."

Demetre laughed. "Because I don't want peace? Father was a fool for favoring you. But he paid the price for that mistake."

My breaths hitched. "He did not…."

Demetre sauntered over to my fallen blade. He bent and picked it up, inspecting the edge. "He gave you this, a god-blade that my power cannot touch. What a boring sword, simple and useless." Demetre regarded me with our father's eyes. My eyes. "When I look at you, I do not see a hero. I see a failure who never stopped running."

"You think I don't fucking know that!" I choked on the words, blood filling my mouth and pain blurring my vision. My lips were wet, and I tried to laugh, but warm, metallic fluid gurgled in my throat.

Demetre moved in front of me, blocking the last light of the sun. He hefted my god-blade and swung it back. "Give Father my regards."

Demetre's face twisted as he brought the sword down.

I closed my eyes, welcoming the end.

I waited.

Maybe I had died already and not felt it.

I opened my eyes slowly and glanced up. Demetre was frozen before me, the sword raised above his head, his face still contorted with effort.

I quickly created a path from the sky for the lightning to follow, and it struck into Demetre over and over again. Smoking, my brother jolted with each bolt and finally fell.

Behind him, Antolios and Bryan stood at the roof's edge.

The last bolt sizzled into my brother's body, and he stopped twitching, his eyes glazed. The liquid of his armor solidified into chunks and hit the roof. My sword clattered to the tiles.

"Are you both okay?" My throat seized up, and I clutched my abdomen. I thought I was going to be sick, but I had a feeling that would be a very bad idea. Passing out seemed a better plan. Blackness swam around my vision invitingly.

I let go of the storm, exhausted, and the clouds blew away.

Antolios and Bryan strode over to me, and Bryan said, "Antolios found a healing cleric in the rubble and made her heal me!" Bryan paused, and then he muttered, "You look as if you could use a cleric too."

Antolios cupped my chin in his hand and gazed into my eyes with that white light. It seared into my soul and blew the blackness away. I relaxed and pressed my cheek against his hand, taking in wet but easier breaths. The pain seemed further away too.

I looked past his shoulder and for the first time noticed the sea of people below, surrounding the palace. Ilium was swarming with all the armies. The palace was mostly rubble, and the city wasn't much better. Buildings were burning.

"He'll be okay." Antolios considered my brother's body. "Perseus, pick up Demetre, and let's get you to a healer."

I nodded and stood shakily. Blood trickled down my back and dripped out my sandal. I gathered my brother into my arms and lifted him. He was lighter than I thought he would be.

Demetre's singed, snow-dusted hair drifted across one of my arms. It was soft and fine. He had an almost pleasant expression on his face, relaxed and slightly lopsided. I ripped my gaze away and turned toward my companions.

I spat out the blood in my mouth.

Bryan started toward a hole in the roof and a staircase leading back down into the ruined palace. Antolios touched my elbow and urged me forward.

We only shuffled a few steps before rapid footfalls pounded up the stairs and dozens of people rushed onto the roof. Goran was the first to approach us, lithe and wearing the black of Laconia. The elves in gold stormed out of the hole next. They stopped in front of me, blinking at the dead body of the king of Epiro.

My vision faded slightly. I couldn't feel my legs, but I didn't fall. Antolios had his hand on my shoulder, his warm skin against my sweaty neck.

Someone took the king from my arms, and another asked me a question, but I wasn't sure what they said, so I nodded dumbly. A small hand, cold, reached up and touched my cheek, and I gasped from the rush of warmth that flooded my body. It felt as if I'd been dunked in a bath, and I held my bladder. The pain faded further, but the world still swam around me, and I couldn't parse the warbling voices. Antolios guided me down the stairs.

You're doing great, he said in my head. *Perseus?*

"Mmmm?"

Your family is safe. Demetre never had them. We're going to go see them right now.

"Thank you, angel." I was disoriented, and Antolios gripped me harder and pushed me on.

My sword was on my belt, but I didn't remember putting it there. When we cleared the palace ruins, Antolios pulled me into a box chariot. As we started to move, he held the reins, and I slumped against the front of the cart. Something was bothering me, but I couldn't figure out what.

Just a bit longer, Antolios said. *We're going to see your family.*

"Aye." I nodded and smiled, but then I frowned. When I yawned, my body felt too tight somehow, and I tried to stretch a little.

Antolios took one of his hands off the reins and touched my shoulder. *We're almost there.* I couldn't remember where we were going, but maybe when we got there I could rest. Eventually the chariot stopped, and we stepped out.

And then I saw the most beautiful sight in the world.

"Baba!"

"Perseus!" Andromeda and the kids rushed out of a pillared stone house to greet me. My kids slammed into me, and all my worries evaporated. I laughed and stroked their hair, running the fine threads through my fingers. Andromeda held a baby, and tears burned in my eyes.

Cynurus.

I had never met my son. He had olive skin, and black fuzz on his head. And he had my eyes. I wanted to kiss him and touch his pudgy face, but my hands were dark with grime. I cooed at him as the other kids begged me to pick them up.

Andromeda looked me up and down, frowning, and then peeked over my head at Antolios. He said something to her while my children all shouted at me.

"Okay. Take him," Andromeda said, and I glanced up. She waved the kids toward her. "Come to me. You can see Baba soon. Let him get cleaned up."

My kids backed away, and Antolios pushed me forward. When we reached the manor, several clerics in the black-and-white robes of Zeus approached us.

I looked behind me, grinning. "Those are my kids." I pointed them out to the clerics. My children were clustered around Andromeda, waving at me.

The clerics' expressions were oddly grave for seeing the cutest children on the planet. "Son of Zeus, we're going to have to perform surgery on you," the balding cleric said.

I grunted. "I already got healed."

The cleric muttered darkly. "You were healed by a *battle cleric*, and some of the metal was sealed inside of you." He straightened and shook the bag he was carrying. "Don't worry. I have everything I need. We'll get this done and have you cleaned up in an hour. The lady says that this manor has a medical ward of sorts."

"I'm coming too," Antolios said behind me.

I gave a last look toward the foyer, but we had already turned down a hall. I had really wanted to give Cynurus a kiss and to toss the other kids around. Antolios squeezed my shoulder, and I smiled at him reassuringly. "Fine," I said. "Make it quick."

We entered an infirmary and more people joined us, using terse sentences I ceased trying to understand. I was completely stripped and laid out on a cold table. I shivered, nervous.

Antolios placed his fingers on my temples. "I'll do it," he said.

That was the last thing I heard.

I WOKE up in a large bed with ornate posts, wearing the most ridiculously decorated purple chiton and chlamys. Blinking and rubbing my eyes, I tried to remember how I got there. Recent events were still foggy, but I had to piss, so I rolled off the bed and groped under the bed frame, my fingers gripping the cool metal of the chamber pot.

I carried the pot over to an open window and gazed out, lifting my skirt and positioning it in front of me. The cool night air hit my face as a heavy stream of urine pinged at the bottom of the pot. The moon was out, but no one had lit the torches on the streets. A thick smell of smoke was in the air.

And then I remembered.

It had only been hours since I had killed my brother, the king of Epiro.

I sighed and shook myself. Placing the chamber pot back under the bed, I took note that my sword was lying on a chest, and a stand next to it carried a full set of armor. Not as nice as the one my brother had made for me, but nice enough for royalty.

My brother had been right. I kept running, but now there was nowhere else to go.

I stretched my arms over my head and twisted side to side, feeling no twinges of pain. The healers had done a good job, but I was still tired. The mirror on the far wall showed that someone had trimmed my hair to just over my shoulders and completely shaved my face. Had I been groomed by elves?

The door opened, and Andromeda slipped inside the bedroom. She smiled at me and ran into my arms, and I spun her around in a circle and kissed her. She was wearing the most beautiful violet gown, and it matched the designs in the fabric of my chiton.

"I missed you so much," I said. "I'm glad that you and the kids are okay. I was worried. Can I see them now?"

"I missed you too." She buried her nose in my neck. "We have to attend a ball to celebrate the armies taking Ilium. The children want to come too."

I held her tightly, surrounding myself in her flowery scent, and rocked her back and forth. "How much time do we have?" I said.

She looked up at me, tears in her almond-shaped eyes. Her painted lips curved into a sly smile. "It doesn't matter. I don't think we'll need much."

THE NEXT day was full of meetings, and I had barely slept. There were a lot of fires to put out and decisions to be made. Most of Demetre's sons and daughters had pulled away from the capital, but some of them were stirring up trouble in other cities. The royal committee wanted a king on the Epirote throne as quickly as possible and had asked my opinion. Bryan had my full support, since he was a native of Epiro and had been the king's right-hand man for over eighty years. Additionally he was a demigod, so he had the divine right to rule in any kingdom. They had thanked me for my advice, but I still had to sit through hours and hours of deliberation.

In between meetings, I wandered through what was left of the gardens. The week went by slowly, and I had nothing but parties to amuse myself with. Because Antolios was either at Cora's side or hiding somewhere, the only times I was able to speak with him were at formal gatherings.

One morning, tea in hand, I was called to a private meeting with the rulers. They all sat on one side of a long wooden table, and I sat on the other. This wasn't how we had been doing meetings—were they changing their minds about sentencing me to prison for the death of my brother?

Cora was wearing a silver crown with emeralds, and Antolios sat beside her. His face was impassive with its hard lines, and the light from his eyes made it impossible for me to discern his expression.

What do they want? I asked Antolios.

He said nothing back. The rulers stared at me for long minutes, and I fiddled with my cup.

Cora finally addressed me. "Greetings, Perseus, Son of Zeus. As you know, Argos was nearly destroyed by the war and will require much assistance to recover its former strength."

I nodded.

"King Acrisius is an old man, may he continue to live a long life, but he will eventually pass, and you will inherit his throne," Cora said. "That puts you in a unique position to fit our present needs."

I blinked.

"Perseus, would you assume the throne of Epiro?"

I blinked again.

"You and Demetre were brothers, and we believe you may have more authority over his children, your nieces and nephews."

"What about Bryan?" I blurted.

This time King Butades, Zoticus's father, answered. His skin was dark as midnight, and his hair was so black it was bluish. When he spoke, his square jaw moved slowly, reminding me of Zoticus. "We have already spoken with Bryan. He said we would be fools to not accept you as king. While that statement was rather brash, we are all in agreement. You also have the support of many of your colleagues because of the way you handled the peace talks in Argos."

I flushed. Bryan had said that? My mind went to the nights we spent in prison, a lot of them hazy. He had seen… a not very flattering side of me.

It apparently didn't matter how much I fucked up my life. I was born to rule, and I couldn't keep running. The world would accept both me and my flaws because they had to. It was prophecy. This was what I was made for.

"Well, Perseus," Cora said, "will you take the throne?"

I smiled.

Chapter Twenty-Six

Andromeda

ANDROMEDA SAT with her children in the first row of the temple, swelling with pride for her family. Perseus knelt in front of the clerics, intoning words he read from a scroll. In one hand he carried an olive branch; in the other, he held his sword. His simple black-and-white ceremonial robes pooled around his bare feet.

After he had made his oaths to the people, the law, and the gods, a cleric dipped his thumb in oil and anointed Perseus. Thousands of Greeks crammed into the large temple, but it was quiet save for the shuffling of feet. The clerics placed a crown of dried olive branches on Perseus's head, and he was asked to rise as a king. Perseus stood and turned around. A roar went up and people clapped and cheered, their faces smiling.

During the executions of Demetre's sons and daughters—the ones who would not bow to their new king—Andromeda's children became quiet. Andromeda was uneasy at first, since none of them had seen death before, but they watched with rapt attention, and even Cynurus gazed at the executions on the dais, silent. Their unflinching pale blue eyes witnessed their father spilling the blood of those who would not kneel.

She and the children were called up to stand with Perseus in front of the crowd, and their heads were anointed with oil. They made their own promises to the people, the law, and the gods. Andromeda met Princess Danae's glistening eyes.

Andromeda and Danae had had several talks about Perseus and his destiny, and Danae had even spoken a little about sacrifice— something Andromeda understood better now.

The gods had protected Andromeda, but that didn't mean life was easy. She gazed at her children, standing proudly next to their father.

This was the gods' plan, and even though the clerics had said the gods were dead, Andromeda could feel them with her.

Andromeda had sacrificed everything for this. Her legacy was pure and eternal.

Chapter Twenty-Seven

I SAT at a table in a large dining room with King Acrisius, my mother, and my wife. I was already into several cups of brandy. My mother and wife droned on to my grandfather about my childhood, my children, my heroics, and my favorite time to take a shit.

I tapped my cup for a refill, and a servant poured brandy to the brim.

King Acrisius had lived a long life, much to my amazement. His skin was papery, translucent, with spidery blue veins running everywhere and little blotches of brown. He had a tremor that he tried to conceal with constant movement, and his beard was scraggly and sparse over a weak chin. My mother and I must have gotten our looks from my grandmother, but I hadn't met her and never would.

At least my grandfather was allowing me into Argos for the new Great Games. The flame ceremony had been that morning. Since Mount Olympus had collapsed, each kingdom brought fire and lit the torches together, symbolizing a new era of peace.

Andromeda told my grandfather that Perses had come of age and left to go on adventure.

Acrisius's voice shook. "Where is he traveling?"

"He wouldn't say, but he is sailing across the oceans with one of his boyhood friends. Perseus gave Perses his god-blade." Andromeda watched me expectantly. My mother did the same.

I tried not to sigh. "King Acrisius, I applaud your hosting of the first Great Games in many years. The capital looks beautiful," I said.

Acrisius smiled, showing yellowing teeth.

The truth was that the capital was the only thing in Argos that looked beautiful. The rest of the land had been torn by war, and everyone knew that the kingdom was broke from making repairs. The other rulers and I had brought gifts of gold so the king could save face.

"In what events are you planning to participate?" Acrisius asked me.

"Discus, wrestling, and the marathon. I haven't decided on chariot racing yet. I brought two horses, but honestly I don't favor either."

Acrisius nodded his approval and pointed a bony finger at me. "When I was a boy, I used to drive my father's horses, and when I became king, King Demetre gifted me with two good racers. Best horses I ever had. If you care for me to, I can take a look at the ones you brought."

"I would be honored." I didn't see any harm in that, and it would make my mother happy. The king's egg-like eyes glowed in youthful anticipation.

After supper, I escorted my wife back to our rooms in the palace. Andromeda was heading to bed, and before she went inside the bedroom she raised her brow at me in invitation.

I smiled at her. "I admittedly drank too much. I'm going for a walk."

She smiled knowingly. "Be careful. While you're out, will you check on the children?"

"That's a fantastic idea." I gave her a kiss on the head, and we parted ways.

Andromeda had certainly been enthusiastic about our sex life of late. Not that I was complaining, but the reason for this change was a depressing one. She had finally admitted that with the birth of Cynurus, she'd had more complications, and the clerics hadn't been able to fully heal a tear in her womb. It wasn't safe for her to get pregnant anymore. She took herbs so she wouldn't conceive, and I tried to convince her that nine children was plenty, but I knew she was still upset.

I paid Ava and Aiden now to keep them around just in case, and Andromeda probably knew their skills, but she hadn't questioned me. My courtesans served their purpose, and I didn't ruin my marriage. I should have been doing this ages ago. My youthful arrogance astounded me.

I still wasn't sure where Antolios fell into all of this.

I exited the palace into the night. It was early fall and cool in the mountains. Taking a breath of crisp piney air, I wove my way down the long drive to the fields where the events would begin the next day. Past those fields were rows of large white tents. There hadn't been enough room in the palace, so they had erected tents for the rest of the guests, and the older kids had wanted to stay in the midst of the action. I couldn't blame them.

I was just striding past the track when a white light lit me from behind, casting my shadow onto the grass.

I spun around. "Antolios!" I threw my arms open with a big smile.

Antolios wrapped his arms around me and squished me to his chest. He smelled wonderful, and I inhaled deeply.

"How long have you been here?" he asked.

My smile slipped, and I peeked up at him. "About a week."

"Where have you been?" He scowled. His hair flowed past his shoulders, naturally curled and golden. I wanted to run my fingers through it, but his irritation flamed through our bond.

I stepped away from him, and the feelings from the bond cut out. "Doing kingly things," I said. "My kids wanted to see the battlegrounds, and we traveled a bit. I was going to call on you, but I had to check on them first. Want to come with me?"

"I haven't seen you in ages," Antolios said.

I shrugged as we continued down the path together. "Seems as if it's been less time than we usually go without seeing each other."

Antolios blinked, and I could feel his gaze on me. "You're drunk."

"I *know* I'm drunk." I rolled my eyes. "You're probably drunk too, you're just better at hiding it than I am."

Antolios pulled a flask out of his coat and took a swig. "I'm not going to argue with that."

I laughed, and the sound echoed as we entered the maze of tents. The grass had been completely trampled, and the paths were now straw and dirt. Voices chattered on all sides of us, and lamps glowed within the tents.

"Hey," I said. "I'm glad you're here, because I don't actually know where my kids are. Did you bring yours?"

"Six came with us, including my first grandchild. A boy."

"A boy!" I said. "Congratulations! It just took a different set of balls than yours!"

"Shhh!" Antolios hit me on the shoulder, but he was smiling. I giggled.

We stopped before a large set of tents, and Antolios pointed at the far one. "They're fine." His eyes widened, and then he smiled.

"What?" I said.

Antolios's grin grew. "Gorgophone is *with* someone."

"What? Who?" I said.

"Shhh!" Antolios slapped me upside the head. "Katina."

I rubbed the back of my head. "Who?"

"*My daughter*, Katina," Antolios said.

I froze. "You mean *your* Katina is with *my* Gorgophone? Alone? Right now?"

"Yes." Now we were both grinning fools.

"Our families will be joined!" I broke into dance, which probably looked more as if I was trying to ride a horse backward. I stopped just as suddenly. "Do they like each other?"

Antolios shook his head. "I try not to pry."

"Bullshit!" I bellowed, which earned me another "Shhh!" and a slap.

"I can't believe you're asking me this," Antolios sighed.

"I'm drunk!"

"That you are. Okay... uh... they seem to be happy. Gods, Perseus, I need more to drink." Antolios put his finger on his chin. "You know, that's interesting, because I knew that two men could do that together, but I didn't know girls could. From what I can gather, Gorgophone is—"

My fist connected with Antolios's angular jaw before I knew I was swinging my arm.

He crumpled to the ground.

I bent over his unconscious form and put a finger to my lips. "Shhh!" Throwing him over my shoulder, I whistled as I stumbled back to the palace.

As I entered through the palace doors, the guards lifted their brows. I grinned and slapped Antolios's ass. "He can't handle his liquor," I said, and they chuckled. I took Antolios to the back where the kitchens were and set him on a chair. A man with a shaved head eyed Antolios warily and asked if I needed anything.

"A cup, some ice, and brandy." I grinned.

Doubt flashed across his face, and then was gone. He returned with the drink, and I put my hand on Antolios's cheek, healing him.

Antolios gasped awake and then glared. I held out my peace offering, and he took the booze, still scowling. "You ass." He gulped the brandy. "You could have healed me sooner."

I nodded judiciously. "But this was more fun. And what did we learn?"

"That spying on my daughter having sex is a lose/lose situation for me, even when you ask me to," Antolios said.

"What are friends for?" I smiled.

Antolios flinched and looked away. I swayed slightly in the uncomfortable silence, and finally Antolios sighed. "Do you want to get drunk and fuck?"

My cock grew heavy, and I supposed I wasn't *too* drunk. "I'm already halfway there."

We gathered more alcohol and another cup and hurried out of the kitchens. The palace didn't have any empty rooms because of the Games, even the ballrooms were full, so we climbed upstairs to Antolios's suite.

We stumbled inside, and Antolios shushed me. He tiptoed into the bedroom where Cora was sleeping, and I was struck with how much older she looked, with her long blonde hair streaked with white and wrinkles around her eyes. Antolios had said that she hadn't been pregnant for many years. I was over forty years old, and both Antolios and I should have gray in our hair… if we were human. I suddenly felt both old and young.

Antolios put his hand on Cora's head and then came back out with a leather bag. He stood next to me for I didn't know how long, and then said, "She's not going to wake. You don't have to stare."

Startled out of my musings, I jerked. "Sorry. I was just thinking."

Antolios snorted, ambled across the room, and set the bag on a low table in front of the white couch. I joined him and tossed back the drink he poured me, not even feeling the alcohol slide down my throat.

I stifled a belch. "When Perses left, I was worried that we'd have to wait for Electryon to come of age. This makes it so much easier. And who's to say we can't marry more of our children?" I drained my glass.

"It's so tempting to *encourage* things," Antolios said.

"Now you sound like a meddling old woman." I set my cup down. "Come sit on my lap."

Antolios leaned his long frame over and dug into his bag. He pulled out a vial of oil.

"Fantastic." I looked around. "Do we have a towel?"

"That would be polite." Antolios rose, setting down the vial. He disappeared into the washroom and threw a towel at me. I spread it on the couch, placed my silver-coated olive-leaf crown to the side, and stripped.

"Are you afraid we're going to break it?" Antolios said, glancing at my crown.

I grimaced. "Andromeda would kill me."

Antolios sighed and removed his circlet, lying it next to mine. "I was hoping we could fuck with our crowns on."

"Maybe later." I plopped down on the couch and snatched the vial, coating my cock with oil.

Antolios eyed my large erection, so I wagged it at him. He stepped forward and put his hands on my shoulders, then placed his knees along my hips. I held my cock by the base as he reached his hands back and spread his cheeks. Gripping my hips with his thighs, he slowly slid onto me and swallowed my cock into his tight heat.

I groaned but kept my eyes open, watching his face crease in concentration. He worked himself up and down in short strokes, taking me further into him, and slid onto my lap. I pulled him into a hug, squeezing him to me and kissing him, my tongue probing into his mouth. His hair fell around our heads and I rubbed his back, fingering the mole that sat just along his spine.

I started to thrust, but Antolios ripped his body away from me and stood, turning around and gripping my cock. He slid back down my shaft, his back to me, and grabbed my thighs in the vise of his hands. His head rolled forward, his back folding and his hair falling over his face. Sweat beaded on his nape.

"Gods, I never get tired of this." Charging my hands, I tickled the energy down his spine and massaged my thumbs up his long back.

Antolios breathed loudly through his nose. "Shut up and move faster."

I thrust into him and built up momentum, getting as much length in his ass as possible while still maintaining a smooth motion. Antolios moaned softly and reached around, stroking himself rapidly. He panted and bobbed his head while his skin blushed, and the earthy smell of sex intensified and hit my nose in heady waves. His ecstasy bloomed in my mind through the bond.

I clenched my eyes shut and leaned my head back against the cushions of the couch. Seizing his hips, I shook up the rhythm, jerking my cock in and out.

Antolios's body stiffened and he groaned. Through the bond I felt him take his pleasure, and it sent me over the edge. Grunting, I slammed him onto my cock and came. I panted, my jaw tight and neck muscles bulging, and then slowly relaxed my tingling hips against the couch and let out an explosive sigh.

Antolios chuckled and lifted himself off me.

"What?" I huffed.

"I came on our crowns."

"Of course you did."

Antolios, still chuckling, sauntered into the bathroom, and I used part of the towel to clean off. On his way back, he filled our cups with brandy and handed me mine. He winked. "I may have come in that too."

I smirked and took a sip. I was about to place my hand on his thigh when he shifted and gazed at me, bathing me in his white light.

"What?" I said.

"You called out Hermes's name."

I scoffed. "No I didn't. What? When?"

"Yes you did. In your head. When we were...."

Shit, I thought.

"I heard that," Antolios said, tensing.

Shit, I thought again. *I'm too drunk for this.* I refilled our glasses with brandy, but my hands trembled, and I slopped some brandy over his pale leg. He didn't seem to notice, his eyes still glaring into mine.

Antolios sighed and then dug into his bag at the table, pulling out a pipe, a bag of herbs, and a striker. He set everything in a dribble of dried semen, and packed the pipe. Working the striker, he lit the pipe, got it smoking, and handed it to me.

"What is it?" I took a puff.

"It's a type of herb," he said. "Good stuff." He slugged back the rest of the bottle of brandy.

I stared at him while handing him back the pipe and setting down my brandy. I held out my hand. "Angel?"

He tossed the empty bottle aside but frowned at my hand incredulously.

"Come on," I said, but he refused to touch me.

He took a few more puffs. His breaths quickened, and his heart raced.

"Listen." I shook my head, the world tilting dizzyingly. "It's meaningless. I'm married to Andromeda, you're my best friend, and the gods are gone."

Antolios stood up quickly. "You should go. I'm not feeling well."

"Maybe because you just drank enough brandy to kill a small horse." I rolled my eyes.

Antolios had his back to me, but I watched his muscles tighten. "I have been patient with you."

My eyes widened.

When he turned to face me, his mouth was a white line. The light from his eyes seared into me. "So fucking patient."

I crossed my arms and legs warily, covering my naked body.

"You and your fool heart." He cocked his head. "I suppose I should be thankful for that."

"Angel—"

"Shut up," he spat out. "I'm talking. I've been understanding of your behavior."

My face heated. "You broke it off with me!"

"Because I love you!"

"That doesn't—"

"Shut up! How am I supposed to feel about you and all those men and women and—whatever? They're in your head, and every time I see you there are more of them!"

My mouth dropped open. "Wh—? Not lately!"

"They are countless, Perseus. There is no room for me."

"That's not true!" My head throbbed. "I love you."

Antolios's lip curled cruelly. "What about Hermes?"

"We're all meant to love the gods!" The pain pulsed at my temples and sank into the back of my head, making me nauseated. My nose ran, and I lifted my hand to wipe it. My fingers came back bright with blood. Antolios didn't seem to notice.

"That's not what I mean, and you know it. He touched you in ways I can't. You experienced each other in ways I can't."

"You can't hold that against me. He was a god. What is this about?" My head swam.

Antolios snorted. "So you can be reckless and wild, and I have to take it because of your curse? I have to shut up and watch you use people and get used? I have to watch you die?"

"Die?" Shit, I felt as if I was dying. I slumped against the couch and tried to turn away from his stare, but I couldn't. "What are you talking about?" I mumbled.

"Eros," Antolios growled.

I dreaded his next words, but I asked anyway. "What about him?"

"I've seen it buried in your mind. You and he, together. It was nothing short of the most repugnant and terrifyingly beautiful thing I have ever witnessed." He crossed his arms, the muscles of his neck taut.

My head was in agony, but I tried to listen.

"You coupled for three days straight, doing things to each other that I don't even have the vocabulary for. At the end of the third day, he took you into the heavens. You flew so high you suffocated in the thin air. You *died*."

"But—"

Antolios screamed at me, his breath blasting in my face. "He ejaculated your life and soul back into your corpse and then dumped you behind the stables of that fucking tavern!"

I tasted blood. "I died? I don't remember."

He drew back, disgust plain on his face. "Does it matter? You did it. You did all of it."

"I was mindless. My curse."

"Were you? After *three days*?"

I tried to sit up but couldn't. "I was insane, and he was a god. I was helpless."

"Then there's Andromeda."

My entire body jerked. "Don't fucking bring her into this."

Antolios huffed. "Fine. I have so many other wonderful examples to choose from."

"It was meaningless sex, angel!"

Antolios thrust a finger at the door. "Out. Now."

I threw my hands into the air. "This is bullshit!"

"Get out now, or I will remove you." He turned his back to me.

My mouth worked soundlessly for a moment, and then I glared at his back. "Fine!" I said, but I couldn't move. The blood ran freely down my chest and pooled at my navel.

Antolios spun around, his face a mask of fury and loathing, and my heart broke into a billion pieces. He gripped me by the shoulders and tugged me up, dragging me to the door. He threw it open and shoved me into the hall.

I fell in a heap. The guards at the door put their hands on their spears but stood there dumbly, looking from me to Antolios, not sure who they should be helping. As soon as Antolios disappeared inside, the vise that had been gripping my head vanished. Relieved, I sucked in a few breaths.

I managed to stand before Antolios stomped back with my things and chucked them at me. Catching my crown out of the air, I then bent and gathered my clothes. I threw them on, not bothering with my sandals. The guards stood pointedly at attention again, purposefully staring over my head. I scowled and wiped the semen off my crown. Muttering darkly, I turned toward my room, but then changed my mind and stumbled out of the palace for a walk.

This was fucking ridiculous.

THE ARGIVE guards pushed me into a cell and locked the door behind me. My mouth still tasted like the bitter fairy bells they had shoved down my throat.

I was in jail. Again. Still naked and lubed up with olive oil from the morning's events, I sat on the cot in the corner. I had killed my grandfather.

Running my hands through my hair, I tried to piece together what had happened. I had thrown a discus—an ordinary discus. I was the first one to throw, so maybe it had been tampered with, but probably not. There were clerics and mages all over the fucking field, making sure everything was safe.

And I had thrown it normally, I thought. I watched the discus pass the fifty meters, then the seventy-five, and then it had sailed out of the pit and into the stands. I hadn't even burst.

And of course the discus flew right into my grandfather's skull.

I took a few deep breaths, calming myself, trying not to feel my awareness of the storm lessening. The air closed in on me. In and out. In and out. I glanced around the cell. Nothing much to see. Stone. A cot. A chamber pot. Instead of metal bars, there was a wooden door. Not specifically designed for demigods, then. Say what you wanted about Demetre, but the man knew how to make a prison. I kept trying to distract myself with something other than the events of earlier, but then my thoughts drifted to Antolios.

He wasn't speaking to me—hadn't been since our fight a few nights ago. He was still mad at me, and I wasn't sure why. He had never begrudged me my other lovers, my courtesans, or even my wife.

I shifted on the cot as anger flicked through me. Antolios was the one who had beseeched me to assist him in achieving peace among the demigods at the Trench. He was the one who told me to tell them that our race was dying—it was—and that we had to accept peace if we wanted to survive. Before, demigods hadn't been allowed to make their own kind, or at least it had been highly frowned upon, like discussing our curses had been.

So, in front of the demigods of Greece and their generals, I had repeated everything Antolios had said to me.

He had probably known what was going to happen next.

After arguments that stretched days, it was finally agreed that the demigod women who wanted to volunteer to breed with other demigods could. And they could have their choice of partners. It was assumed that any man would be willing.

When Selene and Alena voiced their desire to mate with me, I had looked to Antolios. He must have known how that was all going to go down. And of course I accepted Selene and Alena. What right did I have to refuse? It was for peace.

The day before, Selene and Alena had introduced me to my three children. A boy from Selene, and a pair of twins from Alena: a boy and a girl. They all had my eyes. I was sure Antolios has seen them, but I hoped Andromeda never found out about this. Seeing the continuation of my race had almost been worth it. However, it didn't change the fact that Antolios had used me like a whore. And then knowing what he knew, knowing what I'd been through, he had the nerve to condemn me because I slept around.

My head hit the stone wall as I slumped back. Sure, maybe I should have been sleeping with whores a long time ago, and not slumming around the docks for a quick fuck. I should have probably brought Sarah and Marta, my slaves at Seriphos, with me to Delos, and I could have even hired different ones, and Andromeda probably wouldn't have cared. She knew Ava and Aiden weren't there to just get me dressed in the morning, but she hadn't treated me with the same disgust as she had for my philandering in Delos. It was expected for someone of my birth to have well-bred whores. Yes, I had been a fool, but I wasn't anymore, and Antolios should have fucking known that. He could read my mind.

I hadn't realized how long I'd been stewing in my thoughts until I became aware of raised and muffled voices outside the room. My hearing was dimmed, I knew, from the fairy bells, and I sat up slowly, adjusting to the feeling of weakness. I tried not to think about the dead air, slowly breathing it in and out, and watched through the square hole in the door.

A door opened around the corner, and several pairs of boots marched in. The guards were followed by a pinched-faced Andromeda, swinging her arms in determination. She saw me through the hole in the door and ran, reaching out and holding my hands. The guards made a move to break us up but then stopped and stood stoically off to the sides.

"Perseus!" Andromeda breathed out a sigh. "I'm sorry it took me so long to get in here to see you. Your friend, Antolios, had to help me. They weren't going to let me in!"

I smiled and squeezed her hand. "I'm okay. They're just holding me until they decide what to do. I had no idea I could throw that far."

Andromeda brushed a strand of auburn hair from her flushed face. "It's not your fault! The clerics have all spoken with each other, and no one saw you use any powers. No mortal has ever thrown the discus that far, and to make a point, Zoticus threw a discus with a burst, and his didn't leave the sand pit. Almost everyone is saying you are a victim of divine prophecy. The gods still have sway!"

The fevered look on her face was unsettling, so I quickly said, "How are the kids?"

"They're fine. Everyone's fine. It's you we're worried about."

"King Acrisius was old, and as you said, this had been prophesied since before I was born. According to all witnesses it was an accident, and all the rulers chose to put me on the Epirote throne. This is mostly a formality while they tidy things up. I'm in no danger, and they'll have to let me go soon." Pain stabbed my stomach, and I winced.

"Are you okay?" Andromeda said.

"I'm fine, honey. Could you tell Antolios that I need to speak with him? I'll see you tomorrow. I promise I'll be out soon."

Andromeda nodded and kissed me through the bars. She left with the same determination as she'd had when she came in, her hips swinging.

Not long after she left, a white light lit the wall in front of my cell, and Antolios stepped into view. He had deep shadows under his eyes and held his lips in a tight line.

"I'm sorry," I said.

Antolios crossed his arms over his chest. "That's not what I'm mad about."

I grabbed the door, sagging from another stab in my abdomen. "Then what the fuck are you mad about?"

"You're different...."

My gaze bored into him, and he looked away.

Finally, he said, "You don't think of me like you used to. You're too busy."

I laughed. "It was foretold I would be king, and you, my mother, and all the gods have been drilling this into me all my life. Now I'm a king, and you're complaining that I'm too busy to run off and be with you? You had your chance."

Antolios's mouth tightened further. "I thought you would be king of Argos. That we'd be closer."

I let go of the door and stumbled to my cot, slumping onto the mattress. "You know I can't. I can't take both thrones."

"Says *you*."

I shot him a look through the opening. "Says *me*, and I am *king*."

He took a breath. "That's what you want? We'll see less of each other."

"You don't know that, and yes, this is the right thing to do," I said.

His chin trembled. "Fine," he said. "I'll talk to Cora and see what I can do."

"Thank you," I said.

He nodded and turned his back to me.

"I love you," I said.

Antolios paused. "I love you too, but sometimes I wish I didn't." He left, the guards following him out.

Sometimes I wished I didn't love him either. I rolled onto my side and tried to ignore the growing unease in my stomach.

A FEW days later, the kids and I packed up to head out of Argos—leaving behind Gorgophone and Andromeda. Of course the rulers had released me from prison, and when my mother gave me the rights to the Argive throne, I passed mine to Gorgophone.

My mother was staying as Gorgophone's advisor, and Andromeda had planned to remain for a few months, just to make sure that Gorgophone settled in. I wasn't worried. Our children were divine-blooded, and unlike me they seemed to enjoy the idea of being royalty.

The coaches were packed, and my kids and I were ready to go to Mycenae. The palace in Ilium had been destroyed and would probably take decades to rebuild, so we'd had to relocate. Mycenae had a summer palace, smaller and by the ocean, facing Elis. Living in Mycenae was almost a relief, because I hadn't known anything but the sea.

With a sigh, I trudged up the steps to the upper floors. It was time to say good-bye to Antolios. It was early, before breakfast, and Antolios should still be in his suite. I knocked on his door. One of the servants answered and then vanished to hail Antolios for me. I waited in the hall, picking my nails. My and his servants probably would have been happier if I had sent one of my servants to talk with one of his, but I had a penchant for wandering off. It kept everyone on their toes.

Antolios stepped out wearing long silver mage robes and slippers, his hair tied back and still damp. He looked at me silently.

I sighed. "Care for a walk?"

He dropped his chin in acquiescence, and we headed downstairs and out of the palace. The morning light was just cutting through the clouds, and the grass was heavy with dew. It was cool, and I could smell the animals in the trees.

When we were farther down the path, the trees grew thick, and the palace disappeared. Antolios took me by the shoulders and shoved me up against the trunk of a tree, nibbling my neck and breathing heavily into my ear. His hand slid under my tunic to my thigh and started to hike my skirt up.

"I can't," I breathed. I was shocked at the heady rush coming through the bond. "I have to get going soon."

He groaned, and the vibration shook my chest. "We won't take long."

Closing my eyes, I shook my head. "I'm sharing a coach with my kids...." Finally he stepped away from me, and I smoothed my hair into place. "I love you."

His gaze dropped, illuminating a fern. "Do you?"

"What kind of question is that?"

He shrugged a shoulder. "I don't know."

"A ridiculous one," I answered for him and put my hand on his arm. "You know I do. You feel it." As the bond opened between us, I could feel him pulling away from me. I was an open book to him, but he was closed to me—always had been.

Antolios crossed his arms over his chest. His pulse pounded under the pale skin of his throat. "When am I going to see you again?"

I dropped my arm. "I have a lot of company, and now I'll probably have to meet with all of Slayer's suitors, or whatever she decides to do. We'll see each other eventually, just as it's always been. We knew this day was coming, you more than I."

"It should have worked out better."

"It was shit from the beginning, so I'm not sure why you would think that," I said. Antolios swung his gaze toward me, and I squinted into the brightness. I could barely see the rainbow of his irises. I glanced away. "I have to get going. We'll keep in touch, yes?"

"Okay...," Antolios said.

I nodded and leaned over, giving Antolios a quick peck on the lips. Then I worked my way around him, heading out of the woods. I didn't see if he followed me.

As I approached the coaches, I spied Pegasus off in the grass, grazing. He was ignoring all the people ogling him. The winged stallion had appeared as I was hooking up my racehorse for the chariot events. At first I had been worried that I was in some kind of danger, especially after he frightened off the horse I was harnessing. But then he had not so subtly taken his place, baffling me. We had won the chariot event, and he'd been hovering around me since. I'd thought that maybe he'd hold hard feelings—I had killed his mother, but perhaps he looked at me as some kind of godparent. Technically we were both demigods, but he was admittedly a bit more special.

I hopped in the coach and patted all my children on the heads.

Electryon was holding the only laurel crown I had won for the week. He peered out where Pegasus was grazing. "Baba, is he going to follow us home?"

"Looks like." I pounded on the roof. As we moved out, my children talked excitedly about all the things they had seen—including Pegasus—and I sat back and listened to their chatter, smiling.

CHAPTER TWENTY-EIGHT

"I HATE spinach, Baba!" Autokthe said. She was the spitting image of her mother, with her auburn hair and creamy skin, but her eyes were blue. Her six-year-old mouth was downturned, and her little brows pinched. Even grumpy, she was adorable.

Andromeda had sent me a letter a month before.

She had said that Gorgophone was doing well, and it was a really good idea on my part to let her friend Katina stay with her. Andromeda had never seen Gorgophone so happy. So maybe Antolios and I had meddled a little.

In a week, Andromeda would head back to Mycenae, and I was admittedly relieved to be getting some help from her soon. The palace staff let the children run circles around them.

"But you used to *love* spinach!" I said. "Your mother said that you would run out of the house and singlehandedly eat all the spinach in the garden. Just like a goat." I bleated, and the children laughed. "Your poop was green. What a mess."

Autokthe squealed with laughter and proceeded to eat her spinach, bleating, and Sthenelus thought that looked fun, so he did too.

My chest ached. I had missed so much of their growing up. I just had stories, and two of my children were already gone. So much time lost.

Electryon and Heleus finished and asked to shoot arrows while the light lasted, so I let them leave the table early. Alcaeus and Mestor ran to catch up, even though neither of them could hit objects from as far.

I helped Cynurus keep the bits of vegetables on his plate so he could grab them with his pudgy fists and shove them into his gaping mouth, his pink gums dotted with little white teeth.

After supper, I took the younger kids to the nursery while I signed documents and opened mail. At dark, the older kids came in, and I tucked everyone into bed, smelling their sweet, young scents. After a few more letters, I hopped into bed with my courtesans.

TITRONIS WOKE me later that night. The older man's face was downcast. "Apologies, Your Majesty, but there is a courier who says he has urgent news from Argos, for your eyes only."

I rubbed my eyes and rolled out of bed, heading out the door.

Titronis coughed. "Perhaps a robe, my king? Or a tunic?" He was already holding one up for me, complete with a belt and sandals.

I rolled my eyes and took the offered clothing, throwing it on and resuming my way to my suite's reception room. The door was open, and a courier was pacing back and forth, still breathing heavily from the run here. He held a scroll clenched in his hand, stamped with Argos's gray wax seal. My daughter's seal.

My stomach dropped, and I approached the courier in slow motion. I must have been moving faster than that, though, because the man didn't even see me until I was in his face and snatching the letter out of his hands.

I unfolded the letter and read the first few lines.

The scroll dropped from my fingers and hit the rugs.

The courier was saying something, and Titronis was talking too, but I couldn't process any of it. I had to hurry. Bolting out of the room, I didn't bother with the stairs. I jumped from the third floor to the second and then from the second to the first. I took off toward the main doors at a sprint.

My guards made surprised noises as I blurred by them into the breezy night air.

"Pegasus!" I roared into the sky. "Pegasus!"

The men at the gates barely got them open before I was running outside the palace grounds, stoking the storm. When the sky had enough power, I created a cyclone and dropped it onto my head, soaring up. The guards, who had foolishly been following me, were tossed away from the winds. I tore up the road north.

I hadn't gone far when a flash of white appeared next to me in the sky. I looked at Pegasus, and he looked back with black eyes. I dropped the cyclone.

As I fell, the skirt of my tunic flipped up, and my hair whipped around my head. Pegasus flew under me, and I landed on his back just before we hit the ground. With a few powerful strokes, the winged horse had us back up in the air.

"To Argos," I said.

Pegasus snorted as we sailed.

IT TOOK us several days to fly to Argos, stopping only so Pegasus could sleep. We spent nights where we could, and I didn't recall if I ate or not. I didn't think I slept. I prayed I wasn't too late to save her. It was my job to save her.

When Pegasus and I spied the palace of Argos in the distance, we dove out of the sky. Pegasus hadn't yet landed when I jumped off his back and onto the grass. I ran toward the palace doors, and the guards must have recognized me or Pegasus, because they let me in without question.

Someone in the livery was standing in the reception hall. "Where is Slayer?" I asked him. My voice was broken and gravelly.

The man gaped at me. "Uh…. Sir?"

Gorgophone glided down the stairs, wearing black.

I swallowed and hurried up the stairs to meet her. I hugged her, pulling her to me. She had her dark hair done up in jewels, and her gown was fine silk. "Where's Mama, Slayer?" I held my daughter at arm's length, searching her face.

She looked at me in shock and horror. "Baba, what's happened to you?"

"Please, Slayer, where's Mama?"

Her big blue eyes filled with tears. "Didn't you get my letter?"

I nodded. "Where's Mama? I just need to see her to know she's okay." Gorgophone started to cry, and I rubbed her shoulders. She was shaking. "It's okay. I'm here now."

She took a large breath and wiped her eyes. "Okay, Baba. I'll take you to Mama." I followed her down the stairs, trying not to be impatient, but I couldn't understand her lack of urgency. Where was Andromeda?

Gorgophone took us past the reception hall to the last ballroom door at the end of the long hall. She stood outside the white double doors, looking at me expectantly.

What was Andromeda doing back there? I didn't want to go in.

"Slayer, could I have a minute?" I started to cry and put my hand on the door. Tears were streaming down Gorgophone's cheeks, but she nodded and touched my arm before she walked back down the hall. I took a breath and opened the door.

And there, on a stone slab in the middle of the room, was a figure wrapped in white linen.

My sobs strangled in my throat. As I approached the bed of rock, the smells of the fragrant oils they had soaked the cloth in wafted around me. I couldn't see much of her shape, but I touched what I thought was her arm, bound to her side, and then slid to the floor. I lived in that one moment of pain forever, the ache in my chest unbearable. Tumbling into darkness, I was unable to open my heavy eyelids, and my cheeks burned. The river that had been running down them had dried up long ago.

Footsteps pulled my head up, and the blurry shape of my mother approached me, her arms outstretched. I pulled her to me and buried my face in her neck, inhaling her wonderful smell. I sobbed with heaving wet noises, but I had no more tears to give. My mother held me and smoothed my hair.

I had to swallow a few times before I could speak. "Mama, what's happened?"

My mother sighed. "She died in her sleep. No one knew her condition."

I pulled away and gazed into my mother's face. She was old now. Creases ran along her mouth and eyes, and her hair was mostly gray. Her lips were flakey and pale. She hadn't worn makeup.

"What do you mean?" I said.

She spoke slowly to me, her voice softer and higher than usual. "The clerics said she had a weak spot in her womb, so she couldn't carry the pregnancy."

"But she couldn't be pregnant. She took herbs. We knew about this," I said. My mother squeezed me. "Did they check the herbs? Were they bad?"

"My beautiful boy." She shook her head.

"Maybe they were old herbs? Shouldn't we check?" My lip trembled.

My mother squeezed me again.

I stared at the ceiling, then past the ceiling, and I sent my awareness into the rainy sky. "Is she up there?" I said.

"You can see her tonight." My mother rubbed my arms.

I nodded and rose laboriously. Andromeda wasn't in this body anymore. She was up in the heavens where she belonged and where I would join her soon. I walked heavily out of the ballroom, my mother holding on to my arm. She led me upstairs as the faces around me floated in a haze.

We reached the doors to a suite on the upper levels, but I stopped and didn't go inside. "I want to be in the room she was in," I said.

My mother sighed but nodded. "It may take some time."

I trudged to the rail, looking down over the reception hall. I wasn't sure how long I stood there, staring at the mosaic on the floor in front of the palace doors, but finally my mother took my arm again and led me farther down the hall.

I knew we were in the right place before we stepped inside. It smelled more of Andromeda in here than her body in the ballroom had. It also smelled of blood, but I tried to ignore that. I shuffled toward the bedroom, the smells getting stronger, and slipped off my sandals and clothes and crawled into the fresh sheets. I placed my crown reverently on the nightstand, and found a pillow that smelled more like her than the others. I clutched it to my chest.

My mother kissed me on the head. I tried to tell her that I loved her, but I was trapped in my own head. She smiled at me, her eyes filling with tears, and told me she loved me. She left and shut the bedroom door.

In the hall, a deep familiar voice spoke with my mother. I fell asleep.

WHEN I awoke it was quiet, late. The days before echoed in my mind as if I were in a nightmare, but I knew they were the truth. It was dark, and I was alone, and I would be in the dark and alone forever.

I put my feet on the rugs on the floor. My toes were caked with filth, and my nails were chipped in several places. I must have smelled terrible, but it was hard for me to notice it, as if it weren't my body, so I didn't care. I was gone, somewhere else.

I had been left a full assortment of fresh clothing, but I threw on the simple tunic, not bothering to belt it. I pushed my greasy hair behind my ears and stepped out of the bedroom into the suite and then lumbered into the hall.

The guards at the door nodded to me, and one of them said something, but I was already moving away. I had an odd feeling—the world was washed-out and gray. I was probably hungry. That seemed right, but I didn't feel my stomach growling. I entered the kitchen on the bottom floor, and a serving girl asked if she could get me anything.

"No, I'm all right," I heard myself say. The knives on the chopping block caught my attention, and I grabbed one. I touched it to my thumb, drawing a drop of blood, and glanced over my shoulder, but the serving girl had left, so I took the knife with me.

I also snagged a bottle of brandy on my way out.

I trudged out of the palace and onto the path that led through the woods, past the place where Antolios had wanted to have sex. Another lifetime ago. My breath bloomed in front of my face, but I didn't feel cold. The tall dark trees eventually opened up to a giant clearing with a lake where the moon and stars were reflected off the surface of the water. I sat on a giant rock at the edge, leaning back and gazing into the sky.

There she was.

The pattern of stars was bright, freshly born.

"Hello, honey," I said to her. The constellation twinkled at me as tears welled in my eyes. "I'm sorry. I know we could have been happy."

I gazed at Andromeda for a long time, absorbing as much of her light as I could. Then, as if my hand were not my own, my fingers found the knife, and I picked it up, turning the point toward my heart. The tightness in my chest seemed to ease as I pulled it back. I could finally breathe.

I sighed and thrust the knife.

My muscles seized before I could pierce my body. I couldn't move from my neck down. I made a noise as the knife fell out of my hands, clattering to the stones. Swinging my head around, a tall pale figure stood at the edge of the woods.

"That is not the way back to Andromeda," Antolios said. His face was grim, but his eyes were soft. He pitied me. He strode up to my rock and grabbed the bottle of brandy. Opening it, he chugged a quarter of the bottle, coughing when he pulled it from his lips. He glanced at the knife that had dropped and kicked it with a slippered foot, sending it into the lake.

Antolios regarded me, but I didn't feel the light on my face. I was already on the other side, or I would have been if it weren't for him. "This isn't what she would have wanted, Perseus. She wouldn't want you to abandon your children."

"It's your fault." The world crashed around me. My eyes burned, and my nose clogged. I was still *here*, and it *hurt*.

Antolios shook his blond curls. "You're wrong."

"Bullshit! You knew!" I strained against his hold on me, using my will.

Antolios watched me sadly. "You don't understand."

"I could have saved her," I said. "But you didn't tell me. You knew and you lied."

"You couldn't have stopped it," he said.

"So you're saying you knew!" I tried to move, grunting with effort. My body was useless, and my brain wasn't much better.

"She thought the gods were protecting her," Antolios said softly.

Spit frothed at my lips, and I couldn't stop the tears from running down my face. "Let me go!" I called the storm, ready to strike Antolios with lightning, but then my muscles released and I fell to the ground. I glared up at Antolios, shot to my feet, and ran in the opposite direction. I entered the woods and heard him following me. "I never want to see you again!" I shouted over my shoulder. "I hate you!"

The footsteps stopped, and he gasped. "You don't mean that."

I staggered forward, not looking back. "We're through. It wasn't even someone else who separated us. It was *you*. It was always you."

I ran and ran and ran.

CHAPTER TWENTY-NINE

Four years later
Antolios

ANTOLIOS SAT in his chair with a blanket over his legs. A cleric came in, and he presented his arm to her. She touched him and filled him with empty light, and then left. It wasn't really for him, it was for everyone else.

It was to keep up appearances.

Similarly, the trays of food were brought in and then taken back uneaten. They kept bringing them anyway, for appearances. If Cora groused enough, Antolios would take a bite or two, but luckily for him she was too busy to nag him much. When she did yell at him about eating, it was only because she wanted to yell at him for something.

He'd had two jobs: being the general of Thessaly's armies and producing a royal lineage. Now he had none. His chest felt heavy, and not for the first time he wondered if this was what it was to be human—weak.

Selene came into Antolios's room and pulled up a chair next to his. She stared out the window with him. "How are you feeling?" She always said the same things.

"Fine." He always said the same things.

She was pregnant again. She barely wore clothing, preferring to show off her round, silver belly. Her pregnancy had taken her away from the army and her other duties and had given them more time with each other. This time she was pregnant with Palamedes's child. She had fantastic taste in men.

"Adrastus was playing with clay the other day, and he sculpted it into a beautiful castle," Selene said. "There weren't any clerics around, but I think he may have knowledge of art as his power."

"That's great," Antolios said when he realized that Selene wanted him to say something.

Selene gave him a furtive glance. "Have you heard anything from Perseus?"

"No." Antolios toyed with his hot alcoholic beverage that also had beef stock in it. The cooks thought they were being so clever. He drank some of the alcoholic broth.

Selene touched his leg. "What are you going to do?"

Antolios pointed out the window. "Do you see the northern geese? They've come back for the summer."

Someone handed Selene a cup of tea, and she thanked them. "He's a stubborn man, everyone knows that. Just give him some more time."

Antolios nodded.

"How's Cora doing?" she asked.

Antolios sighed. "I don't know." He sighed again and closed his eyes. "I'm sorry. I meant to say that I wish I didn't know. She's not as angry anymore, at least. Now she feels burdened, as if I were a sick dog she has to take care of until it dies."

Selene sipped her tea.

"Did I ever tell you about the fight I had with Zoticus over Perseus?" Antolios said suddenly.

"I didn't know you got into fights."

Antolios chuckled. "I usually don't. A week after I had paired with Perseus, Zoticus confronted me after class. He said I was no good for Perseus, and I would destroy his innocence and break his beautiful heart. Even then, I knew he was right...." Antolios took another sip of his broth, probably the only thing keeping him alive at this point. "I told Zoticus to back the fuck off, or I'd turn his brain to squid goo."

"You didn't." Selene laughed.

"Not only that, but when he came at me, I took him out, left him lying in the grass for hours. He didn't bother Perseus or me again, but it seemed so out of character of me. Then Perseus proposed a way for us to be closer, and I think that was the moment I fell in love with him. His mind baited me, but I was forever his when I discovered his heart."

"He loves you too, you know."

"He did. I don't know why, but he did. He's beautiful, kind, a force of nature. I'm manipulative, and a recluse."

Selene shook her head. "You stopped a war to be with him."

"Look at how that turned out."

"Antolios...." Selene lifted her arm and shaped her hand into a long silver blade. "You can't be like this forever."

The light from the candles flickered off of the blade. The reflections across its planes distorted as if they were from another world. Antolios's gaunt face stared back at him, and his light wavered.

"These hands have bathed in so much blood, but I would spill more for your sake," she said.

Antolios laughed, a dry cough. "I'm too much of a coward. I'd stop you."

"Better to die fighting." She shrunk her hand back down and flexed her silvery fingers.

"Probably true." Antolios put his hands on the armrest and tried to push himself up. Selene set her tea to the side and easily yanked him to his feet. "I think I'm going to lie down." He shuffled off to his bedroom but then paused. "Thank you for your offer."

Selene's mournful thoughts followed him to the bedroom until he shut the door.

Chapter Thirty

"My, look at all of you. Electryon, you look just like your father," Vora said.

I smiled. That's what my mother had always said about my second son. Now that Electryon was older and more filled out, other people were seeing it too.

Vora, one of Antolios's daughters, was visiting from Thessaly. It wasn't unusual for me to host royalty, but she had come a long way, and I had a feeling it wasn't just a social call. Nothing ever was anymore.

Electryon smiled with my soft lips. "I'll be eighteen next year," he said.

"You'll be a man," Vora said. "Heleus, you look like Perses, except he was flame-haired if I recall."

Heleus grinned. "Aye, but I don't have freaky freckles." He pointed to Vora. "You have purple eyes. That's awesome."

I was about to chastise my son's rudeness, but Vora winked at me. She turned back to Heleus. "Yes. The god-blood runs strong in our families, no? All of my sisters have different-colored eyes."

"How many different colors?" Autokthe said, whistling slightly because she was missing teeth.

Vora leaned forward. "All of the colors of the rainbow." The kids gasped.

"Even red?" Autokthe said.

"I have two sisters with reddish eyes," Vora said.

Autokthe giggled. "Red is my favorite color."

The servants brought the next dish in, a soup in colorful pots filled with feta, sausage, peppers, and bread in a delicious broth. I poked through the bread and cheese layers, mixed it up, and dunked into the steaming soup with my spoon. Bringing it to my lips, I blew on it.

"This is wonderful," Vora said. "Is this a regional dish?"

"It's Mama's recipe," Autokthe said.

The table dropped into silence, and all the kids glared at Autokthe. Her cheeks became rosy, and she hunched in her chair.

I smiled at Vora. "It's a specialty of the lost island of Crete, and the only thing that Andromeda knew how to make when I met her. Hers was the best." On the outdoor terrace, the sounds of gulls and the ocean breezed into the dining hall, but not even a spoon clinked. Vora placed her hands in her lap.

"How's Davus?" I asked.

Vora perked her head up and smiled. "He is well, a good kid."

"It's been a long time since I've seen him."

Vora picked her spoon back up. "I have two others now."

"Really?" I raised my brows. "How time flies."

The kids finally started eating again, and we finished the rest of the meal rather pleasantly.

After supper, I sat with Vora in the drawing room and drank wine in front of the fireplace. The kids were outside or running around the palace giving the nursemaids fits.

"How was the trip?" I said.

Vora sipped her wine. "Long, but pleasant. It's quite warm this time of year."

I smiled. "It's only spring."

Vora's nails tapped her cup with tiny *plinks*. "My mother wanted to know if you got her letters."

I tensed. "Yes."

"Then why haven't you responded to them?"

I set down my cup and folded my arms. "I have. I've signed trade agreements, hosted parties for her nobility, and last month I allowed an entire contingent of her soldiers to cross into Epiro as they searched for Nicanor, the fugitive."

"Not *those* letters," she said.

"She doesn't need to worry. My falling-out with the crown prince is a personal matter and does not affect my politics with Thessaly. Please assure her of that. If I have been absent from recent political gatherings, it is merely because I am still in mourning."

"I'm sorry for your loss," she said softly.

"Thank you."

Vora dragged her finger across the rim of her elven glass, creating a high-pitched whining noise. She saw my pained expression and stopped. "I don't know if you care, but he's sick."

I took a sip of wine.

"I saw him when he came back from Argos. I was standing at the window to my room. His guard had arrived weeks earlier to warn us of his coming. To *warn* us.

"Father rode into the port dirty and greasy. He didn't say hello, wave, or anything. He disappeared into a manor and didn't leave for a month. The only times I saw him was when we were both looking out our windows.

"He still isn't okay. He barely eats. Now he takes herbs so he can be around us when he's upset, but they make him sick. He cut his hair. He doesn't even look like my father anymore." Vora snuck a peek at me.

"He'll be okay." I stared into my glass. I hadn't even tasted the wine, even though it was from my old farm.

Vora drained her glass and set it down. "I know about you two."

I let out a breath and eyed her. "What do you want from me?"

"Write to him," she said.

"What do you want me to say?" I pinched my nose.

"I don't know what happened," she huffed. "But surely there is something you can say?"

"I have nothing to say."

"But he needs you," she said.

I pushed myself off the armrests and strode across the tiles to the balcony, my back to her. "Stay as long as you will, Vora, but I will speak no more of this." The breeze was still warm, but I felt a chill.

"No." Her voice was hot and sharp, but I didn't turn around. "You broke my family, and Katina and Gorgophone can't marry because of you two!"

I stiffened. "They're getting married?"

"They want to have a ceremony, but our fathers are fools."

I turned around. Vora's face was twisted, and her cheeks blushed. When I had first met her, she was a girl. Now she was tall and blonde, as both of her parents. Her eyebrows were delicate, like Antolios's. She had lost her knobby knees and was quite beautiful. She wasn't a girl any longer.

"It's his fault, not mine," I said, feeling foolish.

She rose and came toward me, the silver rings in her ears glinting in the candlelight, and took my trembling hands, enclosing them in her firm, warm ones. She had long fingers like her father too. "He wants you to say something."

I swallowed the lump in my throat. "He's a fool for wanting this." Vora's irises were large and violet, a piece of his beautiful rainbow. Gods, how I missed his rainbow.

"Then say it to me," she said. "If you say it to me, he will see."

I lifted my arm, so heavy, and grabbed her chin, pulling her gaze down to mine until we were eye to eye. She held her breath.

"Enjoy what you have left, Antolios, as I do." I dropped her chin and walked out.

Behind me, Vora sobbed. "Is that it?"

I kept walking.

CHAPTER THIRTY-ONE

Antolios

ANTOLIOS STOOD in front of the brazier. For the last few months he'd had dreams, and other demigods were having them too. The gods were coming back—some had even been seen for short periods at their temples—but they were not at their full strength. He hoped they were strong enough for this.

He signaled to have the hyacinths dropped into the brazier. There were thousands. Belief equaled power. As the aroma of burned flowers filled the air, Antolios put his hands behind his back. The yellow ceremonial robes glared in the light of the sun, and his bare toes poked through the hem.

It didn't take long.

"Hyacinths," said a smooth, light voice behind him, "while appreciated, were not necessary."

Antolios turned and couldn't help but smile. A laurel-leaf circlet nestled in his father's golden curls, and a bow with a quiver holding arrows hung on his back.

"I know," Antolios said.

Apollo stepped up to the brazier and inhaled the fragrance of the sacrifice. "It tastes sweet and yet horribly bitter."

"I thought it would be appropriate."

Apollo looked at him, his blue eyes soft. "The time has come to give my Icarus better wings so that he may catch the sun."

Antolios eyes stung. "Then you'll do it?"

Apollo reached up, pulling Antolios's head down to his shoulder and into the crook of his neck. He smelled of honey and wine, and every breath made Antolios feel safe and loved. His muscles became liquid, and his eyelids drooped. He hadn't realized how tired he had been.

"You are my son. I'd do anything in my power for you."

They wandered to a pond and dangled their feet in the water, the fish nipping at Apollo's toes. Antolios smiled at the goldfish. Even the smallest species worshipped the gods in their own ways.

"What will you do if he decides on another path?" his father said.

Antolios watched the fish. "I don't know. I've been complacent for too long, and I may be too late, but I have to try, and if he decides he doesn't want that, then maybe he'll have me in some other way. I can't be without him anymore."

"And this is how you want to be with him?"

"He's always felt one step behind me, as if I was manipulating him. I want him to trust me." Antolios glanced at his father. "Why? Do you know something?"

Apollo shook his head and gave an enigmatic smile. "We gods can't know everything. Mortals have free will, and even prophecy is written in the fabric of the universe and oftentimes doesn't mean what we think it does. For example, the telling of our supposed deaths."

"What do you mean?" Antolios said.

Apollo stared into the sun, looking wistful. Finally he said, "Some thought we would die as mortals or be reborn, but we remained unchanged, though there have been changes. Uranus is alive, and he and Gaia retook the throne. The Olympians are demoted, and the Titans are free again. Everything has come full circle, and although it will take some getting used to, perhaps now there will be peace in heaven and earth."

Antolios smiled. "You changed the subject."

Apollo winked. "I think it's safe to say that the both of you will have to learn how to communicate."

"I will," Antolios said earnestly. "I'm going to do things the way I should have from the beginning."

Apollo smiled, pulled his lyre from somewhere, and began to play. Antolios lay down in the grass, his legs still in the pool, and listened as he watched the clouds lazily move across the sky. They reminded him of Perseus's eyes, when Perseus desired him. He missed Perseus desiring him.

Antolios's eyes drifted closed.

"It's done," Apollo said and rose.

Antolios jerked awake and knew that time had passed, but he wasn't certain how much. He stood as well, and Apollo took his head in his hands and kissed his forehead.

"I love you," Apollo said. "All you have to do is call."

"So you say." Antolios smiled.

"You never really needed me before." Apollo winked.

"Sometimes it's nice just to chat."

Apollo tilted his head and grinned boyishly. "Godspeed, son." He vanished into a sunbeam.

Antolios sat heavily onto the grass, watching the fish, watching the sky, and hoping it wasn't too late.

CHAPTER THIRTY-TWO

A LONG leg reached out of the big black carriage parked in the drive at my palace in Mycenae. Antolios stepped out wearing a tunic. He locked gazes with me, smiling. All at once, many other tall pale figures ran out of the coaches and flooded the drive.

One of the younger girls ran up to me and tugged on my purple chiton. I looked down at her. "This is my dolly." She held up a doll for me to see.

I smiled and picked up the little girl, sitting her on my hip, and we climbed the steps to the palace. "What's your dolly's name?"

"Andromeda. She's a princess, but she's going to be a beautiful queen when she's big."

I glanced at the dark red hair sewn on the doll's head and smiled. "She looks just like her."

The last year had been good.

The greatest easing of my broken heart had been when Perses had visited from across the seas. He was the king of a kingdom called Persia, and his queen and son were dark, darker than the Greeks. His wife, Banu, didn't speak Greek, but she was clearly in love with him. The looks she gave my son surpassed the boundaries of language.

I had a grandson, Adar, born two years ago. When I saw those little halos of hazel and wisps of auburn hair, my breast ached with understanding. This was what Andromeda had worked for. She was still alive in this child, and in all of our children.

This was our legacy.

Perses and I fought hydras attacking the coastal byways, with him wielding the god-blade I had given him. Gorgophone and Katina finally had their wedding ceremony. Afterward, Perses had sailed back to Persia, and I had ridden home to Mycenae.

And I had only seen Antolios in brief glimpses.

We hadn't really spoken during the festivities, but I had invited him and his family here to try and mend some bridges—they were family now. And I had to see what else this could be.

THE NEXT morning, Antolios met me at breakfast. His hair was short, all the way up to his ears. I hadn't asked him about it, but it made his shoulders look even broader. I was given a report of killer sharks in the area that were attacking people off the coast. Antolios and I agreed that we could handle the problem, just the two of us.

We got ready for the trip. For me, that meant bringing spears; for Antolios, that meant bringing booze. It took four men to carry our boat to the water's edge, even though we could have easily taken it ourselves. Antolios and I rowed the craft into the surf, and soon the white sands of the shore drifted away. I threw the oars down and grabbed the chum buckets, spreading the fishy bloody mess in the water. We didn't attract the sharks right away, but the gulls perched on the edge of our boat and dove for fish hunks. It was bright out, and I was already sweating. I wished I had brought my hat as I stripped naked.

Antolios didn't have to worry about getting burned, one of the reasons he never got any color. He pulled a cork from a brandy bottle and slugged the liquid back.

"You aren't going to fight?" I eyed the bottle.

Antolios grinned and pulled down the front of his tunic, exposing his hard abs. "Do I look like I need to exercise?"

I had to agree that he didn't. If anything, he could use a bit more meat on his bones. I sat on a bench and watched for signs of my prey, and Antolios continued to drink heavily. He cleared his throat and turned my head to him.

His face was fallen, gaze on the boat deck. "Perseus," he said. "I'm sorry."

My heart sank into my gut. I knew we needed to talk, but I wasn't certain if I was ready.

Antolios took another long pull off the bottle. "I didn't mean for things to happen the way they did."

I shook my head, wanting him to stop and yet needing to hear it.

"I swear on heaven and earth that I never meant to harm her. I was only trying to respect her wishes. There have never been any rules for who

I am and what I do. Being in my position...." Antolios's shoulders heaved once, and then he slouched. "I made a mistake. I'm sorry."

I wiped my tears away with my palms. I wished I could see his real eyes and not just his sterile white light. "You should have told me." I sniffed. "But I was wrong saying what I did. You didn't kill her. I did. I killed her the moment I rescued her from Cetus. We lived a lie born of my stubbornness and fear."

We both stared out onto the ocean. I was tired of regret, and I didn't want to be this way for the rest of my life. "We all did the best we could," I whispered. I gazed at Antolios. "I accept your apology."

Antolios smiled, but then his smile fell. "I have something else to say."

I raised a brow.

He cleared his throat. "I had my father take away my ability to read your mind."

I frowned. "What? Why? Is this a game? To what end?"

Antolios shook his head. "No game. And I don't want to talk of endings." He took a deep breath and smiled. "I want to talk of new beginnings. Be my friend, be whatever you can find in your heart to be with me, from now until we both go to the Underworld."

Wasn't that why I had brought him here? To say as much? My mind was still reeling when Antolios made a noise.

"One is here," he said.

I stood up, watching for the crest in the water.

Antolios chuckled and pointed. "It's over there. Go get it."

I took me a second to realize that Antolios had already killed the shark—with his bloody brain. I sighed and set my spear down, and then dove where Antolios had pointed. About twenty strokes out, I came across the shark, belly up, and I grabbed its tail and dragged it back to the boat. I hoisted myself up and hauled the shark in. It was easily as long as our craft. Antolios had to scoot over to make room for the fins.

I sat back down, and Antolios said, "How are things?"

I scanned the water. "Good. Mestor will be a man next year, and I think he'll join the other boys on adventure. Autokthe is turning into a beautiful woman, just like her mother. How are your kids?"

"Doing well. Only Varana lives at the palace anymore. Everyone else has been married off or has their own manor on the grounds. Have you talked to Gorgophone about heirs?"

"They said they would think about it," I said. "Why?"

"As much as they enjoy being referred to as the 'virgin queens,' I think they may use Bortos for heirs."

My jaw dropped, and I glared at Antolios. "What? Why? No." I stood up, my fists clenching. "It's not necessary. I told Gorgophone that one of her brothers could take the throne when she passed, or even one of their children."

Antolios shrugged. "It's their decision."

I growled and paced the boat, causing it to list from side to side. "Bortos? He's smarmy and two-faced. Gods, you remember him during the peace talks! Impossible."

Antolios chuckled.

I glared at him. "What?"

"I had forgotten about this. I've had so many daughters. I had to get used to seeing their thoughts about their lovers, and the accompanying graphic images." Antolios shuddered. "Sometimes the *smells*...."

My neck itched, and I snatched up a spear.

Antolios was still laughing at me. "Another shark is to the north. Why don't you go get this one?"

I snorted air from my nose and jumped into the water, swimming to where Antolios had pointed.

The fish apparently sensed my frustrations, because as soon as it caught wind of me, it turned around, swimming away. I sped up, slicing through the water, and reached a hand out, gripping its tail.

The shark flipped toward me and snapped its jaws, but I stuck my spear through its mouth and thrust up into its brain, twisting it around in its skull. By the time I was done stabbing the fish, I couldn't really recover any of the parts. My arm was bleeding, and I had to yank out a few shark teeth, but I was feeling decidedly better. I spotted the boat and made smooth strokes toward it.

I hoisted myself into the boat and brushed my wet hair from my face. Water ran down me in rivulets. I grabbed the other brandy bottle and popped the cork with my teeth, spitting it over the side and taking a gulp.

Antolios cleared his throat. He was watching me.

I wiped my mouth.

He rubbed his legs and glanced to the side. "So... have you met anyone?"

At first I didn't know what he was talking about. I met all kinds of people. It was also weird that he was asking so many questions, but I supposed that meant he wasn't lying about not being able to read my mind. And then the realization of what he was asking hit me in the gut. I dabbed my bleeding arm with my tunic, and threw it in the corner. Sitting down, I sipped on the brandy bottle. Fighting the shark had helped clear my head some.

"No," I said. "I haven't."

Antolios snuck a peek at me.

I gazed out over the water. "But since my mother's death, I've been speaking with my father again. I think we've both changed."

"I was sorry to hear about your mother. She was a good woman," Antolios said.

I nodded my thanks, and we were silent for a while.

Finally I said, "One of her friends is looking after the school in Seriphos until I can make more permanent arrangements. My mother hadn't really been there in a while anyway. She had been traveling back and forth from Mycenae to Argos constantly. She was even talking about starting a school in Argos, not just for demigods, but other children too. She wanted to spread the philosophy of peace."

"It's a good idea." Antolios sounded melancholy. "I killed another shark."

I was grateful for the break and dove into the water to drag the shark to the boat.

The sun beat down on my head and shoulders, and by the time we quit for the day, our boat was packed with sharks. I sat staring out the bow of the ship, oars in hand, getting ready to row back to shore.

"Are we going?" Antolios's voice floated over the sound of the waves.

I dropped the oars and turned to him. His long legs were firmly planted on the boards, his pale muscles tight, responding to the tilt of the boat. His thighs disappeared into his tunic, and my fingers twitched with the desire to spread his knees, to reveal what I knew was between them. My penis stirred against my leg, and I started talking before my desire became obvious.

"Like I said, I've changed. I'm done running, and I'm not afraid to ask for what I want anymore, what I need." I gazed into the glow of his eyes. "I want you to stay for a while after your family leaves."

"A while?" He looked right at me so that I could see his swirling rainbow irises through the white glare.

"Will Cora mind?" I said.

Antolios set down his oars and snagged a bottle of brandy, finishing it off. He shuffled over and sat next to me. I slid down the bench to give him some room, a shark fin digging into my side. "She won't mind. It's not exactly known, but we haven't been together for a while."

A weight dropped into me. "I'm sorry. What happened?" I already knew the answer.

"She found out about us. After my mental breakdown, my daughters told her. They are annoyingly perceptive at times." Antolios's mouth twitched into a wry grin.

"Didn't you… try to take Cora's memory away or something?"

Antolios shrugged. "I didn't want to anymore."

"Oh." I set my hand on Antolios's leg, squeezing it. A feeling came over me slowly, a layer of sadness over my own. It took me a moment to realize that I was feeling the bond open up between us. We hadn't touched in years.

Antolios gasped and jerked, and I yanked my hand away reflexively. I was about to apologize when he began to cry. His face twisted into a horrifying grimace, and his shoulders lurched with every sob. I sat there for a second, not knowing what to do, and then edged closer and put my arms around him.

The bond opened up, and Antolios sobbed harder. Tears sprang to my eyes, and I sank into this bitter joy of ours. "Don't cry, angel," I said.

"I'm sorry," Antolios stammered. "My father and I never discussed what would happen if he took away my ability to read your mind. I didn't know I could still have this connection. It's been so hard. I've missed you more than anything."

"I'm sorry." I rubbed my face into his soft short curls. "I didn't think I'd ever be okay again, but it's been a long time. I need you."

Antolios hugged me closer, and I buried my nose in his dirty scent. Our hands found each other, light and dark fingers twining together.

"I miss your long hair," I said.

"I'll grow it out." He sighed. "I love you."

"I love you too." I unclasped my hands from his and smoothed a hand down the hard planes of his back to cup his ass. Then I slid a finger up his crack, feeling the heat emanating from it. Antolios twitched against me.

Our arousal hit us, and in the next moment we were on the floor of the boat, lips pressed together, sharks all around us. Our tongues and teeth gnashed as we rutted against each other, the boards of the boat digging into my body.

Antolios's wave of pleasure hit me again, and my eyes rolled into the back of my head. Our hands slipped between our stomachs, and we grasped each other.

"Oh gods," he groaned.

I panted, and the stench of shark assaulted my nose. "Wait." I let go of his cock. "Not here. Not in fish guts."

"I can't wait." Antolios stroked me faster.

I pushed him away, and we both stared at each other, crouched and tense. Antolios's jaw was hard, and his pale neck was flushed. I had torn the collar of his tunic. I licked my lips, and I knew we were thinking the same thing. We scrambled to our benches and took up the oars.

Two mortals had never rowed a boat that fast.

We hit the sand, and Antolios took off his tunic as we ran. I gave him another hot look and we burst into a sprint, tearing up the dunes, through the grass, and to the palace doors.

"Here they come," said one of the guards.

"There they go," said another as we breezed past.

We flew up the stairs, taking them ten at a time. My burst faded right as I crashed through the bathroom door to my suite. I fell as Antolios, still bursting, slammed into me from behind, and we skidded across the floor and rolled into the sunken tub. Our limbs tangled, and the areas where I had left some skin on the tiles burned. My head was submerged in the water against the steps, my feet sticking straight in the air. Antolios grabbed my ankles and rolled me as we roughly washed the sand from our bodies. I popped back to the surface and crawled over to the jug of olive oil.

Antolios launched himself out of the water and got to the jug first, running with it into the bedroom as if it were the torch to the Games. I scrambled to my feet and chased after him.

We hit the covers on the bed, and the cork on the jug came off, spilling oil everywhere. At first our bodies squeaked together from being wet, but as we rolled around in oil, our skin slipped and slid.

I had Antolios's cock in my face, and he had mine down his throat. I nibbled his foreskin and then teased his balls with my tongue and his ass with my fingers. Antolios tapped my asshole, and I gasped.

"Yes, like that!" I said. He licked up and down my crack, then slid his tongue into me. I lay there with his cock half in my mouth, making inarticulate noises around it.

He stuck several long fingers into me.

"Fuck," I said. As he turned me onto my stomach, I rubbed my face against the sheets and spread my knees, displaying my ass to him.

Antolios's desire pulsed through the bond to the point where it was impossible for me to tell whose was whose. When he entered me, my eyes crossed.

"Fuck," I said again. "Oh gods...."

Panting into my ear and nuzzling my hair, Antolios pressed his chest against my back. The whoosh of his breath tickled my cheek as he smelled me. "Mine," he growled. "Only mine." He slammed into me.

"Only yours!" I lifted my hips and arched my back into him, our cheeks brushing together. He bit my neck, and I begged him, "Harder!"

His hips snapped, jerking my entire body. I reached a hand down and stroked myself as my urgency overwhelmed me. Antolios groaned, and we burst into the last seconds of our orgasms. We collapsed, smearing my puddle of semen into my chest hair. Antolios pressed his breathless lips to my cheek, and I smiled.

"Only yours," I told him again, "for the rest of our lives."

EPILOGUE

WATER POURED over our heads, until I could barely see the light from Antolios's eyes filtering through it. Our hands clasped. The weight of the water pulled my hair forward as a black curtain. When the cool flow stopped, and Eros and Hymenaeus flew back to the sidelines, I pushed my hair back and took Antolios's hands again. The ocean and setting sun backlit the silhouettes of our fathers in front of us.

Antolios and I knelt before them in the shallow water of the pool. The Academy at Seriphos was behind us, with our friends and family watching. We had agreed to take over the school in my mother's stead, stepping down from both of our royal positions.

It was time for a new beginning.

Words too old and powerful for me to understand boomed from our fathers and tumbled around me, shaking me to the core. I felt small and lost as I rocked with the sounds.

My ears still rang when they were done. A hand touched my head, and I was lifted out of the pool. Red silk came down over my head, the shift mostly see-through. It smelled of pomegranates.

Zeus and Apollo smiled at us proudly, and everyone clapped and cheered. We joined the revelers. I was offered bread and fruit, but I kept my right hand in Antolios's. Dear friends, family, and gods greeted us.

Electryon was there, a crown on his head. He was king of Epiro now. He had a wife and twin infants, a girl and a boy. Zeus had taken an interest in Electryon's daughter, and it was rumored that she would grow to be the mother of the greatest hero that ever lived.

The greatest hero that ever lived.

My life made more sense now. My heroism, my marriage, and being king—they were all so that this great hero could be *from* someone. I might not have accepted this reason for my misery when I was younger, but looking back it gave me a certain measure of peace. My part of the prophecy was complete, and it was time for me to make my own way with Antolios. My father had been the first to offer his blessings for our union.

Antolios kissed my temple and excused himself, wandering into the crowd.

Thom and Vano barreled up to me, their hair snowy and faces wrinkled. Vano had a rounder belly, and his jowls wagged in merriment. They handed me a cup full of wine and punched me on the shoulder. We wandered over to a nearby cask and drank again to absent friends. Kell had been gored and killed by a nest of horned lizards a few seasons before, but we had sacrificed some wine and a bull to him earlier so he could be here in spirit. He never missed a party.

"So, who's going to have the babies?" Thom asked, covering his smile with his cup. Vano snickered.

I put my finger to my chin. "My father gave birth at least twice, so I guess that it would have to be me."

My friends stopped laughing and uneasily peeked to where Zeus was standing across the clearing. I smiled. Partying with the gods was thrilling but dangerous too, such as everything worth doing.

"This is some serious wine." Thom stared hard into his goblet. I neglected to tell them that it wasn't standard wine, but the nectar of the gods. They'd probably be hungover for *days*. Thom grinned exaggeratedly. "I'm glad you're happy."

"Me too," Vano said. He had tears in his eyes, and I stifled a laugh.

"Thanks," I said. "Be careful at the party, okay? Don't do anything I wouldn't do."

"Well, that leaves our options wide open," Vano said.

I gave my friends hugs, which they more than enthusiastically returned, and while I was still snickering, I wandered over to where my father was talking with Poseidon. The two brothers were nearly alike, with their broad chests and flowing white hair. My father's eyes were soft blue, while Poseidon's were dark blue, almost black.

Poseidon took my hand and congratulated me and then excused himself. Zeus smiled.

"Hail, Patéras." I bent my head.

Zeus crushed me in an Olympian hug. "Congratulations, son," he said.

When he let me go and I could breathe again, I said, "Thank you for the ceremony, sir."

"I'm pleased that you asked me to do this," Zeus said. He took a deep breath and surveyed the party, smiling. "It's nice to be here with family and friends, standing in the sun and fresh air."

"Better than the Underworld?" I tried to say lightly.

Zeus considered me. "Indeed. My time there was well spent, however. I also listened to prayers."

I blinked. "Prayers?"

Zeus nodded. "Prayers spoken by the old, the young, and even the small oaths people said on their breath. My subjects could no longer see or hear me, but they still believed. I had not expected that. I heard yours."

My face fell. "I didn't know."

My father put a hand on my shoulder. "I'm sorry."

"No, I'm sorry, sir. My entire life I've been bitter toward the gods. It seems like such a waste."

"If anything, being a god shows us that mortality isn't easy, and we are better gods when we remember that. As you well know, there are some things that even the divine struggle with," Zeus said.

I blinked back tears.

"Come, let's go pay our respects to Hera," he said.

"What?"

"She'll appreciate it, and I'll be there," Zeus said. He wrapped his arm around me and led me toward her.

My heart skipped a few beats, and I started to sweat. "What do I say?"

"Compliment her on her peacocks and hair or something. Maybe thank her for not killing you?" Zeus said with a chuckle.

Antolios was suddenly at my side, holding my hand. I breathed easier when he smiled at me. "We're ready," I said.

"Good boy," Zeus said.

The three of us walked across the sparse grass, ready for anything.

B. A. BROCK has lived most of his life in the Pacific Northwest, with a couple years in Oklahoma. He graduated with a Bachelor of Science in 2007 at Portland State University—which he mostly uses to contemplate how we can achieve a civilization more closely aligned with *Star Trek*.

While playing *Dungeons and Dragons*, he discovered a desire to write out a few scenes from his character's story. Those scenes became an obsession, that obsession led to writing classes, and an author was born.

When not writing, Brock spends his time reading/reviewing novels, training for marathons, hanging out with his dog, and bemoaning the fact that the world has yet to make a decent gluten-free donut.

You can find more of his works, as well as reviews and his blog at www.babrockbooks.com.

Facebook: www.facebook.com/BABrockBooks

Goodreads: www.goodreads.com/BABrockBooks

E-mail: babrockbooks@gmail.com

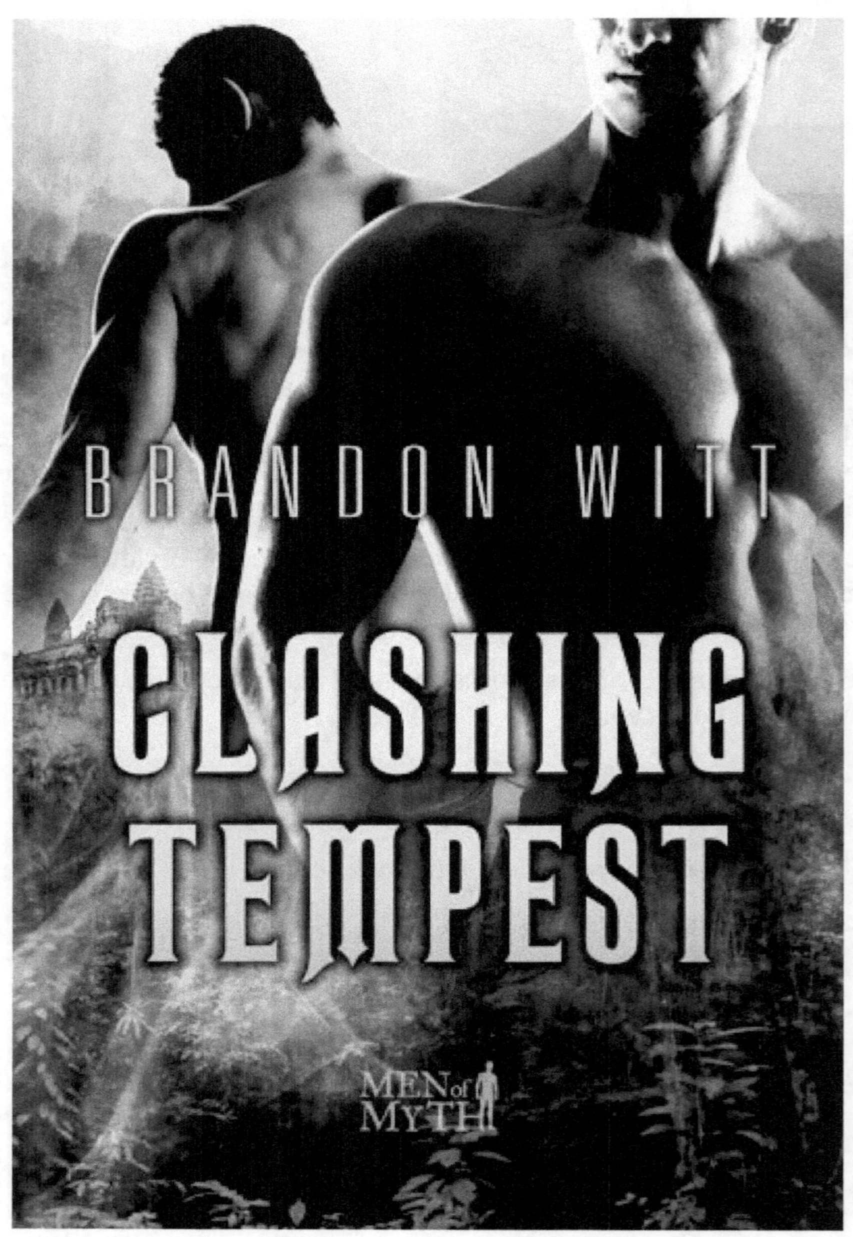

www.dsppublications.com

www.dsppublications.com

DSP PUBLICATIONS

visit us online.
WWW.DSPPUBLICATIONS.COM